nowledge.
知識工場
Knowledge is everything！

面試"零"痛點，這樣口說最高分

隨書附贈 MP3
字記範本 瞬間反應

🎯 最具體！深入高分關鍵，搶得先機。

求職、升遷、考試
絕對通關！

張翔 / 編著

Let's Stand
Out In Oral
Exams.

PASS

效率 100% 高頻口試題庫，這本幫你整理！

稱霸 100% 高分應對法，通通寫給你！

實力 100% 對補充的需求，無一遺漏！

讓你一開口就說得
巧妙、打動人心，

POINT 1

一目瞭然的情境分類

將精選的口試題目依**情境分為 10 大
主題**，分類有系統，學習效率自然
能提升。想要專攻自己不熟悉的題
目也很方便。

UNIT 01 慶祝生日的方法

Q How do you celebrate your birthday?
你會如何慶祝生日？

你可以這樣回答

MP3 001

I like to celebrate¹ with my family because that has been the tradition² in our household³ for as long as I can remember. Normally, my mother cooks us traditional pig knuckle⁴ rice noodle soup and a boiled egg to celebrate that we are now one year older and wiser. The pig knuckle rice noodle soup is for good luck in the future, and to peeling the boiled egg⁵ symbolizes⁶ rebirth and getting rid of bad luck from the past. Instead of having a birthday cake, I much prefer celebrating the traditional way.

我喜歡跟我的家人一起慶祝，因為這一直以來都是我家的傳統。我媽媽通常會煮傳統的豬腳麵線和一顆水煮蛋來慶祝我們長了年紀與智慧——吃豬腳麵線是為了祈求來年的好運；剝水煮蛋的動作則代表重生，把過去的壞運丟掉。和吃蛋糕相比，我比較喜歡這種傳統的慶祝方式。

1 celebrate 動 慶祝
2 tradition 名 傳統
3 household 名 一家人；家庭
4 pig knuckle 片 豬腳
5 a boiled egg 片 水煮蛋
6 symbolize 動 象徵；標誌

換個立場講講看

When it comes to my birthday, I spend months planning for a big night out! I love to do crazy things with my friends. On my 18th birthday, my friends

POINT 2

命中率 NO.1 的熱門考題

精選**150 題**口試最常出現的熱門題目，
掌握這些，口試自然十拿九穩，要學就
學一定會考的內容！

POINT 3

讓面試官驚艷的多元表達

在每一題目之下，編寫三段立場、觀點
各異的的回應。拋開千篇一律的教科書
內容，現在就用**獨具特色的回答**打動面
試官。

證照檢定、國外進修,通通搞定!

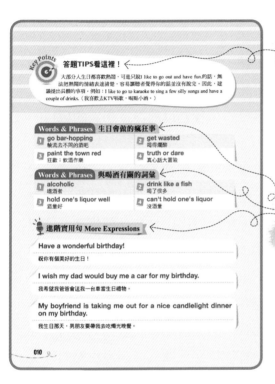

Key Points 答題TIPS看這裡!

大部分人生日都喜歡熱鬧,可是只說I like to go out and have fun.的話,無法把熱鬧的情緒表達清楚,容易讓聽者覺得你的話並沒有設定。因此,建議提出具體的事項,例如:I like to go to karaoke to sing a few silly songs and have a couple of drinks. (我喜歡去KTV唱歌,喝點小酒。)

Words & Phrases 生日會做的瘋狂事
1. go bar-hopping
   輪流去不同的酒吧
2. get wasted
   喝得爛醉
3. paint the town red
   狂歡;飲酒作樂
4. truth or dare
   真心話大冒險

Words & Phrases 與喝酒有關的詞彙
1. alcoholic
   嗜酒者
2. drink like a fish
   喝了很多
3. hold one's liquor well
   酒量好
4. can't hold one's liquor
   沒酒量

🎤 進階實用句 More Expressions

Have a wonderful birthday!
祝你有個美好的生日!

I wish my dad would buy me a car for my birthday.
我希望我爸爸會送我一台車當生日禮物。

My boyfriend is taking me out for a nice candlelight dinner on my birthday.
我生日那天,男朋友要帶我去吃燭光晚餐。

010

📢 POINT ④

一次掌握解題關鍵

除了回答內容之外,在此補充答題時要注意的撇步,以及其他參考答案。**掌握答題核心**,回應時自然能更準確。

📢 POINT ⑤

單字 / 片語 / 替換句再進化

根據每一個單元的題目,補充相關**單字與片語 & 三句進階實用句**。用這些詞彙和句子替換,打造獨一無二的回應內容。

📢 POINT ⑥

進階補充,坐穩口試 NO.1 殿堂

最後提供兩大附錄──**片語補給站 & 口試實用句型**。每一個片語及句型都會附上例句,即學即用,多種表達一次囊括,口試時自然開口無礙。

附錄一 片語補給站 *Level Up!*

Part 1 性格與特質

❶ be accustomed to 習慣於……

A couple of years after I moved to the UK, I got accustomed to the lifestyle here.
搬到英國住了幾年後,我開始習慣這裡的生活方式了。

附錄二 口試實用句型 *Express yourself!*

❶ sb. decided to... 某人決定要……。

This is not the first time Laura busted her boyfriend cheating; therefore, she decided to break up with him.
這不是蘿拉第一次發現男友在外面有小三,她決定要分手。

這樣說，什麼樣的口試都一次過關！

　　大多數人在英語的四大基礎，聽、說、讀、寫中，會先從讀與寫這兩方面下手。這樣的訓練在一般的考試基本足夠，但是，在全球化的影響下，各大英語檢定開始著重於一項我們以前從沒想過的項目，即為「口試」。

　　在我教過的學生當中，也有不少人在看到納入口試的英檢後，習慣性地先避開這類考試，但是，這樣的幫助究竟有多少呢？除了雅思之外，就連新多益也出現口說測驗，足以看出口試為一種趨勢，逃避下去絕非良策。但是，一想到口試，就會有不少人感到苦惱。第一個遇到的關卡是「該講什麼？」想不出來自己該怎麼回答，或者擔心自己講的內容不夠好，所以在臨場更容易因緊張而變得結巴。其實。不管是檢定考的口試，還是工作的面試，面試官都會希望你的回答有條理、具備清楚的邏輯性，這樣的回答往往會比講太多卻沒重點的好，更令面試官滿意。

　　對於平常沒有太多經驗的人來說，要在短期內訓練出條理清晰的英語表達，並不簡單。因此，我花了不少時間於構思這本書，思考「該如何於短期內幫助學生於口試中取得高分，又不至於太困難。」在經過許多討論之後，我最後決定以「一題三解」的方式編寫本書，希望能以最容易的方式，提升學生的口語表達能力。

　　本書中的所有題目，都會提供三組立場各異的回應。之所以會這樣設計，是因為口試並非單一選擇題，沒有絕對正確的答案，甚至是

可以發揮自己想法的一種測驗方式，所以我希望能盡量提供豐富的參考答案給讀者。根據三段不同的回應，讀者可自行挑選最貼近自己想法或立場的內容，再依個人情況替換單字或句子。這樣的話，一方面能幫助讀者省下很多功夫，二方面也能視自己的情況調整。

　　或許有的人會認為單一解答更省事，但在考量面試官的立場後，我還是決定編寫三段不同的回應。單一解答對讀者而言或許簡單，但就面試官的立場來說，若聽的都是千篇一律的內容，等於聽不到你的獨特性在哪裡，這樣的方式並不能幫助讀者於口試中脫穎而出，因此，我最後還是堅持以這種方式編寫本書。

　　其實，口試並不像多數人想的那麼可怕，只是因為在我們學習英語的過程中，聽與說這兩塊領域的訓練不足，所以到真正要用的時候，才會感到慌張。編寫這本書，也是希望讀者能藉此降低自己對口試的恐懼感，「選定參考解答 → 替換少量單字」是人人都能做到的事，接下來，就是熟練，正所謂「熟能生巧」，如此訓練就能幫助學習者在面試官面前條理清晰地開口。

　　學英文是一輩子的事，無論如何，都需要投注一定的心力，最後才能嚐到甜美的果實。身為一位執教者，我能做的就是提升學生的學習效率，如果學生投注了百分之五十的努力，那我想要讓他們品嚐到的成果，當然是在百分之五十之上。看著學生開心地與我分享成績的那個瞬間，就是最讓我感到喜悅的時刻，也許，這就是為什麼我始終熱衷於教學，也始終放不下編寫語言書籍工作的原因吧。無論如何，都希望各位讀者能從本書中獲益，無論你在準備什麼樣的口試，都能一次打動面試官的心，達成目標。

張翔

Contents 目錄

Part 1

性格與特質
About Personality

 動 動詞　　 **形** 形容詞　　 **連** 連接詞

 名 名詞　　 **介** 介系詞　　 **片** 片語

 副 副詞

UNIT 01 慶祝生日的方法

Q **How do you celebrate your birthday?**
你會如何慶祝生日？

你可以這樣回答

MP3 001

I like to celebrate[1] with my family because that has been the tradition[2] in our household[3] for as long as I can remember. Normally, my mother cooks us traditional pig knuckle[4] rice noodle soup and a boiled egg to celebrate that we are now one year older and wiser. The pig knuckle rice noodle soup is for good luck in the future, and peeling the boiled egg[5] symbolizes rebirth[6] and getting rid of bad luck from the past. Instead of having a birthday cake, I much prefer celebrating the traditional way.

　　我喜歡跟我的家人一起慶祝，因為這一直以來都是我家的傳統。我媽媽通常會煮傳統的豬腳麵線和一顆水煮蛋來慶祝我們長了年紀與智慧——吃豬腳麵線是為了祈求來年的好運；剝水煮蛋的動作則代表重生，揮別過去的壞運。和吃蛋糕相比，我比較喜歡這種傳統的慶祝方式。

❶ celebrate
動 慶祝

❷ tradition
名 傳統

❸ household
名 一家人；家庭

❹ pig knuckle
片 豬腳

❺ a boiled egg
片 水煮蛋

❻ rebirth
名 再生；復活

換個立場講講看

When it comes to my birthday, I spend months planning for a big night out! I love to do crazy things with my friends. On my 18th birthday, my friends

took me to a club. We danced and drank way too much beer[7]! It was such a wonderful experience, but I was also very embarrassed[8] because I had a terrible hangover[9] which lasted for two days. I had to struggle to stay focused[10] at school, but it was really worth it! I will definitely do it again if I have a chance to!

說到過生日，我會提前好幾個月計劃晚上要去哪裡瘋！我最愛跟好友一起做些瘋狂事。十八歲生日那天，他們帶我去酒吧，我們狂歡跳舞、喝到掛，真的很過癮，但我因此宿醉了兩天，很丟臉，回學校上課時根本無法專心，但那次經驗真的很值得，要是有機會，我還要再瘋一次！

延伸note
a night out字面上意指「晚上出門」，依情境會產生「狂歡、夜遊」…等意思。

❼ beer
名 啤酒

❾ hangover
名 （口）宿醉

❽ embarrassed
形 尷尬的；窘的

❿ stay focused
片 保持專注

 試著更與眾不同

I like to keep my birthday as low-key[11] as possible. I don't think many people remember[12] my birthday. Besides, I don't really feel like doing anything special for myself. Most likely, I will buy some takeaway[13] and rent a DVD to watch at home. Once, my co-workers[14] bought me birthday cake and sang Happy Birthday to me. I thought it was rather nice. I enjoyed it a lot, but I can't expect people to do it for me every year.

我生日的時候會盡量低調一點，反正應該也沒什麼人記得我的生日。而且，我也沒有特別想做的事，頂多就是叫個外賣，租片DVD回家看吧！我同事有一次在我生日的時候買了蛋糕，還幫我唱生日快樂歌，讓我很感動，也真的很開心，但我不能期待每年都有人幫我慶生。

⓫ low-key
形 低調的

⓬ remember
動 記得；想起

⓭ takeaway
名 （餐館的）外賣

⓮ co-worker
名 同事

延伸note
low-key用來形容事物的低調；若要形容為人低調，則要用sb. keep a low profile。

Words & Phrases　生日會做的瘋狂事

1. **go bar-hopping**
輪流去不同的酒吧

2. **get wasted**
喝得爛醉

3. **paint the town red**
狂歡；飲酒作樂

4. **truth or dare**
真心話大冒險

Words & Phrases　與喝酒有關的詞彙

1. **alcoholic**
嗜酒者

2. **drink like a fish**
喝了很多

3. **hold one's liquor well**
酒量好

4. **can't hold one's liquor**
沒酒量

 進階實用句 More Expressions

Have a wonderful birthday!

祝你有個美好的生日！

I wish my dad would buy me a car for my birthday.

我希望我爸爸會送我一台車當作生日禮物。

My boyfriend is taking me out for a nice candlelight dinner on my birthday.

我生日那天，男朋友要帶我去吃燭光晚餐。

UNIT 02

衝動購物的經驗

Q Have you ever bought something but seldom use it?

你曾經買了什麼很少使用的物品嗎？

 你可以這樣回答

MP3
002

All the time! I always want to try new things out[1], especially when I see products with a lot of different functions. For example, I bought a bread maker a couple of months ago. Other than make a loaf of bread, it can also make muffins, sticky[2] rice cake, red bean paste[3] and fruit jam. It was 20% off. Don't you think that is too hard to resist[4]? However, I really should have thought it over before I purchased it. I live right next to a bakery. Why do I need a bread maker?

經常如此！我總會想要嘗試新東西，尤其是看了具備多功能的產品時，更是如此。看看我幾個月前買的麵包機，它除了可以做麵包之外，還可以做鬆餅、麻糬、紅豆餡和果醬，再加上打八折，怎麼能不買呢？不過，我當時真該在購物前想清楚的，我家隔壁就是麵包店，怎麼會需要麵包機呢？

❶ **try out**
片 試用；試驗

❷ **sticky**
形 黏的

❸ **paste**
名 糊狀物；醬

❹ **resist**
動 反抗；抗拒

> **延伸note**
> think it over的意思是「想清楚」，通常涉及決定。如果是把某問題想透徹，用think it through。

 換個立場講講看

Most of the time, I am quite careful[5] with what I spend my money on. But I sometimes buy things that I end up regretting[6] buying. To give one example, I bought a movie projector[7]. It seemed like a great idea at the time. I was thinking that I could watch DVDs at home with a big screen. But what I didn't realize[8] was, the sound system was not as good as those in theaters. My girlfriend still prefers going to the movies anyway. So, I put it away in the original box somewhere in my house.

對於錢要怎麼花，我通常都很精打細算，但我有時也會買些讓我事後後悔的商品。就像我買的電影投影機，當初覺得很值得，因為我可以在家用大螢幕觀賞DVD，可是我沒想到音響效果仍不比電影院，我女朋友還是比較喜歡去電影院，所以我已經把那個東西放回原來的箱子，收起來了。

延伸note
面試的時候，即便出現Yes/No Question，回答時也不用都以Yes/No開頭，讓對話更自然。

❺ careful
形 小心的；仔細的

❻ regret
動 懊悔；因…而遺憾

❼ projector
名 投影機

❽ realize
動 領悟；認識到

試著更與眾不同

Not usually. I am still paying off[9] my car, so my disposable[10] income is very limited. I have to think twice before I purchase[11] something. However, I once got carried away and got a coffee machine. I thought I could save a bit of money by making my own coffee instead of[12] buying it all the time. However, it was too much work to clean up, so I ended up[13] selling the machine, and now I drink instant[14] coffee.

不太會，因為我還在付車貸，可以花的閒錢很有限。在買東西之前，我一定要考慮很久。不過，我之前還是鬼迷心竅地買了一台咖啡機，原本是想，在家煮咖啡可以省下買咖啡的錢，沒想到清理咖啡機太麻煩，所以我最後賣了那台機器，現在只喝即溶咖啡。

❾ pay off
片 償清債務

❿ disposable
形 可自由使用的

⓫ purchase
動 買；購買

⓬ instead of
片 代替

⓭ end up
片 以…做終結

⓮ instant
形 即溶的；速食的

答題TIPS看這裡！

無論是多理智的人，或多或少都應該有衝動購物的經驗。因此，建議回答時避開「絕對不會」這種機率極低的答案。回想一下有什麼東西是你買回家，卻一直放在櫃子裡的東西，這些就是舉例的好來源。

Words & Phrases　認識特殊廚具

1 **air fryer**
氣炸鍋

2 **pressure cooker**
壓力鍋

3 **thermal cooker**
悶燒鍋

4 **bar mixer**
手持型果汁攪拌機

Words & Phrases　折扣與好康

1 **clearance**
出清

2 **on sale**
特價

3 **10% off (10 percent off)**
打九折

4 **buy-one-get-one-free**
買一送一

進階實用句 More Expressions

I am not an impulsive buyer.

我不是衝動型的消費者。

I have a garage full of things that I hardly use.

我有一車庫很少用到的東西。

I would rather buy something I needed than something I wanted.

我會買我需要的東西，而非想要的東西。

UNIT 03

對鞋款的偏好

Q **Do you like comfortable or fashionable shoes? Why?**

你喜歡舒適款還是流行款的鞋子？為什麼？

 你可以這樣回答

MP3 003

I am totally in love with wearing pretty shoes. I know they are not all that comfortable[1]; some of them have even given me blisters[2], but I feel so much more confident[3] when I am wearing fashionable[4] shoes. They perfectly match my stylish dresses. Do you know Carrie from "Sex and The City"? She has a whole wardrobe[5] dedicated to[6] her pretty shoes, which are designer brands and the latest styles. I really wish that was my shoe wardrobe!

　　我真的很愛穿漂亮的鞋子，我知道有些穿起來並不舒服，甚至會讓我的腳長水泡，但一穿上時髦的鞋款，我就會很有自信，因為它們和我的流行洋裝很搭。你知道《慾望城市》裡的凱莉嗎？她有一整個衣櫃拿來放鞋子，全部都是設計師品牌和最新的樣式，真希望那是我的衣櫥！

❶ **comfortable** 形 舒適的	❷ **blister** 名（皮膚上的）水泡	❸ **confident** 形 有自信的
❹ **fashionable** 形 流行的；時髦的	❺ **wardrobe** 名 衣櫥；衣櫃	❻ **dedicate to** 片 奉獻給

 換個立場講講看

M aybe a bit of both. Actually, I prefer something that is comfortable. The problem is, I am too short to wear flats. Some of my clients[7] even thought I was a student when we first met. To make myself look professional[8], I usually choose a pair of fashionable shoes and put soft gel foot cushions[9] in each shoe. This way, I can still keep the professional look with the minimal[10] discomfort. And after a whole day's work, I don't get swollen[11] and sore[12] feet.

兩種都有吧，其實我比較喜歡穿舒適的鞋子，問題是，我太矮了，不能穿平底鞋，我有些客戶在第一次見面的時候甚至以為我還是學生呢！為了讓自己看起來專業一點，我通常會選雙時髦的鞋子，再放凝膠鞋墊進去，這樣我除了看起來夠專業之外，也能減輕許多不適感，而且穿了一整天後，腳也不會腫痛。

| ⑦ **client** 名 客戶 | ⑧ **professional** 形 專業的 | ⑨ **foot cushion** 片 鞋墊 |
| ⑩ **minimal** 形 最小的；極微的 | ⑪ **swollen** 形 浮腫的 | ⑫ **sore** 形 痛的；疼痛發炎的 |

試著更與眾不同

I would love to wear fashionable shoes, but my feet just can't bear the pain. So what I look for is something more on the comfortable side. I have a bad ankle[13]. As a result, wearing high heels is out of the question[14] for me. I asked a doctor what if I need to dress up on some special occasions. He told me wedges[15] could be an option, but my ankle hurts after three hours of wearing them. Basically, fashion is not what I consider most when I go shopping[16].

我很想穿流行的鞋款，但我的腳受不了那種痛，所以我會買舒適的鞋款。我的腳踝受過傷，不能穿高跟鞋，我問醫生我如果在某些場合需要特別打扮時怎麼辦，他建議我試試楔型鞋，但我穿了三個鐘頭後，腳踝就會很痛。基本上，流行並非我挑鞋的考慮因素。

| ⑬ **ankle** 名 腳踝 | ⑭ **out of the question** 片 不可能的 |
| ⑮ **wedges** 名 楔型鞋 | ⑯ **go shopping** 片 逛街 |

延伸note
platforms(厚底鞋)包含 wedges(楔型鞋)。厚底鞋裡的另一種，是前厚底＋後高跟的設計。

答題TIPS看這裡！

其實，普通人兩種鞋款都會有，只是依據不同場合，會有不同選擇。舉例來說，必須表現出專業度的工作，就會偏重流行款；藍領階層的勞工通常會選擇舒適又耐穿的鞋款；從事戶外活動時較可能會選舒適的鞋子；但去參加舞會時就會選時髦的款式。先選定要從哪個方面切入，舉例時就容易許多。

Words & Phrases　常見的鞋子種類

1	**high heels** 高跟鞋	2	**platforms** 厚底鞋
3	**flats** 平底鞋	4	**sandals** 涼鞋
5	**flip-flops** 夾腳拖	6	**sneakers** 球鞋
7	**ankle boots** 短靴	8	**canvas shoes** 帆布鞋

進階實用句 More Expressions

It is not acceptable to wear sandals to work.

不能穿涼鞋來上班。

This pair of sneakers is too small. Does it come in size 25?

這雙球鞋太小了，請問有25號的嗎？

I can't stand wearing high heels all day long, so I brought my flip-flops to the office.

我沒辦法穿一整天的高跟鞋，所以我把夾腳拖帶去公司。

UNIT 04

偏好漫畫或小說

Q Do you like to read comic books or novels?
你喜歡看漫畫還是讀小說呢？

你可以這樣回答

MP3 004

I have been reading novels[1] since I was a teenager[2]. What I enjoy the most is love stories. When I was younger, I loved to picture meeting a good-looking man like the female characters[3] in those stories did. The best thing about novels is that you can let your imagination[4] run wild because there is no actual picture of the characters. Thus, I can always have a Mr. Right of my own choosing in each love story.

　　我從十幾歲的時候就喜歡看小說，我最喜歡看的是愛情故事。年輕的時候，我很愛想像自己就和小說裡的女性角色一樣，遇見英俊瀟灑的男主角。小說最棒的地方在於，你可以盡情發揮想像力，因為並沒有圖片來限制主角們的長相，所以每一本愛情小說，我都能描繪出一個一百分的完美男主角。

❶ **novel**
名 （長篇）小說

❷ **teenager**
名 十幾歲的青少年

❸ **character**
名 （小說的）人物

❹ **imagination**
名 想像力

延伸note
和romance不同，love story 雖涉及戀愛，但也可能包含其他議題，且結局不一定皆大歡喜。

換個立場講講看

Definitely comic books! I am such a big fan of that type of fiction[5]. I love the superhero-themed series. I even have a complete collection[6] of "Spider-Man" and "The Flash". I don't like reading novels because there is too much information to process[7]. In contrast[8], comic books are very straightforward. There is a lot of visual[9] imagery[10], which is easy to take in. I feel totally relaxed when I am in my comic book world.

當然是漫畫啊！我是科幻漫畫的頭號粉絲，我最喜歡英雄主題系列，我有一整套的《蜘蛛人》和《閃電俠》。我不喜歡看小說，因為小說裡有太多資訊得理解。相比之下，漫畫就直接多了，有很多圖像，又容易了解，只要沉浸在漫畫的世界裡，我就會感到很放鬆。

5 fiction 名 虛構；想像	**6 collection** 名 收集	**7 process** 動 處理；辦理
8 in contrast 片 相比之下	**9 visual** 形 視覺的	**10 imagery** 名 圖像

 ## 試著更與眾不同

I used to like comic books when I was a kid. However, as I got more mature[11], I started to take an interest in reading novels. I couldn't get enough satisfaction[12] from comic books because there is nothing to reflect on[13] after I finish reading. On the other hand, reading a novel is like going on a journey[14]. Through the words, I feel like I am experiencing a different life. Although novels sometimes are quite deep and require a lot of concentration to read, I think that is the beauty of them.

我小時候喜歡看漫畫，可是當我漸漸成熟後，我開始喜歡看小說。漫畫已經無法滿足我了，因為看完漫畫之後，並沒有什麼能回味討論。另一方面，讀小說就像去旅行一樣，藉著小說的文字，我彷彿體驗了不同的人生。雖然小說的涵義有時候很深奧，需要聚精會神地去閱讀，但我覺得這正是小說的魅力。

11 mature 形 成熟的	**12 satisfaction** 名 滿意；滿足
13 reflect on 片 深思；考慮	**14 journey** 名 旅行；旅程

延伸note
used to表示「過去習慣」，現在有可能已經沒有這個習慣；be used to則表示「現在習慣」。

 Key Points

答題TIPS看這裡！

小說與漫畫最大的差異就是一個藉由文字打動人，一個則以圖像傳達訊息。如果本身對小說不熟悉，不妨拿出小時候看漫畫的經驗，列舉一些著名的漫畫來舉例，如：小叮噹。

Words & Phrases 常見的小說主題

1 romance
愛情小説

2 thriller
恐怖小説

3 science fiction (sci-fi)
科幻小説

4 fantasy novel
奇幻小説

5 Chinese chivalry novel
武俠小説

6 historical fiction
歷史小説

7 detective novel
推理小説

8 crime novel
犯罪小説

進階實用句 More Expressions

I love reading novels, especially thrillers.

我特別喜歡讀恐怖小說。

Comic books are so addictive; I can spend hours reading them.

看漫畫很容易上癮，我可以花好幾個小時看漫畫。

I have always imagined that I would meet the right person at the Eiffel Tower. My friends think I live in a fantasy world.

我總幻想會在艾菲爾鐵塔遇見那個對的人，朋友都覺得這個想法太夢幻了。

UNIT 05 才藝搶先跑的經驗

 Q Did your parents force you to learn anything when you were young?

小時候，你的父母曾經強迫你學什麼嗎？

MP3 005

你可以這樣回答

I wish they had done so. My dad had to work two jobs to support[1] our family when I was little. Therefore, we did not have a lot of spare money[2] to spend on after-school classes. Unlike my friends, who went to different classes from jazz to mathematics[3], I spent most of the time helping my mother minding[4] the family. The only thing I learned was cooking because I had to make breakfast for my sisters. But if I could choose, I'd like to take piano lessons.

如果有的話就好了。小的時候，我爸爸必須兼兩份工作來養家，根本沒什麼錢讓我去上才藝班，不像我的朋友們，又學爵士舞、又上數學課，我大部分的時間都跟著媽媽，幫忙照顧家裡。唯一學到的是烹飪技巧，因為要幫妹妹們做早餐才學會的。不過如果可以選擇的話，我真的很想去上鋼琴課。

❶ **support**
動 扶養；贍養

❷ **spare money**
片 剩餘的錢

❸ **mathematics**
名 數學

❹ **mind**
動 照料；看管

延伸note
與過去事實相反的假設，wish後面加had+V(過去分詞)，如本段回答的第一句。

換個立場講講看

Absolutely[5]! My parents believe music helps a person develop[6] a better personality, so they think every kid should take music classes. My mother took piano lessons when she was a little girl, so she forced me to take piano lessons, too! She even spent lots of money to buy a brand-new piano for me to practice[7] at home. However, piano is really not what I enjoy learning. I have been trying to talk to my mother about it, but she just does not listen to me. I had such a bad experience[8] with piano.

當然！我爸媽相信學音樂的人不會變壞，所以每個小孩都應該學音樂。我媽媽小時候學過鋼琴，所以她硬逼我去學，甚至還花錢買了一台全新的鋼琴，好讓我在家練習，可是我對鋼琴真的一點興趣都沒有，我一直嘗試跟我媽媽溝通，可她就是不聽，學鋼琴對我來說真是件糟透了的回憶。

延伸note
學才藝不一定都是美好的回憶，也有因被逼迫而討厭的人，只要內容具體，可以自由發揮。

❺ **absolutely**
副 絕對地；完全地

❻ **develop**
動 使成長；發展

❼ **practice**
動 練習；訓練

❽ **experience**
名 經驗；體驗

 試著更與眾不同

I think it was my mother's dream to become a ballerina[9]. Ever since I was a little girl, she told me a lot of stories about being a ballerina. I started to go to ballet[10] classes when I was three. I am not quite sure whether she forced me to go or if it was because of my asking for it. I can't recall[11] any memories[12] about not wanting to go to the class. Actually, I loved wearing the pretty little tutu[13] and getting my hair all done up for the stage performances[14].

我覺得成為芭蕾舞者好像是我媽媽的夢想。從小，媽媽就會一直跟我說些和芭蕾舞者有關的故事。我三歲就開始上芭蕾課，我不太確定是我父母硬逼我去，還是我自己想去上課的，我不記得自己有不想去上課的時候，老實說，我很愛穿著小巧美麗的芭蕾澎澎裙，將頭髮梳理漂亮地上台表演。

❾ **ballerina**
名 女芭蕾舞者

❿ **ballet**
名 芭蕾舞

⓫ **recall**
動 回憶；使想起

⓬ **memory**
名 記憶；回憶

⓭ **tutu**
名 芭蕾舞短裙

⓮ **performance**
名 演出；表演

答題TIPS看這裡！

若沒有這方面的經驗，不妨先列出一些比較熟悉的才藝或補習項目，或者舉他人為例也可以，千萬不要以No, they didn't.來結束這個問題。你可以說 I can't think of anything in particular, but they did insist that I had to go to the after-school tutoring class for chemistry. (沒有特別印象，但他們有堅持要我去補化學的家教班。) 再簡單補充你對這件事的感覺即可。

Words & Phrases　常見的才藝項目

1 **taekwondo**
跆拳道

2 **karate**
空手道

3 **tap dancing**
踢踏舞

4 **flute**
長笛；橫笛

Words & Phrases　補習與進修課程

1 **tutoring class**
家教課

2 **language school**
語言學校

3 **adult school**
成人進修學校

4 **curriculum**
（一門）課程

 進階實用句 More Expressions

I took many different classes when I was little. I lost count!

我小時候上了很多課程，都算不清楚了！

My favorite class was pottery because I could bring the finished work home.

我最喜歡上陶藝課，因為做好的成品可以帶回家。

I don't know what my parents were thinking. I am only 150cm tall and they expected me to be a ballerina.

真不知道我爸媽在想什麼，我只有150公分，他們竟然期望我成為芭蕾舞者。

工作效率高峰時段

Q **Are you a morning or an afternoon person?**
你早上工作比較有效率,還是下午呢?

 你可以這樣回答

Well, I am much more productive[1] and alert[2] in the afternoon. I struggle to wake up[3] every day. I am too much a late-night person to be a morning one. I am used to staying up late[4]. If I don't have my coffee right after I wake up, I just can't function[5]. Because of this, I am always worried about morning meetings, especially when it is a big one. I just don't want to make silly[6] mistakes which would cost me my job!

　我下午會比較有效率,精神也比較好。我每天早上都爬不起來,當不成早起的鳥兒。我是個夜貓子,很習慣熬夜,所以,如果我早上起床沒馬上喝杯咖啡,我的腦袋就完全無法運作,也因為如此,早上的會議總是讓我緊張萬分,尤其是重大的會議更是如此,我可不想因為犯了愚蠢的錯誤而被炒魷魚!

① **productive**
形 多產的

② **alert**
形 機敏的;靈活的

③ **wake up**
片 起床

④ **stay up late**
片 熬夜

⑤ **function**
動 發揮作用

⑥ **silly**
形 愚蠢的;糊塗的

 換個立場講講看

I am definitely a morning person. I really enjoy the glory[7] of morning. I prefer to get up an hour before going to work. That way, I have a bit of time to go out for a jog by the river. I make myself a glass of fruit juice and eat a low-fat breakfast after I get home. I feel very energetic[8] in the morning when I can complete more complicated[9] tasks. However, I do get tired[10] quite early in the day. I normally go to bed around 9 p.m., which is still early for a lot of people.

絕對是早上，我喜歡享受早晨的美好，我每天會提早一個小時起床，這樣一來，我就有時間在上班前去河邊慢跑，慢跑回家之後，我會打一杯果汁，準備一份低熱量的早餐。我每天早上都覺得精神很好，所以我上午能完成相對複雜的工作。不過，我也滿早就會感到疲倦，我的就寢時間大約為晚上九點，對很多人來說，這個時間還很早呢！

延伸note
除了本段的表達之外，「早起者」和「夜貓子」還可以說an early bird和a night owl。

❼ glory
名 壯麗；壯觀

❽ energetic
形 精神飽滿的

❾ complicated
形 複雜的

❿ get tired
片 感到疲倦

試著更與眾不同

I don't really have a preference[11], but I noticed that I have better concentration[12] after a good night's sleep. I normally visit my clients and do the important jobs in the morning while I feel energetic. I do paperwork[13] in the afternoon because I start to slow down after lunch time, especially when I don't take a nap[14]. There was one time that my co-worker caught me falling asleep at my desk. What an embarrassing moment!

我並沒有特定的偏好，但我發現如果前一天晚上睡得好，那我的集中力也會比較高，所以我通常會趁早上精力充沛的時候去拜訪客戶，或處理比較重要的工作，下午就做些文書處理，因為過了中午，我的精神就開始變差，尤其當我沒有午睡的時候。有一次，同事發現我在辦公桌前睡著，真是超丟臉的！

⓫ preference
名 偏好；喜好

⓬ concentration
名 集中；專注

⓭ paperwork
名 文書工作

⓮ take a nap
片 小睡片刻

延伸note
catch sb.+V-ing意指「逮到某人在做某事」。類似例子還有caught me cheating（逮到我作弊）。

 答題TIPS看這裡！

> 每個人的生活習慣不同，有人喜歡早睡早起，有人天生是夜貓族，可以參考自己的習慣來舉例。另外，無論是白天或晚上，只要精神好，做事就比較有效率。不管是morning person還是afternoon person，都要解釋原因。

Words & Phrases　與精神有關的詞彙

1 energetic 精力充沛的	**2 perky** 有精神的
3 refreshed 恢復精神的	**4 alert** 靈敏的
5 tired 疲倦的	**6 dizzy** 頭暈目眩的
7 exhausted 筋疲力盡的	**8 be not there** 無法專心的

🎤 進階實用句 More Expressions

I just can't get my head around it in the morning.

早晨的時候，我的頭腦都不夠清楚。

You probably noticed that I am a bit slow after lunch.

你可能有注意到，午餐過後，我的反應會變慢。

If I don't take a nap in the afternoon, I will pass out on the couch straight away the moment I get home.

如果我下午沒午睡，我回到家就會直接倒在沙發上昏睡。

當地的街頭市場

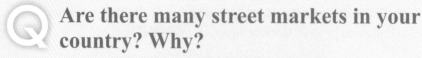

Q Are there many street markets in your country? Why?

你的國家有很多街頭市場嗎？為什麼？

你可以這樣回答

MP3
007

No, street markets are not very common[1] in my country. It is not part of our life, but you will see them during festivals[2] or summer months when the daylight is so much longer. It's when people are more willing to[3] go out. Most of the items you see in the street markets are homemade[4] arts and crafts, ladies fashion, and maybe some preserves[5] made by the local farmers. It is not stuff[6] that you buy every day, so I don't go there often.

　　街頭市場在我的國家並不普遍，那並非我們的日常文化，但遇到節慶，或白晝時間較長的夏季，因為大眾出門逛街的意願較高，所以能看到街頭市場。大部分在街頭市場販售的產品都是手工藝品、女裝或農家自製的蜜餞與果醬，並不是每天要買的東西，所以我其實不太會去逛街頭市場。

❶ **common** 形 普通的；常見的	❷ **festival** 名 節日	❸ **be willing to** 片 樂意；願意
❹ **homemade** 形 自製的	❺ **preserve** 名 蜜餞；果醬	❻ **stuff** 名 東西；物品

換個立場講講看

Yes, street markets are very popular[7] in my country because of the tourists[8]. The markets which aim for tourists mostly sell local souvenirs[9], such as T-shirts, bikinis and sarongs[10], and they are everywhere near the major hotels. We also have a lot of traditional markets which are designed for locals shopping for groceries[11]. People believe things are cheaper in the street markets because you can haggle[12]. Don't be shy. I got quite a lot of nice bargains by doing this.

是的，因為觀光客的關係，街頭市場在我的國家很受歡迎。客群鎖定觀光客的市場賣的多為當地紀念品，像T恤、比基尼、紗籠裙之類的，主要飯店附近都找得到。傳統市場也很多，供當地人採買雜貨，因為可以殺價，大家都會覺得去傳統市場買東西比較便宜。不用不好意思，像我就因此買到很多物超所值的東西呢！

7 popular
形 受歡迎的

8 tourist
名 觀光客

9 souvenir
名 紀念品

10 sarong
名 紗籠裙

11 grocery
名 食品雜貨

12 haggle
動 討價還價

 試著更與眾不同

No, we don't. The weather is really bad in my country, so we literally[13] can't set up[14] street markets. The city is covered in snow for four to five months of a year. Even during the warmer[15] months, it is still too cold to be outside. Therefore, we normally get our groceries from the supermarket in the shopping mall. There is central heating in the mall. Besides, we can go for a coffee or haircut[16] as well as grocery shopping. If the mall weren't open, it would be really inconvenient.

　　沒有，因為我們國家的天氣很差，實在無法擺設街頭市場。市區一年裡有四到五個月都被白雪覆蓋，即使在比較溫暖的月份，一般大眾也無法待在室外，因此，我們通常會去購物中心的超市買東西，那裡有空調，而且我們不只可以買東西，還能去喝咖啡、剪頭髮之類的。假如購物中心沒開，就會很不方便！

13 literally
副 實在地

14 set up
片 擺放某物

15 warm
形 溫暖的

16 haircut
名 剪頭髮

> 延伸note
> 街頭市場與天氣相關，所以若是冬季被雪覆蓋(be covered in snow)的國家，也可以如實描述氣候。

答題TIPS看這裡！

如果本身有很豐富的旅遊經驗，也可以應用其他國家的例子，像街頭市場在東南亞就很常見。除了天氣之外，經濟發展的情況、消費習慣…等也都會影響市場型態。發展較落後的國家基本上不太會有大型的購物中心（shopping mall）；而西方國家大多習慣到超市（supermarket）購物。

Words & Phrases　各種街頭市場

1 **night market**
夜市

2 **night bazaar**
夜間市集

3 **traditional market**
傳統市場

4 **flea market**
跳蚤市場

5 **flower market**
花市

6 **farmers' market**
農產品市集

7 **seafood market**
海鮮市場

8 **swap meet**
二手交換會

進階實用句 More Expressions

If you go to the night market, you must try their local dishes.

如果你去夜市，一定要嚐嚐他們的在地菜餚。

I am not used to the bargaining culture in the street market. I find going to the mall is much easier.

我不習慣街頭市場的殺價文化，去購物中心買東西簡單多了。

You can get the best produce from the farmers' markets. Some of the vendors are the growers themselves.

你可以在農產品市集買到最新鮮的農產品，因為很多小販都是自耕農。

習慣的交通工具

Q Do you drive or use public transport?
你自己開車還是搭乘大眾交通工具？

你可以這樣回答

MP3 008

I drive most of the time because where I live is not near any sort of public transportation[1]. It doesn't matter if I am going to work or just picking up a liter[2] of milk from the shops. I have to drive anyway. I think the Road and Traffic Department should really look into this issue. It would make my life so much easier if they added a bus route[3] near my house. You have no idea how much I spend on gas[4] every week!

　　我通常都自己開車，因為我的住處附近沒有任何的交通站，所以不管是去上班，還是到商店買一公升的牛奶，我都一定得開車。我覺得交通部應該正視這個問題，如果在我家附近加開一條公車路線，生活不知道可以輕鬆多少。現在，光是我一個禮拜的油錢就令人難以想像！

❶ transportation
名 交通工具

❷ liter
名 公升

❸ route
名 路線；航線

❹ gas
名 汽油

延伸note
pick up後面接「人」時，表示到某處接某人；接「物」時依情境，可能有「購買」之意。

換個立場講講看

I always take public transportation because I live right next to an MRT station and a bus terminal[5]. They are only a 5-minute walk away! The MRT and the buses pretty much take me anywhere I want to go. I take the MRT to work because my office is near an MRT station. Besides, the MRT always gets me there on time[6]. I never need to worry about[7] traffic jams[8]. Only when a place is not close to public transportation do I drive.

　　我住的地方離捷運站和公車總站很近，走路只要五分鐘，所以我都搭乘大眾交通工具。基本上，想去任何地方，只要有捷運和公車就夠了。我的辦公室就在捷運站附近，所以我搭捷運上班，而且捷運總是讓我準時抵達公司，完全不用擔心塞車的問題。只有在目的地附近沒有交通站的時候，我才會自己開車。

延伸note
right next to和only a 5-minute walk away都能用以表示「旁邊就有」的便利性。

⑤ terminal
名（火車、巴士等的）總站

⑥ on time
片 準時

⑦ worry about
片 擔心

⑧ traffic jam
片 塞車

試著更與眾不同

Well, I don't have a driver's license[9], so driving is not an option[10] for me. If I want to go out, I have to take the bus to the MRT station first. It's fine during the day, but the bus doesn't come as frequently[11] after 9 p.m. I have to take a taxi from the MRT station to my place if I don't want to wait for the bus. Sometimes, I car-pool[12] with my co-worker during work days. And I will chip in[13] some money for the gas for him. That way, I don't need to worry about the bus connection[14] if I work overtime.

　　嗯，我沒有駕照，所以根本不可能開車。如果我要出門，我必須搭公車到捷運站轉車。白天還算方便，但晚上九點之後，公車班次就沒那麼多，如果我不想等公車的話，就必須坐計程車回家。平常上班的時候，我有時會搭同事的便車，再幫他分攤油錢，這樣我如果加班，就不用擔心轉乘公車的問題。

⑨ a driver's license
片 駕照

⑩ option
名 選項

⑪ frequently
副 頻繁地

⑫ car-pool
動 共乘

⑬ chip in
片 共同出錢

⑭ connection
名 接駁轉運的交通工具

答題TIPS看這裡！

開車和搭大眾交通工具都各有優缺點，如：地鐵/捷運不用擔心塞車，但也許要轉接駁車（shuttle bus），時間上可能無法配合。若自己開車就能直達目的地，但可能會面臨尖峰時段容易塞車的問題，還要付停車費跟油錢。

Words & Phrases　與火車相關的詞彙

1　**night express**
夜快車

2　**through train**
直達火車

3　**lounge car**
休憩車廂

4　**dining car**
餐車

Words & Phrases　認識汽車款式

1　**hatchback**
掀背車

2　**sedan**
轎車

3　**recreational vehicle**
露營車

4　**truck / lorry**
卡車

🎤 進階實用句 More Expressions

Make sure you stick to the speed limit and drive carefully.

切勿超速，小心駕駛。

This bus app is so handy; it updates the timetable every minute.

這個公車APP很好用，它每分鐘都會更新時刻表。

I am going to the Metropolitan Museum. Can you tell me which stop to get off at, please?

我要去大都會博物館，請問要在哪一站下車呢？

UNIT 09

週末的活動安排

 你可以這樣回答

 MP3 009

It depends on[1] whether I need to work on Saturday or not. I get a full Saturday off every two weeks. If it is a working Saturday, I get off work[2] at 5 p.m. I grab[3] something to eat, and then head to my friend's house for a drink. If she feels like it, we play some video games together. Sometimes I stay at her place because I get too drunk. On Sunday, I sleep in[4] during the day. And I go to my parents' house for dinner since I don't see them a lot during the week.

要看我星期六要不要去上班，我的工作是隔週休。如果遇到要上班的星期六，五點下班之後，我會先去吃個東西，再到朋友家喝個小酒，如果她想的話，我們會一起玩電動。喝得太醉時，我會直接在她家睡一晚。星期天我則會補眠，再到我爸媽家吃晚餐，畢竟我星期一到五都沒什麼機會見他們。

❶ **depend on**
片 取決於；視…而定

❸ **grab**
動 抓取

❷ **get off work**
片 下班

❹ **sleep in**
片 補眠

延伸note
採用輪班制(shift)的工作，休假時間不固定，就很有可能用到every two weeks(隔週休)的說法。

 換個立場講講看

I love outdoor activities[5] and to get close to nature. So, I normally go hiking in the woods or go to the beach on weekends. I sit around the office for the whole week, so I really don't want to stay indoors when I can go out. If I get more time, I

organize[6] a camping trip with my friends. I really enjoy a camp fire BBQ under the stars with a couple of beers. I even enjoy listening to the owls at night. I find it very peaceful[7] and relaxing. I can really refresh[8] myself with this kind of activity.

　　我喜歡戶外活動和親近大自然，所以我週末通常會去森林漫步或到海邊玩。星期一到五我整天坐著工作，所以能出門的時候，我不想待在室內。如果有比較多的時間，我會和朋友一起去露營，我真的很喜歡在星空下，圍著營火烤肉喝酒的感覺，也喜歡聆聽貓頭鷹的叫聲，我覺得這很詳和、放鬆，藉由這些活動，真的會有替自己充電的感覺。

延伸note
熱愛大自然的人英文稱a nature lover，這種人很喜歡郊外和鄉下，親近野生動物和大自然。

⑤ activity
名 活動

⑥ organize
動 組織；安排

⑦ peaceful
形 平靜的；安寧的

⑧ refresh
動 使恢復精神

 ### 試著更與眾不同

Well, I will sleep in in the morning first. And then go for a nice brunch with my boyfriend at the local café near my apartment. They have the best brunch selection[9]! After finishing our meals, we might go shopping at the department store or watch the latest movie. If we don't feel like doing those things, we might just go for a walk. Sometimes, my boyfriend gets too busy to go on a date[10]. In that case, I make an appointment at a spa center. The full-body exfoliating[11] and massage[12] are my favorites!

　　上午我都會先補眠，再跟男朋友到我公寓附近的咖啡店吃早午餐，那家咖啡店的早午餐很美味！用完餐後，我們可能會去逛百貨公司，或看剛上映的電影，如果不想做這些的話，就會去散散步。我男友有時候很忙，沒時間約會，這時候我就會打電話向SPA中心預約，全身去角質和按摩可是我的最愛呢！

⑨ selection
名 選擇；精選品

⑩ go on a date
片 約會

⑪ exfoliate
動 使…片狀剝落

⑫ massage
名 按摩

延伸note
三餐時間外的飲食除了brunch(早午餐)之外，還有tea time(下午茶)以及a night snack(消夜)。

答題TIPS看這裡！

Key Points

如果平常週末真的沒有什麼特別活動好提，補眠（sleep in）永遠都可以當作答案。沒事做的週末稱為quiet weekend（寧靜的週末），通常會在家睡覺、看雜誌、打電腦、澆花、陪家人/寵物…等，著重在個人活動；忙碌的週末則稱hectic weekend，通常是與人有約的活動，如：跳舞、騎車、朋友聚會、烤肉、應酬、去海邊玩…等等。

Words & Phrases　描述週末活動

1. **music festival**
   音樂祭
2. **barbecue**
   烤肉
3. **speed dating**
   快速換桌約會
4. **blind date**
   相親
5. **clubbing**
   去舞廳
6. **play softball**
   打壘球
7. **hit the gym**
   上健身房
8. **catch up with friends**
   與朋友聊聊

進階實用句 More Expressions

Switch to the party mode. It is the weekend!

準備好去狂歡，週末到了！

Everyone has different plans for the weekend. Some want to rest, while others want to party.

週末的計畫每個人都不一樣，有人想要好好休息，有人則想瘋狂玩樂。

My weekend was so hectic. I went on two blind dates, and both turned out to be disappointing.

我這個週末很忙，去了兩場相親，結果都很糟。

034

UNIT 10

推薦一本好書

Q Can you recommend a good book? Why or why not?

你能推薦一本好書嗎？為什麼(不)？

你可以這樣回答

MP3
010

I am afraid not. I think I am more of a visual[1] and audio[2] person. I need the stimulation[3] of sounds and pictures to keep me focused. I get information a lot quicker from watching TV or videos. The only printed material I read is tabloid[4] magazines. I really don't know how people can take a book and read by the pool when they are on holidays[5]. I can't imagine[6] anything worse than that!

　　恐怕沒辦法，聲音和影像比較吸引我，而且聲音和圖像的刺激才能提高我的專注力。看電視和錄影帶的時候，我接收資訊的速度很快。我唯一會看的書只有八卦雜誌。真搞不懂怎麼會有人在度假的時候選擇在游泳池邊看書，我覺得這種度假糟透了！

❶ visual	❷ audio	❸ stimulation
形 視覺的	形 聽覺的；聲音的	名 刺激
❹ tabloid	❺ on holidays	❻ imagine
形 轟動式的；庸俗的	片 度假	動 想像

換個立場講講看

I enjoy reading a lot, especially novels that have been adapted into[7] movies. My favorite is "Forrest Gump" by Winston Groom. It is a story about how life presents itself with all kinds of surprises to a not-so-intelligent[8] man. The main character makes the best out of the situations[9] when he just takes things as they come. Although the storyline[10] might be different from the original[11] novel, it's still interesting to see how the director interpreted[12] the story.

　　我熱愛閱讀，尤其是改編成電影的小說。我最喜歡的是溫斯頓・格盧姆所寫的《阿甘正傳》，故事是說一個不太聰明的人，在難料的人生際遇裡以順應的態度面對，卻意外得到最好的結果。雖然電影與原著小說略為不同，但看導演如何詮釋也是很有趣的一件事。

7 adapt into 片 改編	**8** intelligent 形 聰明的	**9** situation 名 處境；境遇
10 storyline 名 情節	**11** original 形 原作的；原本的	**12** interpret 動 詮釋；解釋

 ### 試著更與眾不同

I don't really read for leisure[13], so novels are not my type of thing. I like those self-help books. Whenever I come across problems or need some guidance[14], I always turn to[15] books for answers. Recently[16], I read a book named "How to Manage Your Debts[17]". I found this book really useful. I was not very careful with money when I graduated from college. So I am struggling to pay my bills. I've followed the instructions[18] the book mentioned, and they actually worked. I believe I could be debt-free in the near future!

　　我不太會為了休閒而讀書，所以不喜歡小說。我喜歡與自我成長相關的工具書，每當我遇到問題，或需要指引的時候，我總會從書裡找答案。我最近讀的一本書叫《如何管理你的債務》，我覺得這本書很實用。大學剛畢業的時候，我花錢不夠節制，所以到現在還必須想辦法支付那些帳單。我有照著書裡的方式做，真的有用，相信過不了多久，我就能從卡債中解脫了！

13 leisure 名 空閒時間	**14** guidance 名 指導；引導	**15** turn to 片 向…尋求幫助
16 recently 副 最近	**17** debt 名 債務；借款	**18** instruction 名 指示；講授

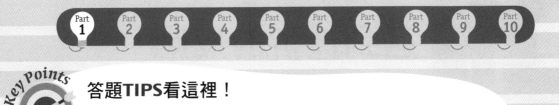

答題TIPS看這裡！

並不是每個人都有閱讀的習慣，無法推薦也有理由，可能是沒有興趣（have no interests），或沒時間閱讀（don't have time/have no time reading），記得提供足夠的資訊，讓對方理解你之所以無法推薦的原因。

Words & Phrases　表達喜好的用語

1 prefer A to B
更喜歡A

2 rather than
勝過；而非

3 like sth. better
比較喜歡(某物)

4 would rather
寧願；情願

Words & Phrases　電影的工作人員

1 screenwriter
編劇

2 director
導演

3 producer
製片人

4 boom operator
收音員

進階實用句 More Expressions

I don't really spend much time reading.

我沒花什麼時間讀書。

If you don't mind the adult theme, "50 shades of Grey" is a very unique book to read.

如果你不介意成人主題，《葛雷的50道陰影》是一本相當特別的書。

My friend recommended this book to me; she said it would help me with my English.

我朋友推薦這本書給我，她說對我的英文會有幫助。

UNIT 11
遇到挫折的反應

Q If you can't do something well, will you give up or keep on trying?

當你做不好某件事時，你會放棄還是繼續嘗試呢？

 你可以這樣回答

I will give up[1] right away, but not completely[2]. I will spend time looking for an alternative[3] and work on it. From my point of view, if you keep working on[4] something that just won't work, it is a waste of time. It is much better to find another way out. For example, I am a technology[5] moron[6]. One time, I spent hours trying to get the GPS to work, but it just wouldn't. I decided to give up and use a traditional paper map instead: problem solved right away!

　　我會馬上放棄，但不會完全放棄，我會花時間找替代方案，試著用替代方案取代原本的作法。我覺得花時間在不可行的事情上，純粹是在浪費時間，不如找其他的方法。像我本身是個科技白癡，有一次我花了很多時間想搞定GPS，可是一直弄不好，我就決定放棄，直接拿紙本地圖來看，問題立刻就解決啦！

❶ **give up**
片 放棄

❷ **completely**
副 徹底地

❸ **alternative**
名 替代方案

❹ **work on**
片 致力於；從事

❺ **technology**
名 科技

❻ **moron**
名（口）傻瓜

 換個立場講講看

I will keep on trying until I get it right. I am not a person that gives up easily. I believe success[7] is the result of endless[8] trial[9] and error. However, there is no point trying the same thing over and over again. So I stop and take a minute to

think what might be the cause of the failure[10] before I retry. Of course, I get frustrated[11] when things do not turn out the way I expected. But look at those famous scientists, which one of them did not keep on trying until he or she had a breakthrough[12]?

　　我會一直試驗到成功為止。我並不是會輕易放棄的人，我相信成功是不斷反覆嘗試的結果。不過，一直重複做同一件事也沒有必要，所以，在我重新嘗試之前，我會停下來想一想，找出導致失敗的可能原因。當然，結果不如預期時，我也會感到灰心，可是看看那些有名的科學家，哪一個不是一直試驗到有突破為止的呢？

❼ **success**	❽ **endless**	❾ **trial**
名 成功	形 不斷的	名 考驗；磨煉
❿ **failure**	⓫ **frustrated**	⓬ **breakthrough**
名 失敗	形 失意的；洩氣的	名 重大突破

 **試著更與眾不同**

It depends. If it is something I am interested in, I would keep trying until I lose patience[13]. For example, I enjoy building models[14]. When I get stuck, I always keep trying until the model is completed. On the other hand[15], if it is something that I am not interested in, I give up easily. I was never a big fan of puzzles[16]. My friend once gave me one for my birthday. And you know what? I never had patience to finish it.

　　不一定，如果是我有興趣的事，我就會一直試到失去耐性為止，就像我喜歡做模型，當我做到一半卡住，我一定會一直試，到完成模型為止。反之，如果我沒興趣，那我很快就會放棄。像我從來就不喜歡拼圖，我朋友之前曾經送我拼圖當生日禮物，結果你猜怎麼著？我根本沒耐性拼完它。

⓭ **patience**	⓮ **model**
名 耐心	名 模型
⓯ **on the other hand**	⓰ **puzzle**
片 另一方面	名 拼圖

延伸note
keep (on) trying表示努力不懈；反義詞為stop trying，也可以用quit表示放棄。

答題TIPS看這裡！

事情做不好有很多原因，每個人面對的方式都不同。面對本題，放不放棄不是重點，容易放棄的人可能只是不想浪費時間（waste one's time on sth.），或在尋找其他方法（find an alternation），其實這也是另一種思考方式，這些都可以在舉例時說明。口試時盡量強調自己的優勢，別著重於會繼續還是放棄，而要多加敘述自己會如何處理。

Words & Phrases 描述個性與做法的詞彙

1 stubborn
固執的；強硬的

2 arrogant
高傲的

3 truant
玩忽職守的

4 indifferent
無所謂的

5 hesitant
遲疑的；躊躇的

6 determined
有決心的

7 concentrated
全神貫注的

8 stick it out
堅持到底

進階實用句 More Expressions

Fixing this engine really is testing my patience.

修這個引擎真是在測試我的耐性。

I am a very determined person. I don't give up easily.

我是個很有決心的人，不會輕易放棄

We have done everything we could, but it still doesn't work. It is frustrating not being able to fix things.

我們什麼方法都試了，但都沒用，事情怎樣都無法順利進行，真令人灰心。

UNIT 12 談迷路的經驗

Q Have you gotten lost? Describe your experience.

你迷路過嗎？請描述當時的情況。

 你可以這樣回答

MP3 012

Yes, although it was seven years ago, I still remember it clearly. I was a backpacker[1] on a working holiday in Australia. I was in Perth and all the roads there change their names in different sections[2] of the same road. It is awfully[3] confusing, especially for a newcomer like me. It was raining and windy[4], and I could barely keep my scooter stable[5]. I just wanted to get home, but I had no idea where I was going. Luckily, I saw a landmark[6] of the city, which gave me an idea of my location.

有，即使那是七年前的事，我依然記憶猶新。那時，我到澳洲的伯斯打工度假當背包客，當地同一條路的每個地段都有不同的名字，對像我這樣剛到的人來說，實在太困擾了！那天颱風又下雨，我差一點連機車都牽不住，我只想回家，但根本不知道我在哪裡，還好後來看到市區的地標，讓我取得大概的方向。

❶ backpacker	❷ section	❸ awfully
名 背包客	名 地段；區域	副（口）極度地
❹ windy	❺ stable	❻ landmark
形 刮風的；風大的	形 穩定的；平穩的	名 地標

 換個立場講講看

I don't get lost often; I have a pretty good sense of direction[7]. But if I am going to a place I have never been to before, I need GPS. One time, I decided to take my girlfriend to a beautiful garden café on the outskirts[8] of the city. I took a wrong turn and got lost[9]. We ended up near a cemetery[10], which was very scary. Luckily, it was in the middle of the day, and we found our way pretty soon. What an experience!

我不常迷路，我的方向感滿好的。但如果是要到沒去過的地方，我就需要GPS了。有一次，我帶女朋友前往位於郊區的美麗花園咖啡館，我轉錯彎，因而迷路，開到墓園去，那真是恐怖。還好那時是中午，而且我們很快就找到了路，這經驗真令人難忘！

❼ a sense of direction
片 方向感

❽ outskirt(s)
名 郊區

❾ get lost
片 迷路

❿ cemetery
名 公墓；墓地

試著更與眾不同

Definitely! I am terrible with directions. I get lost even with the help of a map[11]! I remember[12] one time when my friends and I went to a party at night. I was pretty sure how to get to the place because I had been there before. However, it looked very different at night. I pulled out the map to take a look, but I was very confused about where we were on the map. At the end, we gave up and got out the GPS. Thank God for that invention[13]. I am hopeless[14] with a map!

當然有！我的方向感超差的，連看個地圖都可以迷路！有一次我和朋友們參加晚宴，那個地方我之前去過，所以很有自信能找到，但一到晚上，那附近看起來完全不同。我拿出地圖來看，但是看了半天也看不出我們在哪，最後只好放棄，拿GPS出來，感謝老天，還好有人發明這東西。我對地圖完全沒轍呀！

⓫ map
名 地圖

❷ remember
動 記得

⓭ invention
名 發明物

⓮ hopeless
形 （口）無能的；不行的

Key Points 答題TIPS看這裡！

大家應該都有迷路的經驗，幾乎都是因為對某個地方不熟，建議舉實例，聽起來比較具體。提到迷路，當然可以敘述看地圖或使用衛星導航GPS的經驗。如果遇到秀逗的GPS導錯路，也可以提出來增加故事性喔！

Words & Phrases 開車可能遇到的情況

1 break down
壞掉；熄火

2 a flat tire
爆胎

3 engine overheated
引擎過熱

4 out of petrol/gas
沒油了

5 take the wrong turn
轉錯彎

6 car accident
車禍

7 get caught in traffic
塞車

8 heavy fog
濃霧

 進階實用句 More Expressions

I get so lost that I have no idea where I am.

我迷路到完全搞不清楚現在的所在地。

Can you direct me to the nearest highway entrance, please?

你可以告訴我最近的高速公路閘口怎麼去嗎？

I always get confused at this intersection; I am not sure which way to turn.

每次到這個路口我都很困惑，不知道該轉哪一邊。

UNIT 13

記憶中的童年

MP3
013

Q **What did you usually do during your free time as a child?**

在你小時候，有空時你通常會做什麼呢？

你可以這樣回答

I loved to play "tea party" with my little sister. We would set up a picnic[1] mat in the back yard and take some of the plates[2] from the kitchen to pretend[3] that we were having a picnic. Sometimes, we brought our favorite snacks and put them on the mat. Mostly, my sister and I would be the hosts and our dollies were our guests. It was really fun until my brother came with his toy robot[4]. He always tried to crash our tea party. That's the reason why we didn't welcome boys.

我很愛跟我妹妹玩扮家家酒。我們會在後院擺上野餐布，再從廚房拿碗盤，假裝在野餐，我們有時候會帶自己喜愛的點心，擺在野餐布上。大多數的時間，我妹妹和我會當茶會主人，我們的娃娃則充當客人，在我弟弟拿著他的機器人來搗亂之前，我們的茶會都很有趣。我弟弟總是想要破壞茶會，這也是我們為什麼不讓男生加入的原因。

❶ **picnic**
名 郊遊；野餐

❷ **plate**
名 盤子；碟

❸ **pretend**
動 佯裝；假裝

❹ **robot**
名 機器人

> **延伸note**
> 提到妹妹，除了本段提到的 little sister 之外，younger/baby sister 等用法也很常見。

換個立場講講看

We lived near a little creek[5]. What we often did was ride our bikes to the nearby[6] bridge and jump into the creek. We loved going for a swim in it.

There were a lot of fish and frogs. We sometimes took home some tadpoles[7] and watched them grow into frogs[8]. It is such a good memory. But come to think of it now, it was actually very dangerous to jump off the bridge. There was no adult supervision[9]. Luckily, we didn't injure[10] ourselves by doing this.

我們住在一條小溪附近,我們通常會騎腳踏車到附近的橋墩,從橋上跳進小溪,大家都超愛在那裡游泳的。溪裡有很多魚和青蛙,我們有時候會抓蝌蚪回去,看他們變成青蛙,這真是一段很美好的回憶。不過,現在回想起來,從橋上跳下去其實很危險,而且又沒有大人在旁邊,還好我們都沒因此受傷。

⑤ creek
名 小河;溪

⑥ nearby
形 附近的

⑦ tadpole
名 蝌蚪

⑧ frog
名 青蛙

⑨ supervision
名 監督

⑩ injure
動 傷害;損害

試著更與眾不同

My parents were always working, so I spent a lot of time either at after-school classes or at home with the nanny[11]. I did a lot of drawing and coloring. Sometimes I got so bored that I even played with my imaginary[12] friend. There are only a few things you can do on your own[13]. I usually looked forward to the weekends[14] because it was when my parents took me out to places like parks and zoos. We finally had some family time together.

我爸媽的工作很忙,所以我小時候不是待在補習班,就是回家和保姆一起。我很常畫畫和著色,有時候自己一個人會無聊到跟想像的朋友一起玩,一個人真的沒什麼好玩的。我通常很期待週末,因為爸媽會帶我去公園或動物園等地方,終於有全家相聚的家庭時光。

⑪ nanny
名 保姆

⑫ imaginary
形 想像中的

⑬ on one's own
片 獨自

⑭ weekend
名 週末

> **延伸note**
> few/little和a few/a little的用法要分清楚。a few/a little=some(一些),few/little表示「沒幾個」。

答題TIPS看這裡！

小時候的回憶，大多與玩樂有關，男生可能比較會玩泥巴、抓蟲、釣魚、打球、打彈珠、玩機器人之類的；女生的話，大概就跟扮家家脫不了關係。現代小孩則不同，可能對線上遊戲（online games）或iPad等物有興趣。回答時盡量選自己親身經歷過的事情，才容易往下延伸內容。

Words & Phrases　兒時的遊戲

1 hide and seek
躲貓貓

2 paper, scissors, stone
剪刀石頭布

3 play house
扮家家酒

4 Simon says
老師説

5 make mud pies
玩泥巴

6 skip rope
跳繩

7 fly a kite
放風箏

8 play hopscotch
跳房子

 進階實用句 More Expressions

I loved to raid my mother's wardrobe and put on her dresses.

我喜歡搜刮我媽的衣櫥，偷穿她的洋裝。

I used to draw on the wall when my parents were not watching.

我會趁爸媽沒看到的時候偷畫牆壁。

When I was little, I liked to climb trees and often came home with cuts and bruises.

我小時候很愛爬樹，常常回家後才發現身上有很多傷口和瘀青。

UNIT 14

穿衣服的喜好

Q **What do you like to wear?**
你喜歡穿什麼衣服呢？

 你可以這樣回答

MP3 014

Instead of[1] wearing pants and tops, I prefer to wear dresses. Dresses are easy because I don't need to worry about which top goes with which pants or if the style and color match each other. However, when I need to go to the factory[2] or field for a site visit, wearing dresses can be inconvenient[3]. After all, I don't want others to see my underpants[4] when I am climbing[5] a ladder[6]. So, pants and shirts are the only option then.

　　和褲子搭配上衣的穿法相比，我比較喜歡穿洋裝。洋裝很方便，既不用擔心上衣和褲子要怎麼搭配，也不用考慮款式和顏色。不過，當我必須去工廠或工地實地勘查時，穿洋裝就不方便了。我可不希望在爬梯子的時候，被其他人看到內褲，所以那時候就只好穿褲子和襯衫。

❶ **instead of** 片 代替；與其	❷ **factory** 名 工廠	❸ **inconvenient** 形 不方便的
❹ **underpants** 名 內褲	❺ **climb** 動 爬；攀登	❻ **ladder** 名 梯子

 換個立場講講看

Casual[7] is my favorite style. I don't really care about how good I look. Instead, I care about if the clothes are comfortable[8] or not. My standard[9] outfit[10] consists of[11] a T-shirt, shorts and sandals[12]. I don't worry about being too casual.

However, my girlfriend doesn't like my casual style very much. She even bought me a suit last year. The problem is, I don't have many opportunities to wear it. I guess it will be my wedding suit.

隨興風是我的最愛，我不在意衣服穿起來好不好看，只要穿起來舒適就好。我的標準穿搭是：T恤、短褲加涼鞋。我並不覺得這種隨興的穿著怎麼樣，但我女友不太喜歡，她甚至買了一套西裝給我，問題是，我根本沒什麼場合穿，我猜那套西裝要到我結婚那天才會亮相。

❼ casual
形 隨便的；非正式的

❽ comfortable
形 舒適的

❾ standard
形 標準的

❿ outfit
名 全套服裝

⓫ consist of
片 由…構成

⓬ sandal
名 涼鞋

試著更與眾不同

I love to make myself look good, so I will dress up[13] whenever I can. I spend a lot of money buying the right clothes for work. It has to be a little sexy but still classy[14]. I don't want to look dorky[15] like most of the older ladies in my office. If I'm going out on a Saturday night, I usually put on my favorite black dress, which shows my curves[16]. People have mistaken me for[17] a celebrity[18] before, and that has actually happened quite a few times!

我喜歡把自己打扮得漂漂亮亮，只要有機會，我都會盡量打扮。我花了很多錢購買能穿去上班的衣服，看起來要有點性感，但款式也必須高雅，我不想跟辦公室裡那些年紀大的女人一樣，看起來呆呆的。如果是星期六晚上要出門，我會穿上我最愛的黑色洋裝，那件洋裝能修飾身材曲線，別人還會誤認我是明星，這之前發生過好幾次呢！

⓭ dress up
片 盛裝打扮

⓮ classy
形 漂亮的；別緻的

⓯ dorky
形 呆呆的

⓰ curve
名 曲線；弧度

⓱ mistake for
片 誤認…為

⓲ celebrity
名 名人；名流

Key Points 答題TIPS看這裡！

喜歡穿什麼樣的衣服，其實一句話就可以回答完，口試的時候，建議提供解釋。假如你喜歡穿牛仔褲，不要只說 I like to wear jeans.，而要試著加上原因，例如：I like to wear jeans because it makes my butt looks good!

Words & Phrases 常見的衣服款式

1 **cardigan** 羊毛衫

2 **blouse** 女襯衫

3 **camisole** 小可愛

4 **turtleneck** 高領衫

5 **pullover** 套頭毛衣

6 **hoodie** 連帽T恤

7 **crops** 七/八分褲

8 **straights** 直筒褲

進階實用句 More Expressions

I always pack my tank tops and shorts when I go on holidays.

我去度假時，都會帶背心和短褲。

I prefer to wear slim-fit shirts to work. They make me look younger and perky.

我喜歡穿合身的襯衫去上班，這樣看起來比較年輕有活力。

I like to bring a scarf in my bag. It comes in handy when the weather suddenly turns.

我習慣在包包裡放一條圍巾，如果突然變天，就很方便。

UNIT 15 對屋內空間的偏好

Q **Do you prefer a big or a small house? Why?**
你喜歡住大房子還是小房子？為什麼？

你可以這樣回答

MP3 015

If money were not a concern[1], I would definitely go for a big house. I have always dreamt of living in a house with 4-5 bedrooms and a decent[2]-sized living room. There would also be a beautiful kitchen and a nice balcony[3]. I like to invite my friends over, but where I am living now is only a small rooftop[4] flat. I wish my boss would give me a pay raise soon, so I could afford to move to a bigger place.

如果不用考慮金錢，我一定會選大房子，我一直夢想可以住在有四到五間房及寬敞客廳的房子，裡面還有漂亮的廚房和陽台。我喜歡邀請朋友來家裡作客，但我現在住的地方只是頂樓加蓋的小公寓，希望我的老闆可以趕快幫我加薪，這樣我就能搬到更大的房子了。

❶ **concern**
名 關心的事

❷ **decent**
形 體面的

❸ **balcony**
名 陽台

❹ **rooftop**
形 屋頂上的

延伸note
無論自己的住處怎麼樣，每個人都會有自己理想的房屋(dream house)，回答時盡量多加敘述。

換個立場講講看

I don't mind if it is a big house or a small one as long as the rent[5] is reasonable[6] and affordable[7]. I might actually choose to live in a big house and rent the rooms out. In that case, I could enjoy the space of a big house without paying full

rent. I work at a full-time[8] job, so I don't have much time to do the housework. If I were sharing a house with someone, I would hope that person would help to do the household chores. As you know, cleaning up a big house could be really tiring.

我不介意住大房子還是小房子，只要租金合理、負擔得起就好。不過，要我選的話，我應該會選大房子，再把房間分租出去，這樣我能享受大房子的空間，卻又不必支付全額租金。我是全職員工，沒有太多時間整理家務，所以如果要找室友，我希望他能幫忙做家事，你也知道，大房子整理起來很累人的。

延伸note
和租屋有關的重要單字有：lease(合約)、deposit(押金)、landlord/landlady(房東)…等。

5 rent
名 租金

7 affordable
形 負擔得起的

6 reasonable
形 合理的

8 full-time
形 全職的

 ## 試著更與眾不同

Personally[9], I prefer a small house. I am still single[10], so I don't need a very big place. Besides, living in a small house doesn't require much cleaning up. I am currently[11] living in a one-bedroom apartment. There isn't much to worry about when I do the household[12] chores. The living room and the kitchen are rather small. Normally, it only takes me 1.5 hours or so to finish cleaning. Also, I eat out most of the time, so I don't need to do the washing-up during the week. For now, a small place is better for me.

我個人比較喜歡小房子，我還單身，所以不需要很大的空間。除此之外，小房子也比較不需要整理。我目前住的是一房的公寓，做家事的時候，要整理的地方並不多，客廳跟廚房都滿小的，通常只需要花一個半小時就能打掃完。而且我很常外食，所以星期一到五根本連碗都不用洗，就現況而言，這樣的小房子較適合我。

9 personally
副 就個人而言

11 currently
副 目前

10 single
形 單身的

12 household
形 家庭的；家用的

延伸note
小房子一般分為有隔間的房子(one-bedroom apartment)與套房(suite)。

答題TIPS看這裡！

回答這個問題可以簡單敘述目前住的房子，再敘述自己對它的感想，是喜歡還是不喜歡？原因為何？這樣就能發展對話。如果不想談目前的住處，可以從夢想屋（dream house）著手，描述想要的房子。建議把自己的意見和想法加入答案，聽起來更具體。為了能在口試中流利地表達，事前理解各種屋型和基本傢俱該怎麼說，也是很重要的喔！

Words & Phrases 國外的房屋類型

1 house
獨棟房屋

2 apartment
公寓

3 duplex
聯式房屋

4 mansion
官邸；宅第

5 town house
連排住宅（大多為二到三層樓）

6 studio
（出租的）套房

7 hostel
青年旅館

8 commercial building
商業用屋

進階實用句 More Expressions

My studio apartment is the size of a shoe box.

我的套房空間大概只跟鞋盒一樣大。(形容超小)

My dream house is a big mansion with ocean view and a heated pool in the backyard.

我的夢想屋是海景別墅，後院還有溫水游泳池。

I had to share a bedroom with my sister when I was little. I am glad I have my own bedroom now.

我小時候必須和我妹妹同睡一間，真高興現在有自己的房間了。

Part 2

食物與旅遊
Food and Travel

 動 動詞   形 形容詞   連 連接詞

 名 名詞   介 介系詞   片 片語

 副 副詞

UNIT 01

速食的Yes與NO

Q **Do you like fast food? What do you think about it?**

你喜歡速食嗎？你對速食的看法如何？

 你可以這樣回答

I prefer home-cooked food over fast food because the former[1] is usually healthy and fresh[2]. However, I do not have enough time to cook for myself, so I have to turn to fast food every now and then[3]. It would be good if I had a boyfriend who enjoyed cooking and was willing to make dinner for me every night. If that were the case, I would not even need to rely on[4] fast food!

　　和速食相比，我其實比較喜歡自己煮的菜，因為那通常都比較健康、新鮮。但我實在沒那麼多時間下廚，所以有時候還是會去吃速食。如果我有個熱愛下廚的男朋友，願意每天煮晚餐給我吃，那就太棒了，如果有這樣的對象，我才不會去吃速食呢！

❶ former
形（兩者中）前者的
❸ every now and then
片 有時；偶爾

❷ fresh
形 新鮮的
❹ rely on
片 依靠；依賴

延伸note
every now and then表示「有時」或「偶爾」，也等於from time to time / occasionally。

 換個立場講講看

I love it! I really enjoy the taste of fast food. I mean, who doesn't like fried chicken and hot French Fries? Crispy[5] and juicy fried chicken is impossible to resist! But to balance my guilty[6] conscience[7], I normally would order a serving of salad. It makes me less guilty when I eat that greasy[8] and high-calorie food.

Sometimes I even swap^9 a soda for a glass of fresh juice. At least, that way I get some fiber^{10}.

　　我超愛！我覺得速食很美味，誰不喜歡吃炸雞和熱騰騰的薯條啊？炸雞酥脆的外皮和多汁的雞肉根本讓人無法抗拒啊！不過，為了減低我的罪惡感，我通常會另外點一份沙拉，這能讓我在吃完油膩和高熱量的美食後，感覺稍微好一些，有時候我甚至會把汽水換成新鮮果汁，這樣至少還有吃到一點纖維質。

⑤ crispy
形 酥脆的

⑥ guilty
形 內疚的

⑦ conscience
名 良心

⑧ greasy
形 油膩的

⑨ swap
動（口）與…交換

⑩ fiber
名 纖維質

試著更與眾不同

Well, I believe eating fast food has a very negative^{11} impact^{12} on our health, especially for its high in fat and low in fiber. Look at the increasing^{13} number of people who suffer from obesity^{14} and two type 2 diabetes^{15}. It is alarming^{16} for us to think about what we are eating compared to what we should be eating. Do you know Jamie Oliver? He's a famous English cook and TV host. He tries really hard to promote a healthy and organic diet for kids. It's difficult to follow, but I totally agree with his opinion.

　　我認為吃速食對我們的健康有害，尤其速食就是高油脂、低纖維的食物。看看現況，遭肥胖及第二型糖尿病所擾的人口日益增加，這對我們來說是個警訊，讓我們注意平常都吃了什麼，並思考應該吃些什麼才對。你知道傑米・奧利佛嗎？他是一位英國知名的廚師與節目主持人，他大力提倡兒童的餐點必須走向健康與有機，這很困難，但我完全同意他的觀點。

⑪ negative
形 負面的

⑫ impact
名 影響；作用

⑬ increasing
形 增加的

⑭ obesity
名 肥胖；過胖

⑮ diabetes
名 糖尿病

⑯ alarming
形 令人驚慌的；告急的

答題TIPS看這裡!

無論你喜不喜歡速食,記得要針對原因多加解釋,並盡量具體(be specific),不要單單只是說好還是不好,尤其英文裡的good / bad其實很抽象,所以建議加上具體的原因或實際例子,例如:I don't like fast food because most of the items are deep fried, which is really bad for my health.(速食大部分都是油炸物,對健康有害,所以我不喜歡。)

Words & Phrases 國外的人氣速食

1 fish and chips
炸魚加薯條

2 coke and soda
汽水(碳酸飲料)

3 pizza
披薩

4 burgers & fried chicken
漢堡及炸雞

Words & Phrases 替速食加分的美味醬料

1 ketchup
番茄醬

2 mayonnaise
美乃滋

3 mustard
黃芥末醬

4 chilli sauce
辣椒醬

進階實用句 More Expressions

Fast food is not everybody's cup of tea.

並非每個人都喜歡速食。

I know soft drinks are full of sugar, but I just can't resist them.

我知道汽水的糖分很高,但我就是無法抗拒。

I only eat boiled vegetables and lean meat. There is no way I would go to a fast food restaurant.

我只吃燙青菜和瘦肉,所以絕對不可能去速食餐廳。

UNIT 02

喜歡的食物類型

Q What kind of food do you like? When do you usually eat this food?

你喜歡什麼食物？你通常會在什麼時候吃呢？

MP3 017

你可以這樣回答

My favorite food is sticky[1] rice dumplings[2]. It was originally[3] a type of food that we ate during Dragon Boat Festival. The food is from an ancient[4] story. The dumplings were made to throw into the river to feed the fish, so that they wouldn't eat the body of a famous poet[5]. He committed suicide[6] by jumping into a river. Although sticky rice dumplings were originally created for Dragon Boat Festival, they have pretty much become a kind of food we buy every day.

我最喜歡的食物是粽子，它原是端午節才吃的食物，那源自於一個古老的歷史故事，當時的人包好粽子，丟進河裡餵魚，以保護一名投江自盡的詩人，保全他的屍體，不被魚吃掉。雖然粽子原本是端午節特有的食物，但現在其實天天都買得到。

❶ **sticky**
形 黏的

❷ **dumpling**
名 餃子

❸ **originally**
副 起初；原來

❹ **ancient**
形 古代的

❺ **poet**
名 詩人

❻ **commit suicide**
片 自殺

換個立場講講看

I love to enjoy Yum Cha. Those individual[7] small servings of steam[8] dumplings are so nice, and the flavor[9] is really delicate[10]. Yum Cha originated in Hong Kong; it means tea drinking in Cantonese[11]. Most apartments in Hong Kong are very small. In order to get away from home, people often go to Yum Cha restaurants for a break[12]. Traditionally, Yum Cha is more like a brunch; but here in Taiwan, we have it mostly for lunch or dinner.

我喜歡吃港式飲茶，那一籠籠小份的現蒸點心真的很美味，味道也很精緻，這類點心是源自於香港的傳統食物。「飲茶」其實是從廣東話Yum Cha音譯過來的字。香港人的住處空間大都很小，所以為了出門透透氣，香港人會去飲茶餐廳休息一下。傳統上，香港人把飲茶當作早午餐，但在台灣，我們反而會將它視為正式的中餐或晚餐。

❼ individual 形 個別的；單獨的	**❽ steam** 動 蒸；煮	**❾ flavor** 名 味道
❿ delicate 形 鮮美的	**⓫ Cantonese** 名 廣東話	**⓬ break** 名 暫停；休息

試著更與眾不同

I like Italian food most. My favorite is spaghetti[13] marinara[14] in a rich, tomato-based sauce with a hint of chilli[15]. I don't have it very often. Normally, it's only when my boyfriend and I want to celebrate certain holidays that we go to an Italian restaurant. I like to have my dish with a glass of red wine and a serving of garlic[16] bread. It feels so exotic[17] and romantic[18].

我最喜歡義大利菜，尤其是淋上濃郁的番茄醬、又帶點辣味的海鮮番茄義大利麵。我不常吃義大利菜，通常只有在男友和我想慶祝特定的節日時，我們才會上義大利餐廳用餐。吃義大利菜時，我喜歡搭配紅酒與大蒜麵包，感覺很有異國情調、又浪漫。

⓭ spaghetti 名 義大利麵	**⓮ marinara** 名 大蒜番茄醬	**⓯ chilli** 名 辣椒
⓰ garlic 名 大蒜；蒜頭	**⓱ exotic** 形 異國情調的	**⓲ romantic** 形 羅曼蒂克的

答題TIPS看這裡！

聽到對方詢問food（食物）的時候，不用太緊張，因為食物的範圍很廣，早晚餐、中西餐、葷素餐、甜點和鹹點…等，這些全部都包括在內。回答的範圍可大（如Italian food 義大利菜）可小（如spaghetti 義大利麵）。

Words & Phrases 有特色的異國料理

1. **Indian curry**
   印度咖哩

2. **Vietnamese noodle soup**
   越南河粉

3. **taco / burrito**
   墨西哥捲餅

4. **German style pig knuckle**
   德國豬腳

5. **kimchi**
   韓國泡菜

6. **fried rice cake**
   炒年糕

7. **foie gras**
   鵝肝醬

8. **cheese fondue**
   乳酪火鍋

進階實用句 More Expressions

I just can't turn down desserts. I must have one after dinner.

我完全無法抗拒甜點的誘惑，晚餐後我一定要吃甜點。

I am a big fan of a nice and juicy steak. I have it at least once a week.

我超愛多汁的牛排，一星期至少會吃一次。

Sandwiches are my favorite food for lunch, especially the ones made to order.

我中午最愛吃三明治，尤其是現點現做的。

UNIT 03

挑選午餐的餐點

Q What's the restaurant or place you often have lunch at?

你午餐常到哪間餐廳吃呢？

你可以這樣回答

MP3 018

I bring my lunch from home most of the time. If there aren't enough leftovers[1] the day before, I go to the famous noodle[2] shop near my office. It's right on the corner of the block. Wonton noodles are their specialty[3]. The restaurant is always packed[4] during lunch hour, so I would have it to go. There is no way I can get a seat there.

　　我通常會自己帶午餐，如果前一天的剩菜不夠我裝便當，我就會去公司附近的麵店，那間店很有名，就在公司街口的轉角，餛飩麵是他們的招牌菜色。午餐時間去總是門庭若市，所以我會外帶，否則絕對找不到位子坐。

❶ **leftovers**	❷ **noodle**
名 剩菜；廚餘	名 麵條
❸ **specialty**	❹ **pack**
名 特產；名產	動 擠滿；塞滿

延伸note
到國外點餐，若聽到櫃台店員問你For here or to go?，就是在問「要內用還是外帶」。

換個立場講講看

I prefer something light for lunch, such as sandwiches[5] or ciabattas[6]. Subway is a good choice because their sandwiches are all made to order. I like the freshness of their bread. It doesn't get soggy[7]. Sometimes when I feel like something different, I go to the local café. There is a good selection of light lunches, such as quiches[8], chicken and vegetable pies and pita bread. The best part of it is, they all

come with a serving of side salad and a free drink. Without paying too much, I can acquire enough nutrition.

　　我中午喜歡吃清淡一點的食物，像三明治或義式托鞋麵包之類的。Subway是不錯的選擇，因為他們的三明治都是現點現做，我喜歡它的新鮮麵包，都不會軟掉。如果我想換個口味，就會去附近的咖啡店，裡面輕食的選擇性滿多的，有法式鹹派、雞肉蔬菜派跟口袋餅，最棒的是，餐點都有附一份沙拉和一杯免費飲料，這樣我不用花太多錢就能獲得充足的營養。

延伸note
light用來形容餐點，表示為份量少、對身體較無負擔，在國外通常指三明治、麵包等。

5 sandwich
名 三明治

7 soggy
形 潮濕的

6 ciabatta
名 義式拖鞋麵包

8 quiche
名 法式鹹派

試著更與眾不同

I normally go to the restaurants with lunch specials[9]. There are quite a lot near my office. I like a teppanyaki restaurant about two blocks[10] away from my office. Their food is good and the price is even better. For NT$100, you can get a teppanyaki beef combo[11], which comes with rice and two stir-fry vegetable dishes. If the restaurant is too busy, I go to the local self-service buffet[12] restaurant instead. It has a good selection of food, and the price is quite fair, too.

　　我通常會去有商業午餐的餐廳，我公司附近還滿多的。我喜歡距離公司兩個街口的鐵板燒餐廳，食物美味，價格又優惠，一個鐵板燒牛肉套餐只要台幣一百元，附飯和兩道炒青菜。如果這間餐廳太多人，我就會去附近的自助餐，它的菜色挺豐富，價錢也公道。

---

9 lunch special
片 商業午餐

11 combo
名 套餐

10 block
名 （美）街區

12 buffet
名 自助餐；快餐

延伸note
到國外點套餐時，講 number one和combo one 都能表示「一號餐」。

答題TIPS看這裡！

回答本題最常出現的狀況是「答了自己常去的餐館後就不知道要說什麼」。建議從「喜歡的原因」（reason）、招牌菜（signature dish）…等角度切入。除了回答自己的午餐吃什麼以外，若有特殊情況，例如客戶來訪時，不得已必須有午餐會議（lunch meeting）的話，就可能要帶客戶去比較安靜或是離客戶較近的餐廳，此時就不用執著於究竟吃哪一間。

Words & Phrases 可挑選的中餐菜式

1	**spicy hotpot** 麻辣火鍋	**2**	**pork dumplings** 豬肉水餃
3	**cuttlefish soup** 魷魚羹	**4**	**fried rice noodle** 炒米粉
5	**braised pork rice** 滷肉飯	**6**	**beef noodle** 牛肉麵
7	**teppanyaki** 鐵板燒	**8**	**lunch box** 便當

進階實用句 More Expressions

I don't have a favorite restaurant. I like to find new places and try new dishes.

我沒有特別偏好的餐廳，我喜歡去新的餐廳嚐鮮。

I wish I could go to the steakhouse for lunch, but I only have forty minutes for my lunch break.

真希望能去牛排館吃午餐，但我的午休時間只有四十分鐘。

I am meeting a client for lunch. I guess I have to take him to a better place if I want to seal the deal.

我中午跟客戶約吃午餐，看來我得請他去好一點的餐廳，才有機會跟他簽約。

UNIT 04

詢問你的廚藝

 Q Can you cook? Who cooks in your house?
你會煮菜嗎？你家裡掌廚的人是誰呢？

MP3
019

你可以這樣回答

I can make simple dishes like fried rice[1] and vegetable soup, but my mother was always in charge of our meals. There was no need for me to step into[2] the kitchen while I stayed with my family. However, since I moved out[3] last year, I need to cook for myself. I really miss my mother's cooking and the time when there was someone cooking for me! Anyway, I eat out quite a lot because I am too busy with[4] my job.

　　如果是炒飯或蔬菜湯那種簡單的餐點，我會煮，不過，一向都是我母親在張羅大家的餐點，我還住家裡的時候，根本不用進廚房，但自從去年從家裡搬出來之後，我就得下廚了。真懷念母親的手藝，和有人煮飯給我吃的日子！總之，因為工作太忙碌，所以我習慣吃外食。

❶ **fried rice**
片 炒飯

❷ **step into**
片 走進

❸ **move out**
片 搬出來

❹ **be busy with**
片 忙著做某事

延伸note
be busy with後面要接名詞或動名詞，表示「忙著做某事」。

換個立場講講看

My mother never taught me how to cook. I think I am pretty lucky since my mom has cooked all my meals at home in the past. Ever since my brother got married[5] last year, my sister-in-law has taken up the responsibility[6] of cooking.

It is good that my mother can get more rest now; but frankly speaking[7], I like my mother's dishes more. Now, she only cooks for the important festivals like New Year's Eve. I strongly recommend[8] her rice balls which she makes on the winter solstice[9]. It's her secret recipe[10]. I've never seen anyone who can resist it.

　　我母親從來沒教我怎麼煮飯。我很幸運，在家都是媽媽煮給我吃，我哥哥去年結婚以後，就換我大嫂掌廚了。母親可以多休息固然是件好事，但老實說，我還是比較喜歡母親的手藝。現在她只有在重要的節慶才下廚，像年夜飯她就會煮。我強烈推薦她每年冬至煮的湯圓，那可是她的獨家配方，到目前為止，我還沒看過有人能抗拒這道菜的呢！

❺ **get married**
片 結婚

❻ **responsibility**
名 責任

❼ **frankly speaking**
片 坦白說

❽ **recommend**
動 推薦

❾ **solstice**
名 （夏或冬）至；至點

❿ **recipe**
名 食譜

 ## 試著更與眾不同

I had to cook for myself quite a lot when I was young. I moved away from home and went to university[11] in Taitung. I got my own apartment outside of the campus[12], so I had to cook most of the time. Things like fried rice and corn chowder[13] were a piece of cake for me. I could even make pork buns[14] and seafood dumplings. I have my own family now, and my kids all love my cooking.

　　我年輕的時候經常要下廚。大學的時候，我離家到台東唸書，住在校外的公寓，所以大部分時間都得自己煮飯。像炒飯或玉米濃湯這種菜色，對我來說根本不是問題，我還會做肉包跟海鮮水餃呢！我現在有自己的家庭，我的小孩都很愛我煮的菜。

⑪ **university**
名 大學

⑫ **campus**
名 校園

⑬ **corn chowder**
片 玉米濃湯

⑭ **pork buns**
片 肉包

延伸note
廚藝好的人，不妨具體一點，點出那些自己擅長的菜名，聽者會因此對你更有印象。

 答題TIPS看這裡！

聽到這樣的問題，可先從家裡的掌廚者開始講起。介紹母親、祖母或其他家人的廚藝，再簡單帶到自己的情況，如果是不會下廚的外食者，大可直接說自己偏好外食。另外，如果對烘焙有興趣，也可以在最後額外說明。

Words & Phrases 各式各樣的烹調方式

1. **boil** 水煮
2. **blanch** 川燙
3. **pan-fry** 煎炒
4. **deep-fry** 油炸
5. **roast** 烤
6. **smoke** 煙燻
7. **simmer / stew** 煨；燉
8. **steam** 蒸煮

進階實用句 More Expressions

My boyfriend cooks really well, so he does most of the cooking.

我男友很會做菜，所以通常都是他下廚。

I miss living at home. My mother took care of everything, so I didn't need to lift a finger.

真懷念住家裡的生活，我媽媽包辦一切，所以我什麼都不用做。

I live right next to a night market. I can get whatever I want there, so cooking is unnecessary.

我住的地方旁邊就有夜市，什麼都買的到，根本不需要煮飯。

UNIT 05

對素食者的看法

Q **What do you think about vegetarians?**
你對素食者的看法如何？

你可以這樣回答

MP3 020

I am a vegetarian myself. I respect[1] the life of animals just as much as I do to the life of human beings. I couldn't live with the idea of killing a life simply[2] to satisfy[3] my hunger. I'd rather give up a serving of juicy[4] steak for a plate of salad or stir-fried cabbage[5]. There are quite a lot of benefits to eating fruit and vegetables. I think it actually improved my health after I became a vegetarian. For example, I never need to worry about my fiber intake[6].

　　我自己就是素食者，對我來說，動物的生命跟人的生命一樣重要，所以我不能接受為了填飽肚子而去殺生。我寧願吃沙拉或炒高麗菜，也不吃多汁的牛排。蔬菜水果對身體有益，我覺得自從吃素之後，我的健康情況改善了不少，比方說，我從來不用擔心纖維質攝取不足的問題。

❶ **respect** 動 尊重；重視	❷ **simply** 副 僅僅；只不過	❸ **satisfy** 動 滿足；使滿意
❹ **juicy** 形 多汁的	❺ **cabbage** 名 甘藍菜；高麗菜	❻ **intake** 名 吸收

換個立場講講看

I feel very sorry for them. I think they are missing out on all the tasty[7] food. Let's face it. It must get pretty boring eating only vegetables every day. I couldn't think of many ways to make vegetables appealing[8]. And if you are not a good

cook, I am sure you will get sick of[9] being a vegetarian very soon. I found it very inconvenient to go out with my vegetarian friends. It is impossible to share[10] a meal unless I also eat vegetarian food; honestly, I am not a big fan of vegetarian food.

　　我覺得素食者很可憐，什麼美食都不能吃。算了吧，只吃菜一定很無趣，只用蔬菜，我想不出太多美味的煮法。而且，如果你不太會煮菜，那肯定很快就會厭倦吃素。和素食者的朋友出去很不方便，根本無法和他們一起分享餐點，除非你也點素食來吃；但老實說，我並不喜歡吃素食。

> **延伸note**
> 若你不贊同素食，答題時建議以自身的經驗為例，千萬不要淪於偏見與批評。

❼ tasty
形 美味的

❽ appealing
形 吸引人的

❾ get sick of
片 感到厭倦

❿ share
動 分享；共享

試著更與眾不同

I respect their choice of food. It is all about choice. Some people don't eat seafood, while others don't eat red meat, for example. I know many vegetarians are doing it for religious[11] reasons. They have strict[12] rules to follow. Things like garlic, spring onions[13] and leeks[14] are not allowed to be part of their diet. I don't think I could be a vegetarian because I enjoy garlic bread. If it weren't for such strict rules, I might be able to be a vegetarian for a while, but not for long.

　　我尊重他們的選擇，每個人都有選擇的自由，就像有些人不吃海鮮，有些人不吃紅肉。我知道很多人吃素是因為宗教，他們有嚴格的戒律要遵守，大蒜、蔥跟蒜苗都不能吃。我不覺得自己能成為素食者，因為我很愛吃大蒜麵包。如果不是因為嚴格的戒律，我應該可以吃素一陣子，但也不會很久。

⓫ religious
形 宗教的

⓬ strict
形 嚴格的

⓭ spring onion
名 蔥

⓮ leek
名 蒜苗

> **延伸note**
> 肉品在英文裡分為red meat(紅肉，如：牛、羊、豬)和white meat(白肉，如：海鮮)。

答題TIPS看這裡！

素食者大多有自己的理由，比如宗教（religion）或健康（health）因素，想要深入表達意見時，可以從這兩點切入。另外，國外吃素的定義與台灣有所不同，vegetarian 在某些國家除了吃蔬食之外還能吃海鮮或雞肉（不吃紅肉），vegan則表示吃純素食（不吃肉類）的人。

Words & Phrases 宗教以外的吃素原因

1 respect life
尊重生命

2 love our planet
愛地球

3 dislike the taste of meat
不喜歡肉的味道

4 pray for
為…祈願

Words & Phrases 吃素者的常見分類

1 vegetarian
蛋奶素者

2 vegan
吃純素者

3 pescetarian
魚素者（吃海鮮）

4 flexitarian
彈性素食者（偶爾吃葷）

進階實用句 More Expressions

It is hard to make vegetarian food taste good.

要把素食做得好吃不容易。

I am wondering whether mock chicken tastes as good as real chicken.

我在想素雞是不是跟真的雞肉一樣好吃。

I am curious about the taste of meat. It's not because I want to eat it; I have just never tried it before.

我很好奇肉的味道，不是因為我想吃，只是因為從來沒有試過。

UNIT 06

在自家種植蔬菜

Q Do people grow vegetables at home in your country?

你國家的人們會在自家種植蔬菜嗎？

你可以這樣回答

MP3 021

It depends. For those who live in the city, it is impossible for them to grow vegetables in their tiny[1] apartments. On the other hand, people who live in rural[2] areas might have big yards or farmland. In that case, they could grow[3] vegetables or fruit trees. Things like potatoes[4] and carrots[5] are quite commonly grown. However, the quantity[6] is not enough in winter, so people who grow their own food still need to go to the supermarket then.

要看情況，如果是住在市區的人，就不可能在小公寓裡種菜；反之，那些住在鄉村地區的人可能會有大院子或農地，就能種植蔬菜和果樹，其中馬鈴薯和紅蘿蔔都是很常見的作物。不過，冬天的產量可能不夠，所以還是需要上超市購物。

❶ **tiny**
形 極小的

❷ **rural**
形 農村的

❸ **grow**
動 種植

❹ **potato**
名 馬鈴薯

❺ **carrot**
名 蘿蔔

❻ **quantity**
名 數量

換個立場講講看

Not really. In our country, most of the farm produce is imported[7] because there is hardly[8] any farmland available[9]. We live in a high-rise since there is barely enough room for people, let alone vegetables. In addition, the lifestyle is quite fast-paced[10] here. For example, my colleagues[11] and I stay in the office late a lot.

a lot. So, even if we had fresh vegetables at home, we wouldn't bother to cook them up. For some retirees[12], growing flowers and plants on their rooftops is an option.

不太會，因為國內的農地不足，所以我們國家的農產品多半仰賴進口，我們住在高樓大廈，居住空間都不夠了，還談什麼種菜？生活步調也滿緊張的，比方說，我同事和我經常都留在公司加班，所以就算家裡有新鮮蔬菜，也根本不想煮。退休人士可能才會在屋頂養花種草吧。

7 import
動 進口；輸入

8 hardly
副 幾乎不；簡直不

9 available
形 可得到的

10 fast-paced
形 節奏快的

11 colleague
名 同事

12 retiree
名 （美）退休人員

 試著更與眾不同

Yes, it is very popular to have a small vegetable garden at home in my country. One of my friends even grows beans and snow peas in her garden. She always keeps some for me when they are ripe[13]. I don't have a big yard, but I really enjoy fresh herbs[14]. Therefore, I have a small indoor vertical[15] garden to plant certain fresh herbs. I have got chilli, basil[16] and mint. I usually use them to make Vietnamese or Thai dishes. Those fresh herbs really make the food taste much better.

會啊，在我們國家，大家很流行在家弄個小菜園。我朋友還在她的花園裡種豆子跟碗豆莢呢！每當作物熟成了，她都一定會留一些給我。我家沒有很大的院子，但我很喜歡新鮮的香料，所以我在室內搭建垂直式的花園，種植辣椒、九層塔跟薄荷。我經常用這些香料煮越南菜和泰國菜，新鮮的香草真的讓食物美味不少。

13 ripe
形 成熟的；適宜食用的

14 herb
名 香草；藥草

15 vertical
形 垂直的；立式的

16 basil
名 九層塔；羅勒

延伸note
herbs(香草類植物)因為體積小、種植方便，公寓裡可以栽種，所以現在也非常流行。

Key Points

答題TIPS看這裡！

在家裡種花草或蔬菜是外國人很普遍的興趣，除了一些季節性的蔬菜外，香草（herb）是很常見的居家作物，能用盆栽種植，不僅不佔地方，而且還可以用於料理上呢！

Words & Phrases　可以在家栽種的香草

1 **rosemary**
迷迭香

2 **basil**
九層塔（羅勒）

3 **parsley**
歐芹（洋香菜）

4 **sage**
鼠尾草

5 **dill**
洋茴香（蒔蘿）

6 **peppermint**
薄荷

7 **thyme**
百里香

8 **coriander**
中國香菜；芫荽

 進階實用句 More Expressions

It doesn't take much to grow celery in the garden.

芹菜很好種，不用花太大功夫就能在菜園裡種植。

My grandmother has a vegetable patch in her front yard.

我奶奶家的前院有一個菜園。

I like to garnish my pasta with some fresh parsley from my garden.

我喜歡用自己菜園種的新鮮的洋香菜點綴我的義大利麵。

UNIT 07

餐館 vs. 在家煮

Q Do you like meals cooked at home better than at a restaurant?

你喜歡家裡煮的飯，還是餐廳的餐點？

你可以這樣回答

MP3 022

Yes, I really enjoy home-cooked meals because they are made with love! My mother is a very good cook. She goes to the market and picks the fresh ingredients¹ for our meals every day. She puts in a lot of effort² to make every meal different and presentable³. Her dishes are as good as a restaurant⁴ meal if not better. We feel warmer and more comfortable dining at home together. This is the reason why I prefer a home-cooked meal more.

　我很喜歡家裡煮的飯，因為家裡的飯是用愛心煮出來的！我媽很會做菜，她每天都會上超市，挑新鮮的食材來煮給我們吃。她很用心地變化菜色，也很重視擺盤，就像餐廳做的一樣，甚至更好。全家在家一起用餐，我們感到更溫暖、自在。所以我才比較喜歡家裡煮的菜。

❶ **ingredient**
名 食材

❷ **effort**
名 努力；盡力

❸ **presentable**
形 漂亮的；可見人的

❹ **restaurant**
名 餐廳

> **延伸note**
> be made of意指「用⋯做出來」，像是木屋的建材是木頭，就可以用⋯be made of woods.形容。

換個立場講講看

Well, although home-cooked meals are probably⁵ healthier, I personally prefer restaurant meals. Chefs in the restaurants ensure⁶ the taste and the presentation of the plates. They might be a bit oilier⁷, but they are surely tasty.

Besides, dining[8] in a restaurant is a complete dining experience. The service and decoration[9] count, too. After all[10], I can't expect my girlfriend to bring my food to me and say, "Enjoy your meal!"

雖然自己煮菜比較健康，但我還是比較喜歡上餐廳。廚師們會確保餐點的味道與擺盤，雖然菜餚可能會比較油膩，但味道絕對是一絕。除此之外，上餐廳吃飯是一套完整的用餐體驗，服務與餐廳的裝潢一應俱全。我總不能期望我的女朋友送餐給我，還向我說聲「用餐愉快！」

⑤ **probably**
副 可能

⑥ **ensure**
動 保證；擔保

⑦ **oily**
形 多油的

⑧ **dine**
動 用餐；進餐

⑨ **decoration**
名 裝飾

⑩ **after all**
片 畢竟

 試著更與眾不同

I like home-cooked meals because you know exactly[11] what is in it. Some restaurants might use ingredients that are not very fresh. My friend works in a restaurant and he told me that they sometimes deep-fry the food and add artificial[12] seasoning[13] to make it tasty. It sounds scary! That kind of restaurants' aim[14] is to make a profit, so they might use cheap but unhealthy ingredients. I feel more secure when cooking at home. At least, I know what is in my food.

我喜歡家裡煮的飯菜，因為這樣我才知道用了什麼原料。有些餐廳的食材可能沒有那麼新鮮，我有一位在餐廳工作的朋友，他說他們會直接油炸那些食物，再加一些人工調味料，讓食物的味道吸引人，真可怕！那種餐廳的目的就只是賺錢，所以他們可能會用便宜但有害健康的食材。還是在家煮我比較有安全感，畢竟，我知道那些菜是用了些什麼食材。

⑪ **exactly**
副 確切地；精確地

⑫ **artificial**
形 人工的

⑬ **seasoning**
名 調味

⑭ **aim**
名 目標；目的

延伸note
make profit表示賺錢，若想表示虧錢、虧損，則可用be in deficit。deficit是「赤字」的意思。

答題TIPS看這裡！

喜歡在家吃的人通常是因為家裡有人煮得一手好菜，或是喜歡在家吃飯的輕鬆感，以現在來說，還有一個原因就是食安（food safety）問題。至於上餐廳，往往是因為多樣化的菜色以及美味，如果是較高檔的餐廳，也會有服務（service）及用餐環境（dining environment）的考量，舉例時都可以多加說明。

Words & Phrases　形容食物的味道與口感

1	**delicious / tasty** 美味的	**2**	**spicy** 辛辣的
3	**oily** 油膩的	**4**	**light** 清淡的
5	**whet one's appetite** 刺激食欲	**6**	**a turn-off** 倒胃口的東西
7	**tender** 口感很軟的	**8**	**tough** 口感很硬的

進階實用句 More Expressions

I like home-cooked meals as long as I am not the one cooking them.

只要別叫我煮，我就喜歡吃家裡做的菜。

Restaurant meals are normally greasier and there is usually MSG in them.

餐廳的餐點通常比較油膩，而且通常都會加味精。

I can't cook steak as good as a restaurant. Their tastes are much more tender.

我的牛排沒辦法煎得像餐廳一樣軟嫩。

UNIT 08

談旅遊部落格

Q **Do you read blogs before planning your travel?**
你去旅行之前會參考別人部落格上的文章嗎？

你可以這樣回答

MP3 023

I think blogs are worth reading to get a general[1] idea about the destination[2], but they shouldn't be your only source. I like to plan my trip based on some prestigious[3] travel books like "Lonely Planet[4]". The information in the books is very detailed. They even list many suggested itineraries[5] for people. In addition, the books are good for traveling on a budget[6]. Information like this is not available in most blogs.

我覺得部落格能讓我對目的地有個大致的概念，但那不會是我唯一的參考資料。我喜歡參考大部分人推薦的書籍，像《寂寞星球》這類的旅遊書來規劃行程，書上提供的資訊很詳細，列出許多條旅遊路線；此外，對讀者在預算內完成旅行也很有幫助。這類資訊在部落格上就找不到。

❶ **general** 形 大體的；籠統的	❷ **destination** 名 目的地	❸ **prestigious** 形 有名望的
❹ **planet** 名 星球	❺ **itinerary** 名 旅程；路線	❻ **on a budget** 片 在預算內

換個立場講講看

Definitely! Once I decide where to go, I start my research[7] by viewing several blogs to get an idea of what I can do there. Some bloggers[8] provide the contacts[9] they used while they were at the places. I find them very useful. If I can't find anything better, I can use the same contacts. It can save a lot of effort. Besides, I can avoid[10] planning things that did not work for the bloggers.

一定會！一旦我決定了地點，我就會上網搜尋部落格文章，看看當地有哪些活動。有些部落客會提供他們旅行當時的聯絡人，我覺得這很有用，如果找不到更好的資訊，我就會跟那些人聯絡，可因此省下很多時間。除此之外，藉由部落客的失誤經驗，我還能避開那些地雷行程。

延伸note
若是經常自己規劃旅程的人，應該對部落格(blog)的資訊相當熟悉，可多加發揮喔！

❼ **research**
名 調查；探究

❽ **blogger**
名 部落客

❾ **contact**
名 聯絡人；門路

❿ **avoid**
動 避免

 **試著更與眾不同**

Well, I usually won't unless[11] I am looking for particular[12] information that is not available on the official[13] tourism bureau[14] website. I am not very confident in the information in the blogs because you have no idea how truthful[15] the information is or how recent it is. Some information even contradicts[16] itself. To me, the articles in blogs are more like a journal of the bloggers' travel experience. I won't rely on it fully.

不太會，除非我在觀光局的官方網站上找不到我要找的資訊，我才會去看旅遊部落格。我對部落格的資訊沒什麼信心，因為不知道資料的真實性，無法確認那是否是近期的資訊，有些資料甚至還自相矛盾呢！對我來說，部落格的文章比較像是個人的旅遊紀錄，我不會完全相信。

⓫ **unless**
連 除非

⓬ **particular**
形 特殊的；特定的

⓭ **official**
形 官方的

⓮ **bureau**
名 局；司；署；處

⓯ **truthful**
形 真實的；如實的

⓰ **contradict**
動 與…矛盾

 答題TIPS看這裡！

近年來，部落格興起，在網路上可以找到很多有關旅遊的部落格，答題時盡量以自身的想法切入。除了部落格之外，還有很多不同的資源，如：觀光局網站，旅遊書、旅遊節目…等等，可依個人需求變化答案。

Words & Phrases　安排旅遊行程

1 **destination**
地點；目的地

2 **itinerary**
（班機）行程表

3 **reservation**
預約；預定

4 **waiting list**
候補名單

Words & Phrases　不同的行程種類

1 **package tour**
套裝行程

2 **tour group**
團體旅行

3 **city tour**
市區旅行

4 **independent travel**
自助旅行

進階實用句 More Expressions

I am currently on the waiting list.

我目前在等候補。

According to the train timetable, I should reach the destination by lunch time.

根據火車時刻表，中午前應該會抵達目的地。

I made a booking online, but I haven't received the confirmation from the hotel.

我在網路上預約了房間，可是一直沒收到飯店的確認信。

UNIT 09

想去的旅遊地點

你喜歡旅遊嗎？你想去旅遊的國家或地點為何？

你可以這樣回答

MP3 024

Yes, I love traveling. I have been to quite a few countries in Europe[1], and I am hoping to travel to Italy for my honeymoon[2]. I have heard a lot about the canals[3] in Venice. You can take a gondola cruising[4] around the city while the gondolier[5] sings for you. This is definitely romantic for any honeymoon. Besides, I've also heard Italy's specialties are diverse in different regions. I want to try local Italian cuisine[6] from the country where pasta originated.

　　是的，我熱愛旅行，我去過歐洲的幾個國家，真希望能去義大利渡蜜月，我聽說水都威尼斯很美，可以坐威尼斯的傳統交通工具——貢多拉——繞遊市區，船夫還會唱歌助興，真是太浪漫了，很適合蜜月。另外，我也聽說義大利各區的招牌菜都不同，我想去義大利麵的故鄉品嚐當地的義大利菜。

❶ **Europe**
名 歐洲

❷ **honeymoon**
名 蜜月

❸ **canal**
名 河渠；運河

❹ **cruise**
動 航遊；巡航

❺ **gondolier**
名 貢多拉船夫

❻ **cuisine**
名 菜餚

換個立場講講看

I haven't been doing a lot of traveling overseas[7] because I am scared of[8] taking airplanes[9]. However, my girlfriend and I sometimes go for a small weekend getaway[10] to the countryside to relax and unwind[11]. We have been to most of the

towns in northern Taiwan. And we are hoping to explore more in the southern part. I was told that Guanziling is a nice place to visit for their famous muddy[12] hot spring. I've never tried anything like that before, so I'm really interested in it.

因為我怕坐飛機,所以我沒有什麼出國旅遊的經驗。不過,我女朋友和我週末有時會去郊外度個小假、放鬆減壓。北台灣的小鎮我們大部分都去過了,之後我們想去看看南部的城鎮。我聽說關子嶺的泥漿溫泉很有名,我從來沒有試過,所以很有興趣呢。

7 **overseas**
副 在海外

8 **be scared of**
片 害怕

9 **airplane**
名 飛機

10 **getaway**
名 逃走

11 **unwind**
動 使心情輕鬆

12 **muddy**
形 泥濘的

試著更與眾不同

Absolutely! I especially like to visit places with historical value. I went to Angkor Wat in Cambodia a couple of years ago. The architecture[13] and the temples[14] were breathtaking[15]! I couldn't help thinking what it might have been when it was in its golden days. I took several beautiful pictures there. Actually, I dream to visit Machu Picchu in Peru one day. I was told that it is even more remarkable[16] than Angkor Wat.

當然喜歡!我最愛有歷史價值的景點。我幾年前去過柬埔寨的吳哥窟,那些建築物和廟宇真是令人嘆為觀止!令我不禁想像起它們以前的樣貌,在全盛時期肯定更風光。我在那兒拍了許多漂亮的照片。事實上,我夢想有一天可以到秘魯參觀馬丘比丘,聽說那裡比吳哥窟更令人驚嘆。

13 **architecture**
名 建築物

14 **temple**
名 寺廟

15 **breathtaking**
形 驚人的

16 **remarkable**
形 非凡的

> **延伸note**
> 搭乘交通工具的搭配動詞,會有take a bus/MRT/train/plane與ride a bicycle/scooter的差別。

Key Points

答題TIPS看這裡！

本題的問題重點在「是否喜歡」以及「想去的地點」，所以並不一定要有實際的旅遊經驗，可以從日常生活中找靈感，不管是以前聽過的故事、看過的照片、甚至是旅遊節目的介紹，都可以拿來發揮。如：I wish to visit the Disneyland in Tokyo. I have seen it on television, and the firework looks amazing.（我想去東京的迪士尼，我看過電視介紹，煙火很美。）

Words & Phrases　出名的國際景點

1 **Cape Town**
開普敦

2 **Sydney Opera House**
雪梨歌劇院

3 **Pyramids of Egypt**
埃及金字塔

4 **Great Wall of China**
中國萬里長城

5 **The Grand Canyon**
美國大峽谷

6 **Great Barrier Reef**
大堡礁

7 **Taj Mahal in India**
印度泰姬瑪哈陵

8 **Maldives**
馬爾地夫

進階實用句 More Expressions

I would like to visit northern Thailand to see the Golden Triangle.

我想要去泰國北部看金三角。

We are planning a trip to Nepal, and we are making a stop in India on the way there.

我們計劃前往尼泊爾，去程會在印度停一下。

I just saw a great deal with one of the budget airlines to Singapore. I would love to visit the Marina Bay Sands Casino.

剛剛看到廉價航空有去新加坡的特惠機票，我好想去金沙賭場。

UNIT 10

旅行時愛做的事

Q **What do you usually do when you go traveling?**
你去旅遊時通常會做些什麼？

MP3 025

你可以這樣回答

When I first arrive in a place, what I would do is go and explore[1] the surroundings[2]. I don't plan my itinerary in detail in advance. Usually, I talk to the inhabitants[3] and ask about the activities they recommend. Local markets are my favorites because I really love to try the local food. Trust me, visiting markets is the best way to experience the local lifestyle. Normally, I come home with a variety of souvenirs[4] and local specialties, which I share with my family and friends.

我剛抵達一個新地方時，會到附近逛逛。我不會事先規劃太細節的行程，我通常會和當地居民聊天，問他們推薦哪些活動。當地市場是我最喜歡去的地方，因為我熱愛品嚐當地的小吃美食。相信我，去市場是體驗當地生活最好的方式。我通常會買各式各樣的紀念品和當地特產回家，再分給親朋好友。

❶ **explore**
動 探究；探索

❷ **surroundings**
名 環境

❸ **inhabitant**
名 居民；居住者

❹ **souvenir**
名 紀念品

延伸note
a variety of的意思為「種種」，和僅指出數量的many相比，更強調種類上的多樣化。

換個立場講講看

Travel is all about relaxation[5] for me, so I normally book[6] hotels with spas. Having a massage is a good way to rejuvenate[7] from the tiring plane ride.

That's why I usually don't plan too many outdoor activities. It's certain that the fee charged[8] by a day spa is expensive. But based on my experience, you get what you pay for. It is worth it!

對我來說，旅行就是用來放鬆的，所以我通常會選擇附SPA的飯店。在長時間的飛行過後，按摩能幫助放鬆，感覺會很舒服，這是我之所以不會規劃太多戶外活動的原因。當然，有些SPA中心的收費很昂貴，但根據我的經驗，貴有貴的價值，很值得。

延伸note
第一句的all about在口語中經常用到，表示「純粹是…」，用以表示重點。

⑤ relaxation
名 放鬆；鬆弛

⑦ rejuvenate
動 恢復精神

⑥ book
動 登記；預訂

⑧ charge
名 費用；價錢

 試著更與眾不同

I usually get excited when I go traveling. I like to stay up and check out the night life. Normally, I jump in a taxi and ask if there are popular clubs or bars the driver recommends. Hopefully[9], I can meet some nice people who are willing to show me around the city. Once, a friendly guy took me to view local fascinating night scenes. However, if that plan falls through[10], I just hire[11] a taxi for the day and get the driver to be my tour guide[12].

去旅遊的時候，我通常都很興奮。我喜歡熬夜探訪當地的夜生活。我通常會招一台計程車，請司機推薦有名的俱樂部或酒吧，看看是否能遇到好人願意陪我逛市區。有一次，有個友善的小夥子就帶我去欣賞當地的迷人夜景。如果計畫失敗，就只好包計程車，請司機當導遊了。

⑨ hopefully
副 但願

⑪ hire
動 雇用；租借

⑩ fall through
片 成為泡影

⑫ tour guide
名 導遊

延伸note
show sb. around sth.指帶某人認識某地的環境，通常會去好幾個地點（如：城市的重要地標）。

Key Points 答題TIPS看這裡！

渡假時想做的事，其實與旅遊地點有關。有些人喜歡人文歷史，就可以舉有古蹟（a historic spot）的國家；以此類推，有些人喜歡購物玩樂（go shopping）；有些人則熱愛美食（local delicacy），先確定喜好就容易舉例。

Words & Phrases　常見的海邊活動

1	**sunbathing** 日光浴	**2**	**surfing** 衝浪
3	**waterskiing** 滑水	**4**	**jet-skiing** 水上摩托車
5	**parasailing** 玩拖曳傘	**6**	**scuba diving** 潛水
7	**snorkelling** 浮潛	**8**	**sand sculpting** 做沙雕

進階實用句 More Expressions

I always reserve a rental car in advance.

我一定會事先完成租車手續。

Why don't we charter a boat to take us snorkelling?

為什麼我們不包船出海浮潛呢？

Don't forget to bring your phrase book with you when you go traveling.

旅遊的時候，別忘了帶你的翻譯書。

UNIT 11
具體的旅行經歷

Q **Describe your latest trip. Where did you go and how was it?**

描述你最近一次的旅行。你去了哪裡？旅程如何呢？

你可以這樣回答

MP3 026

I went to Bali with my best friend last month. To be honest[1], it was very disappointing[2]. I read a lot of information[3] on it before we went, and the itinerary from the travel agent[4] also looked really attractive[5]. However, things were totally different once we got there. The beach was dirty and the food was just terrible. The portions[6] offered were very small, and they were not freshly made. I don't think we will go with a tour group again.

　　我上個月和好友去峇里島，老實說，那趟旅程讓人失望透頂。出發前，我看了很多資料，旅行社的行程規劃也很吸引人，可是當我們抵達當地後，實際上經歷的和事前規劃的根本是兩回事。海邊很髒亂，食物又難吃，份量少又不是現做的，我們下次不會再跟團了。

❶ **to be honest**
　片 老實說

❷ **disappointing**
　形 令人失望的

❸ **information**
　名 資訊

❹ **travel agent**
　片 旅行社

❺ **attractive**
　形 有吸引力的

❻ **portion**
　名 （食物的）一份

換個立場講講看

I took my girlfriend to Sydney last year because it was the place she had always wanted to visit. We had dinner at the revolving[7] restaurant in Sydney Tower. After dinner, we walked down to see the Opera House. It is situated[8] in a circular[9]

quay[10] with the Harbor[11] Bridge on the other side. The view was magnificent[12]. We were there during the Mardi Gras parade. People wear colorful or creative costumes in the parade. It was a spectacular experience!

　　我去年帶女朋友去雪梨，因為那是她一直很想去的地方。我們先去了雪梨塔的旋轉餐廳吃飯，再走路去看歌劇院。歌劇院位於一個環狀碼頭，另一邊是雪梨港大橋，景觀令人驚豔。我們去的時候剛好遇上同性戀大遊行，遊行隊伍穿著繽紛多彩或具有創意的服裝，真是令人大開眼界！

7 revolving
形 旋轉的

8 situate
動 使位於

9 circular
形 環形的

10 quay
名 碼頭

11 harbor
名 海港

12 magnificent
形 極美的

試著更與眾不同

We went on a 5 day 4 night ocean cruise with my family to the Caribbean[13] ocean from Miami. The cruise ship facilities were very impressive[14]. There was an outdoor swimming pool, a pool side bar with live music and a rock climbing facility. The room was not very big, but it was clean and tidy[15]. We spent a lot of time in the pool during the day and watched the performances at night. We even visited[16] the Bahamas as one of the stops. It was wonderful.

　　我們參加了五天四夜的加勒比海郵輪之旅，郵輪從邁阿密出發，設備很棒，有室外游泳池、附現場音樂表演的池畔酒吧、及攀岩設備。臥室是小了一點，但很整齊乾淨。我們白天的時候大多待在游泳池，晚上則去看表演，中途還在巴哈馬停了一站，這趟旅程真的很棒。

13 Caribbean
形 加勒比海的

14 impressive
形 予人深刻印象的

15 tidy
形 整齊的

16 visit
動 拜訪；參觀

延伸note
in the evening和at night都指晚上，若嚴格區分，evening為傍晚，night則指日落後的時間。

Key Points

答題TIPS看這裡！

旅行不限於國內外，如果沒有印象深刻的旅行經驗，畢業旅行（graduation trip）、騎車環島（cycling around the island）、露營烤肉（go camping）或是聯誼（group dating）的經驗都可以舉例。例如：We took the ferry across to the Cijin Island to visit the local fishing village.（我們坐渡輪過去旗津看當地的漁村。）

Words & Phrases　旅館的設施與設備

1 **balcony**
陽台

2 **roof garden**
屋頂花園

3 **gym**
健身房

4 **central heating**
暖氣

5 **air-conditioned**
附空調的

6 **bedside lamp**
床頭燈

7 **shutter**
百葉窗

8 **French casement**
落地窗

進階實用句 More Expressions

I didn't realize there were so many jellyfish in the ocean. We got stung badly.

我不知道海裡有這麼多水母，我們被螫的很慘。

I went rock climbing in the mountains but accidently fell and broke my ankle.

我去山裡面攀岩，但不小心摔斷了腳踝。

We went to see the FuLong Music Festival at the beach. I enjoyed the music, and we had a great time.

我們去海灘看福隆音樂祭，音樂很棒，我們也玩得很開心。

UNIT 12

我的最佳旅伴

Q **Describe someone you like to travel with.**
請描述一位你想與之共同旅行的對象。

你可以這樣回答

MP3
027

I like to travel with my sister. She speaks not only English but also Spanish. I can totally rely on[1] her when we ask for directions[2]. Besides, she is very organized and has a lot of traveling experience. So, she is very capable[3] of dealing with the unexpected. She always remains calm and collected[4] when there is trouble. Traveling with her makes me feel secure and protected.

　　我喜歡跟我姊姊一起去旅行，她除了會說英文之外，還懂西班牙文，需要問路的時候，交給她就對了。除此之外，她很會計劃，也有很多旅遊經驗，所以很會處理突發狀況。有問題發生的時候，她總是很穩重、鎮定，和她一起旅行讓我很有安全感。

❶ **rely on**
片 依靠；信賴

❷ **direction**
名 方向

❸ **capable**
形 有…的能力

❹ **collected**
形 鎮定的

延伸note
回答時的著眼點要放在對方能讓你放心的原因，這些原因才是面試官想聽的答案。

換個立場講講看

If it were possible[5], I would love to travel with Janet, who is the travel show host of "Fun Taiwan". She does a wonderful job promoting[6] Taiwan through the travel show. What I love the best is her personality[7]. She seems to be smart, bold[8] and daring[9]. Traveling with her would be so much fun as I would definitely[10] try something I never have tried before. I can imagine how thrilling going rock climbing and riding horses with her would be.

　　如果有可能的話，我想跟旅遊節目《瘋台灣》的主持人謝怡芬一起旅遊。我覺得她成功地用旅遊把台灣推廣出去。我最喜歡的是她的個性，看起來很很聰明、開放又大膽，跟她一起旅行肯定會很好玩。我絕對會去嘗試從沒做過的事，我可以想像和她一起攀岩和騎馬有多刺激。

⑤ **possible**
　形 可能的

⑥ **promote**
　動 促進；發揚

⑦ **personality**
　名 個性

⑧ **bold**
　形 大膽的

⑨ **daring**
　形 勇於冒險的

⑩ **definitely**
　副 肯定地

 試著更與眾不同

I want to travel with my boyfriend because I know he will take good care of me. What's more, he always carries my bags, so I don't need to lift a finger[11]. He is also quite experienced in planning the trips and surprises[12]. If we go on a trip together, I am pretty sure that I will be spoiled[13] most of the time. He is also very good with directions, so renting a car to do a self-guided tour would not be a problem[14] for him at all. Actually, we did it once when we went to California last year.

　　我想跟我的男朋友一起去旅行，因為他會很照顧我。他一定會幫我提包包，所以我什麼都不用做。在安排行程和驚喜方面，他的經驗豐富。如果我們一起去旅行，我十之八九會備受寵愛。他的方向感也很好，開著租車自助導覽對他而言也完全不是問題。事實上，我們去年去加州時就這麼做過了。

⑪ **lift a finger**
　片 盡舉手之勞

⑫ **surprise**
　名 驚喜

⑬ **spoil**
　動 寵壞；溺愛

⑭ **problem**
　名 問題

> **延伸note**
> spoil帶有負面意涵，如：a spoiled kid指被寵壞的小孩，此處則強調被捧在手掌心般的照顧。

答題TIPS看這裡！

每個人安排行程的方式都不同，放的重點也不一樣。有的人注重安全，喜歡懂得規劃的旅伴；有人則喜歡能同樂狂歡的朋友，可以一起好好放縱一下。答題時不妨思考自己的旅遊重點，再思考適合的旅伴。

Words & Phrases 人的特質及性格

1	**calm and collected** 穩重鎮定的	**2**	**caring** 很關心人的
3	**organized** 有組織力的	**4**	**clumsy** 笨拙的
5	**energetic** 精力旺盛的	**6**	**helpful** 有幫助的
7	**fun-loving** 愛找樂子的	**8**	**clued-up** （口）十分了解的

進階實用句 More Expressions

It is difficult to travel with my grandmother because she is really picky.

和我奶奶一起旅遊是件很困難的事，因為她非常挑剔。

My father plans a big family trip once a year. He is very good at planning.

我爸爸每年都會安排一次家族旅遊，他很擅長規劃行程。

I couldn't believe that my brother forgot to bring his passport. I just reminded him of it this morning!

不敢相信我哥哥竟然忘了帶護照，我今天早上才提醒他耶！

UNIT 13

推薦國內景點

Q What's the tourist spot/attraction in your country you would recommend to foreigners?

你會推薦給外國人的國內旅遊景點為何？

你可以這樣回答

MP3 028

If it's a family traveling with young children, I would definitely recommend a Zoo café near Kaohsiung International Airport. It is mind-blowing[1] to be greeted[2] by two big hippopotamuses[3] when you arrive. Their African-themed bird park is outstanding, too. There are lots of different species[4] of birds. The best part of it is, you can feed the animals like alpacas[5] and little piglets[6]. I am sure kids will love it.

　　如果是帶著小孩的家庭，我強烈推薦去高雄國際機場附近的動物園咖啡館。一抵達門口，就會看到門口有兩隻大河馬在歡迎你，這一幕真的會讓人大吃一驚！他們的非洲鳥園也很棒，有很多種類的鳥兒。最精彩的是可以餵食像羊駝和小豬這樣的動物，小朋友肯定會喜歡。

❶ **mind-blowing** 形 讓人印象深刻的

❷ **greet** 動 問候；迎接

❸ **hippopotamus** 名 河馬

❹ **species** 名 種類

❺ **alpaca** 名 羊駝

❻ **piglet** 名 小豬

換個立場講講看

I definitely recommend the night markets. Even if they don't have the courage to try the local delicacies[7] like chicken hearts or chicken feet, it would still be interesting for them to walk around. In night markets, vendors display various clothes, snacks, and games. Foreigners can play darts and net fish. They can even try snake blood if they go to the right place. But honestly, I think most of them would be happy just to have a cup of bubble[8] tea or BBQ corn[9] on a stick[10].

　　那我肯定推薦夜市，就算他們沒有勇氣嘗試雞心或雞爪這類的小吃，單純逛逛也會很有趣的。夜市攤販陳列各式各樣的衣服、小吃、遊戲，外國人可以玩玩射飛鏢、撈金魚，如果選對地方去的話，甚至還能喝到蛇血呢！不過老實說，我想大部分的外國人應該對珍珠奶茶或烤玉米更滿意吧。

> **延伸note**
> 對於擁有許多特色小吃的台灣來說，推薦夜市絕對是個好主意，提到具體的菜名會更好。

7 delicacy
名 美味；佳餚

8 bubble
名 泡狀物

9 corn
名 玉米

10 stick
名 棒狀物

試著更與眾不同

If they come during summer, I recommend they visit Taitung and take a ferry[11] across to Green Island. The island is isolated[12], but most of the scenery there is still unspoiled[13]. If it's someone who loves aquatic[14] activity, Green Island would be like paradise[15]. There are so many snorkelling spots and beautiful beaches. By the way, if they want to try something unique, they can try venison[16]. I heard that it's very popular on the island.

　　如果他們夏天來，我會推薦到台東搭船去綠島。綠島的位置比較偏遠孤立，所以大部分的景觀都還沒有被破壞。如果他們喜歡水上活動，綠島對他們來說肯定如天堂一般，因為島上有很多適合浮潛的地點和美麗的沙灘。對了，如果真的想試試獨一無二的東西，可以嚐試鹿肉，聽說鹿肉在綠島很受歡迎。

11 ferry
名 渡輪

12 isolated
形 隔離的

13 unspoiled
形 未受破壞的

14 aquatic
形 水上的

15 paradise
名 天堂

16 venison
名 鹿肉

答題TIPS看這裡！

本題重視的是「個人推薦」，只要是你能多加著墨的地點都可以，不侷限於旅遊書上的景點。如go to the tribal villages to experience the aboriginal lifestyle（到部落去體驗原住民的生活方式），或go to the Hakka villages in Mei Nong to learn how to make paper umbrella（去美濃客家村學做油紙傘）…等等。

Words & Phrases 台灣的觀光景點

1 Maokong Gondola
貓空纜車

2 Jiufen & Jinguashi
九份與金瓜石

3 Sun Moon Lake
日月潭

4 Chingjing Farmland
清境農場

5 Kenting Baisha Beach
墾丁白沙灣

6 Chimei Museum
奇美博物館

7 Taroko Gorge
太魯閣

8 Penghu Island
澎湖

進階實用句 More Expressions

Visiting the islands is not a good idea in winter. It usually gets windy and cold.

冬天不太適合到離島，因為風通常都很大、而且很冷。

You can take the cable car from Sun Moon Lake to the Formosan Aboriginal Culture Village.

從日月潭可以直接搭纜車到九族文化村。

If you go to Yang Ming Shan National Park in spring, you'll see a clock made of flowers.

如果你春季到陽明山國家公園，就能看到花鐘。

UNIT 14

意料之外的旅行

Q Have you ever had a holiday that turned out to be different from what you planned?
你曾經有過不照你計畫進行的假期嗎？

 你可以這樣回答

MP3 029

Yes, one year we went to Vietnam. We signed up for a 2 day 1 night tour to explore one of the underground[1] tunnels[2] during the Vietnam War. The bus broke down not long after it picked us up[3] at the hotel. Then it suddenly[4] started to rain. It rained heavily, so the roads were flooded. In the end, the tour guide arranged for us to get on scooter taxis. That was an interesting experience.

有啊，有一年我們去越南，參加了兩天一夜的旅行團，去看越戰留下的地下坑道。公車到旅館接我們之後，沒多久就拋錨了，而且突然下起大雨，雨勢大到馬路都淹水，最後我們的導遊只好安排計程摩托車來載我們，真是個有趣的經驗。

❶ **underground**
形 地下的

❷ **tunnel**
名 地道；隧道

❸ **pick up**
片 用汽車接某人

❹ **suddenly**
副 突然

> **延伸note**
> 除了敘述經驗之外，別忘了點出你對這件事的觀感（不用過於情緒化，但也別太官方）。

 換個立場講講看

I do have one, and it was a terrible experience. I went to Italy to get some cheap designer[5] handbags[6], but my purse and passport[7] were stolen on the second day! Luckily, the hotel had been prepaid[8], so I didn't get kicked out. But as you can imagine, for the next ten days, I was pretty much stuck in the embassy[9] trying to get the passport replacement[10] sorted. I didn't see much of Italy nor buy any designer handbags!

是有，那次的經驗實在太慘了。我去了義大利，想說可以買一些便宜的名牌包，可是我的錢包和護照在第二天就被偷了！還好飯店的錢已經提前付清，我才沒有被趕出去，你可以想像接下來的十天，我幾乎都待在大使館等我的新護照辦好，根本就沒怎麼去義大利觀光，更別說買名牌包了！

⑤ designer
名 設計師

⑥ handbag
名（女用）手提包

⑦ passport
名 護照

⑧ prepay
動 預付

⑨ embassy
名 大使館

⑩ replacement
名 更換

 試著更與眾不同

Yes, I went to the Gold Coast with a friend. We flew to Brisbane Airport and planned to take the bus down to the Gold Coast. All of a sudden, some guy came and approached[11] me, asking whether we had organized transportation[12]. He was there to pick someone up, but his guest cancelled the trip at the last minute. He offered us a discounted[13] rate, which was the same as the bus fare. We decided to take it. And then we realized that he was a limo[14] driver. We traveled in a big, fancy limo at the cost of riding on a bus!

有，我跟朋友去黃金海岸。我們搭飛機到布里斯本機場，打算坐公車去黃金海岸。突然間，有一個人靠近我，問我們是否已經決定交通工具。他是來機場接客人的，但客人卻臨時取消。他提供了很優惠的價格，和公車一樣，所以我們就同意了。後來才發現原來他是開加長型禮車的司機，我們居然以巴士的價格坐到加長型禮車耶！

⑪ approach
動 接近；靠近

⑫ transportation
名 交通車輛

⑬ discount
動 打折扣

⑭ limo
名（縮）大型豪華轎車

延伸note
lime是limousine的縮寫，指的是豪華轎車。國外機場常見的接駁公車則稱shuttle bus。

Key Points 答題TIPS看這裡！

出外旅遊一定會碰到預料之外的事，尤其是自助旅行的時候。不按照計畫不一定是壞事，有時可能是意外的驚喜。例如：I got lost but accidently ran into Brad Pitt in a café.（我迷了路，但卻在咖啡廳意外地遇見布萊德彼特。）

Words & Phrases 旅遊可能會遇上的窘事

1 language barrier
語言不通

2 bad weather
天氣不佳

3 on the wrong bus
搭錯車

4 feel sick
身體不適

5 get lost
迷路

6 miss the flight
錯過班機

7 sth. be stolen
（某物）被偷

8 sb. be robbed
（某人）被搶

 進階實用句 More Expressions

You must have a plan B just in case Plan A does not work.

你一定要有備案，以防原來的計畫無法執行。

I have the telephone number of an overseas helpline just in case I get into trouble.

為防出問題，我會帶國際救援專線的電話號碼。

"Always expect the unexpected." I think this is important when you go traveling.

「要為了各種無法預期的狀況做好準備。」我覺得這點在旅遊時很重要。

UNIT 15

何謂一家好旅館

Q **What are the most important things that a good hotel should have?**

一間家好旅館最重要的是什麼？

 你可以這樣回答

 MP3 030

I think the service is the most important thing for a hotel. I know things cannot always be perfect, but a good attitude[1] minimizes[2] the problem. Once, I went traveling to Europe. At night, I decided to have a couple of drinks in the hotel. When I sat at the bar, a rushing waiter spilled[3] my wine, and it stained[4] my dress. The waiter apologized and assured[5] me that he would dry-clean my dress as soon as possible. He offered me a tequila[6] sunrise for free. It was his attitude that made me less angry.

　　我覺得服務是最重要的。雖然事情不可能盡善盡美，但好的態度能將問題減到最低。我有次去歐洲旅遊，晚上，我決定在飯店裡喝幾杯酒，當我坐在吧檯邊時，有一位匆忙的服務生打翻我的酒，灑得我身上都是，那位服務生向我道歉，並保證會幫我將洋裝送乾洗，還免費請我喝龍舌蘭日出，他的態度讓我的火氣消了不少。

① **attitude** 名 態度	② **minimize** 動 使減到最少	③ **spill** 名 使溢出；使濺出
④ **stain** 動 玷汙；染汙	⑤ **assure** 動 擔保；保證	⑥ **tequila** 名 龍舌蘭

 換個立場講講看

G ood facilities are what I look for in a hotel. I pay for it, so I believe the hotel should make me feel comfortable and relaxed. The decorations[7] should be

tasteful[8] and modern. I can't stand dated wallpaper and damp[9] carpets[10]. Although this is a tiny problem for some people, I just won't walk into a hotel feeling like I am walking back in time.

飯店設施會是我最看重的一項要素。我付了錢，所以飯店當然要讓我覺得舒適、放鬆，內部裝潢應該要有品味、具現代感。我無法忍受老舊的壁紙跟潮濕的地毯，有些人覺得這是小事，但我絕對不會走進一家會讓我覺得好像重返過去的飯店。

延伸note
facility(設施；設備)除了指房內的設備之外，舉凡游泳池、健身房…等等，這些都包含在內。

❼ decoration
名 裝飾；裝潢

❽ tasteful
形 雅緻的

❾ damp
形 潮濕的

❿ carpet
名 地毯

試著更與眾不同

I can't stand staying in a hotel with poor hygiene[11] standards[12]. I don't mind if the hotel is a bit old as long as it is clean and tidy. I know someone else has used that room, but I really don't want to see any evidence[13] of it. I can't tolerate[14] seeing hairs in the drain[15], lip stick stain on the drinking glasses, or a dirty toilet. That really bothers[16] me, regardless if it is a 5 star hotel or not. Keeping the hotels clean and tidy is basic for me.

我無法接受環境髒亂的飯店。地方有點老舊沒關係，只要看起來乾淨整齊就好。我知道別人也用過這個房間，可是我不想看到用過的痕跡。如果看到排水口有頭髮、玻璃杯有口紅印、或是骯髒的馬桶，不管是不是五星級飯店，都會讓我很受不了。維持飯店的整齊與清潔對我而言是最基本的事項。

⓫ hygiene
名 衛生

⓬ standard
名 標準

⓭ evidence
名 證據

⓮ tolerate
動 容忍；忍受

⓯ drain
名 排水管

⓰ bother
動 煩擾；打擾

答題TIPS看這裡！

外出旅行，大家都有找旅館的經驗，所以有人說「旅館就是外出的第二個家（home away from home）」。如果無法講出深入的內容，不妨想想自己最討厭在飯店遇到的情況，例如：環境衛生（hygiene）、服務態度（service）、飯店的餐點（meals/afternoon tea）…等等問題，就能答出飯店應該注意的地方了。

Words & Phrases 飯店的服務人員

1 **concierge**
門房

2 **switchboard**
總機接線員

3 **receptionist**
櫃台接待員

4 **bellhop**
（旅館）侍者

Words & Phrases 認識飯店的各部門

1 **food and beverage**
餐飲部

2 **room service**
客房服務

3 **maintenance**
維修部

4 **reservation**
訂房部

 ## 進階實用句 More Expressions

Remember to tip the hotel staff when traveling abroad.

出國旅行時，記得給飯店人員小費。

I want to swap to a different room. There are stains on my sheets.

我想換房，我的床單上有污漬。

All the kitchen staff are required to wear masks and hair-nets to meet the hygiene standards.

所有的廚房員工都必須戴口罩及髮網，這樣才符合衛生標準。

Part 3

音樂與電影
Music and Movies

 動　動詞

 名　名詞

 副　副詞

 形　形容詞

 介　介系詞

 連　連接詞

 片　片語

UNIT 01 電影院 vs. 看DVD

Q **What's the difference between going to the movies and watching DVDs at home?**
去電影院和在家看DVD有何不同？

 你可以這樣回答

MP3
031

The best thing about watching movies in the cinema[1] is the sound system[2] and the big screen. The characters[3] seem so much more life-like on the big screen. Movies, especially thrillers and adventure films, are livelier in the theater. It is a different kind of sensation[4] compared to[5] watching DVDs at home. However, there is one good thing about watching DVDs at home. That is, I can pause and rewind[6] at any point. So, I can take a toilet break whenever I want.

　　去電影院看電影最棒的地方在於大螢幕和音效。大螢幕上的電影人物顯得更栩栩如生，尤其是像驚悚片和冒險片這類電影，在電影院看更能讓人身歷其境，聲光效果是在家看DVD時感受不到的。不過，在家看DVD有一個好處，就是可以隨時暫停或倒帶，內急的時候隨時都能跑洗手間。

❶ **cinema**	❷ **system**	❸ **character**
名 電影院	名 系統	名 角色
❹ **sensation**	❺ **compare to**	❻ **rewind**
名 感覺；知覺	片 與…相比	動 轉回

 換個立場講講看

The difference between going to the movies and watching DVDs at home is the privacy[7] and freedom. I really miss going to the movies, but ever since I had kids, it has been impossible for my wife and I to go and see a movie. I am sure no

one wants to be disturbed[8] by screaming[9] kids at a movie. Therefore, I can only watch Walt Disney and Pixar animations at home with my kids. I guess I can only wait for my kids to grow up[10] so that I can go to the movies again.

　　去電影院和在家看DVD最大的不同在於隱私和自由度，我非常懷念去電影院，但自從有了小孩之後，我跟我太太根本沒辦法跑電影院，相信沒有人會想被鬼叫的孩子們打斷看電影的興致吧？所以我只能在家陪孩子看迪士尼和皮克斯的動畫片，想去電影院看電影，大概只能等孩子們長大再說了。

延伸note
can only wait for意指「只能等到…」，是在表達無奈；後面接時間則不用加for。

❼ **privacy**
名 隱私

❽ **disturb**
動 妨礙；打擾

❾ **scream**
動 尖叫

❿ **grow up**
片 長大

試著更與眾不同

To me, there is no difference between going to the movies and watching a DVD at home. First of all[11], I have a movie projector[12], so it is literally a big screen. I also invested[13] a lot of money to upgrade[14] the sound system. With the equipment, watching DVDs at home are not less pleasurable than going to the movies. If you ask me, I'd rather stay at home and watch DVDs unless there is something I can't wait to watch.

　　對我來說，去電影院跟在家看DVD沒什麼差別。第一，我家裡有電影投影機，所以看的同樣是大螢幕；而且我投資了很多錢升級音響，有了這些設備，在家看DVD和去電影院一樣享受。如果要我選，除非有什麼我等不及的片子上映，否則我還是比較喜歡待在家看DVD。

⓫ **first of all**
片 首先

⓬ **projector**
名 投影機

⓭ **invest**
動 投資

⓮ **upgrade**
動 使升級；提升

延伸note
除了would rather之外，prefer to同樣也能表達喜好。如：prefer coffee to tea（比較喜歡咖啡）。

答題TIPS看這裡！

一般而言，電影院的優勢除了專業的硬體設備之外，就是可以觀賞到剛上映的院線片；相比之下，DVD比較沒有時效性，但方便性卻無可取代。答題的時候，可以針對不同的優點，闡述你之所以喜歡某一方的原因。不同種類的電影，也適合不同的觀看場所：驚悚片、恐怖片、動作片、冒險片在電影院看會更過癮，而動畫片、文藝片、劇情片、偵探片則較不受觀看地點的影響。

Words & Phrases　與電影院相關的詞彙

1　**box office**
　售票處

2　**screening room**
　放映廳

3　**blockbuster**
　很賣座的電影

4　**new release**
　新上映的院線片

Words & Phrases　DVD放映機的操作

1　**pause**
　停止；暫停

2　**rewind**
　倒轉；倒帶

3　**forward**
　向前快轉

4　**skip**
　跳過（不想看的部分）

進階實用句 More Expressions

I like to go to the movies during film festivals.

我喜歡在電影節的時候去看電影。

I prefer to watch movies in the cinema because I won't be disturbed.

我喜歡在戲院看電影，這樣比較不會被打擾。

I like to have my dinner while watching a DVD, which is not allowed in a cinema.

我喜歡一邊吃晚餐一邊看DVD，但電影院禁止觀眾這樣做。

UNIT 02

看電影的習慣

Q **Do you like to go to the movies alone or with other people?**

你喜歡獨自看電影，還是呼朋引伴一起去呢？

你可以這樣回答

MP3 032

I like to go with my friends. Normally, we will go out for dinner after the movie. It is like a big day out. We will vote to decide the movie we want to see before it starts. We will discuss[1] the storyline[2] after it finishes. There might be some disagreements[3], but it is very interesting to hear various opinions. My opinion about going to the movies with friends is the more the merrier[4].

我喜歡跟朋友一起去看電影，看完電影後，我們通常會一起去吃飯，就像有什麼大型活動般，約出來度過一整天。電影開始前，我們會投票決定看哪一部電影，看完之後，我們會討論劇情，當然，意見多少都會不合，但能聽到各種不同的意見真的很有趣。我覺得看電影是人越多越熱鬧。

❶ **discuss**
動 討論

❷ **storyline**
名 故事情節

❸ **disagreement**
名 意見不一

❹ **merry**
形 愉快的

延伸note
這種回答是比較容易延伸內容的方法，以平日的經驗著手，不僅內容清楚，聽起來也夠具體。

換個立場講講看

Most of the time, I like to go to the movies on my own[5] because that way I don't need to worry about making plans with everyone. I can just go whenever it suits me. The movies I like are pretty dark[6] and not very popular among my classmates. I am not sure whether others will be interested in it or not.

Besides, I don't want to make others feel that they are being forced[7]. After all[8], watching movies should be relaxing.

　　大部分的時候，我喜歡一個人去看電影，因為這樣我就不用費力安排大家的時間，只要我有空，隨時都能去。我喜歡的電影類型都比較晦暗，不是那種同學間會討論的片子，我不確定其他人會不會喜歡，也不想逼大家陪我去看，畢竟，看電影就是為了放鬆嘛。

延伸note
這段回答中的dark，絕不是指電影的色調或光線，而是只看完會令人感到鬱悶的電影類型。

❺ on one's own
片 獨自

❻ dark
形 陰暗的；陰鬱的

❼ force
動 強迫

❽ after all
片 畢竟

試著更與眾不同

I don't like going to the movies on my own because it feels odd[9]. I think going to the movies is a group activity. You go with your friends, family or a date[10]. If I go to a movie by myself, I will feel lonely and depressed[11] when surrounded by so many groups in a theater. Anyway, I would definitely ask around and see if anyone wanted to go to the movies with me. If I found no one who wanted to go with me, I would just wait until the DVD is released[12].

　　我不喜歡獨自去看電影，因為那種感覺很怪。我覺得看電影是團體活動，不管是跟朋友、家人，還是某位約會對象，總之就是要有人一起。如果我自個兒看電影，被電影院三三兩兩的人群包圍，就會感到特別地孤單、沮喪，所以要看電影的時候，我絕對會到處問人，看有沒有人想跟我一起去，找不到人一起的話，我就會等DVD出來再看。

❾ odd
形 奇特的；古怪的

❿ date
名 （美）約會對象

⓫ depressed
形 沮喪的；憂鬱的

⓬ release
動 發行；發表

延伸note
不喜歡獨自看電影的人，除了感覺奇怪(odd)之外，也可能是因為感覺很孤單(lonely)。

答題TIPS看這裡！

喜不喜歡和人一起看電影，除了和個性有關之外，也可能涉及約人看電影的優缺點。除了比較內向或不擅交際的人可能偏好獨自看電影外，約人一起看電影，最重要的因素應該就是看大家有沒有空了。

Words & Phrases 電影的正／反評價

1 thought-provoking
發人深省的

2 epic
經典的

3 a tight plot
劇情緊湊

4 a highlight
亮點；高潮

5 be tired of
感到厭倦

6 run out of steam
電影冷場

7 nothing new
了無新意

8 waste one's time
浪費時間

進階實用句 More Expressions

Which movie are we going to watch?

我們要看的是哪一部片呢？

I am free this afternoon. I think I will go to the movies on my own.

我今天下午有空，我應該會自己去看場電影。

My friends are all busy, so no one is able to go and watch the new release with me.

我的朋友最近都很忙，所以無法陪我去看最新上映的電影。

UNIT 03 最後一次看的電影

Q What was the last movie you saw?
你最後一次看的電影是什麼？

你可以這樣回答

MP3
033

Oh, that was a while ago. I think it was "Twilight". It is a love story, and there were a few different parts to the movie. The storyline is about a teen vampire[1] falling in love with his classmate[2] Bella, who is a human being. To stay together, Bella decides to turn herself into a vampire, too. The series[3] is really popular among teenagers[4]. Well, I guess I don't like romance[5] that much, so I didn't find it appealing[6].

噢，我上次看電影是滿久之前的事了，好像是《暮光之城》，那是一個愛情故事，一共有好幾集。劇情是說有一個十幾歲的吸血鬼愛上了人類的同學貝拉，為了在一起，貝拉決定也變成吸血鬼。這部電影很受青少年族群歡迎，不過，我可能沒那麼喜歡愛情電影吧，所以我覺得沒什麼特別的。

❶ **vampire** 名 吸血鬼	❷ **classmate** 名 同班同學	❸ **series** 名 系列；連續
❹ **teenager** 名 青少年	❺ **romance** 名 愛情故事	❻ **appealing** 形 吸引人的

換個立場講講看

The last movie I watched was "Gone Girl". It is a psycho-thriller film starring[7] Ben Affleck. The story is about this so-called "perfect couple". They have been living in lies and been unhappy for a long time. One day, the wife disappears[8] from their house and all the evidence points to someone possibly abducting[9] or killing her. It was not certain[10] whether she was alive or not. The ending is so not what I expected. It is very tense and exciting. You've got to watch it.

　我上次看的電影是《控制》，是一部懸疑驚悚片，由班艾佛列克主演。故事講述一對令人稱羨的夫妻，他們長久以來都活在謊言中，婚姻其實非常不幸福。有一天太太失蹤，所有的證據都說明她被某人綁架或撕票了，且生死未卜。結局完全令人意想不到，是一部緊張又刺激的電影，你一定要去看。

延伸note
只要是和自己原本預想不同的結果，都可以用 not what I expected，記得用過去式表示。

❼ star
動 由⋯主演

❽ disappear
動 消失

❾ abduct
動 誘拐；綁架

❿ certain
形 確鑿的；確信的

試著更與眾不同

The last movie I watched was a comedy called "The Hangover". It is such a funny movie and full of surprises! It is about a group of friends who decide[11] to go to Las Vegas to celebrate[12] their friend's upcoming wedding. They have no recollection[13] of what happened the night before when they wake up in a hotel room with a real live tiger in the bathroom. I was laughing my head off! You are missing out[14] if you haven't seen this movie.

　我上一次看的電影是一部叫《醉後大丈夫》的喜劇。這部電影超好笑，處處充滿驚奇！故事講述一群朋友決定去拉斯維加斯，幫朋友慶祝即將到來的婚禮。隔天，他們在飯店裡醒來，浴室多了一隻活生生的老虎，他們卻對前一晚發生的事毫無印象。我看這部電影的時候笑到不行！如果你到現在還沒看過這部片，那可就落伍了。

⓫ decide
動 決定

⓬ celebrate
動 慶祝

⓭ recollection
名 回憶；記憶

⓮ miss out
片 損失很大

延伸note
funny意指「滑稽可笑」，用來形容搞笑電影，如果只是覺得有趣，建議用 interesting。

答題TIPS看這裡！

因為題目很明確地問是哪一部電影，所以建議挑一部電影，簡單的形容一下劇情，或是加以解釋之所以會挑這部片看的原因，也可以敘述自己看完電影的感想與評論。其實就算不是最後看過的電影也無妨，只要是讓你印象深刻的電影，就方便舉例，如：That horror movie is highly recommended.（那部恐怖片深受好評。）

Words & Phrases　挑選電影的標準

1 a film review
影評

2 actor / actress
男演員 / 女演員

3 a plot summary
劇情大綱

4 film genre
電影類型

Words & Phrases　形容看完電影的感受

1 touched
深受感動的

2 impressed
印象深刻的

3 motivated
有動機的

4 disappointed
失望的

進階實用句 More Expressions

I don't think the director picked the right actress.

我覺得女主角沒挑對人。

I went and watched "Mr. & Mrs. Smith". The ending is disappointing.

我去看了《史密斯夫婦》這部電影，結局真令人失望。

I was impressed that the actor could play two different roles in the movie. That really shows his excellent acting.

男主角一人分飾兩角讓我印象深刻，完全體現出他精湛的演技。

UNIT 04 對音樂類型的偏好

Q What kind of music do you like or dislike?
你喜歡或討厭的音樂類型是什麼？

你可以這樣回答

MP3 034

I really enjoy a bit of light jazz in the background[1] when I am at home. It makes me feel really relaxed. Light jazz creates the wonderful holiday atmosphere. I often beat time[2], especially when I am doing housework like mopping[3] the floor or doing the washing up. One time, I got into a taxi which was playing light jazz. The driver's and my taste in music were exactly the same. It just put me in a good mood[4] for the whole day.

在家的時候，我喜歡放輕爵士樂當背景音樂，輕爵士樂營造出美好的假日氛圍讓我覺得很放鬆，我做家事的時候經常跟著音樂打拍子，拖地或洗碗時尤其會這麼做。有一次，我搭的計程車剛好在放輕爵士樂，司機和我對音樂的喜好一模一樣，讓我一整天的心情都很好。

❶ **background**
　名 背景

❷ **beat time**
　片 打拍子

❸ **mop**
　動 用拖把拖洗

❹ **in a good mood**
　片 心情好

> **延伸note**
> 搭乘轎車或計程車的慣用說法為get in(to) a car/taxi，用on會讓人誤以為你坐在車頂上喔。

換個立場講講看

I can't stand heavy metal. It is just too much bass[5] and screaming. I don't find it enjoyable[6] at all! Instead, it stresses me out[7] when I hear it. I remember once seeing a live band with my friend. And gosh! It made me very agitated[8] and irritable[9]. My friend asked me if I liked the performance. I simply said "not bad" just to avoid[10] hurting his feelings. Honestly, I just can't understand why some people enjoy heavy metal.

　　我無法忍受重金屬音樂，實在太多貝斯聲和鬼叫聲了，我完全不覺得那好聽！重金屬音樂只會讓我的壓力直線上升而已。我記得有一次陪朋友去看樂團的現場表演，天啊！那鬼音樂讓我異常焦躁。朋友問我那場表演如何，因為不想讓他太難過，所以我說「不差」，但說實話，我真的搞不懂怎麼會有人喜歡重金屬音樂。

| ❺ **bass** 名 低音樂器；低沉的聲音 | ❻ **enjoyable** 形 有樂趣的 | ❼ **stress sb. out** 片 使某人緊張 |
| ❽ **agitated** 形 焦慮的 | ❾ **irritable** 形 煩躁的 | ❿ **avoid** 動 避免 |

 ## 試著更與眾不同

I enjoy listening to pop music[11] regardless of the language. Pop music is usually catchy[12]. And even if you don't understand a word of the lyrics[13], it is still easy to sing along with. Like most Korean pop music, so I can sing along with it easily because there are plenty of[14] English words in the lyrics. Besides, pop music is what my friends and I sing together at KTV. I love the music everybody enjoys.

　　我喜歡流行音樂，不管什麼語言我都愛。流行樂通常都很容易朗朗上口，即便完全看不懂歌詞，也很容易就能跟著唱。就像大部分的韓國流行樂，我都能跟著唱，因為歌詞用了很多英文字。除此之外，在KTV的時候，流行樂是最能點來和我的朋友一起唱的，我喜歡這種大家都能同樂的音樂。

| ⓫ **pop music** 片 流行音樂 | ⓬ **catchy** 形 動聽而易記的 |
| ⓭ **lyrics** 名 歌詞 | ⓮ **plenty of** 片 充足；大量 |

延伸note
regardless of(不管；不顧)
後面接名詞/動名詞，意思
等同於 in spite of 和
despite。

Key Points

答題TIPS看這裡！

對於喜歡或討厭的音樂，每個人有他的理由，記得用幾句話說明。比方說：I hate Rap because it is not singing. It is more like people arguing. （我討厭饒舌歌，因為那根本不是唱歌，比較像在吵架。）

Words & Phrases 談論音樂的種類

1 **pop music**
流行音樂

2 **classical music**
古典音樂

3 **symphony**
交響樂

4 **reggae**
雷鬼音樂

5 **hip-hop music**
嘻哈音樂

6 **anime song**
動畫歌曲

7 **R&B**
節奏布魯斯

8 **country music**
鄉村音樂

 進階實用句 More Expressions

I think the café next door has a very good selection of lounge music.

隔壁咖啡廳播的沙發音樂都很好聽。

My neighbor plays reggae the whole afternoon. Can you ask him to stop for a while?

我鄰居整個下午都在放雷鬼音樂，你可以要求他停一下嗎？

Super Junior is my favorite Korean pop singers. I can even dance to their music video.

Super Junior是我最喜歡的韓國流行歌手，我甚至能跟著他們的音樂錄影帶跳舞呢！

UNIT 05 與音樂相關的回憶

Q **Is there a song that reminds you of something?**
有哪首歌會讓你回想起某件事嗎？

你可以這樣回答

MP3
035

Yes, there is a very old song called "Moon River". It reminds me of[1] my first date with my ex-boyfriend back in college. We were having a ball[2], and the song was playing in the background. That was when he came and asked me whether he could dance with me. We broke up[3] soon after we graduated[4], but the memory is still very sweet.

　　有一首很老的歌叫《月河》，那首歌總讓我想起我和大學時的男朋友初會時的情形。我們當時參加舞會，背景音樂就是這首歌，也就是那個時候，他過來問我是否能當他的舞伴。雖然我們畢業後沒多久就分手了，但過往的回憶依然很甜蜜。

❶ **remind sb. of**
片 使某人想起

❷ **ball**
名 舞會

❸ **break up**
片 分手

❹ **graduate**
動 畢業

延伸note
提到老歌，還有另外一個英文單字oldie可用，不僅能用來指老歌，也可指老電影。

換個立場講講看

Every time I hear "Last Christmas", I remember the Christmas gift exchange[5] back in high school. Everyone would agree on a budget[6] and go get a present for someone else. Everyone would be nervous[7] while drawing lots[8]. The most exciting moment was when we tore off[9] the wrapping paper and saw what gifts we got. Sometimes I got girly stuff. It was really embarrassing[10], but I didn't know who gave it to me and couldn't return it. Hence, I would just give it to my sister. All in all, it was really fun.

　　每當我聽到《去年的聖誕節》這首歌，就會想起高中時期的聖誕節交換禮物活動。我們會訂出預算，再依預算去挑禮物，抽籤的時候，大家都很緊張，最令人興奮的就是拆開包裝紙，看抽到什麼禮物的那一刻。我有時候會抽到女生的東西，尷尬死了，但我不知道是誰送的，所以也無法退回去，因此只好把禮物送給我妹妹。無論如何，交換禮物真的很有趣。

⑤ exchange
名 交換

⑥ budget
名 預算

⑦ nervous
形 緊張的

⑧ draw lots
片 抽籤

⑨ tear off
片 撕掉

⑩ embarrassing
形 使人尷尬的

 試著更與眾不同

Yes, but it is not a proper[11] song. It is the theme song[12] for the cartoon[13] called "Chibi Maruko Chan". I went on a grand[14] camping trip in my sophomore[15] year of high school. Every class had to prepare a performance for the night of the camp fire, so our class did a dance with that song. We mimic the cartoon characters' actions. There were lots of silly[16] moves in it. My friends and I still laugh about it now.

　　有，可那不是一首正式的歌，而是卡通《櫻桃小丸子》的主題曲。我高二的時候去參加學校的露營活動，每一班都必須為營火之夜準備一段表演，所以我們班跳了那首歌，我們模仿那部卡通中的人物動作，設計了很多搞笑的舞蹈動作，我和我朋友現在談起這件事都還會笑呢！

⑪ proper
形 適合的；適當的

⑫ theme song
片 主題曲

⑬ cartoon
名 卡通

⑭ grand
形 盛大的

⑮ sophomore
名 高二生；大二生

⑯ silly
形 蠢的

答題TIPS看這裡！

音樂往往會伴隨過去的記憶，只是平常不見得會記得，通常是聽到音樂時才想起。回答時，記得敘述音樂播放的場合和因此引發的事件。實在想不出特別的曲子時，也可以從節慶歌曲下手，例如聽到恭喜發財就會聯想到過年，敘述節慶的氣氛也是一種回答方式。

Words & Phrases　東方重要節慶

1 Chinese New Year
農曆新年

2 Dragon Boat Festival
端午節

3 Moon Festival
中秋節

4 Tomb Sweeping Day
清明節

Words & Phrases　西方重要節慶

1 Christmas
聖誕節

2 Easter Holiday
復活節假期

3 Thanksgiving Day
感恩節

4 Halloween
萬聖節

 進階實用句 More Expressions

Christmas carols always remind me of my childhood.

聖誕頌歌總會讓我想起我的童年。

Whenever I hear this love song, I can't help thinking about my wedding day.

每當我聽到這首情歌，總會想起結婚的那一天。

It reminds me of my graduation ball whenever I hear "Take A Bow" by Madonna.

每次聽到瑪丹娜的《謝幕》，我都會想起畢業舞會的景象。

UNIT 06 最喜歡的歌手

Q **Who is your favorite singer? Why?**
你最喜歡的歌手是誰？為什麼？

 你可以這樣回答

MP3 036

My favorite[1] singer is Michael Jackson. Although he passed away[2] a few years ago, his songs are still popular. It's almost like he never left us. He was a very talented singer and dancer. Young kids are still trying to copy his signature[3] "Moon Walk" move. He not only had a beautiful[4] voice, but also danced like no one else can. I know all his songs and some of the dance moves.

我最喜歡的歌手是麥可傑克森，雖然他已經過世好幾年了，可是他的音樂依然很受歡迎，就像他還在世一般。他是一個很有天分的歌手與舞者，年輕小孩到現在都還在學他的招牌舞步「月球漫步」。他不僅擁有美麗的嗓音，也有超群的舞技。他所有的歌我都會唱，也會跳一部份舞步。

❶ **favorite**
形 最喜愛的

❷ **pass away**
片 過世

❸ **signature**
名 特徵

❹ **beautiful**
形 出色的

延伸note
如果你喜愛的歌手並非像麥可這樣的國際級名人，記得要多介紹歌手的特色和歌路。

 換個立場講講看

It has to be Lady Gaga. She is so different from most of the singers these days. Her songs are very catchy. She used to sing country[5] music but didn't succeed[6] at that time. Now she is well-known both for her music and daring style. Her music videos feature creativity and queerness. What impressed me the most was she once wore a dress that was completely[7] made of[8] raw meat. I don't know what other people think of her, but she is amazing in my eyes.

一定是Lady Gaga啊，她跟現今的歌手很不一樣，她的歌很容易唱。她曾經是鄉村音樂的歌手，但當時沒有成功，現在她則以音樂和大膽作風聞名，她的音樂錄影帶特色就是有創意又古怪，我印象最深刻的是她穿過一件生牛肉裝。我不知道別人怎麼想，但在我的眼裡，她實在太棒了！

延伸note
舉出歌手實際表演的例子，能讓面試官感受到你的喜愛之情，會更有說服力。

⑤ country
名 鄉村；鄉下

⑥ succeed
動 成功

⑦ completely
副 完全地

⑧ be made of
片 由…製造

試著更與眾不同

I really like Jay Chou. He is not only a popular singer but also a talented record producer. He has a very unique[9] tone when he sings. Sometimes it sounds like he is talking to you. I admire[10] his talent in composing[11] songs. Besides his own album, he writes songs for other famous singers. He has also made a few films, but I prefer his music. I went to one of his concerts[12], and I could tell that he put in a lot of effort to make his performance different from others.

我很喜歡周杰倫，他不僅是一位人氣歌手，還是個很有天分的音樂製作人。他唱歌的聲調很獨特，有時候就像在和你說話一樣，我很崇拜他在音樂創作方面的天分，除了他自己的創作專輯，他也幫其他知名歌手寫曲。他也拍過幾部電影，可是我還是比較喜歡他在音樂上的表現。我以前去看過他的演唱會，看得出來他花了很多心思，讓表演獨樹一格。

⑨ unique
形 獨特的

⑩ admire
動 欽佩；欣賞

⑪ compose
動 作（詩、曲等）

⑫ concert
名 音樂會；演唱會

延伸note
如果講的是演歌雙棲的歌手，除了歌曲之外，也可以提到他在演戲方面的表現。

Key Points 答題TIPS看這裡！

選一個有特色的歌手，形容他的外表、個性、表演風格、歌曲或舞蹈，甚至是值得學習的地方也可以。例如：I like Ricky Martin. His songs are passionate.（我喜歡瑞奇馬汀，他的歌曲都很熱情。）

Words & Phrases 談論藝人的魅力

1 gifted
有天賦的

2 good-looking
外貌帥氣/美麗的

3 a sense of humor
幽默感

4 have a strong work ethic
敬業

Words & Phrases 不同類型的音樂人

1 idol
偶像

2 singer-songwriter
創作型歌手

3 diva
天后

4 vocalist
聲樂家

進階實用句 More Expressions

Jody Chiang is a wonderful singer of Taiwanese songs.

江蕙是一個很棒的台語歌手。

If you like great dancing, you should watch Aaron Kwok's live concert.

如果你喜歡舞蹈表演，你應該去看郭富城的演唱會。

Justin Bieber was so innocent when he first started singing, but now he seems to be all over the place.

小賈斯汀剛出道的時候很清純，可是他現在很亂七八糟。

UNIT 07

關於KTV這檔事

Q **Do you like to go sing karaoke?**
你喜歡去KTV嗎？

你可以這樣回答

MP3 037

Yes, it is my favorite thing to do on Friday night. My co-workers and I usually get off work about 8 p.m. Then we head straight[1] to a karaoke[2] place. They normally offer Friday specials for NT$500 per person. We can have our dinner there, including[3] unlimited[4] beer. If we arrive earlier, we can even get a big room at a discounted price. We have a great time whenever we go there. That is definitely a great deal[5] for food and entertainment[6].

　　當然喜歡，那是我星期五晚上最喜歡做的事。我同事和我通常會趕在八點左右下班，接著直奔KTV。星期五通常會有特價優惠，一個人只要五百元台幣，我們可以在那裡用餐，啤酒也能無限暢飲。如果早點到的話，甚至還能以折扣價訂到大包廂，我們每次去卡拉OK都很開心。不僅有飯吃，還含娛樂，真的很划算。

❶ **straight**
副 直接地

❷ **karaoke**
名 卡拉OK

❸ **include**
動 包含；包括

❹ **unlimited**
形 無限制的

❺ **deal**
名 交易

❻ **entertainment**
名 娛樂；消遣

換個立場講講看

Well, I wouldn't say I like karaoke, but I will go there if I am invited[7] for a birthday or other gatherings[8]. I am not good at[9] singing, so singing in public[10] makes me feel embarrassed. However, I do want to catch up with my

friends, so I will go when there is a special occasion[11]. I just sing a few songs. Instead, I have a lot of food and drinks which are offered there. It doesn't happen[12] often anyway, maybe once every couple of months.

我不是那麼愛唱歌，但如果是有人生日或聚會，我就會去。我不擅長唱歌，所以在大家面前唱會讓我覺得很尷尬，但我還是會想見見朋友，所以有特殊場合的話，我就會參加，我只會唱幾首歌，相較之下，享用食物和飲料的機會還更多。不過，這種情況也不常發生，幾個月才一次吧。

7 invite	**8** gathering	**9** be good at
動 邀請	名 集會；聚會	片 擅長
10 in public	**11** occasion	**12** happen
片 公開地	名 場合；時刻	動 發生

試著更與眾不同

Honestly[13], I don't like karaoke because I don't sing. I hardly listen to pop music, so whenever I go to a karaoke place, all I do is sit there and watch. That is very boring[14]. If somebody invites me, I try to get out of it however I can. However, if it is a work function, I have to attend[15]. But hearing some people sing is such torture, so I don't stay for long. I make up[16] an excuse and leave early.

老實說，我不喜歡去KTV，因為我不唱歌，也幾乎不聽流行音樂，所以去KTV的時候，我都只坐在一旁看人唱歌，很無聊。如果有人邀請我，我會試著拒絕，但如果是公司聚會，我就非去不可，不過聽某些人唱歌，真的讓我如坐針氈，所以我會找個藉口提早離開。

13 honestly	**14** boring
副 老實說	形 無聊的
15 attend	**16** make up
動 參加	片 編造

延伸note
常見的make it up to sb.則表示「補償某人」，用在表示歉意的場合。

Key Points 答題TIPS看這裡！

每個人都有喜歡或不喜歡去KTV的原因，答題時盡量多加解釋。例如：想練歌而獨自去，或者喜歡和朋友同樂（party with friends），喜歡那裡的氣氛或供應的食物…等等。現在也有人會在家中裝KTV設備，或是住家的公共設施有KTV室 ，這些都可以提出來說，描述時建議盡量舉出與人同樂的實例，比較容易延伸話題。

Words & Phrases　去KTV慶祝的理由

1 **birthday**
生日

2 **one's promotion**
某人升職

3 **stag party**
（男生）告別單身趴

4 **hen party**
（女生）告別單身趴

Words & Phrases　去KTV的討人厭行為

1 **grab one's mike**
搶麥克風

2 **cut one's song**
卡掉某人的歌

3 **a drunken brawl**
酒醉鬧事

4 **don't pay the bill**
不付錢

進階實用句 More Expressions

It would be cheaper if you go to a KTV during weekdays.

平日去KTV會比較便宜。

I have reserved a private room in a KTV for New Year's Eve.

我已經訂好跨年夜那天的KTV包廂了。

I always know what songs I am going to sing before I go to a karaoke.

去KTV之前，我都會想好要唱什麼歌。

Q **Do you like to listen to music while you are working?**

你喜歡邊聽音樂邊工作嗎?

 你可以這樣回答

No, I can't have music on when I am working. I find it very distracting[1]. I tried playing light jazz before. I just couldn't concentrate[2] on my job at all! Furthermore[3], I am an accountant[4]. I need to deal with[5] numbers all day long. If I got distracted, I would very likely make mistakes, like adding up the wrong figures[6]. It would take forever to locate what went wrong once the mistake was made, so I avoid all possible distractions.

不,我無法邊聽音樂邊工作,音樂會讓我分心。我曾經放過輕爵士樂,但我完全無法專心在工作上。除此之外,我是會計師,整天都要確認數字上的細節,一分心就容易犯錯(像加錯總數之類的),要再找出錯誤會很花時間,所以如果有導致分心的事物,我都會盡量避免。

❶ **distracting** 形 分心的	❷ **concentrate** 動 集中	❸ **furthermore** 副 此外;再者
❹ **accountant** 名 會計師	❺ **deal with** 片 處理	❻ **figure** 名 數量;金額

 換個立場講講看

Most definitely! I don't like sitting in a real quiet office. It would only stress me out. So the first thing I do after arriving at my studio[7] is to turn the radio[8] on. The radio will stay on until I get off work at the end of the day. I think the time goes faster when there is music in the background. My co-workers also agree with me that it makes the working hours more tolerable[9]. I have even become more efficient with music. Sometimes when I hear the songs I like, I will sing along[10]!

　　一定要的啊！我不喜歡太過安靜的辦公室，這只會讓我感到緊張。所以我抵達工作室之後，就會馬上打開收音機，我會開一整天，到我下班為止。我覺得有背景音樂相伴，時間過得比較快，我的同事也跟我一樣，覺得這樣上班會比較好熬，有音樂陪伴，我的工作效率甚至更好了。有時候，當我聽到喜歡的歌時，還會跟著唱呢！

延伸note
上班時間稱為working hours；描述店家的營業時間時，則用opening hours。

❼ studio
名 工作室

❽ radio
名 收音機

❾ tolerable
形 可忍受的

❿ sing along
片 跟著唱

試著更與眾不同

Yes, I do, but I can only use headphones[11] because I work in an open-plan[12] office. If I have the speakers[13] on, it will disturb my co-workers. Most of them do not like the extra noise[14] in the office. I wish everyone could agree on having light music in the background because sometimes I can't hear the phone ringing when I'm wearing my headphones.

　　喜歡是喜歡，但我只能用耳機聽音樂。因為我們的辦公室是開放式設計，所以開音響會打擾到同事，他們大部分都不喜歡辦公室有額外的噪音。真希望大家都能接受輕音樂的播放，因為用耳機的話，我有時候會聽不到電話鈴聲。

⓫ headphone
名 頭戴式耳機

⓬ open-plan
形 （建）開啟式的

⓭ speaker
名 揚聲器；喇叭

⓮ noise
名 噪音

延伸note
speaker是指音響類的喇叭，如果要表示對著嘴、手拿式的擴音器，則用megaphone這個單字。

 Key Points

答題TIPS看這裡！

在表達喜好的同時，不妨補充工作性質，某些需高度專注力的職業（如：會計師），就必須避免音樂干擾；邊上班邊聽音樂無非是希望能有輕鬆感（feel relaxed），任職店員或簡單文書工作的人可能比較能這樣做。

Words & Phrases 不適合邊聽音樂的職業

1 **accountant**
會計師

2 **lawyer**
律師

3 **engineer**
工程師

4 **doctor**
醫生

Words & Phrases 與專注力有關的詞彙

1 **focus on**
專注在…

2 **distract from**
使分心

3 **attention**
注意力

4 **distraction**
分散注意力的事物

進階實用句 More Expressions

I can't have the music on because I might make mistakes.

我不能聽音樂，因為我可能會因此出錯。

I enjoy working as a barista because there is always nice music in the café.

咖啡廳裡總是會播放好聽的音樂，這也是我喜歡咖啡師傅這份工作的原因。

The company policy says that listening to music during office hours is not allowed.

公司規定上班時間不能聽音樂。

喜歡的電影類型

Q Do you like movies? What kind?
你喜歡看電影嗎？喜歡哪一類的呢？

你可以這樣回答

MP3
039

Yes, I like movies. My favorite is comedies. After a whole week's hard work, all I want to do is sit there and zone out[1] for a bit. This is why I usually don't pick a drama or psycho-thriller, even it's a blockbuster[2]. These two are a bit too much for me. On the other hand, a comedy doesn't take much brain[3] power, so it will be the perfect way to relax myself. It feels great to laugh after a stressful[4] week at work.

是的，我喜歡電影，我最愛喜劇片。努力工作了一整個星期後，我只想坐在某處好好放空，所以我通常不會挑劇情片或心理驚悚片來看（就算是人人推薦的熱門電影也一樣），這兩類電影對我來說過於沉重；相比之下，看喜劇不用花什麼腦力，是一種很棒的放鬆方式。工作了一個星期，放聲大笑才能讓人感到身心舒暢。

① **zone out**
片 放空發呆

② **blockbuster**
名 風靡一時的電影

③ **brain**
名 腦；腦袋

④ **stressful**
形 壓力重的

延伸note
既然題目問的是電影類型，就要把最重要的「類別」點出來，再簡單地敘述原因就可以了。

換個立場講講看

I don't have much patience[5] for movies because they last for at least an hour and a half without a break. My girlfriend loves going to the movies, so we watch movies together quite often. However, I fall asleep[6] most of the time. She gets mad at[7] me when she catches me falling asleep. Honestly, it's nothing to do with the movie. I just don't like sitting in a dim[8] room for such a long time. I actually[9] prefer to watch a TV series at home since each episode[10] is much shorter than a movie.

　　我沒什麼耐性看電影，你想想嘛，一部電影至少要演一個半小時，中間還沒有休息時間耶。我女友很喜歡看電影，所以我們還滿常一起去電影院的。不過，大部分的時間我都會睡著，如果她發現我睡著，就會很生氣。老實說，這跟電影在演什麼一點關係都沒有，我就是不喜歡長時間待在那個昏暗的房間裡。我其實比較喜歡在家看電視影集，因為每集播放的時間短多了。

⑤ **patience** 名 耐性	⑥ **fall asleep** 片 睡著	⑦ **get mad at** 片 對…生氣
⑧ **dim** 形 微暗的	⑨ **actually** 副 實際上	⑩ **episode** 名 （連續劇的）一集

試著更與眾不同

I love watching horror[11] movies in the cinema. The surround sound system makes me feel like the ghosts[12] are just in front of me. My boyfriend hates watching horror movies, but I sometimes pressure[13] him into going with me. It gives him nightmares[14], but I am okay with it. I might be scared for a couple of hours, but once I am distracted by something else, I forget about being scared right away.

　　我愛到電影院看恐怖片，立體聲的效果超棒，鬼就像在我面前似的。我男朋友討厭看恐怖片，但我有時候會強迫他陪我去看。他看了恐怖片會做惡夢，我就還好。雖然我也會害怕，但一旦有什麼其他吸引我的東西，剛剛看的恐怖片情節就會完全被我拋在腦後。

⑪ **horror** 名 恐怖；毛骨悚然	⑫ **ghost** 名 鬼；幽靈
⑬ **pressure** 動 迫使	⑭ **nightmare** 名 惡夢

延伸note
horror movies是刻意要讓觀眾感到害怕的電影(如：鬼片)；thriller則是帶有懸疑感的電影。

答題TIPS看這裡！

每個人喜歡的電影類別都不同，甚至會因不同的心情和狀態，選擇不同種類的片子，比方說，想要沉澱心情的人可能會選擇劇情片和溫馨片；尋求刺激的人則偏好恐怖片或動作片。如果沒有特別喜歡的也可以說：I don't like watching movies, so I don't have any preference.（我不喜歡看電影，所以也沒有特別喜歡的類型。）

Words & Phrases 各種電影的類型

1 **chick flick**
文藝片

2 **rom-com**
愛情喜劇片

3 **comedy**
喜劇片

4 **action movie**
動作片

5 **horror movie**
恐怖片

6 **musical**
音樂劇

7 **documentary**
紀錄片

8 **animation**
動畫片

進階實用句 More Expressions

Comedy is the best remedy for a hard day at work.

一天辛苦的工作結束後，看喜劇是最棒的充電方式。

I enjoy watching psycho-thrillers because I can never guess the ending.

我喜歡看心理驚悚片，因為結局總是出人意料。

I love science fiction. I believe it illustrates our life in the future, but I don't think I will live that long to witness it.

我愛科幻片，我相信未來生活就像電影裡演的那樣，但我有生之年應該看不到了。

參加演唱會/音樂會

Q Have you been to a concert before? Whose concert was it?

你參加過演唱會或音樂會嗎？是誰的呢？

你可以這樣回答

MP3
040

Yes, I have. It was a Britney Spears concert. The concert was meant to start at 7:30 p.m., but we waited until 8:45 p.m. I was not impressed with the venue[1] because the stage[2] was far away from the spectator[3] area. Honestly, I can't tell who was performing on the stage. The only way to see Britney was through the big projector[4]. Well, if I had known this, I would definitely have bought the Blue-ray DVD instead.

我去過小甜甜布蘭妮的演唱會，演唱會預計七點半開始，但我們等到八點四十五分才正式開始。我不喜歡那個場地，舞台離觀眾席太遠，老實說，我根本看不清楚是誰在舞台上表演，要看布蘭妮的唯一方法就是盯著會場的投影布幕。早知如此，我還不如買藍光DVD回家看呢！

❶ venue 名 場地	❷ stage 名 舞台
❸ spectator 名 觀眾	❹ projector 名 投射器；放映機

> **延伸note**
> 問題沒有標準答案，脈絡清楚才是重點，所以如果你不喜歡某場演唱會，照實說即可。

換個立場講講看

Of course! I once went to watch my favorite band, "Mayday", in Kaohsiung on New Year's Eve. The vocalist's[5] singing was powerful. I just couldn't take my eyes off[6] them. In addition to[7] their performance, I enjoyed their interaction[8] with the audience. It was interesting to see them throwing in jokes here and there. The best part was they did the New Year countdown[9] with us. It was absolutely memorable[10]!

當然有！我曾經為了看我最愛的五月天的表演，去高雄跨年。主唱的聲音很有渲染力，我的目光完全無法從他們身上移開。除了表演之外，我也喜歡他們和現場觀眾的互動，他們會不斷開玩笑，很有趣。最棒的是，他們陪我們一起倒數，那真是令人難忘的跨年！

❺ vocalist
名 主唱

❻ take one's eyes off
片 移開目光

❼ in addition to
介 除…之外；此外

❽ interaction
名 互動

❾ countdown
名 倒數計秒

❿ memorable
形 難忘的

 試著更與眾不同

I don't like going to concerts. You can never see who is on the stage. Besides, the tickets[11] are expensive[12]. Some cost you an arm and a leg. The worst part of it is I have to line up[13]. And once I get in, it is almost impossible for me to go to the toilet[14] because I might lose my spot. There's one more thing. Things may go wrong with equipment. A poor sound system really drives me nuts.

我不喜歡去看演唱會，你根本就看不清楚舞台上的人是誰，而且有的票價貴到你無法想像。最糟的地方在於得跟著排隊，進去之後，連跑廁所都簡直是「不可能的任務」，因為位子會被搶走。對了，現場設備還可能出錯，如果遇到差勁的音響效果，我真的會很抓狂。

⓫ ticket
名 門票

⓬ expensive
形 昂貴的

⓭ line up
片 排隊

⓮ toilet
名 廁所；洗手間

延伸note
真的不喜歡演唱會的話，也不需要硬是講一個，說明自己之所以不去看現場的原因即可。

Key Points 答題TIPS看這裡！

concert是大型演唱會/音樂會，現在還有一種小型的活動，稱為fan meeting（粉絲見面會），通常為非正式的活動，重視與粉絲的互動，如果沒有看演唱會的經驗，也可以從這方面切入。

Words & Phrases 與演唱會相關的詞彙

1. **live performance** 現場演出
2. **rehearsal** 彩排
3. **stage props** 舞台道具
4. **costume** 表演的戲服
5. **light effects** 燈光效果
6. **glow stick** 螢光棒
7. **up close and personal** 很靠近的
8. **general admission** 搖滾區（美）

進階實用句 More Expressions

I was lucky to get an autograph of Jolin Tsai.

能拿到蔡依林的簽名實在太幸運了。

I loved the costumes in the concert. They looked so unique.

我好喜歡那場演唱會的服裝，每一件看起來都好特別。

We got there really early. The singers were still doing the final rehearsal.

我們很早就抵達，歌手們還在做總彩排。

129

UNIT 11 我的專長樂器

Q Can you play any musical instruments?
你會演奏任何樂器嗎？

 你可以這樣回答

MP3
041

I like to play drums and jam with my band. I started learning on a drum kit[1] in my childhood[2]. But I hadn't thought about joining a band until my college friends invited me to be their drummer. We often practice[3] in the university gym[4] because it gets quite loud. I would get complaints[5] from my neighbors[6] if I practiced at home. We now play in a small pub on Saturday nights. We don't make much money, but it is something fun to do.

　　我喜歡打鼓和跟樂團的團員即興合奏。我從小就開始學爵士鼓，但在我大學朋友邀請我擔任樂團的鼓手之前，我從沒想過要加入樂團。因為練習的聲音很吵，所以我們通常都在學校的體育館練習。如果我在家練習，鄰居就會抗議。我們現在每週六晚上會在一間小酒吧表演，錢不多，但是很有趣。

❶ **drum kit** 片 爵士鼓	❷ **childhood** 名 童年	❸ **practice** 動 練習；訓練
❹ **gym** 名 體育館	❺ **complaint** 名 抱怨	❻ **neighbor** 名 鄰居

 換個立場講講看

I didn't learn how to play a musical[7] instrument[8] until I was in high school. I joined the ukulele[9] club. I was planning to pick up the guitar[10] at first, but then I realized the ukulele was becoming more and more popular. I found that I could

still impress the girls with my singing and performing. With less strings than a guitar, the ukulele is not difficult for me to learn. Besides, the ukulele is easier to carry around. Most importantly, it actually worked! My girlfriend was totally impressed by my playing.

　　我一直到高中才開始學樂器，我加入了烏克麗麗的社團。我原本想學吉他，但後來我發現烏克麗麗越來越風行，我可以藉著自彈自唱來追女生。烏克麗麗的弦比吉他少，對我來說比較好上手，又方便攜帶，最重要的是，它真的有用！我女朋友當時對我的彈奏可印象深刻了。

延伸note
美國高中為9～12年級稱呼為 f r e s h m a n 、 sophomore、junior和 senior。

❼ **musical**
形 音樂的

❽ **instrument**
名 樂器

❾ **ukulele**
名 烏克麗麗

❿ **guitar**
名 吉他

試著更與眾不同

I have taken violin classes ever since I was five. My parents' dream is to see me turn out to be like Yo-Yo Ma one day. I enjoy playing violin, but I have never gotten good at it. Maybe I am just not gifted enough to be a professional[11] violinist[12]. I just regard playing the violin as amusement[13] instead of serious practice. Sometimes I will take out my violin and play a few songs. But to be honest, I don't think I will pursue the idea of being a professional musician[14].

　　我從五歲就開始就學小提琴，我父母的夢想是有一天能看到我拉得像馬友友一樣。我滿喜歡小提琴的，可是我拉得不好，我大概沒什麼當小提琴家的天份吧。拉小提琴對我來說只是種消遣，不是嚴肅的練習，所以我有時候還是會拿出我的小提琴，拉幾首曲子來聽，但老實說，我不會認真地想成為職業音樂家。

⓫ **professional**
形 職業的

⓬ **violinist**
名 小提琴家

⓭ **amusement**
名 娛樂；消遣

⓮ **musician**
名 音樂家

延伸note
弦樂四重奏(string quartet)為室內樂，標準的配置為兩把小提琴、一把中提琴與一把大提琴。

答題TIPS看這裡！

每種樂器都有不同的演奏場合與調性，回答時可以就自己本身的氣質和資質解釋自己學習某種樂器的目的。如果真的沒有學任何樂器的經驗，笛子（flute）會是個好選擇。一般的學校大概都有教，例如：I can play flute, I learned it from the music class in elementary school.（我會吹直笛，國小的音樂課有教。）

Words & Phrases　常見的西洋樂器

1 viola 中提琴	**2 cello** 大提琴
3 harmonica 口琴	**4 trumpet** 喇叭；小號
5 French horn 法國號	**6 keyboard** 電子琴
7 timpani 定音鼓	**8 saxophone** 薩克斯風

進階實用句 More Expressions

I can play harmonica rather well.

我的口琴吹得很好。

I learned to play trumpet after I joined the school marching band.

加入了學校的儀隊後，我學會吹小喇叭。

The sound of cello is very soothing. That's the reason why I chose the cello to be my major instrument.

大提琴的聲音很舒服，所以我才選大提琴做主修樂器。

UNIT 12

音樂偏好的變化

Q **Has your taste in music changed from when you were younger?**

和年輕時相比，你對音樂的偏好有改變嗎？

你可以這樣回答

MP3
042

Yes, I used to think that I would love slow love songs forever. But I started to like Latino[1] love songs with stronger beats[2] after I graduated. Furthermore, the rhythm[3] is more passionate[4]. I even took some classes to learn Latino dances like the salsa and samba. Dancing was first introduced[5] to me by one of my friends. She loves ballroom dance[6] and joined a club back in college. We took the dancing classes together, and I fell in love with it, too.

　　有，我曾經以為我一輩子都只會喜歡抒情歌曲，但畢業之後，我慢慢喜歡上節奏較強烈的拉丁情歌。其實拉丁樂不只節奏，聽起來還更熱情，我甚至還去學拉丁舞蹈，薩爾薩舞曲和森巴我都有學。一開始是我的一個朋友介紹我去跳舞，她熱愛國標舞，大學時期是國標舞社的一員，我們一起去上課，後來我也愛上了。

❶ **Latino**	❷ **beat**	❸ **rhythm**
形 拉丁美洲的	名 拍子；節奏	名 節奏；韻律
❹ **passionate**	❺ **introduce**	❻ **ballroom dance**
形 熱情的	動 介紹	片 國標舞

換個立場講講看

I never thought much about the symphony[7] orchestra[8] until one day I was given a free concert ticket to go and see one. I used to think the symphony orchestra must be really boring, but after I went to see one, I realized how powerful music can be. Thanks to that performance! It really touched[9] me, and now I am a big fan. I actually booked[10] a ticket to see the National Symphony Orchestra next weekend.

我一直對交響樂沒什麼興趣，直到某天有人送了我一張免費的音樂會門票，才有了改變。我以前覺得交響樂很無趣，但我實際去聽了之後，我才發現音樂的力量有多大，感謝去看了那場音樂會！那次讓我深受感動，也因此成為交響樂迷。事實上，下星期國家交響樂團有一場表演，我票都訂好了呢！

延伸note
第一句的never think much about表達的是不討厭也不喜歡，表示說話者對交響樂「無感」。

❼ **symphony**
名 交響樂

❽ **orchestra**
名 管弦樂隊

❾ **touch**
動 觸動；感動

❿ **book**
動 預定；預約

 試著更與眾不同

I have always liked pop music, but I fell in love with jazz when I traveled abroad[11] last year. Compared with pop songs, jazz is more relaxing. I especially like bossa nova. It's a style[12] of jazz from Brazil. Singers like Lisa Ono and Olivia Ong are my favorites. I first heard bossa nova in a jazz bar. I love it so much that I even made up my mind[13] to visit the famous[14] "Blue Note" in New York next year.

我一直都喜歡流行音樂，但當我去年出國接觸了爵士樂後，我就不可自拔地愛上這種曲風了。和流行音樂比起來，爵士樂聽起來更舒適宜人，而爵士樂當中，我特別喜歡巴莎諾瓦，這是一種源自巴西的爵士樂派，小野麗莎和王儷婷是我最愛的巴莎諾瓦歌手。第一次聽到這種曲風，是在一家爵士酒吧裡。我超愛這類音樂，甚至已經下定決心明年要去紐約，到那家有名的Blue Note酒吧朝聖。

❶ **abroad**
副 在國外

⓬ **style**
名 風格

⓭ **make up one's mind**
片 下定決心

⓮ **famous**
形 出名的

延伸note
被爵士樂影響而出現的還有jazz dance(爵士舞)，搭配節奏較為強勁的音樂盡情舞動。

 答題TIPS看這裡！

在音樂類型的偏好（preference to music）上，大部分人多多少少都會有些轉變。例如有人會因為心情成熟之後，喜歡上古典音樂（classic）或交響樂（symphony）；也有人會隨著時代的變化，而喜歡上新式的音樂流派。

Words & Phrases　描述各式各樣的改變

1 **make changes**
刻意改變

2 **transform into**
將…改成

3 **alter to**
修改（衣服等）

4 **change one's mind**
改變心意

Words & Phrases　從小到大的年齡階段

1 **children**
兒童

2 **teenager**
青少年

3 **adult**
成年人

4 **in middle age**
中年的

進階實用句 More Expressions

I like contemporary music more.

我更喜歡現代音樂。

I like to play calm music before going to bed. It helps with my sleep.

我睡前喜歡播放平靜的音樂，可以幫助睡眠。

This love song sounds very sweet. I think it's the best choice for your wedding.

這首情歌很甜蜜，我覺得是最適合你婚禮的一首歌。

UNIT 13 對歷史劇的喜好

Q **Do you like to watch historical films?**
你喜歡看歷史劇嗎？

 你可以這樣回答

MP3 043

Yes, I like historical films. Some of them represent[1] history correctly, and some turn history into fiction[2] to attract a larger audience. A true historical film might be dull[3] to some people, so certain adaptations[4] are necessary[5]. Through historical films, I learn a lot about leadership[6] and interpersonal relationships. For instance, I understand that showing off leads to dangers. I wish to avoid making the same mistakes in my life.

　　我喜歡歷史劇，有些歷史劇會依史實拍攝，有些則會為了吸引更多觀眾而改編。對部分人來說，完全照史實拍攝的劇情很乏味，所以適度的改編是必要的。我從歷史劇中學到很多和領導力、人際關係有關的事情，例如，我了解到太愛出風頭會導致災禍。希望我能將這些應用到生活中，避免犯下同樣的錯誤。

❶ **represent**	❷ **fiction**	❸ **dull**
動 上演；表現	名 虛構；捏造	形 乏味的；單調的
❹ **adaptation**	❺ **necessary**	❻ **leadership**
名 改編；改寫	形 必須的	名 領導

 換個立場講講看

No, I am not interested in historical films at all. I was never good at history when I was in school. Seeing those nobles[7] interacting[8] with each other and figuring out[9] what is going on in the drama are just tiring[10] to me. I always forget

the characters' relationships when watching historical films. Some people believe you can learn from those films, but things have changed rapidly[11]. What worked in the past might not work now. It is like comparing apples with pears[12].

　　我對歷史劇一點興趣都沒有，在學時期，我的歷史就沒好過。看電視劇裡的貴族互動，還得理解當中發生了什麼事，對我來說實在太難了，所以看歷史劇的時候，我總會忘記人物間的關係與互動。有些人相信能從過去的歷史中學到很多，但時代快速變遷，過去有效的方式，到了現代未必有用，就好像是拿兩個不對等的東西來比較一樣。

❼ noble 名 貴族	❽ interact 動 互動	❾ figure out 片 理解；明白
❿ tiring 形 令人疲倦的	⓫ rapidly 副 迅速地	⓬ pear 名 梨子

 ## 試著更與眾不同

I will watch historical films only if they are recommended by my friends. Some historical films happen to[13] be good movies, too. In that case, I will go and watch it. But if I could choose[14], I would not watch historical films. To me, they are generally[15] dull and serious[16]. The plots are all about men struggling for power or women fighting for attention. History sometimes can even put me to sleep when I am really tired.

　　我只會看朋友推薦的歷史劇，有些歷史劇很精采，那種的我會去看。可是如果可以選擇的話，我不會選歷史劇看，因為那對我來說很枯燥、過於嚴肅，情節不外乎是男人爭權，或女人爭寵，疲倦的時候看歷史劇，我真的會睡著。

⓭ happen to 片 碰巧	⓮ choose 動 選擇	延伸note only if在此處點出條件，後面的子句(朋友推薦)是前提，符合此前提才會去看。
⓯ generally 副 通常；一般地	⓰ serious 形 嚴肅的	

答題TIPS看這裡！

歷史劇並非人人都會喜歡的戲劇類型，可以先確定你對歷史劇的感受，再加以形容舉例。如果你對歷史劇沒有特別想法，可看可不看，不妨說：I don't really get interested in historical films, but I wouldn't refuse to watch one.（我並沒有特別喜歡歷史劇，但也不會排斥。）

Words & Phrases　與歷史有關的詞彙

1 historic
歷史性的；歷史悠久的

2 historical
與歷史有關的

3 archeology
考古學

4 event
事件；大事

Words & Phrases　講述來源或根據

1 according to
根據

2 be based on
以⋯為基礎

3 be determined by
由⋯決定

4 in terms of
就⋯而論

🎤 進階實用句 More Expressions

What happened today is history tomorrow.

今天發生的事，明天就變成歷史了。

Some historical films are a true reflection of an actual event.

有些歷史劇完全依史實拍攝。

Historical films sometimes get quite heavy, so I wouldn't watch them to relax.

歷史劇有時候很沉重，所以我想放鬆時不會看。

UNIT 14 傳統音樂與舞蹈

MP3 044

Q **Do you like traditional music or dances?**
你喜歡傳統音樂或舞蹈嗎？

你可以這樣回答

Yes, I am a big fan of Irish step dance, aka[1] Riverdance. All the dancers have to keep a very stiff[2] posture[3] and move their legs and feet very quickly. I find this fascinating[4] and unique. The dancers' fast-moving dances attract the audience. The dance has been around for over 2,000 years. I think the dancers do a very good job of keeping the tradition[5] alive. I have a lot of respect[6] for them.

是的，我很喜歡看愛爾蘭的踢踏舞，這種舞蹈又叫大河之舞。舞者的身體必須挺直，腳又要動得很快，我覺得這種舞蹈很吸引人，也夠獨特，舞者的快節奏舞步令觀眾看得入迷。這種舞蹈已經有兩千年左右的歷史了，在維持傳統這方面，我覺得舞者們做得很棒，我很尊敬他們。

❶ **aka**
縮 亦稱為

❷ **stiff**
形 挺的；硬的

❸ **posture**
名 姿勢

❹ **fascinating**
形 迷人的

❺ **tradition**
名 傳統

❻ **respect**
名 尊敬

換個立場講講看

No, I like neither traditional music nor dance. I think those are for the older generation[7]. It is not like we don't have any choice in music or dances these days. There are so many pop music singers and they make really good music, too. Maybe I should introduce this kind of modern[8] music to people who only listen to the traditional music. Maybe they haven't had a chance[9] to be exposed to[10] pop songs.

我不喜歡傳統音樂或舞蹈，我覺得那些是給老人家看的。又不是沒有其他的音樂或舞蹈可以選擇，很多流行音樂歌手的歌也不錯啊！也許我應該把這些現代音樂介紹給那些只聽傳統音樂的人，搞不好他們沒聽過也不一定。

試著更與眾不同

Yes, I like the traditional music that is performed[11] with the Chinese zither[12]. I find it very peaceful[13] and soothing[14] to listen to. It is not very popular among the younger generation, but it is quite common in film scores[15], especially for movies based on Chinese history. In addition, some pop music accompanied by the instrument can create a mysterious[16] atmosphere. I took a few Chinese zither classes, and it is actually difficult to play. Therefore, I gave it up after several classes.

我喜歡古箏彈奏的傳統樂曲，我覺得這類音樂很有安撫作用，聽了之後內心會變得比較平靜。年輕人不太會喜歡，但這類音樂滿常出現在電影配樂中，尤其是那些和中國歷史相關的電影，而以此樂器伴奏的流行樂則能創造神秘的氛圍。我之前上過幾堂古箏課，彈起來其實比想像中困難。因此，在上了幾堂課之後，我就放棄學古箏了。

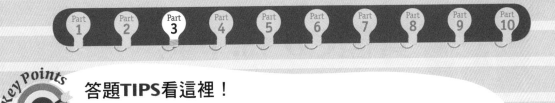

Key Points 答題TIPS看這裡！

雖然與現代音樂的差別很大，但傳統音樂有其存在的價值，兩者可以共存，所以也有人是兩種音樂都喜歡的，如果你正好是這樣的人，也可以用：I like..., but I also like...這個句型表示兩者皆喜歡。

Words & Phrases 傳統音樂或舞蹈

1 Taiwanese Opera
歌仔戲

2 Chinese Opera
國劇

3 classic ballet
古典芭蕾

4 Kabuki
日本歌舞伎

5 folk dance
土風舞；民族舞蹈

6 belly dancing
肚皮舞

7 flamenco
佛朗明哥

8 hula
草裙舞

進階實用句 More Expressions

I love watching the hula. It is very welcoming.

我喜歡看草裙舞表演，讓人覺得備受歡迎。

Although Taiwanese Opera seems a bit old-fashioned, I enjoy watching it.

雖然歌仔戲有點過時，但我很愛看。

I went to Taitung last year to experience the Aboriginal Harvesting Festival.

我去年去台東參加原住民的豐年祭。

UNIT 15
實體CD vs. 下載

MP3 045

Q **Do you prefer to buy CDs or pay and download the music from certain websites?**
你喜歡買CD還是付錢從網站下載音樂呢？

 你可以這樣回答

I prefer CDs because I am still used to CD players. My brother once taught me how to pay for MP3s and download[1] them through the Internet[2], but those steps are just confusing[3] to me. Plus, I feel giving my credit card[4] number online is not secure[5]. Although storing CDs takes a lot of room, I still like taking them down from my bookshelf. I guess I am a little bit "old-fashioned[6]" when it comes to CDs.

我個人喜歡買CD，因為我還是比較習慣用CD播放器聽音樂。我哥哥曾經教我從網路上購買以及下載音樂的方法，但我覺得那些步驟好複雜。除此之外，在線上填寫信用卡號碼這件事也讓我覺得很沒安全感。雖然存放CD很佔空間，但我就是喜歡從書架上把CD拿下來的感覺。講到CD，我覺得自己大概是比較「落伍」的那一類吧。

❶ **download**
動 下載

❷ **Internet**
名 網路

❸ **confusing**
形 令人困惑的

❹ **credit card**
片 信用卡

❺ **secure**
形 安心的；安全的

❻ **old-fashioned**
形 過時的

 換個立場講講看

I definitely[7] prefer downloading from websites[8]. I have bought and downloaded lots of songs. It's much more convenient[9]. I can keep them all in my iPhone and

listen to them whenever I want. Of course, I still have some old CDs, but I seldom take them off from my shelf. If I really want to listen to those oldies[10], I need to turn on my computer and use the DVD player for them. It's really inconvenient.

當然是從網站下載啊。我一直都是從網站上購買以及下載音樂的，那樣方便多了，可以直接把音樂存入我的iPhone，想聽的時候隨時都可以聽。當然，我還是買過一些CD，但我很少把那些CD從書架上拿下來。如果我真的很想聽那些老歌，我還必須開電腦，用DVD播放軟體才有辦法聽，真的很不方便。

延伸note
現在有許多線上購買音樂的管道（例如：iTunes、KKBOX等），都可以拿出來舉例。

❼ definitely
副 肯定地；當然

❾ convenient
形 方便的

❽ website
名 網站

❿ oldie
名 老歌；老影片

 試著更與眾不同

Generally, I download them from websites. If it's not something I really like, I just spend time browsing[11] online[12] to find free websites for downloading. I am not a fan of particular singers, so I don't want to own their albums. Buying a CD is usually not an option[13] for me because I only like a few songs from the CD. It makes no sense[14] to pay for the whole thing when I only want some of it.

基本上，我會從網站下載，如果並非我特別喜愛的音樂，我就會花點時間找網路上免費的分享網站。我不是某些歌手的粉絲，不會特別想要擁有他們的專輯，而且我通常也不會選擇買CD，因為我只喜歡其中幾首歌，沒必要為了那幾首而花錢買整張CD吧。

⓫ browse
動 瀏覽

⓭ option
名 選項

⓬ online
副 連線地

⓮ sense
名 道理；效益

延伸note
spend (time/money) on+名詞很實用；若要講「浪費時間/金錢在…上」，將動詞改成waste即可。

答題TIPS看這裡！

在這個網路發達的時代，手機和iPad是許多人聽音樂的媒介，CD甚至被部分人視為過時的產品。儘管如此，還是有人喜愛購買CD，答題時可以先用 prefer A to B這樣的句型點出自己的偏好，再接著敘述原因。另外，即使從網路下載音樂，還是有分為付費和免費的方式，回答時可依個人喜好稍加解釋。

Words & Phrases 讓人跟不上科技發展

1 **dated**
老舊的；過時的

2 **computer moron**
電腦白癡

3 **can't keep up with**
跟不上

4 **live in the past**
活在過去

Words & Phrases 常見的CD唱片種類

1 **album**
專輯

2 **single**
單曲

3 **compilation album**
合輯

4 **original soundtrack**
電影原聲帶

進階實用句 More Expressions

I have a few CDs that were signed by the singers.

我有幾張CD，上面有歌手的親筆簽名。

My computer is very slow. Downloading is time-consuming.

我的電腦跑得很慢，下載要花很久的時間。

I like to keep up with new technology, so I always have the latest cell phone.

我喜歡走在科技的尖端，所以我的手機一定是最新機型。

Part 4

運動與健康
Sports and Health

 動　動詞
 名　名詞
 副　副詞
 形　形容詞
 介　介系詞
 連　連接詞
 片　片語

UNIT 01 游泳池 vs. 海邊

Q Can you swim? Do you prefer to go to the swimming pool or the beach?

你會游泳嗎？你喜歡去游泳池還是海邊？

 你可以這樣回答

 MP3 046

Yes, I have been taking swimming lessons[1] since I was in elementary[2] school. I also did some swimming training back in high school. I was part of the swimming team, and we practiced three times a week. I was also good at open water[3] swimming. I actually prefer to go to the beach because I can do some snorkelling[4] as well. Besides, I can watch the beautiful sunset reflected on the sea. How marvelous it is!

　　我從小學開始就學游泳，高中也受過游泳訓練，我是游泳校隊的，我們一個星期要練習三次。我也擅長在開放式的水域游泳，事實上，我比較喜歡去海邊，還可以順便浮潛。而且，我還能欣賞美麗的夕陽倒映在海面上的景色，多美妙啊！

❶ **lesson**
名 課程

❷ **elementary**
形 初級的；基礎的

❸ **open water**
片 開放水域

❹ **snorkelling**
名 浮潛

延伸note
常見的泳式有：freestyle（自由式）、breaststroke（蛙式）、backstroke（仰式）、butterfly（蝶式）。

 換個立場講講看

I can swim, but I am not very good at it. I almost failed[5] PE class because of swimming in junior high. The pool was quite shallow[6], but I thought I was drowning[7]. Ever since then, I have been scared of water. So, I never enjoy going to the beach. The waves[8] just scare me. Whenever I go with my friends, all I do is

wear a life jacket[9] or sit in the shade[10].

　　我會游泳，可是游得不好，連國中體育課都差點因為游得不好而被當掉。那個游泳池的水還滿淺的，但我當時覺得自己快溺死了。自從那次之後，我就有恐水症，所以我從來沒喜歡過海邊，海浪很恐怖，每次和朋友去海邊，我就只會穿著救生衣坐在陰涼處看而已。

⑤ fail	**⑥ shallow**	**⑦ drown**
動 不及格	形 淺的	動 溺死
⑧ wave	**⑨ a life jacket**	**⑩ in the shade**
名 浪；波	片 救生衣	片 在陰涼處

 試著更與眾不同

N o, I can't swim. I wish I had learned how to swim when I was younger so that I could also have fun swimming with my friends. If they go to a pool[11], I usually don't go because I get really bored just sitting there and watching. However, if they go to the beach, I will certainly go with them. At least there I can lie down[12] on the beach for a bit of sun bathing[13] or take a walk. I especially like dipping[14] my feet in the water. It feels much cooler. Sometimes, it thrills me when the breaking waves cover my feet.

　　我不會游泳，早知道小時候就去學游泳了，這樣現在就能和朋友一起游泳同樂。如果他們打算去游泳池，我通常不會跟著去，因為坐在旁邊看實在太無聊了。但如果他們要去海邊，那我就會跟，至少可以躺在那邊享受日光浴或在海灘上走走，我特別喜歡在海裡泡腳，感覺超級涼爽的，有時候，浪花打上我的腳，就會讓我很興奮。

⑪ pool	**⑫ lie down**
名 游泳池	片 躺下來
⑬ sun bathing	**⑭ dip**
片 日光浴	動 泡；浸

> **延伸note**
> 完全不會游泳的旱鴨子除了用can't swim表示之外，美國人還有一個慣用表達，叫sink like a rock。

答題TIPS看這裡！

會游泳的人可以很直接地回答這個問題。不會游泳的話，可能會比較難回答，因為不能只回答「不會」，還是必須延伸話題。建議針對不會游泳的不便加以解釋或舉例。如：I can't swim, so I never get invited to go on the snorkelling trips.（我不會游泳，所以大家都不會邀我去浮潛。）

Words & Phrases 游泳會用到的物品

1 rescue buoy
救生圈

2 swimming cap
泳帽

3 swimming goggles
蛙鏡

4 sunscreen
防曬乳液

Words & Phrases 游泳池的周邊設備

1 swimming lane
（泳池的）水道

2 swimmer's pool
深水池

3 non-swimmer's pool
淺水池

4 diving platform
游泳池跳台

進階實用句 More Expressions

I forgot to put on sunscreen, so I got terribly sunburned.

我忘了擦防曬乳，所以嚴重曬傷。

I always wear a life jacket if I am doing any water activities.

要從事水上活動時，我都會穿救生衣。

I am not very good at open water swimming. I was rescued by a lifeguard once.

我不太擅長在開放式的水域游泳，之前還曾經被救生員救起來。

UNIT 02

喜歡的運動型態

Q Do you like team or individual sports? Why?
你喜歡團體運動還是單人運動呢？為什麼？

你可以這樣回答

MP3
047

Individual[1] sports suit[2] me a lot better because I have more freedom in deciding when to do exercise. If I engaged[3] in team sports, I would have to consider others' schedules[4] and find a day that suits everyone. And if an emergency[5] came up[6], I might not be able to participate, either. It is just inconvenient for a lover of sports like me.

就我而言，單人運動的時間安排比較自由，所以比較適合我。如果加入團體運動，那我就必須考量所有人的行程，再安排大家都有空的時間，如果突然發生緊急要事，那我很可能就無法參加。對我這種熱愛運動的人來說，這樣實在太不方便了。

❶ **individual** 形 個人的	❷ **suit** 動 適合	❸ **engage** 動 使從事
❹ **schedule** 名 日程安排表	❺ **emergency** 名 突發事件	❻ **come up** 片 發生；出現

換個立場講講看

I like team sports more, such as basketball or baseball. I enjoy being part of the team because I can build up[7] a sense of belonging[8] and friendship[9] with others. I met most of my buddies through sports. We often get together on weekends and have a game. After that, we would find a restaurant[10] and discuss[11] the recent games we've watched. It's really great to have someone to share the same passion[12] with.

我比較喜歡籃球或棒球這類型的團體運動。團體運動會帶給我一種歸屬感，又能和其他人建立友誼，我很喜歡這種感覺。我大部分的好朋友都是藉由運動認識的。我們通常會在週末的時候聚在一起，來場比賽，結束之後，我們會找家餐廳聚餐，討論最近看過的比賽。能找到和我熱愛同樣事情的人，又能一起分享的感覺真的很棒。

7 **build up**
片 增進

8 **belonging**
名 （團體的）緊密關係

9 **friendship**
名 友誼

10 **restaurant**
名 餐廳

11 **discuss**
動 討論

12 **passion**
名 熱情

 試著更與眾不同

To me, exercising is what I'd rather do alone. I go to the gym after work four times a week. It's what I do to unwind and relax, so I don't want to be interrupted[13] or socialize[14] with other people. I normally wear my headphones[15] and listen to music. I do a lot of talking at work because I work in the customer service department. This is also the reason why I like silence[16] after I get off work.

就我而言，運動是我獨處的時間，我下班後會去健身房（一個星期會去四天），那是我轉換心情和放鬆的方式，所以我不喜歡被打擾，也不想與人交際，我通常會戴上耳機聽音樂。我是客服人員，上班時間要一直講話，所以下班之後，能不講話我就不講話。

13 **interrupt**
動 打斷

14 **socialize**
動 交際

15 **headphone**
名 頭戴式耳機

16 **silence**
名 沉默

延伸note
現在常見的運動場所除了gym(健身房)之外，sports center(運動中心)也是很熱門的選項。

Key Points 答題TIPS看這裡！

偏好單人運動的人除了不想跟外界交際之外，也可能是因為生活型態忙碌，所以很難配合團體運動，或是享受一個人的感覺。喜歡呼朋引伴、或是喜歡競爭的人可能就比較喜歡團體運動，因為團體運動通常都會分出勝負。

Words & Phrases 與競賽有關的詞彙

1 tournament
錦標賽；聯賽

2 a draw / tie game
比賽平手

3 1st half of the game
上半場

4 2nd half of the game
下半場

Words & Phrases 認識足球用語

1 goal post
球門

2 goalie
守門員

3 kickoff
（足）開球

4 send off
將（球員）罰下場

🎤 進階實用句 More Expressions

I go jogging every evening unless it rains heavily.

除非下大雨，否則我傍晚都會去慢跑。

Golf is a sport that you can either challenge yourself or others.

高爾夫是一種可以同時挑戰自我及他人的運動。

The LA Lakers are very competitive. I am sure it will be a good game.

洛杉磯湖人隊的實力堅強，我相信比賽一定會很精彩。

多久運動一次

Q **How often do you exercise?**
你運動的頻率為何?

你可以這樣回答

I don't exercise very often because my work schedule is pretty tight[1] during the week. But even when I have got time, exercising is my last choice. I'm not into exercising. If there's a seat[2] on the bus, I won't choose to stand. On the weekends, I definitely sleep in till noon. Although I joined several gyms in the past, I had no patience to go very often. In the end, I transferred[3] my membership[4] to my sister. That was just a waste of money to me. Anyway, I guess exercising is not my thing.

　　我星期一至五的工作很忙,所以我不太有時間運動。不過就算有時間,我也不會去運動,我不怎麼喜愛運動,公車上如果有位子,我絕對不會站著;週末時,我也絕對會睡到日上三竿才罷休。雖然我也參加過健身房的課程,但我根本沒有耐性常去上課,後來就把會員資格轉讓給我妹妹,那對我來說實在很浪費錢,總之,運動和我的個性不合。

❶ tight
形 緊湊的;沒空的

❷ seat
名 座位

❸ transfer
動 轉讓

❹ membership
名 會員資格

延伸note
如果實在不太運動,也可以照實回答,但記得一定要補充足夠的原因,才能讓面試官理解。

換個立場講講看

I am trying hard to make sure I stay fit[5], so I exercise almost every day. I normally do it before I go to work. I do sit-ups[6] and push-ups[7] for about thirty

minutes. On weekends, I won't work out[8] because I think weekends are for fun things. So, I will hang out with my friends or go to some clubs. Indulging[9] myself sometimes is important[10] as well.

　　我很努力地在維持身材，所以我幾乎每天都會運動。基本上，我都是在上班前運動，我會做三十分鐘左右的仰臥起坐和伏地挺身。我週末不會去運動，因為我覺得週末就得好好玩樂，所以我會和朋友出去玩，或是去酒吧，偶爾放縱一下對我來說也是很重要的。

5 **fit**	**6** **sit-up**	**7** **push-up**
形 健康的；強健的	名 仰臥起坐	名 伏地挺身
8 **work out**	**9** **indulge**	**10** **important**
片 做大量運動訓練	動 放縱自己	形 重要的

試著更與眾不同

I try to exercise as much as I can. My exercise schedule is pretty full[11] on. I go swimming on Monday and Wednesday evening and take aerobic[12] classes on Thursday night. I recently joined a badminton[13] team, and the training is on Saturday morning for two hours. I don't plan anything for Tuesday and Friday nights. Those are my days off[14]. On Tuesday and Friday, all I do after work is sit around and watch TV.

　　能運動的時候我就盡量多運動，我的行程表排的可充實了。星期一、三的晚上要游泳，星期四晚上要上有氧舞蹈的課程。我最近加入了羽毛球隊，集訓的時間是星期六早上，一次訓練兩小時。星期二、五的晚上我沒有安排運動，因為這兩天是我的休息日，下班之後，我只想坐下來看電視。

11 **full**	**12** **aerobic**
形 滿的；充滿的	形 有氧的
13 **badminton**	**14** **day off**
名 羽毛球	片 休息日

延伸note
安排運動課程(lesson)也是現代人喜歡的方式之一，這種課程通常每週一次(once a week)。

Key Points 答題TIPS看這裡！

出了社會以後，要找時間運動好像頗為困難，尤其是工作時間很長、或是需要待命的工作更是如此。如果沒時間運動，也可以老實說，如：I have no time to exercise because my job is very demanding.（我沒時間運動，因為工作實在太忙了。）對忙碌的人來說，選擇運動中心的課程或許是一個好方法；當然，也有人會自己去慢跑（jogging）或騎腳踏車（cycling），時間就比較不受限。

Words & Phrases 表達頻率的詞彙

1 all the time
總是

2 often
經常；常常

3 a couple of days a week
一個星期幾天

4 not very often
並不常

5 sometimes
有時候

6 once a year
一年一次

7 seldom
很少

8 not at all
從不

🎤 進階實用句 More Expressions

My sister does exercise in order not to put on weight.

我妹妹是為了避免變胖才做運動。

It would help me a lot if I could go swimming once a month.

如果能一個月去游一次泳，就對我很有幫助了。

I haven't made any effort to exercise ever since I graduated.

畢業之後，我就沒有努力運動了。

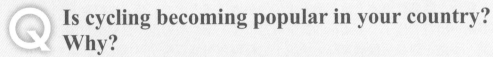

UNIT 04 騎自行車風潮

Q Is cycling becoming popular in your country? Why?

在你國家，騎腳踏車成為流行了嗎？為什麼？

 你可以這樣回答

 MP3 049

Yes, it is getting more and more popular in my country, especially in the city. It is more than just a sport now. A lot of people actually prefer to cycle[1] to work to avoid the traffic congestion[2]. There are some companies[3] promoting this idea, too. They even have shower[4] facilities and lockers[5] for the employees. Some business owners believe that people will become more productive[6] if they exercise in the morning.

是的，在我的國家，騎腳踏車確實變得越來越風行，尤其在市區。腳踏車已經不只是一種運動了，為了避開塞車，很多人選擇騎腳踏車上班。有些公司也鼓勵這樣的作法，公司甚至還設有沖澡設備和置物櫃。有些老闆相信早上運動後，員工的工作效率會提升。

❶ **cycle** 動 騎腳踏車	❷ **congestion** 名 擁塞；擠滿	❸ **company** 名 公司
❹ **shower** 名 淋浴	❺ **locker** 名 衣物櫃	❻ **productive** 形 多產的

 換個立場講講看

Absolutely! I think the number of bicyclers[7] has increased dramatically[8] over the past ten years. You can even see a lot of families riding their bikes on weekends. There must be a great demand[9], or the government wouldn't have

155

started to add designated[10] bike lanes[11]. For a motorcyclist[12] like me, however, it only means finding a parking space for my scooter might be more difficult.

當然！騎腳踏車的人數在過去十年內激增，週末出去的時候也很常看到一家人騎腳踏車出遊的樣子。腳踏車的數量肯定很多，不然政府也不會開始設腳踏車的專用道。不過，對我這種機車騎士來說，這種現象可能只會讓停機車這件事變得更加困難吧。

7 bicycler
名 騎自行車者

8 dramatically
副 戲劇性地

9 demand
名 需求

10 designate
動 指定；指派

11 lane
名 小路；巷；弄

12 motorcyclist
名 機車騎士

 ## 試著更與眾不同

W̲ell, I wouldn't say it is getting popular as a sport because it has been a part of our life for a long time. That's how most people get around in my country. The government[13] started to promote the idea of reducing[14] your carbon[15] footprint twenty years ago. They give out incentives[16] to families that own only one car. That is the reason why it's natural for people to ride bikes everywhere in my country.

這個嘛，不能說是越來越風行，因為騎腳踏車原本就是我們生活的一部分。在我們國家，大部分的人都是騎腳踏車出門。政府早在二十年前，就開始提倡節能減碳的觀念，如果家裡只有一輛車，政府還會給予獎勵，這就是騎腳踏車出門在我們國家之所以這麼普遍的原因。

13 government
名 政府

14 reduce
動 減少；降低

15 carbon
名 碳

16 incentive
名 鼓勵；動機

延伸note
在環境議題日趨重要的現在，eco-friendly(環保的)的物品也跟著越來越風行了。

Key Points

答題TIPS看這裡！

以前大多是以車代步，但現在大眾已經會關心環保與健康的議題，因此造就一股腳踏車風潮。在台灣，政府所設立的YouBike也成為許多人的代步工具，回答時也可以提到類似的政府措施。

Words & Phrases 與腳踏車有關的詞彙

1	**helmet** 安全帽	2	**bottle cage** 水壺架
3	**elbow/knee pad** 護肘/護膝	4	**foot pump** 腳踏式打氣筒
5	**stand** 自行車腳架	6	**pannier bag** 側袋
7	**flat tire** 爆胎	8	**patch up** 補胎

進階實用句 More Expressions

If you need help with your bike, some police stations will help you out.

如果你的腳踏車出問題，需要幫忙的話，有些警察局會幫忙。

Some cities are very bike-friendly. You can find a bike repair shop easily.

有些城市的設計會考量自行車騎士，到處都能找到維修站。

Some of the designated bike lanes are right next to the river. The scenery is stunning.

有的腳踏車專用道會設在河邊，景色很美。

UNIT 05
對戶外活動的偏好

Q **Do you like outdoor activities?**
你喜歡戶外活動嗎？

你可以這樣回答

MP3
050

Not really, I'd like to keep my skin[1] as fair[2] as possible, so I actually avoid outdoor activities. If I need to go out, I always put a lot of sunscreen[3] on. In addition to sunscreen, I also wear a hat and a long-sleeved shirt. If I could choose, I would definitely do indoor activities. For example, compared to going to the beach, staying in an indoor pool is much preferable[4].

不怎麼喜歡，我很介意我的皮膚顏色，不想曬黑，所以我會盡量避免從事戶外活動。如果真的得出門，我一定會擦防曬乳，而且我另外還會戴帽子，並穿上長袖衣物。如果能選擇，我一定會選室內活動。比方說，和去海邊相比，我寧願待在室內游泳池。

❶ **skin**
名 皮膚

❷ **fair**
形 （皮膚）白皙的

❸ **sunscreen**
名 防曬乳

❹ **preferable**
形 更合意的

延伸note
常見的膚色說法有：fair
(白皙的)、brunet(淺黑色
皮膚的)、dark(黝黑的)。

換個立場講講看

Basically[5], I like outdoor activities. However, the weather here gets really hot in summer. Staying outdoors becomes really unbearable[6]. When I play basketball with my friends, I just get sweaty[7]. I even got heatstroke[8] one time. So if it gets too hot, I'd rather pay a bit more to rent an indoor basketball court for a couple of hours. I also enjoy hiking, but there is no alternative for it. After all, I can't move the mountains indoors!

基本上，我喜歡戶外活動，但這裡一到夏天就會變得異常炎熱，待在室外真的很難受。和朋友一起去打籃球的時候，我會熱得滿身大汗，還曾經因此中暑。所以，如果天氣太熱，我寧願多花點錢，租幾個小時的室內籃球場。我也喜愛爬山，但這可就沒有替代方案了，我總不能把山搬到室內啊！

延伸note
中暑的症狀一般會有 dizziness(頭暈目眩)、weakness(四肢無力)與 nausea(感到噁心想吐)。

❺ **basically**
副 基本上

❻ **unbearable**
形 不能忍受的

❼ **sweaty**
形 滿身是汗的

❽ **heatstroke**
名 中暑

試著更與眾不同

Yes, I am totally an outdoor person. I enjoy both the mountains and the water. What I like most is going hiking[9] in the mountains where there are nice creeks. Once I get there, I can go for a swim in the creek and camp[10] by the riverbed[11]. I can also take a lot of nice pictures since the view is beautiful. But I must be very careful about the weather. After all, it is the main cause of the mountaineering[12] disasters.

當然，我最愛戶外活動了，山林和海邊我都喜歡。最喜歡的就是到有溪流的山林去，抵達目的地之後，我可以到河裡游泳，並於河床紮營，我還可以拍很多好看的相片，因為風景很漂亮。但我必須注意天氣，畢竟惡劣的天氣可是造成山難的主要原因呢！

❾ **go hiking**
片 健行

❿ **camp**
動 露營；紮營

⓫ **riverbed**
名 河床

⓬ **mountaineering**
名 登山；爬山

延伸note
對登山者來說，攜帶 compass(指南針)、map(地圖)、flashlight(手電筒)…等物品是非常重要的。

159

答題TIPS看這裡！

戶外活動有很多可以舉例（常見的有登山mountain climbing、游泳swimming、露營camping…等等），再加上自己的經驗，就能延伸話題；如果真的不喜歡戶外活動，建議多加解釋，如：I am not a big fan of outdoor activities because I am scared of creepy crawlers.（我不喜歡戶外活動，因為我怕那些令人毛骨悚然的爬行類動物。）

Words & Phrases 日漸流行的戶外活動

1 **kayaking**
泛舟

2 **marathon**
馬拉松

3 **rock climbing**
攀岩

4 **rollerblading**
溜直排輪

Words & Phrases 露營相關配備

1 **tent**
帳篷

2 **lime powder**
石灰粉

3 **sleeping bag**
睡袋

4 **recreational vehicle**
露營車

進階實用句 More Expressions

My family is kayaking in Hualien in July.

我們家七月要去花蓮泛舟。

I participate in the annual marathon every year.

我每年都參加年度的馬拉松大賽。

I will check the weather forecast before I go deep-sea fishing.

我去海釣之前，一定會先確認天氣情況。

UNIT 06

對健康有益的活動

What's a healthy activity or lifestyle you would recommend?

什麼是你會推薦的健康活動或生活型態？

 你可以這樣回答

 MP3 051

Once a week, I choose one day to be a vegetarian. I've done this for two years, and I have found it to be helpful[1] to my health. Taking in more greens and fruits is beneficial[2] for digestion[3]. Based on some research, people these days don't get enough fiber[4] from fruits and vegetables. I used to suffer from constipation[5] and went to see quite a lot of doctors for this problem. Ever since I started to hold my "vegetarian day", my constipation has improved[6] a lot.

我一個禮拜會挑一天吃素，兩年來我都這麼做，發現對我的健康很有幫助，攝取更多的蔬菜水果可以幫助消化。一些研究報告顯示，現代人所攝取的蔬果纖維很不足。我以前有便秘的問題，還為此看了好幾個醫生，自從我開始訂下「吃素日」之後，便秘問題改善了許多。

① **helpful**
形 有益的

② **beneficial**
形 有益的

③ **digestion**
名 消化

④ **fiber**
名 纖維質

⑤ **constipation**
名 便祕

⑥ **improve**
動 改善；改進

 換個立場講講看

Years ago, I attended[7] a workshop called "Laughing Helps". It is a therapy[8] designed to increase your mental[9] health by doing fake laughs. The goal is to fake it until you make it. Once you are used to laughing, you will embrace[10] it as part of your lifestyle. There are a lot of benefits to laughing. For example, laughing will trigger[11] the release of endorphins[12]. It is a hormone that makes people feel happy. I have found it very useful, so I recommend it to others.

幾年前，我上過一個療程叫「笑很有效」。那是一個以大笑來改善精神狀態的課程。它主要的治療手段就是假笑，假笑到最後就會變真笑了。等你習慣大笑，它就會變成你生活中的一部分，大笑會使大腦分泌腦內啡，那是一種能讓人感到愉悅的賀爾蒙。我發現這種療程很有效，所以推薦給其他人。

❼ **attend**	❽ **therapy**	❾ **mental**
動 參加；出席	名 治療；療法	形 精神的；心理的
❿ **embrace**	⓬ **trigger**	⓬ **endorphin**
動 擁抱；包含	動 觸發；引起	名 腦內啡

 試著更與眾不同

I recommend Yoga classes. I had been suffering from[13] back pain for years until I met my Yoga teacher. Most of the Yoga moves help you to improve your flexibility[14] and muscle[15] strength[16]. I started taking Yoga classes one year ago. My teacher spent time correcting[17] my posture[18]. Surprisingly, it helped. My back pain was gone after six months. I wish I had met my Yoga teacher earlier.

我推薦去上瑜珈課。我背痛了好幾年，直到我接觸瑜珈，背痛的情況才得到舒緩。大部分的瑜珈動作都在幫助我們增進身體的柔軟度及肌肉的強韌度。我一年前開始上瑜珈課，老師當時花了不少時間糾正我的姿勢，令人訝異的是，這麼做真的有效，過了半年，我背痛的問題就消失了，如果能早點遇到我的瑜珈老師就好了。

⓭ **suffer from**	⓮ **flexibility**	⓯ **muscle**
片 受…困擾	名 靈活性	名 肌；肌肉
⓰ **strength**	⓱ **correct**	⓲ **posture**
名 力量；力氣	動 改正；糾正	名 姿勢；姿態

Key Points 答題TIPS看這裡！

坊間有很多所謂的健康課程或療程，強調能放鬆身心、促進健康，例如：瑜珈、舒壓按摩、泡溫泉、低糖少油的飲食方式…等等。傳統的民俗療法（如：針灸、拔罐）也都可以拿來舉例。

Words & Phrases 舒壓與健康

1 **do tai-chi**
打太極拳

2 **acupuncture**
針灸

3 **cupping**
拔罐

4 **go on vacation**
度假

5 **go to a hot spring**
泡溫泉

6 **pressure relief massage**
舒壓按摩

7 **pressure point**
穴道

8 **sauna or steam room**
蒸氣烤箱

進階實用句 More Expressions

I believe laughter is the best medicine.

我相信大笑是最好的良藥。

If you don't want to put on weight, try to finish your dinner before 7 p.m.

如果不想變胖，建議你在晚上七點前吃完晚餐。

The research shows that keeping a regular lifestyle will improve the quality of sleep at night.

研究報告顯示，規律的生活可以改善晚上的睡眠品質。

希望擅長這項運動

Q What's the sport you would love to be good at?
你希望自己能擅長的運動是什麼？

你可以這樣回答

MP3
052

I wish I could be good at diving[1]. If I were good at diving, I could go and collect[2] abalone[3] and catch lobsters[4] from the ocean. Fresh seafood is usually expensive, especially the types I just mentioned. I might be able to supply[5] endless[6] seafood to my family. My mother would certainly be impressed by the seafood I caught! Come to think of it, maybe this is the reason why I love fishing so much.

我希望自己擅長潛水，這樣我就可以到海裡去採鮑魚跟抓龍蝦。海鮮通常都很貴，尤其是鮑魚和龍蝦。我能抓很多海鮮給家人吃，我媽一定會為此讚嘆的！說到這個，這搞不好是我之所以熱愛釣魚的原因呢。

❶ **diving**
名 潛水

❷ **collect**
動 收集；採集

❸ **abalone**
名 鮑魚

❹ **lobster**
名 龍蝦

❺ **supply**
動 供給；提供

❻ **endless**
形 不斷的

換個立場講講看

Being good at basketball would definitely be my choice. I have always dreamt[7] of playing in the NBA like Jeremy Lin. I am very proud of[8] him playing in the NBA. You don't see many Asian[9] players as good as him. Although I am not as talented as him, I still try my best in the training. I practice basketball every day. I also do a lot of cardio training to keep my stamina[10] up. I hope one day, it will be

me that everyone is watching.

　　我絕對會希望自己能精通籃球。一直以來，我都夢想成為NBA球員，並表現得像林書豪一樣。看到他在NBA打球的模樣，令我感到很驕傲。你很少看到像他這樣優秀的亞裔選手。雖然我不像他，那麼有打籃球的天分，但我仍投注了很多努力在訓練中。我每天都練籃球，也持續做心肺訓練以加強耐力，希望有一天，大家在關注的人會是我。

延伸note
have always + 過去分詞表示「從過去一直到現在都…」，帶有持續性。

7 dream
動 想像；幻想

8 be proud of
片 為…感到自豪

9 Asian
形 亞洲的

10 stamina
名 耐力

試著更與眾不同

It would be rock climbing. It looks so cool to be able to climb up a stiff[11] mountain with your bare[12] hands. Tom Cruise did it in one of the Mission[13] Impossible movies. It was amazing[14] to see how he climbed up the rocks. I know it is a movie, and he might not have done much of the actual climbing, but I still wish I could be as good in real life as the character he played.

　　應該會是攀岩吧，徒手爬上陡峭山峰的感覺實在太酷了。湯姆克魯斯在《不可能的任務》中有做過，他攀岩直上的鏡頭看起來實在太令人吃驚了。當然，我知道那些令人讚嘆的鏡頭只是電影裡面的情節，而且大部分的動作搞不好根本不是他本人做的，但我還是會希望自己在現實生活中，能像湯姆克魯斯在電影裡面的角色一樣厲害。

11 stiff
形 陡峭的

12 bare
形 裸的；空的

13 mission
名 任務；使命

14 amazing
形 令人吃驚的

延伸note
攀岩初學者要在climbing wall(人工岩壁)上練習；熟手才會進入free climbing(自由攀登)。

答題TIPS看這裡！

本題的重點在「希望」，和你的能力無關，所以可以大肆發揮自己的想像力。大部分的人會因為自己的喜好或憧憬某人，而升起想精通某種運動的欲望，舉例的時候，重點要放在原因上，聽起來才有說服力。例如：I wish I could play tennis as good as Rendy Lu.（我希望我的網球可以打得跟盧彥勳一樣好。）

Words & Phrases 講述學習成果

1 as good as
像（某人）一樣好

2 be inspired by
被激勵

3 be born with
天生的

4 Practice makes perfect.
熟能生巧。

Words & Phrases 希望與想像

1 suppose
假定

2 imaginative
想像的

3 unreal
不真實的

4 hope for sth.
希望

進階實用句 More Expressions

I started jogging every evening.

我開始於每天傍晚去慢跑。

I wonder if it is possible for me to swim across Sun Moon Lake.

不知道我能不能泳渡日月潭。

If I were good at golf, I might have the chance to become the next Teresa Lu.

如果我擅長打高爾夫球，就有機會成為下一個盧曉晴。

UNIT 08

對極限運動的看法

Q **What do you think of extreme sports?**
你對極限運動的看法是什麼呢？

你可以這樣回答

MP3 053

I think extreme[1] sports are too dangerous. I don't think they should be called sports; they are more like risking your life. It might be very exciting for some people, but I wonder[2] how their families feel about it. My brother once said he wanted to go cliff jumping. My parents almost had a heart attack[3]. There was no way they would consent to[4] it. Besides, I think he would have struggled[5] to find an insurance[6] company that was willing to cover him.

　　我覺得極限運動很危險，那根本不能算運動，而是要命行為。或許有些人會覺得那很刺激，但我真的很想知道那些人的家人怎麼想。有一次，我哥哥說他想去跳山崖，我爸媽簡直要心臟病發了，他們根本不可能同意他這麼做，而且，我想根本就不會有保險公司願意和他簽保單吧。

❶ **extreme** 形 極端的	❷ **wonder** 動 納悶；想知道	❸ **a heart attack** 片 心臟病
❹ **consent to** 片 同意；贊成	❺ **struggle** 動 艱難地行進	❻ **insurance** 名 保險

換個立場講講看

I am a big fan of extreme sports. I always look for excitement[7] in life, and extreme sports satisfy[8] me. I went bungee jumping[9] a couple of years ago. And I am planning to go BASE jumping next month. Some of my friends think I might be risking my life. But I have to say, extreme sports are not that dangerous since the staff checks the equipment[10] very carefully. The only thing you need to prepare is to overcome your fear. The first time is usually the most difficult one. However, once you've tried it, you'll love the excitement.

　　我熱愛極限運動，我永遠都在尋求生活的刺激感，而極限運動完全符合我的期待。幾年前，我參加過高空彈跳，下個月打算嘗試高台定點跳躍。我的一些朋友覺得那是在和自己的生命開玩笑，但老實說，極限運動並沒有那麼危險，因為工作人員都會非常仔細地檢查裝備。你唯一需要準備的，就是克服恐懼，第一次通常會是最困難的一次，不過，一旦你嘗試之後，就肯定會愛上這種刺激感的。

延伸note
不管你有多熱愛極限運動，回答時建議提到安全面，不要讓面試官認為你輕忽安全性。

⑦ **excitement**
　名 刺激；興奮

⑧ **satisfy**
　動 使滿足

⑨ **bungee jumping**
　片 高空彈跳

⑩ **equipment**
　名 裝備

 ## 試著更與眾不同

Personally[11], I won't participate in[12] any kind of extreme sport. However, I don't mind watching them on TV. Some of the things they do look so unreal and pretty cool. What I enjoy the most is BMX because I like riding bikes, too. Those guys must practice the flips[13] and twists[14] really hard. It is fun to watch, but I wouldn't dare to try it.

　　我個人不會去嘗試，但我滿喜歡在電視上觀看這些極限運動的。有些看起來很超現實，又很酷。因為我喜歡騎腳踏車，所以我最愛看越野自行車的比賽，為了做出翻滾及旋轉的動作，那些極限運動員肯定苦練了很久，看畫面是真的很酷，但我可不敢嘗試。

⑪ **personally**
　副 就個人而言

⑫ **participate in**
　片 參加

⑬ **flip**
　名 空翻

⑭ **twist**
　名 旋轉；轉彎

延伸note
個人是否會做極限運動和是否欣賞是不同的概念，如果能從這兩點出發，內容會顯得更有深度。

 Key Points

答題TIPS看這裡！

極限運動（extreme sports）泛指危險性較高，且對技術和體能的要求也比較嚴格的運動。如果你沒有特定的立場，可以說：I have not done any extreme sports, but I don't mind trying it.（我沒做過極限運動，但我不並排斥。）

Words & Phrases 常見的極限運動

1 car racing
賽車

2 rock climbing
攀岩

3 sky diving
空中跳傘

4 whitewater rafting
急流泛舟

5 paragliding
滑翔傘

6 hang-gliding
滑翔翼

7 snowboarding
單板滑雪

8 paintball
漆彈運動

進階實用句 More Expressions

We go whitewater rafting every summer.

我們每年夏天都會去急流泛舟。

I booked myself a hang-gliding adventure in the next week.

我下星期準備去挑戰滑翔翼，已經預定好時間了。

It scared me too much just thinking about the idea of bungee jumping.

說到高空彈跳，我光用想的就怕死了。

UNIT 09 看現場 vs. 電視轉播

Q **Do you prefer to watch a game live or on TV?**
你比較喜歡到現場看比賽還是觀看電視轉播？

MP3 054

你可以這樣回答

I prefer watching a game live more because I can share the passion with other people in the audience[1]. Moveover, I can scream[2] as loud as I can. Sometimes I can even feel the floor move. If it's at home, then my cheering[3] will annoy[4] my mother. Therefore, I have to lower my voice[5]. It is as dull as ditchwater[6]. On the contrary, watching a game live is much fun. You never know what is going to happen next.

　　我比較喜歡到現場看比賽，因為可以和其他觀眾一起沉浸在比賽的氛圍中，盡情地大聲加油，觀眾的吶喊聲有時候都能震撼地板了呢！如果是在家看電視轉播，就得顧慮我媽媽，她討厭我過大的加油聲，因此，我得放低音量，無趣極了。到現場看比賽就不同了，你完全無法預料接下來的比賽走向，所以比窩在家看轉播要有趣多了。

❶ **audience** 名 觀眾	❷ **scream** 動 尖叫	❸ **cheering** 名 喝采；歡呼
❹ **annoy** 動 惹惱；使生氣	❺ **lower one's voice** 片 降低音量	❻ **ditchwater** 名 溝中的死水

換個立場講講看

It might sound strange[7], but I actually prefer to watch a game on TV rather than watch it live. If I go to a game, I might not get a spot[8] up close to the action[9]

and end up getting stuck in the back. In that case, I will barely see what is going on. On the other hand, TV always gives me the best seat. The cameraman[10] will always get the close-up shots. I can even see the athletes'[11] facial expressions[12].

聽起來或許很奇怪，但和現場相比，我其實更喜歡看電視轉播。如果我去球場，可能佔不到靠近球場的位子，最後就會卡在後面，根本什麼都看不到。然而，電視一定會提供最好的位置給我，攝影師會以超近的距離拍攝場上的一舉一動，我甚至還能看到球員的表情呢！

⑦ **strange** 形 奇怪的	⑧ **spot** 名 場所；位置	⑨ **action** 名 活動；行動
⑩ **cameraman** 名 攝影師	⑪ **athlete** 名 運動員	⑫ **facial expression** 片 臉部表情

試著更與眾不同

I do like to watch a game live. However, the tickets sometimes are hard to get, and it is too much work to go to the stadium[13]. I actually prefer to go for the alternative, which is watching the action on TV or a big screen in a sports bar or pub when a big game is on. It is great to watch games in a sports bar. You can cheer along with all the audience but also enjoy the comfort[14] of having air conditioning[15] and cold beer[16]. How great is that!

我喜歡看現場比賽，但有時候票很難買，去球場又很麻煩。如果有重要的比賽，我會選擇另一種替代方案——去運動酒吧或小酒館看電視或大螢幕轉播。在酒吧裡看比賽的感覺很棒，你可以和大家一起吶喊加油，還可以享受店裡的冷氣跟冰啤酒，多棒啊！

⑬ **stadium** 名 體育場；球場	⑭ **comfort** 名 安逸；舒適	**延伸note** 運動酒吧(sports bar)除了提供飲食之外，其中一項特色是會裝設很多台電視，以便轉播比賽。
⑮ **air conditioning** 片 空調	⑯ **beer** 名 啤酒	

Key Points 答題TIPS看這裡！

現場比賽和轉播相比，氣氛（atmosphere）完全不同，除了臨場的刺激感之外，和其他球迷一起鼓譟加油（cheer with others）也往往是人們熱愛看現場的原因；看轉播的人則不同，有些人是想去球場看比賽，卻礙於現實考量無法成行，但也有些人是真的比較喜歡看電視轉播，覺得這樣很舒適（comfortable），要如何選擇，就看個人偏好囉。

Words & Phrases 有關場地的詞彙

1. **playground**
（學校的）操場

2. **football field**
足球場

3. **stadium**
體育場

4. **golf course**
高爾夫球場

5. **volleyball court**
排球場

6. **ice rink**
冰球場

7. **taekwondo hall**
跆拳道館

8. **Superdome**
巨蛋

進階實用句 More Expressions

I love watching games in the Superdome. It is very well-designed.

我喜歡去巨蛋看比賽，因為場地設計得很好。

I know a good sports bar. They always show games on the big screen.

我知道一家很棒的運動酒吧，如果有比賽，他們都會用大螢幕播放。

I like to watch games live because I might be able to meet the players after the game.

我喜歡去現場看比賽，因為賽後可能見到選手們。

UNIT 10

釋放內心的壓力

MP3
055

Q **What would you do to relieve your stress?**
你會如何釋放內心的壓力呢?

你可以這樣回答

I would talk to my friends if something kept bothering[1] me or stressed me out. I feel much better after I talk to them, especially when I need others' opinions. Generally, I am not the kind who can keep things inside[2]. It is just too hard for me. If I didn't talk to others, I would get really anxious[3] and depressed[4]. It is not good for my health.

如果有困擾我很久的事情,或者壓力大到快受不了的時候,我會找朋友聊聊。和他們聊過之後,我就會好很多,尤其是當我需要聽聽他人意見的時候。基本上,我是沒辦法把事情憋在心裡不說的那種人,那實在太痛苦了。如果我不找個人談,我就會變得很焦慮、沮喪,這很不健康。

❶ **bother**
動 煩擾;打擾

❷ **inside**
副 在裡面;往裡面

❸ **anxious**
形 焦慮的

❹ **depressed**
形 沮喪的;消沈的

> **延伸note**
> 「向某人吐露心事」的講法為confide in sb.;「訴苦」則要說vent one's grievance。

換個立場講講看

If I were stressed, I wouldn't want to be around people. Instead, I would like to go to a remote[5] area of Taiwan to refresh[6] myself. I might go on a trip to the mountains in central[7] Taiwan, the beaches on the east coast or some aboriginal[8] tribes[9]. Spending a few days on my own could make me feel relaxed. When I am on vacation, I sometimes do things that I don't normally do for a change. It makes me feel much better by being away from the city[10].

　　有壓力的時候，我不會想和其他人一起。相反的，我會想去台灣比較沒有人煙的地方，比如到中央山脈、東海岸或原住民部落旅遊，過幾天獨自一人的生活能緩和我的情緒。當我在度假時，為了轉換心情，有時候會做些平常不太會做的事情。遠離都市能讓我感到輕鬆許多。

⑤ remote
形 遙遠的；偏僻的

⑥ refresh
動 消除疲勞

⑦ central
形 中心的；中央的

⑧ aboriginal
形 土著的；原始的

⑨ tribe
名 部落；種族

⑩ city
名 都市；城市

試著更與眾不同

Riding a bike is what I do when I am stressed. I can totally zone out[11] when I am riding a bike. When I am mentally[12] stressed, my body usually gets very tense. By doing some exercise, I can stretch[13] my body. It will make me feel better. After I get home, I take a hot shower. It's the best time of the day for me. Then I enjoy a cup of tea and go to bed[14] early. No matter what happened, getting a good sleep is always the best medicine.

　　當我覺得壓力很大的時候，我會去騎腳踏車，騎車的時候可以完全放空。只要我壓力變大，我的身體就會跟著變緊繃，藉由運動，我可以伸展四肢，這會讓我覺得輕鬆許多。回到家以後，我會去沖個熱水澡，這真是一天下來最讓人放鬆的時間了。接著我會喝杯熱茶，再早點上床休息，無論發生了什麼事，好好睡一覺永遠都是一帖良藥。

⑪ zone out
片 放空

⑫ mentally
副 心理上；精神上

⑬ stretch
動 伸直；伸展

⑭ go to bed
片 上床睡覺

延伸note
除了藉由做運動伸展四肢 (stretch oneself)，之後的好眠狀態(a good sleep)也很有放鬆的效果。

Key Points

答題TIPS看這裡！

每個人舒壓的方式不同，回答時別忘了提供原因，以及你的感受，如：I like to go to a quiet café. Sitting there on my own is the best way to calm myself down.（我喜歡找家安靜的咖啡廳，獨自一人待著是最能讓我冷靜下來的方式。）

Words & Phrases 　與舒壓有關的詞彙

1 **listen to music**
聽音樂

2 **scream**
大叫

3 **have a couple of drinks**
喝點小酒

4 **go for a drive**
開車兜風

5 **see a psychologist**
看心理醫生

6 **take a deep breath**
深呼吸

7 **meditation**
打坐冥想

8 **do exercise**
運動

進階實用句 More Expressions

I found meditation really helps to release stress.

我發現打坐冥想對舒壓很有幫助。

When I am upset with my boss, I feel like screaming as loud as I can.

當我很氣我老闆的時候，我會想放聲大叫。

I like to go for a drive in the middle of the night when there is no one around. It feels great.

我喜歡在沒什麼人的深夜開車兜風，那種感覺很棒。

UNIT 11 對健康有害的習慣

Q **Do you have any unhealthy habits that you want to change?**

你有什麼不健康的習慣是想要改掉的嗎？

你可以這樣回答

MP3 056

I have been a smoker[1] since I was a college[2] student. I know it is not a good habit, but it is what I turn to[3] when I am stressed. I really want to quit smoking, but it is more difficult than I thought. I tried nicotine[4] patches[5] and gums[6], but none of them worked. I think I will go and see a specialist to see if he for she can help me quit this old habit. I am getting older now, so I definitely want to live a healthier lifestyle.

我從大學時代就開始抽菸，我知道那不是好習慣，但只要一有壓力，我就會想抽一根。我真的很想戒菸，但這比我原本想的要困難。我試過尼古丁貼片和嚼錠，但都沒有用。我想我應該會去看專門的醫生，看他是否能幫我戒掉這個長久以來的壞習慣。我的年紀也慢慢大了，當然也想要活得健康一點。

❶ **smoker** 名 吸菸者	❷ **college** 名 大學；學院	❸ **turn to** 片 著手
❹ **nicotine** 名 尼古丁	❺ **patch** 名 貼片	❻ **gum** 名 口香糖

換個立場講講看

I like to go clubbing on weekends. Recently, I noticed[7] that I often get a terrible hangover[8] on Sundays. Sometimes it is so bad that I can feel the effect on Monday. I think I am a binge[9] drinker. When I am out with my friends, I just don't care how many drinks I have as long as I am having fun. I regret it every Sunday, but I just can't help myself when the drinks are presented to[10] me. I really need to do something about it.

　　我週末喜歡去夜店，但我最近注意到一件事，星期天我通常會宿醉得很嚴重，宿醉的情況有時候甚至會延續到星期一。我覺得自己有狂飲到爛醉的問題，和朋友出去的時候，只要玩得很嗨，我就完全不在意喝了多少酒。我每個星期天都會後悔自己喝得太不節制，但只要酒杯送到我眼前，我就完全拒絕不了，真的應該要好好注意一下了。

延伸note
a heavy drinker是指酒喝得很多的人，如果已經到酗酒、酒精中毒的程度，就是alcoholic了。

❼ **notice**
　動 注意到

❽ **hangover**
　名（口）宿醉

❾ **binge**
　名 狂飲；狂鬧

❿ **present to**
　片 呈現；贈送

試著更與眾不同

I enjoy comfort food and midnight snacks[11] a lot. That may not sound so bad compared with those habits that are really unhealthy. However, it has given me a weight[12] problem. I have put on five kilograms[13] in the past six months. If I don't do anything about it, I might become massive[14] by end of the year. Plus, I read a study that says it is bad to have excess[15] fat wrapped around the vital organs. I really don't want to suffer from obesity[16] in the future.

　　我很喜歡吃能帶來滿足感的食物和消夜。和那些真的很不健康的生活習慣相比，這聽起來也許不算什麼，但卻已經造成我肥胖的問題了。我半年內胖了五公斤，再這樣下去，年底前我肯定會胖到不行。而且，我看過一則研究說：多餘的脂肪包覆在重要臟器外對人體很不好，我不想變成肥胖症的受害者。

⓫ **snack**
　名 小吃；點心

⓬ **weight**
　名 體重

⓭ **kilogram**
　名 公斤

⓮ **massive**
　形 魁偉的

⓯ **excess**
　形 過量的；額外的

⓰ **obesity**
　名 肥胖；過胖

Key Points 答題TIPS看這裡！

可以舉例的不良習慣很廣泛，從一般大眾所認知的抽菸（smoking）、喝酒（drinking）、賭博（gambling），到生活起居上的不良習慣，如：熬夜（stay up late）、挑食（picky）、缺乏運動（lack of exercise）、宅在家（indoorsy）、沉迷於線上遊戲（be addicted to the online games）…等等，都是答題時可以舉例的切入點。

Words & Phrases 各種戒除的說法

1 get rid of
擺脫

2 abstain from
戒絕

3 get out of
放棄；戒除

4 give up
放棄；戒絕

Words & Phrases 有益健康的生活型態

1 keep good hours
生活規律

2 go on a light diet
養成飲食清淡的習慣

3 a balance diet
均衡的飲食

4 regular exercise
定時運動

進階實用句 More Expressions

I spend too much time playing online games.

我花太多時間在玩線上遊戲。

Binge drinking is such a serious problem in western countries.

狂飲到爛醉的現象在西方國家是個很嚴重的問題。

I suffer from obesity. The doctor told me that I need to lose at least fifteen kilograms.

我已經算是肥胖等級，醫生說我至少得瘦十五公斤。

UNIT 12 生病的時候怎麼做

Q What do you usually do when you get sick?
當你生病的時候，通常會怎麼做？

 你可以這樣回答

 MP3 057

If it is a work day, I will call in sick and take a day off to rest at home. I think it is not good to pass the germs[1] around in the office to make my colleagues sick as well. However, my supervisor[2] doesn't see it that way. He thinks all employees should work as hard as he does. From his point of view, being sick is just an excuse[3] not to go to the office. Therefore, he will give me a hard time whenever I call in sick[4].

如果是上班日，我會打電話去公司請假，在家休息，因為我覺得把病菌傳染給其他同事很不好。但我的主管並不這麼想，他覺得所有員工都要像他那樣努力地工作。在他的眼裡，生病只不過是不上班的藉口，所以每次我打電話去請假的時候，都會被他刻意刁難。

❶ **germ**
名 細菌；病菌

❷ **supervisor**
名 監督人

❸ **excuse**
名 藉口；理由

❹ **call in sick**
片 請病假

> 延伸note
> 所謂留職停薪，有兩種說法，員工主動稱為leave without pay；若是被迫則必須用furlough。

 換個立場講講看

If I felt a bit run down[5], I would run myself a hot bath and see if I could get rid of the tiredness[6] and minor[7] cold before things get worse. If the symptoms persisted[8], I would then go and see a doctor. I know medication will work. I would

179

get a lot better the next day. However, I would try to avoid taking medicine as much as I could. You never know what kind of side effects[9] it could cause. Some of them might not have been discovered[10] yet.

如果我覺得有點不舒服，我會先去泡個熱水澡，看看疲勞感和感冒症狀會不會因此得到緩解。如果症狀沒有改善，那我就會去看醫生。我知道藥物很有效，吃了藥，隔天我就會好很多，但我盡量避免吃藥，因為也不知道那些藥物會有什麼副作用，很多副作用其實都只是還沒有被發現而已。

❺ run down 片 由於過勞而疲憊	**❻ tiredness** 名 疲勞	**❼ minor** 形 不嚴重的
❽ persist 動 持續；存留	**❾ side effect** 片 副作用	**❿ discover** 動 發現

試著更與眾不同

I will give my mother a call to see if she can come and help me when I am sick. No one is as comforting[11] as my mother. She always makes me fish soup when I am sick. For some reason, it does help. Also, I will try to rest as much as I can. So, I usually take a few naps[12] throughout the day. For me, limiting the amount of fluids[13] and getting plenty[14] of rest does the trick.

我生病的時候會打電話給我媽媽，看她是否能來幫我，沒有什麼比我的媽媽更讓人感到安慰的了。我媽媽總是會在我生病時煮魚湯給我喝，說也奇怪，這還滿有用的。除此之外，我會盡量多休息，一整天能睡就睡。就我而言，只要控制好攝取的流質物，不要喝太多，並多休息，就會好很多。

⓫ comforting 形 令人欣慰的	**⓬ nap** 名 午睡
⓭ fluid 名 流質；液體	**⓮ plenty** 名 充足；大量

> **延伸note**
> 感冒時，一定要多休息，就算看醫生，通常也會開些讓人感到sleepy(昏昏欲睡)的藥物。

Key Points

答題TIPS看這裡！

生病的時候大部分的人會選擇休息（take some rest）或看醫生（see a doctor），甚至有些人會採用一些民俗療法來恢復健康，例如：刮痧（skin scraping）、拔罐（cupping therapy）…等等。

Words & Phrases 恢復健康的方式

1 **take herbal medicine**
吃中藥

2 **take painkillers**
吃止痛藥

3 **take injections**
打針

4 **take drips**
打點滴

Words & Phrases 各種形式的藥品

1 **tablet**
藥丸

2 **pill**
藥片（扁平狀）

3 **lozenge**
藥錠

4 **capsule**
膠囊

🎤 進階實用句 More Expressions

I get regular flu shots to avoid getting sick.

我會定期打流感疫苗，以避免感冒。

I put some painkillers in my drawer in case of a sudden headache.

我放了一些止痛藥在抽屜，以防突然頭痛。

I have been taking Chinese herbal medicine for a couple of months.

我已經吃中藥吃了好幾個月。

UNIT 13

有效的減肥法

Q In your opinion, what's an effective way of losing weight?

在你看來，用哪種方式減肥有效呢？

你可以這樣回答

MP3 058

I think the most effective way of losing weight is to cut down[1] the intake[2] of calories[3]. In other words, you need to eat less. The recommended calorie intake for women is 1,200 a day, and for men it is 1,800. If what you eat is less than the recommended intake, the body will start to burn the existing[4] fat. I have lost fifteen pounds by eating less. However, this could be the most difficult way because resisting[5] the temptation[6] of food just doesn't fit our human nature!

　　我覺得最有效的減肥方式就是減少卡路里的攝取量，換句話說，就是少吃。女性每日建議的卡路里攝取量為1200大卡，男性則是1800大卡。如果吃的量比這個建議量少，身體就會開始燃燒現有的脂肪。我曾經用這個方式瘦了十五磅。不過，這可能是最困難的瘦身方法，因為抗拒美食的誘惑根本就不符合人的天性啊！

❶ **cut down** 片 削減	❷ **intake** 名 吸收	❸ **calorie** 名 卡路里
❹ **existing** 形 現存的	❺ **resist** 動 反抗；抗拒	❻ **temptation** 名 引誘；誘惑

換個立場講講看

I found that increasing the amount of daily exercise is the most effective way to achieve weight loss. I lost three kilos in two months simply[7] by increasing the duration[8] and frequency[9] of exercise. I used to go for a short walk after dinner twice a week, but it didn't help much in losing weight. Therefore, I increased it to five times a week. Also, I went for longer walks of about one hour every time. Six months later, I could really see the enormous difference. No wonder my friend always tries to persuade[10] me to go exercising with him.

　　我發現增加每日的運動量是最有效的減肥方法，我這兩個月光靠增加運動的時間和頻率，就瘦了三公斤。我以前一個星期會選兩天的晚餐飯後，去小走一段路，但並沒有多大效果，所以我把運動量增加到一個星期五次，而且一次都會走一個小時左右，半年後，就真的體會到其中的差別，難怪我朋友老是勸我和他一起運動。

延伸note
講到體型，如果胖得很可愛，叫chubby；豐滿則用plump，千萬不要隨便說人fat/obese。

❼ **simply**
　副 僅僅；只不過

❾ **frequency**
　名 頻率

❽ **duration**
　名 （時間的）持續

❿ **persuade**
　動 說服；勸服

試著更與眾不同

I think the most effective way is to eat the right food. Losing weight may be important, but I believe nobody wants to lose his health because of it. I am a nutritionist[11], so I'm totally against the idea of not eating enough. Based on most studies, the idea of substituting[12] bad food with the right food is much more healthful[13]. For example, if you can replace[14] fried chicken with fresh salad, you will reduce the calories you take in by more than half.

　　我覺得最有效的減肥方式是要吃對食物。減肥也許很重要，但我想應該不會有人想要因為減肥而賠掉健康吧。我是營養學家，所以我極度反對用挨餓減肥這件事。根據大多數的研究，把對身體有害的的食物替換成健康食品對身體比較好。例如，如果你能抗拒炸雞，改吃沙拉，卡路里的攝取量馬上少了一半以上。

⓫ **nutritionist**
　名 營養學家

⓭ **healthful**
　形 有益於健康的

⓬ **substitute**
　動 用…代替

⓮ **replace**
　動 取代

延伸note
再怎麼嚮往paper-thin models(紙片人身材的模特兒)，變得過瘦、不健康(angular)就不好了。

答題TIPS看這裡！

坊間減肥的方法很多，從內在的調養到外在的工具輔助都有，可謂五花八門，但不見得每項都有效果，有些太極端的方式甚至對健康有害，這些都可以提出來討論。如：I tired the apple diet, which is eating only apples for three days. It did work, but I got a very sore stomach after the first week. （我試過蘋果減肥法，三天內都只吃蘋果，很有效，可是我吃了一個星期就開始胃痛了。）

Words & Phrases　與運動有關的詞彙

1. **warm-up**
暖身運動

2. **aerobics**
有氧運動

3. **cool-down**
緩和運動

4. **pull-up**
（體）引體向上

Words & Phrases　常見的肥胖部位

1. **bingo wing(s)**
蝴蝶袖

2. **double chin**
雙下巴

3. **love handles**
腰間贅肉

4. **thunder thighs**
粗壯的大腿

 進階實用句 More Expressions

I wish I could get rid of some excess fat in my arms.

真希望能減掉手臂上的肥肉。

I need to be careful of what I eat because I am watching my waistline.

為了避免腰圍發胖，我必須注意我吃的東西。

I really enjoy the fat-burning cardio workout. I actually feel energetic after it.

我很喜歡燃脂有氧舞蹈，跳完之後，我的精神都會變得很好。

定期做健康檢查

MP3 059

Q Do you think a regular physical check-up is important?

你覺得做定期健康檢查重要嗎？

你可以這樣回答

Absolutely! My uncle[1] was diagnosed[2] with early stage cancer[3] in one of his regular physical[4] check-ups. He would not have known about it if it hadn't been for the check-up[5]. He considered himself lucky because the cancer was in the early stage; it was treated by removing the cancer cells and chemotherapy[6]. Thank God he went to his regular check-up. I couldn't imagine what would have happened if it were found afterwards.

　　當然很重要！我叔叔就是在健康檢查的時候發現他患有早期癌症。如果他沒去健康檢查，就根本不可能發現。他覺得自己很幸運，因為發現得早，所以只要移除癌細胞，並配合化療就可以了。幸好他有去做定期健康檢查，我完全無法想像如果之後才發現會怎麼樣。

❶ **uncle** 名 舅舅；叔叔	❷ **diagnose** 動 診斷	❸ **cancer** 名 癌症
❹ **physical** 形 身體的	❺ **check-up** 名 檢查	❻ **chemotherapy** 名 化學療法

換個立場講講看

Well, I think I am still too young[7] to worry about being unhealthy; I probably[8] won't bother getting a physical check-up until I turn thirty-five. I live a pretty healthy lifestyle[9]. I don't smoke and only drink occasionally[10]. I like eating deep-fried food, but I don't do it very often. Other than that, I can't really think of anything that could have a negative[11] impact[12] on my health. I think I am alright without a physical check-up for the time being.

　　我覺得自己還很年輕，不用擔心健康的問題，在三十五歲前我應該都不會操心去做健康檢查的事。我的生活習慣滿健康的，我不抽菸，酒也只是偶爾小酌。我愛吃油炸食品，但並不常吃。除此之外，我實在想不出還有什麼會對我的身體有害，就目前而言，我覺得自己不去做健康檢查也沒問題。

❼ **young**	❽ **probably**	❾ **lifestyle**
形 年輕的	副 大概；或許	名 生活方式
❿ **occasionally**	⓫ **negative**	⓬ **impact**
副 偶爾	形 負面的	名 衝擊

 試著更與眾不同

Yes, I think it is quite important to have regular physical check-ups. Life is unpredictable[13]. You never know what will happen the next moment. Besides, most of our organs[14] are inside our bodies. We can't physically see their condition. To me, the only way to know whether one's organs are doing well or not is to go through a complete check-up. I get a check-up once a year. Although it's quite expensive[15], it's worthwhile[16] to me. I hope they won't find anything bad this year.

　　是的，我覺得定期健康檢查很重要。生命充滿意外，你永遠都無法得知下一刻會發生什麼事。而且，大部分的器官都在身體裡面，肉眼根本看不出來。就我而言，唯一能確認器官是否健康的方式，就是去做徹底的身體檢查。我每年都會做一次健康檢查，雖然費用昂貴，但我覺得很值得，希望今年不會有什麼壞消息。

⓭ **unpredictable**	⓮ **organ**	延伸note
形 出乎意料的	名 器官	固定做身體健康檢查，除了本段的regular之外，還
⓯ **expensive**	⓰ **worthwhile**	可以用a routine physical
形 昂貴的	形 值得做的	check-up表示。

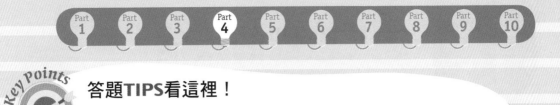

 Part 1　Part 2　Part 3　Part 4　Part 5　Part 6　Part 7　Part 8　Part 9　Part 10

Key Points

答題TIPS看這裡！

大家對身體檢查的態度可能大不相同。如果是剛畢業的學生，可能不覺得檢查有什麼重要性，或覺得年輕就應該是健康的，所以不怎麼在意。隨著出社會的時間越長，越會覺得容易疲倦，此時就可能開始重視起健康檢查了。

Words & Phrases 常見的健康檢查項目

1 **a blood test**
抽血檢查

2 **urinalysis**
驗尿

3 **check one's vision**
視力檢查

4 **take a chest X-ray**
胸部X光檢查

Words & Phrases 檢驗、症狀與治療

1 **infection**
感染

2 **symptom**
症狀

3 **treatment**
治療方式

4 **antibody**
抗體

進階實用句 More Expressions

I got a check-up last week, and the results will be known tomorrow.

我上禮拜去做健康檢查，報告明天會出來。

The doctor believes that I am suffering from a bladder infection.

醫生說我應該是有膀胱感染。

I haven't been feeling well. The doctor referred me for a blood test.

我一直都不太舒服，醫生建議我去做抽血檢驗。

187

UNIT 15 令人恐懼的疾病

Q What's your reaction when you hear about a fatal disease like Ebola?

當你聽聞某致命疾病(例如伊波拉)時，反應為何？

你可以這樣回答

MP3
060

I don't actually care about this kind of news because it seems so far away from me. I don't travel overseas unless it's a business trip[1]. And normally, I try to avoid visiting hospitals[2]. To me, that kind of disease is more like something you see in the movies. People panic[3] because of an uncontrollable[4] outbreak[5]. In the real world, medical teams find most cures[6] quickly before diseases start to spread worldwide. Therefore, we don't need to overreact to these cases.

　　事實上，我對這種新聞不太關心，因為我覺得那距離我很遙遠。我不出國旅行，除非是出差才去，而且我通常會避開醫院那種場所。對我來說，這類疾病簡直像是電影裡才會出現的情節。人們之所以會恐慌，是因為擔憂爆發的大型疾病變得無法控制，但在現實生活中，大部分的疾病在擴及全球之前，醫療團隊就會找出治療的方法，所以我們其實不用大驚小怪。

❶ **a business trip** 片 出差	❷ **hospital** 名 醫院	❸ **panic** 動 使恐慌
❹ **uncontrollable** 形 控制不住的	❺ **outbreak** 名 爆發	❻ **cure** 名 治療；療程

換個立場講講看

I get really concerned when I hear things like that. I still remember when SARS got really bad and all the hospitals were in lockdown ten years ago. People tried to stay at home as much as they could. M95 masks[7] all sold out[8] quickly. You couldn't get any even if you were willing to pay big money for them. It was such a terrible[9] time. I hope it will never happen again[10].

如果有類似的事情發生，我會很擔心。我還記得十年前SARS的疫情有多恐怖，所有的醫院都必須封鎖、隔離；能待在家的時候，民眾就絕對不會出門；M95的口罩賣到缺貨，有錢也買不到，那真的是非常恐怖的回憶，希望類似的事情不會再發生。

延伸note
舉例是個延伸話題的好方法，如果能稍加描述疫情爆發時的社會氣氛，會更有說服力。

❼ **mask**
名 口罩

❽ **sell out**
片 賣光

❾ **terrible**
形 嚇人的；嚴重的

❿ **again**
副 再一次

試著更與眾不同

It depends on how widespread[11] it is. If it were all over Asia[12], then I would get really worried because it could get to us anytime. But if it were isolated in a particular[13] area of the world like Africa or Europe, I would be less concerned since it's quite far away. Furthermore, people going in and out of the infected areas would be strictly[14] controlled and traced[15]. It would be unlikely[16] for that type of virus to spread so quickly to this part of the world.

這要視病毒擴散的狀況而定。如果疫情已經擴及亞洲國家，那我就會擔心，因為隨時都可能擴散到我們這裡。但如果疫情只出現在特定的區域，如非洲或歐洲，因為距離比較遙遠，所以我比較不會那麼擔心。況且，進出疫區的人會被嚴加控管與追蹤，所以疫情不會這麼快就擴散到我們這裡。

⓫ **widespread**
形 普遍的

⓬ **Asia**
名 亞洲

⓭ **particular**
形 特定的

⓮ **strictly**
副 嚴格地

⓯ **trace**
動 跟蹤；追蹤

⓰ **unlikely**
形 不太可能的

答題TIPS看這裡！

聽聞致命疾病，有些人會很擔心，這可能是因為以前曾有過不好的經驗、正處於高風險的地區，或是在擔心疾病到最後仍無法控制，可能會傷亡慘重…等等；也有些人的態度偏冷漠，這本來就是個人意見，沒有什麼對錯。了解相關時事的人可以多加舉例，但若對這個話題了解的不多，建議著重在個人感受層面，不要深入探討自己不熟的專業內容。

Words & Phrases　致命疾病的影響

1 **curfew**
宵禁

2 **lockdown**
關閉；封鎖

3 **quarantine**
醫院的檢疫隔離

4 **death toll**
死亡人數

Words & Phrases　檢驗與抑制傳染病

1 **checkpoint**
檢查站

2 **positive**
（醫）陽性的

3 **negative**
（醫）陰性的

4 **contain**
抑制；控制

進階實用句 More Expressions

There is still so much unknown about the Ebola virus.

關於伊波拉病毒，還有很多需要研究的。

The outbreak is out of control and the whole town is in lockdown.

傳染病的疫情失控，整個城市都被封鎖。

Make sure you take all the necessary precautions to avoid cross-contamination.

為了避免交叉感染，一定要確保你有遵照所有的必要步驟。

Part 5

職業與學習
Job and Academy

 動 動詞

 名 名詞

 副 副詞

 形 形容詞

 介 介系詞

 連 連接詞

 片 片語

UNIT 01 理想的工作

Q **What do you think is the most interesting / ideal job?**

你認為最有趣或最理想的工作是什麼？

你可以這樣回答

MP3 061

I think being a celebrity[1], especially a movie star, would be an interesting job. If I were a movie star, I could have the chance to work with other stars. Wouldn't it be exciting[2] to get close to whom you only see on the big screen? Besides, acting looks fascinating[3]. It is like you are living someone else's life. It must be a wonderful experience. The best part is that I might travel around the world for my work. This kind of lifestyle would be fantastic[4]!

我覺得當明星會是一件很有趣的工作，尤其是當電影明星。如果我是電影明星，就有機會和其他明星搭檔對戲，和那些以往只能在大螢幕上看到的人近距離接觸，不是很令人興奮嗎？除此之外，演戲這件事也很吸引人，藉由演戲，可以體驗到不同的人生，這種經驗肯定很美好。最棒的是，我還能因為不同的演出環遊世界，這種生活方式實在太棒了！

❶ **celebrity**
名 名人；名流

❷ **exciting**
形 令人興奮的

❸ **fascinating**
形 迷人的；極好的

❹ **fantastic**
形 （口）極好的

延伸note
celebrity並不限於演藝明星，舉凡政經界、科技業、體育範疇或文藝界的名人都可以稱呼。

換個立場講講看

I think being a video game tester would be fun. It would be my duty[5] to play video games during office hours[6]. I would even get paid for doing it.

Furthermore, I would be the first one trying the unreleased[7] games out. It would feel like the games were exclusively[8] designed for me. Personally, I enjoy all kinds of video games and play them a lot in my spare time. So, being a video game tester would definitely be the perfect job for me.

　　我覺得當電玩的測試員一定很棒。上班時間的工作就是玩電動，還能因此領到薪水。除此之外，我還會是第一個體驗未上市遊戲的人，感覺那些遊戲就像是專門為我設計的一樣。我本身很喜歡各種類型的電玩，空閒時經常都在打電動，所以，電玩測試員簡直就是我的夢想。

延伸note
常見的電玩類型有 Puzzle(益智類)、RPG(角色扮演)、Simulation Game(經營養成)等。

❺ **duty**
名 職責；職務

❻ **office hours**
片 上班時間

❼ **unreleased**
形 未上市的

❽ **exclusively**
副 專門地

 ## 試著更與眾不同

I would love to be a hotel owner on a beautiful tropical[9] island[10]. It would be wonderful since it would be like I was on vacation every day of the week. People would pay for flights and hotels, but I could enjoy the spectacular[11] scenery[12] for free. I could jump into the ocean for a swim whenever I felt like it. When I was hungry, I could ask the chefs[13] to cook me a meal. I could even enjoy the sunset[14] while having my dinner!

　　我想要成為美麗熱帶島嶼飯店的老闆。那樣的話，每天都像在度假，感覺很棒。其他人必須要付機票與住宿的費用才能享受，我卻能免費欣賞壯麗的景色。想要游泳的時候，我隨時可以跳進大海裡；肚子餓的話，還能請主廚們替我準備餐點，甚至還能在進餐的時候欣賞日落美景呢！

❾ **tropical**
形 熱帶的

❿ **island**
名 島嶼

⓫ **spectacular**
形 壯麗的

⓬ **scenery**
名 風景

⓭ **chef**
名 主廚

⓮ **sunset**
名 日落的景象

答題TIPS看這裡！

談到理想或有趣的工作，多半會是自己感興趣或一直想嘗試的事，答題時可以不考慮自己的能力，只要是自己覺得有趣的工作都可以。另一方面，也可以天馬行空地發揮想像力，就算自創一個工作也可以，例如：月球的房地產銷售員（a real estate agent on the moon），不過如果是幻想中的職業，記得要和面試官講清楚，免得讓對方一頭霧水。

Words & Phrases 較少見的有趣職業

1. **street performer**
   街頭藝人

2. **F1 race car driver**
   F1賽車手

3. **zookeeper**
   動物園的管理員

4. **vet**
   獸醫

5. **cartoonist**
   漫畫家

6. **fashion designer**
   時裝設計師

7. **detective**
   偵探

8. **TV producer**
   電視節目的製作人

進階實用句 More Expressions

Since I love animals so much, being a vet would be the most ideal job for me.

我這麼喜歡動物，獸醫顯然會是最適合我的工作。

I would love to be a pilot so that I could fly to different countries for free!

我想當機長，這樣就可以免費飛往世界各地了！

I wish I could sing as good as an opera singer. That would certainly impress my girlfriend.

我希望自己能唱得跟歌劇表演家一樣好，這樣我女友肯定會印象深刻。

UNIT 02 樂在工作 / 課業嗎？

Q Do you enjoy your job / school life? Why?
你對工作或學校生活樂在其中嗎？為什麼？

你可以這樣回答 MP3 062

I really enjoy my school life at the moment. I am in my senior[1] year of university. Although a lot of my classmates chose to pursue[2] further[3] studies, I decided to join the workforce[4] after graduation. I got a student loan[5], so I'd better pay it off as soon as possible. I am a little bit nervous[6] about what is going on in the real world, but I look forward to the next stage of my life. I am taking a course on preparing for interviews.

　　我很享受目前的學校生活。我現在是大四生，雖然我有很多同學都選擇繼續升學，但我還是決定要直接就業，我有助學貸款，最好儘早付清。我不確定真實的世界如何，所以有點緊張，但能進入生命的下一個階段，也讓我感到很期待，我現在有上一些準備面試的課程。

❶ **senior** 名 大四生	❷ **pursue** 動 從事；繼續	❸ **further** 形 進一步的
❹ **workforce** 名 勞動力	❺ **loan** 名 貸款	❻ **nervous** 形 緊張的

 換個立場講講看

I am a graduate student in history now, and I enjoy my studies quite a lot. I love analyzing[7] the papers I read and attending conferences[8]. However, I am quite worried because I don't plan to be a scholar[9]. I need to support my own family someday, so it's better for me to think about some realistic[10] factors[11]. Deciding on a career is never easy for me, but I believe I can get used to all kinds of jobs since I always keep optimistic[12] towards life.

我現在是攻讀歷史的研究生，我滿喜歡做研究的。我喜歡分析看過的文章內容，也愛參加研討會的活動，不過，因為我沒有做學者的打算，所以有點擔心。未來總有一天，我得賺錢養活家裡，所以我最好考慮現實面的問題。要決定職涯對我來說並不容易，但我一直以來都以積極、正面的態度面對生活，所以我相信無論是什麼工作，我都能適應。

❼ **analyze** 動 分析	❽ **conference** 名 研討會	❾ **scholar** 名 學者
❿ **realistic** 形 現實的	⓫ **factor** 名 因素；要素	⓬ **optimistic** 形 樂觀的

 試著更與眾不同

I have been working for almost ten years at the same company. My working life in general is good, but it is also stressful[13]. If I make a mistake, it might cause serious consequences[14] afterwards. Therefore, I need to be really careful about what I do. I got promoted last year and found out[15] that being a manager is even more complicated[16]. I now have to be responsible[17] for my subordinates'[18] jobs.

我已經在同一間公司工作了十年，我的職場生活很不錯，但壓力也滿大的，如果我犯了錯，之後就可能造成嚴重的後果，所以我對自己的工作必須非常地小心謹慎。我去年獲得升職，但我發現做經理其實更困難，我現在還必須為部屬的工作表現負責。

⓭ **stressful** 形 壓力重的	⓮ **consequence** 名 後果	⓯ **find out** 片 找出；發現
⓰ **complicated** 形 複雜的	⓱ **responsible** 形 承擔責任的	⓲ **subordinate** 名 部屬

Key Points

答題TIPS看這裡！

學校的環境比較單純，一般就是升學壓力；若是上班族，除了工作之外，人際關係（relationship）可能也是影響很大的一環。答題時，就算沒有樂在工作/課業，其實也沒有關係，只要能清楚闡述原因就好。

Words & Phrases   求職的書信與文件

1 **resume**
履歷表

2 **job application**
求職申請書

3 **cover letter**
求職信

4 **portfolio**
代表作選輯

Words & Phrases   令人印象深刻的性格

1 **organized**
有條理的

2 **flexible**
能隨機應變的

3 **adaptive**
有適應力的

4 **persistent**
持之以恆的

🎤 進階實用句 More Expressions

I sent out a lot of job applications. It is time for a change.

我寄出了很多的求職申請信，是時候改變了。

I feel miserable in my current position; there is too much work pressure.

目前的職位令我苦不堪言，工作的壓力太大了。

I really enjoy my college life. I will definitely miss it here after graduation.

我很享受我的大學生活，畢業之後，我肯定會很想念這裡的。

197

UNIT 03 最喜歡的科目

Q What's your favorite course / subject in school?

你在學校最喜歡的一堂課或科目是什麼？

你可以這樣回答

MP3 063

My favorite subject is geography[1]. I love it so much that I even dream about traveling around the world. I sometimes imagine the scenery of a country. For example, when my teacher was introducing France, I couldn't stop picturing the Arch[2] de triumph[3]. It was so much fun to me. I always look forward to geography class. I even bought a sketchbook[4] for drawing the various maps of the countries.

　　我最喜歡的科目是地理，我真的很喜愛這一科，甚至還夢想去環遊世界呢！我有時候還會想像他國的風景。比方說，當老師在介紹法國時，我就忍不住在腦內描繪凱旋門的模樣，這真的很有趣。我總是很期待上地理課的日子，我甚至還為了畫各國的地圖，而買了一本素描本。

❶ **geography**
名 地理

❷ **arch**
名 拱門

❸ **triumph**
名 凱旋式

❹ **sketchbook**
名 寫生簿

> 延伸note
> 地圖上除了position(方位)之外，還會顯示各地點間的distance(距離)、terrain(地形；地勢)…等。

換個立場講講看

I love to study biology[5] because I hope one day I can become a marine[6] biologist to help the sea creatures[7] and promote wildlife conservation[8]. I once got some fish as pets when I was little. But they all died after I changed the water for them.

At that moment, I realized there was a lot more to keeping fish than just feeding them. After that, I did a lot of research on biology. I guess that's when I found the subject interesting.

我喜歡生物學，並希望成為海洋生物學家，以幫助海裡的生物，從事野生動物的保育行動。小時候，我曾經養魚，但就在我替牠們換水之後，那些魚就死光了。那個時候，我才了解到養魚不只是餵食而已，還有很多要注意的。在那之後，我花了很多時間研究生物學，我想那就是我喜歡上這門科目的原因。

⑤ biology
名 生物學

⑥ marine
形 海生的

⑦ creature
名 生物

⑧ conservation
名 保護；管理

延伸note
conserve的保育範圍比preserve大。以動物而言，後者只針對動物，前者則包含生態環境。

 試著更與眾不同

I always looked forward to art class when I was in junior high school. I think that is when I developed a strong foundation[9] of creativity[10]. I really like art projects like creating an object with everyday items such as cooking utensils[11]. I made a robot[12] with cooking pots[13] and utensils one time. My teacher was very impressed with my work and I had fun making it, too. Becoming more and more interested in arts, I chose it to be my major[14] in university.

國中的時候，我就很喜歡上美術課，我覺得那段時期培養出我的創造力。我很喜歡做美術專題，像是用日常用品（比如廚具）製作出新東西。有一次，我用鍋子和其他器具製作出機器人，我的老師很滿意這項作品，而且我也樂在其中，也因為對藝術的興趣越來越濃厚，所以我大學選了它作為主修。

⑨ foundation
名 基礎

⑩ creativity
名 創造力

⑪ utensil
名 器皿；用具

⑫ robot
名 機器人

⑬ pot
名 罐；壺；鍋

⑭ major
名 主修

答題TIPS看這裡！

大家喜歡的科目（subject）都不同，理由也各異，除了本身對科目有興趣外，老師的角色也很重要，很多時候，是因為喜歡老師，因而對那門課有興趣，答題時也可以從「老師」的角度切入，如：I never like mathematics until I met my math teacher in senior high school.（我從來都不喜歡數學這個科目，直到我高中時遇到我的數學老師，才有了轉變。）

Words & Phrases 美國中學常見課程

1	English 英文	**2**	mathematics 數學
3	history 歷史	**4**	social sciences 社會科學
5	foreign language 外國語	**6**	lab science 實驗課
7	physical education 體育課	**8**	elective course 選修科目

進階實用句 More Expressions

History is the subject that I am good at.

歷史這門科目是我的強項。

I like to read novels in English; my favorite subject is English literature.

我喜歡讀原文小說，我最喜歡的科目是英國文學。

I really enjoy doing science experiments. I hope I can become a famous scientist and win a Nobel Prize one day.

我喜歡做科學實驗，希望有一天，我能成為有名的科學家，並贏得諾貝爾獎。

UNIT 04 參加社團活動

Q Did you join a student club? Why or why not?
你有加入學校的社團嗎？為什麼(不)？

你可以這樣回答

MP3 064

I had a great time in the street dance club back in high school. It was one of the best things I ever did. I still think back on those days when we practiced dancing at the MRT station[1] and performed[2] at a New Year's concert[3]. Even though I graduated a long time ago, I still get in touch with[4] some friends I met in the club. I don't dance now, but I really miss the old days.

　　我高中的時候加入街舞社，那段時光真的很棒，算是我最精采的回憶。我偶爾還會想起在捷運站練舞的時光，和參加跨年晚會表演的景象。雖然我已經畢業很久了，但還是有和一些舞蹈社的朋友保持聯繫。我現在已經不跳舞了，但依然很懷念那些日子的事情。

❶ **station** 名 車站	❷ **perform** 動 演出；表演	
❸ **concert** 名 音樂會；演奏會	❹ **get in touch with** 片 與…聯繫	

> **延伸note**
> 表演性社團，大部分都會有成果發表會、演奏會等活動，可以擇一實例闡述。

換個立場講講看

I was too busy to join any student clubs because it took me a lot of time to complete my homework and studying. Furthermore, I had quite a lot of after-school[5] courses back then. Literally, I had no time to do anything else other than studying. I did get jealous[6] seeing my friends attending club gatherings[7] and always wondered why they had time to participate in[8] those activities. If I had a chance to live my high school life again, I would definitely try different things other than studying all the time.

　　我沒有空加入社團，因為我花了很多時間在課業上，那個時候，我有好幾個補習班得上，所以根本就沒有多餘的時間去做別的事。看到朋友去參加社團聚會時，我都很羨慕，總是在想「他們為什麼有空去參加那些活動呢？」如果能重回高中生活，我絕對不會只專注在唸書，而會嘗試各種不同的事情。

延伸note
after-school course是放學後的課程，除了補習班之外，還能用來指稱才藝班。

⑤ **after-school** 形 課外的；課後的	⑥ **jealous** 形 妒忌的
⑦ **gathering** 名 聚會；聚餐	⑧ **participate in** 片 參加

 ## 試著更與眾不同

I joined the entertainment[9] club and planned a group activity in high school. I really enjoyed it. Basically[10], we created scripts[11] and rehearsed[12] for the performances. I was chosen to be the show host[13] several times. I built up my courage for public speaking because I sometimes had to make a fool out of myself and perform in front of other students. I got pretty thick-skinned[14] after three years in the club.

　　我高中時是康輔社的一員，我覺得很有趣。基本上，我們會負責設計表演的橋段和預演，我好幾次都被選為活動主持人，藉由這些經驗，我在公眾面前演說的膽量提升許多，因為我有時候必須在其他學生面前出醜搞笑，這三年的社團經驗讓我的臉皮變厚不少。

⑨ **entertainment** 名 娛樂；消遣	⑩ **basically** 副 基本上	⑪ **script** 名 腳本；底稿
⑫ **rehearse** 動 排練；排演	⑬ **host** 名 主持人	⑭ **thick-skinned** 形 厚臉皮的

Key Points

答題TIPS看這裡！

學校社團是許多人求學過程中的美好回憶，無論是一起準備活動的過程、籌款（fund-raising）、或是聚會（gathering）…等等，都可以拿來舉例。藉由某次的具體經驗，提到自己的成長，也能令面試官印象深刻。

Words & Phrases 國外高中的社團

1 **student council**
學生會

2 **band**
樂隊

3 **cheerleading**
啦啦隊

4 **debating society**
辯論社

5 **academic team**
學術搶答小組

6 **dance ensemble**
舞團

7 **office aides**
辦公室助理

8 **chorus**
合唱團

進階實用句 More Expressions

I play electric guitar in my pop music club.

我在熱音社裡是負責彈電吉他的。

I learned the skills of taking pictures while I was in the photography club.

我的攝影技巧是在參加攝影社時學的。

We used to perform sign language songs at nursing homes to entertain the elderly.

我們以前經常到老人院去表演手語歌，讓老人家開心。

學外語的重要性

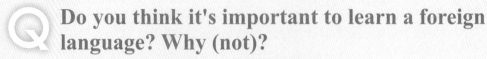

Q Do you think it's important to learn a foreign language? Why (not)?

你覺得學外語重要嗎？為什麼(不)？

 **你可以這樣回答**

I have always been interested in learning languages because I think languages are something I can actually use in daily[1] life. I find fulfillment[2] when I can talk to foreigners[3] in their mother tongue[4]. It's totally different from something like calculus[5]. Although I took a course in calculus, I didn't find it useful at all. I guess it's only for people who are doing advanced[6] studies.

　　一直以來，我都對學語言很有興趣，因為我覺得語言是真的能在生活中派上用場的工具。如果我能用外國人的母語和他們交談，我會覺得特別有成就感，和微積分之類的科目完全不同，雖然我修過微積分這門課，卻完全不覺得那實用，我想只有在做學問的人才會需要微積分吧。

❶ **daily** 形 日常的	❷ **fulfillment** 名 成就（感）	❸ **foreigner** 名 外國人
❹ **mother tongue** 片 母語	❺ **calculus** 名 微積分	❻ **advanced** 形 高等的

 換個立場講講看

I think learning a foreign language is really important because it comes in handy[7] when you get in trouble overseas. My experience[8] of traveling to Japan really taught me a lesson. I thought English would work no matter what happened, but I was totally wrong! Luckily[9], my friend knows a little bit of Japanese, so my problem was solved[10] eventually. The world has becoming an international village[11]. The trend[12] of people speaking more than one language will become more popular in the future.

　　我覺得學習外語很重要，當你在國外遇到困難時，語言就能派上用場。之前去日本的經驗真是讓我好好上了一課。我以為不管發生任何事，只要會講英文就一定沒問題，這個想法實在是太錯特錯！幸運的是，我的朋友懂一點日文，所以問題最後還是順利解決了。全世界正形成國際村，未來會有越來越多人懂得好幾種語言，這是國際趨勢。

❼ come in handy
片 遲早有用

❽ experience
名 經驗

❾ luckily
副 幸好

❿ solve
動 解決

⓫ village
名 村莊；村

⓬ trend
名 趨勢；傾向

試著更與眾不同

Well, I don't think learning a foreign language is that important. Nowadays[13], people can download[14] apps that do the translation[15] work for them. So why do we need to bother wasting so much time learning other languages from scratch[16]? I am sure someone will invent something that can convert[17] my thoughts into words in different languages. That invention[18] might even be available before I could master a foreign language.

　　我覺得學外語並沒有大家說的那麼重要，現在有很多能翻譯語言的APP，下載使用就好，實在沒有必要花那麼多時間從頭學語言。我相信未來會有人發明一種機器，能將我的想法翻譯成不同的語言，在我精通某個語言之前，那個機器搞不好就先被發明出來了呢！

⓭ nowadays
副 現今；時下

⓮ download
動 下載

⓯ translation
名 翻譯

⓰ from scratch
片 從頭開始

⓱ convert
動 轉換；變換

⓲ invention
名 發明；創造

答題TIPS看這裡！

Words & Phrases 常見的外語種類

1 **Spanish**
西班牙語

2 **French**
法語

3 **Italian**
義大利語

4 **Mandarin Chinese**
漢語

5 **Arabic**
阿拉伯語

6 **German**
德語

7 **Russian**
俄語

8 **Portuguese**
葡萄牙語

進階實用句 More Expressions

If I knew Arabic, I could travel around the Middle East without any problems.

如果我會講阿拉伯語，去中東旅遊就能暢行無阻。

I wish I could read German because the operation manual was written in German.

因為那本操作手冊是用德文寫的，所以我很希望自己看得懂德文。

I would like to learn Spanish because it is widely spoken in South America.

我想學西班牙文，因為南美洲有很多國家都講西班牙文。

UNIT 06

上班族還是學生

Q **Do you work or study?**
你是上班族，還是學生呢？

你可以這樣回答

MP3 066

I am a full-time engineer¹ at HTC. My job is to improve the functionality² of our cell phones. I find the job quite challenging and interesting. The surveying³ department gathers the reports⁴ from users to see what they think of our products. Based on the reports, I try to solve the existing problems of the cell phones. I sometimes even work on some projects which aim⁵ to remove the limitations⁶ of our current system.

　　我目前在宏達電任職，做工程師，我的工作是改善手機的功能。我覺得這份工作很有挑戰性、也很有趣。市場調查部門會先蒐集用戶的反應，看他們對我們的產品有何意見。我再根據這些回報，試著解決手機現存的問題。有時候，我還會參加一些企劃，試圖讓我們目前的系統擺脫使用上的限制。

❶ **engineer** 名 工程師	❷ **functionality** 名 功能；機能	❸ **survey** 動 調查
❹ **report** 名 報告；報告書	❺ **aim** 動 致力；旨在	❻ **limitation** 名 限制

換個立場講講看

I am doing my master's degree⁷ at the moment; I am majoring in⁸ business administration⁹ and will earn an MBA one day. I worked in an international trading firm for a couple of years after I graduated from university. I was a manager in the procurement[10] department for mechanical[11] spare parts. It was really hard for me because I didn't have any related background. Therefore, I made up my mind to enroll[12] in an MBA course.

我目前正在攻讀碩士，我的主修是企業管理，也就是所謂的MBA。大學畢業後，我在一家國際貿易公司工作過幾年，我當時是採購部的經理。因為完全沒有相關背景，所以當時真的非常辛苦，也因為如此，我才決定攻讀MBA。

❼ degree 名 文憑	❽ major in 片 主修	❾ administration 名 管理；經營
❿ procurement 名 採購	⓫ mechanical 形 機械的；技工的	⓬ enroll 動 登記；使入學

試著更與眾不同

I am currently doing my bachelor's[13] degree and working part time at McDonald's. It is quite tiring because I work three nights a week from 5 p.m. to 10 p.m. My family can't afford my tuition[14] and other expenses[15], so I need to work enough hours to cover it. Luckily, I don't have lectures[16] every day; otherwise, I wouldn't be able to work and study at the same time. I still need a few credits before I can graduate. I am looking forward to graduation since I am keen to get a full-time job.

我現在一邊讀大學、一邊在麥當勞兼職，這樣的生活其實滿累的，因為我一個星期要上三天班，從下午五點到晚上十點。我的家人無法負擔我的學費和其他開銷，所以我必須要工作以補貼生活費。幸好我不是每天都有課，不然我真的無法半工半讀，我還得再修幾個學分，才達到畢業的門檻。我很想要趕快找到一份正職工作，所以我很期待畢業。

⓭ bachelor 名 學士	⓮ tuition 名 學費
⓯ expense 名 花費	⓰ lecture 名 授課；演講

延伸note
經濟情況沒有那麼好的學生，除了work part time之外，還能申請student loan（助學貸款）。

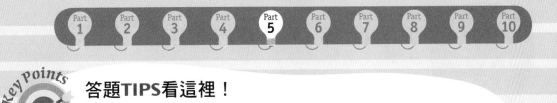

Key Points

答題TIPS看這裡！

答題時不要只偏重在「身分」。如果是學生，不要只簡答 I am a student. 而要補充自己的背景，例如：I study full-time in NTU, majoring in Chinese literature.（我就讀於台大，主修中文。）

Words & Phrases 一般公司常見的部門

1	**marketing and sales** 市場行銷部	2	**accounting dept.** 會計部門
3	**R & D** 研發部	4	**engineering dept.** 工程部門
5	**maintenance dept.** 維修部	6	**customer service dept.** 客服部
7	**HR dept.** 人事部	8	**procurement dept.** 採購部

 進階實用句 More Expressions

I have been working in the HR department for over five years.

我已經在人事部待了五年多。

I am currently doing a double major in law and accounting at NTU.

我目前於台大雙主修法律和會計。

It is challenging to work in marketing and sales. There is always a target to meet.

市場行銷部很有挑戰性，因為總是有要達成的銷售目標。

UNIT 07

擁有的專業證照

Q **What kind of qualifications do you have?**

你擁有什麼專業證照呢？

你可以這樣回答

MP3 067

I took a few training courses outside of school during my junior year. I got an average[1] score of 7.5 on IELTS. IELTS is an English proficiency[2] test recognized[3] worldwide, especially in British Commonwealth[4] countries. On top of that, I got a bartending[5] qualification[6]. My major is in hotel and tourism management. I am pretty sure there won't be any problem for me to get a job in this industry.

　　我大三那年上過幾個校外的訓練課程，我的雅思英語測驗有7.5分，雅思是世界公認的英語檢定考，在大英國協的國家特別有指標性。除此之外，我還取得了調酒執照，我的主修是飯店管理，我對在這一行找到工作相當有信心。

❶ **average**	❷ **proficiency**	❸ **recognize**
形 平均的	名 精通；熟練	動 認可；認定
❹ **commonwealth**	❺ **bartend**	❻ **qualification**
名 共和國	動 做酒保	名 資格證書；執照

換個立場講講看

I am a qualified graphic[7] designer. I have quite a lot of qualifications in different graphic design programs[8], such as Photoshop and Illustrator. I found these certificates[9] very helpful in job hunting. My portfolio plus the qualifications are pretty persuasive[10] to most interviewers. I even got my last job at The Walt Disney

Company because the interviewers were impressed by my professional skills.

　　我是一名有專業證照的平面設計師，我取得的設計軟體執照滿多的，Photoshop和Illustrator的我都有。我覺得這些證照在找工作時很有用，附上作品輯和證照之後，大部分的面試官就會覺得很有說服力，我上一份在華特迪士尼的工作，就是因為面試官對我的專業技能印象深刻，才被錄用的。

延伸note
擁有與面試相關的執照，或有因為執照而加分的經驗，都可以多加敘述。

⑦ **graphic**
　形 繪畫的

⑧ **program**
　名 （電腦）程式

⑨ **certificate**
　名 證明書；執照

⑩ **persuasive**
　形 有說服力的

 試著更與眾不同

Although I have been working at an accounting firm[11] for the past three years, it still took me years to complete[12] my CPA. I got a promotion and a pay raise right after I obtained[13] my CPA qualification. However, the accounting firm I am currently employed by is only a small firm. With my CPA qualification, I hope that I can join an international firm like Deloitte. To me, joining an international firm would be a lot more challenging[14] than what I am doing now. I expect a change in my career.

　　雖然我已經在會計公司工作了三年，還是花了好幾年時間才拿到CPA會計師執照。順利取得CPA之後，公司馬上就替我升職和加薪。可是，我現在的公司規模並不大，取得CPA執照後，我希望能進入國際性的公司（如：勤業眾信）工作，我覺得在國際性的公司任職一定會比現在的工作有挑戰性，我期待自己的職業生涯能有一些變化。

⑪ **firm**
　名 商行；公司

⑫ **complete**
　動 完成

⑬ **obtain**
　動 得到；獲得

⑭ **challenging**
　形 挑戰性的

延伸note
在國際企業和小公司工作各有優缺點，敘述時要偏重在自己對未來的展望上。

211

答題TIPS看這裡！

如果沒有什麼專業證照，可以回想一下是否參加過對就業或職場有幫助的短期課程（short-term course）和專題講座（seminar），如：I am working on getting the real estate agent licence. I even attended a workshop to learn the techniques on price evaluation.（我正在準備考取房屋仲介的證照，甚至參加了研討會，以學習估價的技巧。）

Words & Phrases　專業證照的類型

1 interior design
室內設計

2 bakery and patisserie
烘焙及糕點製作

3 GEPT
全民英檢

4 computer programming
軟體設計

Words & Phrases　與執照有關的詞彙

1 license
許可證；執照

2 permission
允許；許可

3 practicing
開業的

4 legally binding
有法律效力的

進階實用句 More Expressions

I am a qualified scuba diving instructor.

我是領有合法執照的潛水教練。

I want to get my CPA, but it will take a lot of time and effort.

我想考取會計師執照，但這需要花費很多的時間和努力。

I enrolled in a patisserie course. I hope I can be a certified pastry maker some day.

我報名了製作糕點的課程，希望有一天能成為具合格認證的糕點師傅。

加強專注力的方法

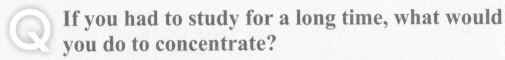

If you had to study for a long time, what would you do to concentrate?

如果你必須長時間唸書，你會做什麼來加強專注力？

 你可以這樣回答

 MP3 068

I would brew[1] a cup of strong coffee for myself. I've tried various methods[2] and figured out that coffee works best in keeping myself awake and alert[3]. I don't do this often. It only happens during mid-terms and final exams. I always push myself to do as much reviewing[4] as possible the night before the exam, so that I can have a clearer memory of what I read. However, coffee[5] only works for a rather short period[6] of time. Therefore, getting more good sleep is also necessary.

　　我會泡一杯很濃的咖啡來喝。我試過很多方法，發現咖啡是最能提高我專注力的東西。我並不常這樣做，只會在期中考和期末考的時候這樣喝咖啡。考試的前一天晚上，我會強迫自己盡量複習，這樣我才會對看過的內容有比較深刻的印象。不過，咖啡的效力並不長，因此，良好的睡眠還是很必要的。

❶ **brew** 動 泡（茶）；煮（咖啡）	❷ **method** 名 方法；辦法	❸ **alert** 形 警覺的
❹ **review** 動 複習	❺ **coffee** 名 咖啡	❻ **period** 名 時期；期間

 換個立場講講看

When I am planning to study for a long time, I set a timer[7] in advance[8]. It can remind me to get up and go for a walk or take a toilet break. Sitting at the desk studying gets tiring after a few hours. Therefore, I usually grab[9] something to eat while I am on a break. Sweets are always the best. After having some, I usually feel much more energetic[10]. Sometimes my mother deliberately[11] comes in my room to make sure I take a proper[12] break.

當我準備要長時間讀書時，我會事先設定鬧鐘，以提醒自己起來走動或上個洗手間。坐在書桌前唸幾個小時的書之後，會感到很疲倦，所以我休息的時候通常會去找東西吃。甜食是我的最佳選項，吃了甜食之後，我通常會覺得有精神許多，有時候，我媽媽也會故意進來我房間，好讓我休息一下。

7 timer
名 定時器

8 in advance
片 事先

9 grab
動 抓取

10 energetic
形 精神飽滿的

11 deliberately
副 慎重地

12 proper
形 適當的

試著更與眾不同

When I am feeling sleepy or losing concentration[13] while studying, I either pinch[14] or slap[15] myself in the face to stay awake. It sounds silly, but it actually works. The trick is to pinch or slap yourself just hard enough so that you don't hurt yourself. You have to feel the pain[16] to stay awake. So, if you do it too softly, it will not work. The other trick I often use is to turn on all the lights in my room.

當我開始昏昏欲睡或開始不專心的時候，我會捏自己或打臉來提神。聽起來很蠢，但這真的有用。最重要的一點是，必須在不受傷的前提下，盡量用力打，一定要感覺到痛才會有效，下手如果太輕就沒有用了。另一個我會採用的方法是把我房間的電燈全打開。

13 concentration
名 集中；專注

14 pinch
動 捏；擰

15 slap
動 摑⋯耳光

16 pain
名 疼痛

> **延伸note**
> 白天的上午時段可細分為
> daybreak/the small hours(凌晨)、morning(早上)、noon(中午)。

Key Points 答題TIPS看這裡！

提神的方式有很多，除了一般的喝咖啡之外，也可以舉一些獨具創意的方法，如：設鬧鐘嚇自己（set the alarm clock to wake me up）、站著讀書（study without sitting down）…等等。

Words & Phrases　學校考試與成績

1 mid-term exam
期中考

2 final exam
期末考

3 review
複習

4 preview
預習

5 result
成績；結果

6 score
（測驗的）成績；分數

7 ranking
排名

8 assignment
作業

進階實用句 More Expressions

I always stay up late the night before my assignment is due.

我總是在作業截止日的前一天熬夜完成它。

Reviewing takes so much time and there seems to be no end to it.

複習很花時間，好像永遠唸不完似的。

Passing the final exam is required for graduation. I'd better spend more time on reviewing.

必須通過期末考才能畢業，看來我最好多花點時間複習。

UNIT 09

如何激勵員工

MP3
069

Q How can you motivate employees to do their jobs better?

你能如何激勵員工提升自己的工作表現呢？

你可以這樣回答

In order to improve the general[1] performance, I think selecting[2] the best employee of the month is a good way to stimulate[3] their sense of honor. This creates a kind of competition among the staff. Customer comment cards are always good tools for this kind of evaluation[4]. Based on a customer's feedback[5], I can not only see the problems to be improved, but also know the customer's feelings[6] towards a particular employee.

為了提升工作表現，我覺得選出「每月之星」是刺激員工榮譽感的好方法，這能夠激起員工的競爭心，提升表現。針對類似的評估方式，顧客意見調查表永遠都是很方便的一項工具。根據顧客的意見，我不僅能看出需要改善的問題，還能得知顧客對員工的評價。

❶ **general** 形 普遍的；一般的	❷ **select** 動 選擇	❸ **stimulate** 動 刺激；激勵
❹ **evaluation** 名 評估；評價	❺ **feedback** 名 反饋	❻ **feeling** 名 看法；感想

換個立場講講看

To me, money would be the best incentive[7] to motivate[8] my employees. Most salary workers nowadays struggle to earn a living. So welfare[9] becomes more and more important for them. If I were the boss, I would set up a sales target for

my staff. If they were willing to go the extra mile, they would be rewarded. Those who work really hard and bring in enormous[10] benefits could get an annual[11] performance bonus[12]. I believe that no one would reject money.

就我而言，錢是最能激勵員工的東西。現在大多數上班族的壓力都很大，想要賺錢養家糊口，所以福利對現代人而言變得越來越重要。如果我是老闆，我會先設定一個業績目標，要求員工達成，如果在此之外，他們願意做得更多，就會得到獎勵。那些努力工作、替公司帶進龐大收益的人能獲得額外的績效獎金，我相信沒有人會和錢過不去的。

❼ incentive
名 動機；鼓勵

❽ motivate
動 給…動機

❾ welfare
名 福利

❿ enormous
形 巨大的；龐大的

⓫ annual
形 一年的

⓬ bonus
名 獎金

 ### 試著更與眾不同

It depends. People work for different reasons. As an executive[13], I always try to know my team members and then determine[14] which reward works the best for him or her. For example, some people care about being paid for all the hours they work. In that case, overtime pay[15] would be my choice. On the other hand, some prefer compensatory[16] leave than money. All in all, knowing my staff is the key to me.

看情況，每個人工作的原因都不同，身為主管，我總是會想辦法了解我的團隊成員，再決定最適合他們的獎勵方式。比方說，有些人認為工作了多久，就該領多少錢，對於這樣的員工，我會給他們加班費；另一方面，有些人就沒那麼在意錢，反而比較想要補休。總而言之，理解員工對我來說是最重要的關鍵。

⓭ executive
名 經理；業務主管

⓮ determine
動 決定

⓯ overtime pay
片 加班費

⓰ compensatory
形 補償的

> **延伸note**
> 事先搞清楚各種獎勵的手段用英文要怎麼說，回答時自然能更有內容。

答題TIPS看這裡！

Key Points

本題詢問的是你個人會採用的作法，如果沒有特別想法，可以直接用你就職公司所採用的作法。一般來說，激勵員工的方式不外乎金錢獎勵和滿足員工心理。金錢獎勵包含加薪（pay raise）、加班費（overtime pay）、年終獎金（annual bonus）…等等；除此之外，休假也是很常見的方式，例如：特休（annual leave）和補休（compensatory leave）…等等。

Words & Phrases 激發更好的表現

1. **motivate**
   刺激；激發
2. **push sb. hard**
   給予某人壓力
3. **go further**
   更進一步
4. **raise the bar**
   提高整體水平

Words & Phrases 懲罰性的員工處置

1. **demote**
   降職
2. **cut one's salary**
   減薪
3. **furlough**
   非自願的留職停薪
4. **lay off**
   資遣

進階實用句 More Expressions

All of us will get a 5% pay raise as a reward.

作為獎勵，我們每個人都會加薪百分之五。

I have found that most people perform better when competing.

我發現大多數人在有競爭的時候，表現得會比較好。

Offering a cash prize for the best employee of the month works well in my company.

發給每月的最佳員工現金獎勵，這種作法在我們公司有很顯著的效果。

UNIT 10

兼職 vs. 全職工作

Q Do you prefer to have a part-time or full-time job?

你喜歡兼職還是全職工作？

你可以這樣回答

I need to work full time because I have a student loan[1] to pay off[2]. The salary of a part-time job won't cover my basic expenses. One of my friends is a freelancer[3]. Her working hours are very flexible. If there aren't any deadlines, she can take days off as long as she wants to do so. I wish I could be like her, too. That way, I would have more spare time to do things I like, such as exercising and volunteering[4] at a nursing home.

　　我必須做全職的工作，因為我還有學生貸款要繳，兼職工作的薪水根本不夠我平日的基本開銷。我有一個朋友是自由作家，她的工作時間很彈性，如果沒有截稿日的壓力，隨時都可以如自己所願地放好幾天假。我也希望能像她那樣，這樣我就有更多時間從事我喜歡做的事，像是運動或到老人院做義工…等等。

❶ **student loan**
片 助學貸款

❷ **pay off**
片 付清

❸ **freelancer**
名 自由作家

❹ **volunteer**
動 自願（做）

延伸note
cover one's expenses在此處指「收入大於支出」，也就是能負擔花費的意思。

換個立場講講看

I prefer to work part time, but it is very hard to find a decent[5] part-time position[6] in an office. I did some part-time jobs, such as being a cleaner and waiter. While I don't like blue collar jobs, finding a part-time job in an international corporation[7] seems impossible for me. They prefer hiring people who work full time. Therefore, if I want to work in an office, I will have to work full time. I wish there were some other options. Sadly, it is not really up to[8] me.

　　我喜歡做兼職，但要在辦公室裡找到不錯的兼職工作真的很困難。我做過像清潔工、服務生這類的打工，我不怎麼喜歡這類的藍領階級工作，但想要在國際性的商社裡找兼職，簡直是不可能的任務。那種大公司都比較喜歡雇用全職員工，因此，如果我想要在辦公室裡工作，就必須做全職的。真希望有其他選擇，可惜的是，這不是我能決定的事。

⑤ decent
形 體面的；像樣的

⑥ position
名 職位；工作

⑦ corporation
名 股份（有限）公司

⑧ up to
片 由…決定

 試著更與眾不同

Personally, I enjoy working full time because I am a very career[9]-driven person. I don't know what to do with my spare time if I am not working. I even work overtime on the weekends. I love being busy and enjoy the sense of satisfaction[10] when I complete a big project. My friends call me a workaholic[11] because of it. I know most people work just to make a living, but I love what I do very much. I never take my days off unless[12] I'm sick.

　　我喜歡全職的工作，因為我很有事業心。閒暇時間不拿來工作的話，我就不知道該做什麼，我甚至連週末都在加班。我喜歡忙碌的感覺，也很享受完成一件大案子的成就感。也因為如此，所以朋友都叫我「工作狂」。我明白大多數人工作只是為了能過活，但我真的很喜歡自己的工作，除非生病，否則我不會請假。

⑨ career
名 職業

⑩ satisfaction
名 滿足；滿意

⑪ workaholic
名 工作狂

⑫ unless
連 如果不；除非

Key Points 答題TIPS看這裡！

工作多數是為了養家糊口，所以畢業之後，多數人會選擇收入穩定的全職工作，這是社會的現實面；但是，也有越來越多人選擇兼職工作，尤其是要照顧家庭的婦女，更偏好在家工作（work at home）的兼職。

Words & Phrases 薪資與紅利

1 salary
（白領階級的）薪水

2 wage
（藍領階級的）工資

3 allowance
津貼；補貼

4 dividend
紅利；股息

Words & Phrases 常見的兼職工作

1 waiter/waitress
服務生

2 tutor
家教

3 bartender
酒保

4 SOHO
在家上班的SOHO族

進階實用句 More Expressions

I work part time, so I get paid based on an hourly wage.

我只是兼職員工，所以薪水以時薪來計算。

In order to increase my income, I might have to find a part-time job.

為了增加收入，我可能要找一份兼職工作。

I went on a working holiday, and most jobs I got were labor-intensive ones like fruit picking.

我參加過打工度假的計畫，大部分做的，都是像摘水果那樣偏重勞力的工作。

獨立或團隊合作

Q Do you prefer to work independently or cooperate with others?

你喜歡獨立作業，還是與人合作？

你可以這樣回答

MP3
071

I prefer working independently[1]. If it's in a teamwork environment, I can't control[2] other people's work since everyone's attitude[3] towards work is different. If my partner[4] were serious about what we do, that would be perfect. However, I am not a prophet[5], so I won't know who is going to work with me. I don't want my partners to drag me down and hurt my performance. Therefore, I feel extremely[6] tired whenever we get group assignments.

　　我喜歡獨立作業。如果是團隊作業，我就無法控制每個人的品質，因為大家對工作的態度都不一樣。假如我的夥伴剛好也很認真，那當然很完美，但我又不是先知，所以根本不可能知道合作的對象是誰。我不希望因為夥伴而拉低我的分數，因此，每次有團隊作業的時候，我都感到非常疲倦。

❶ **independently** 副 單獨地；自立地	❷ **control** 動 控制	❸ **attitude** 名 態度
❹ **partner** 名 夥伴；拍檔	❺ **prophet** 名 預言者	❻ **extremely** 副 極其；非常

換個立場講講看

I like to cooperate with others because no one can finish[7] big projects all by himself. In most cases, you need to work with people with different expertise[8]. For example, if I am planning a residential[9] building project, designers are

absolutely necessary for the layout¹⁰. In addition to the designer, I would also need experienced builders to build the house and a financial¹¹ specialist to make sure that the cash flow is under control¹². There's no way I can do all these on my own.

我喜歡與他人合作，想要成就大案子，光靠一個人是不夠的。就大多數的情況而言，你需要和有不同專長的人合作。例如，要規劃住宅大樓的建案，就需要設計師來規劃空間；除此之外，還得有經驗豐富的建築工人來蓋房子，以及金融專員來確保現金流向是否控制得宜，這些光靠我一個人是做不到的。

❼ **finish**
動 結束；完成

❽ **expertise**
名 專門知識

❾ **residential**
形 住宅的；居住的

❿ **layout**
名 規劃圖

⓫ **financial**
形 財政的

⓬ **under control**
片 在控制之中

 ## 試著更與眾不同

For a project that I am familiar¹³ with, I prefer to work on my own because I am confident¹⁴ in producing something of fine quality. However, if it is something I don't know well, I would prefer to cooperate with others. It would be best if my partner knew the project well, so that he or she could provide¹⁵ me with enough guidance¹⁶. I am communicative and responsible, so I should be a useful member in any situation.

如果是我熟悉的事情，我會喜歡自己做，因為我有信心做出具水準的作品。但如果是我不熟悉的主題，我就會希望有人一起完成，對主題有了解的夥伴當然最好，這樣的話，他就能提供我足夠的建議。我很善於溝通，也很有責任感，所以不管在什麼樣的情況之下，我都應該會是個有用的組員。

⓭ **familiar**
形 熟悉的

⓮ **confident**
形 有信心的

⓯ **provide**
動 提供

⓰ **guidance**
名 指導；引導

延伸note
描述好的品質，可以用 good/high/fine quality；反之，劣質品則用poor quality形容。

答題TIPS看這裡！

Key Points

本題會牽涉到「個性偏好」（personal preference）與「事情性質」（the nature of the job）。答題時可從這兩方面著手，可以先提出自己比較喜歡的作業方式，但如果平常工作或課業上的團隊合作（teamwork）經驗很豐富，也可以拿出來講，就算是喜歡獨立作業，也不要讓面試官覺得你不合群、無法適應團體合作的模式。

Words & Phrases　表示合作的詞彙

1 work with
與…合作

2 do sth. together with
和…一起做某事

3 partner up with
和…搭檔

4 join up with
加入…（做某事）

Words & Phrases　與團體成員交流意見

1 agree with sb.
贊同某人的論點

2 have a disagreement
爭執；爭吵

3 up in the air
懸而未決的

4 compromise on sth.
在某事上妥協

 進階實用句 More Expressions

I worked with Parker before. His is a very reliable man.

我以前跟帕克合作過，他是個很可靠的人。

I prefer working on my own because I don't need to worry about how to partner up with others.

我比較喜歡獨立作業，因為這樣就不用擔心和別人合作的問題。

My friend and I have very good understanding of each other, so there is good chance of winning the competition.

我好友和我很有默契，所以很有機會贏得這次的競賽。

UNIT 12

大公司 vs. 小公司

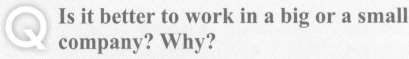

Q **Is it better to work in a big or a small company? Why?**

在大公司工作比較好，還是小公司？為什麼？

你可以這樣回答

MP3
072

Personally, I prefer working in a big company. Projects in a big company generally are divided[1] into several sections[2]. When the manager assigns us jobs, I do the part I am hired for, not the things that I know little of. I once worked as an assistant[3] at a small firm, and all kinds of jobs were assigned to me. Well, I did learn[4] a lot from that job, but I wish I could have focused on things that I was really good at.

　　我個人偏好到大公司工作，大公司的職責分工很細，當經理指派工作時，我處理的業務就是公司聘我來做的事，而非我不清楚的事。我曾經在一家小公司做助理，各式各樣的工作都派到我身上，當然，我是從中學到很多沒錯，但我還是希望能專注在自己真正擅長的事情上。

❶ **divide**
動 分；劃分

❷ **section**
名 部門；處

❸ **assistant**
名 助理

❹ **learn**
動 學習

> 延伸note
> 制度較完善的大公司注重專業分工，job assignment (工作上的指派)也會比較明確。

換個立場講講看

Well, I don't really have a particular[5] preference towards[6] the type of company. For the time being, I prefer a big company. I plan to get married with my girlfriend in three years. If I could find a job at an international corporation, there would be a better chance that I could get a decent salary. However, since I don't have any work experience[7], it would be better to work at a small company. I might struggle[8] at first, but it's a faster way of learning.

　　我其實對公司的型態沒有什麼特別的偏好，就目前而言，我比較想在大公司找到工作。我計劃三年後和女友結婚，如果我能在國際性的商社找到工作，那就比較有可能拿到一份不錯的薪水。不過，因為我沒有任何工作經驗，所以在小公司上班或許比較好，剛開始或許會很辛苦，但這樣學得更快。

延伸note
就算本身沒有特別的偏好，也可能因個人的考量(consideration)而想選哪一種公司。

⑤ particular
形 特定的

⑥ towards
介 朝；向

⑦ experience
名 經驗

⑧ struggle
動 艱難地行進

試著更與眾不同

I think it is much better to work in a big company because I would be less likely stuck with doing the things I don't want to do. In a small company, all the tasks are overlapping[9] and there is no clear[10] instruction[11] who is supposed to[12] do what. For example, a sales representative[13] might have to do the receptionist's[14] job when she is off. It's not like I refuse to help my colleagues. The point is, it will affect my performance if things like this happen.

　　我覺得在大公司工作比較好，因為比較不用做些我不想做的工作。小公司的工作分配很容易重覆，也沒有清楚指示誰應該做什麼。例如，公司的業務可能會因為櫃台小姐請假，而必須負責她的工作。我不是不願意幫助同事，重點在於，這種事情一旦發生，就會影響到我的工作表現。

⑨ overlapping
形 部分重疊的

⑩ clear
形 清楚的

⑪ instruction
名 命令；指示

⑫ be supposed to
片 應該

⑬ representative
名 代表；代理人

⑭ receptionist
名 接待員

 Key Points

答題TIPS看這裡！

大公司通常很講究規模，分工細微，事情有一定的作業程序，比較無法通融。小公司可以變通的地方則比較多，可是也可能因為組織鬆散，而產生分工不均的問題，如果要請假，找人代班就會很困難。

Words & Phrases　企業的各種類型

1 family-owned business
家族企業

2 solely-owned company
獨資企業

3 joint venture
合資企業

4 franchise business
加盟企業

Words & Phrases　談及自我成長的詞彙

1 self-development
自我成長

2 improvement
改善的事物

3 self-awareness
自知；自明

4 enhance
提高；增加

進階實用句 More Expressions

I am thinking about starting up my own franchise business.

我想要建立自己的加盟企業。

I don't like a family-owned business because the people who get promoted are mostly the family members.

我不喜歡家族企業，因為升職的幾乎都是他們自己人。

It is easier to take a few days off in a big company because someone will cover your job while you are away.

在大公司比較好請假，因為有人會在你休假的時候，接手你的工作。

面對棘手的工作時

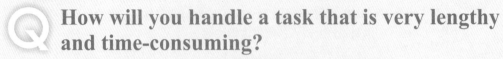

Q How will you handle a task that is very lengthy and time-consuming?

你會如何處理一件冗長且耗費時間的工作呢？

你可以這樣回答

I will divide the task into a few manageable components[1] and set the deadline for each step, and then I will try my best to meet the deadlines[2]. Once in a while, I will go back to review the schedule and make sure I have been realistic[3] with the timeframe[4]. I am pretty strict about the fact whether I am on track with everything or not. I will also make a spread sheet[5] which lists all the tasks and deadlines. I will tick off[6] the tasks once they are completed.

　　我會把案子分成比較容易達成的幾個階段，然後替每個階段設下截止日。接著我會全力在截止日前完成工作。每隔一段時間，我會重新審視時間表，確保那些日期是實際可行的，我很介意自己是否有跟上進度。我還會製作一張表格，標註待辦事項和截止日期，完成之後我就會在上面打勾。

❶ **component**
名 構成要素

❷ **meet the deadline**
片 在期限內完成

❸ **realistic**
形 實際可行的

❹ **timeframe**
名 時間範圍

❺ **spread sheet**
片 空白表格程式

❻ **tick off**
片 用記號勾出

換個立場講講看

First, I will have a good read through of the related files to understand the goal and things I need to deal with. Once I get a good understanding[7], I will prioritize each part and start on the most time-consuming[8] task to avoid delay. If it

requires[9] teamwork, I will also stay in touch with those who are involved in the task to make sure everybody is on the same page[10]. This is not easy. I may need to talk to my colleagues when they don't get along well.

　　首先，我會將相關文件的內容讀清楚，以理解案子的目標和我必須處理的事項有哪些。在理解內容之後，我就會將優先順序安排好，並先著手處理最花時間的工作，才不會搞得最後來不及。如果工作涉及團隊合作，我就會和與相關人員保持聯繫，確保大家的認知都一樣。這並不容易，我可能還必須在同事不合的時候和他們談。

延伸note
容易與on the same page 搞混的片語有on the same boat，意指「處境相同」。

❼ understanding
名 理解；了解

❽ time-consuming
形 耗費時間的

❾ require
動 需要

❿ on the same page
片 有共識

 試著更與眾不同

I am not very good with time management. Therefore, I tend to[11] work with someone else. In that case, they can give me a bit of pressure to keep things on track. In order to remind me of the deadlines, I will also paste a lot of reminders[12] around my desk. Basically, I can deal with various jobs on my own. However, when it comes to lengthy[13] and time-consuming tasks, it is a totally different story. Some kind of pressure[14] is really necessary for me.

　　我不擅長控管時間，因此，我傾向與別人合作，當別人給我壓力時，我才會按時間表來完成工作。為了提醒自己截止日期是哪一天，我還會在辦公桌周圍貼上許多提醒用的便條紙。基本上，不論是什麼工作，我都能獨立完成，但如果是很花時間的任務，那就另當別論，適度的壓力對我來說是必要的。

⓫ tend to
片 傾向；易於

⓬ reminder
名 提醒物

⓭ lengthy
形 冗長的

⓮ pressure
名 壓力

延伸note
面試時，沒有必要隱藏自己的弱點(weakness)，但重點要放在「你如何克服弱點」上。

答題TIPS看這裡！

不是每個人都擅長處理冗長又耗時的工作，在讓工作順利完成的前提之下，每個人都會建立屬於自己的一套時效管理技巧，應用得宜的話，就會有幫助，例如：I have set the deadline for each task and the next step is to meet it. （我已經替每一項工作設定完成期限，接下來就是按時完成了。）

Words & Phrases 時效管理的技巧

1 prioritize
按優先順序處理

2 schedule
安排執行日期

3 goal setting
設定目標

4 set the deadline
設定期限

Words & Phrases 延誤或耽擱期限

1 miss the deadline
超過期限

2 put off
延後

3 procrastinate
拖延

4 over five years
在五年之間

 進階實用句 More Expressions

I am pretty sure that I can meet the deadline.

我確信自己能在期限內完成。

Good time management skills really help when it comes to a lengthy task.

好的時效管理技巧對於處理冗長的工作很有幫助。

I don't know much about time management. I miss deadlines most of the time.

我不太懂時效管理到底是什麼，大部分的時候，我都會延誤。

UNIT 14

學習語言的欲望

Q Do you plan to learn another language in the future?

你將來有想要再學其他語言嗎?

你可以這樣回答

MP3 074

I am quite happy with how I am doing now. I really don't see the need to learn another language in the future[1]. Learning a new language takes so much time and effort[2]. I think I am too old for that. Spending time on going to class and studying isn't the life I am pursuing. Besides, even if I spend ten years on a specific[3] language, I might not be able to master[4] it, either. I'd rather spend time doing something I really enjoy, such as cooking and reading novels.

　　我對目前的生活相當滿意,完全不覺得自己有必要去學新語言。學語言會花上很多時間,也必須投注許多心力,我覺得我自己年紀太大,已經不適合做這件事,花時間在上課和唸書並非我追求的生活型態。況且,就算我花了十年去學某個語言,也不一定就能精通那個語言啊!我寧願把時間花在我真正喜歡做的事情上,像是烹飪或閱讀小說之類的。

❶ **future** 名 未來	❷ **effort** 名 努力;盡力
❸ **specific** 形 特定的	❹ **master** 動 精通

> **延伸note**
> sth. take time/effort指的是「某事耗費的時間/精力」;人當主詞時則要用sb. spend time on sth.。

換個立場講講看

I would love to learn another language[5] if I had time. However, it is quite impossible[6] for me. My job is really busy[7]. I not only need to work overtime during the week[8], but also go to the office on weekends. It is too difficult for me to get several hours for a language class. Furthermore, I am thinking of marrying my girlfriend next year. Once we started a family, life would be even busier. Come to think of it, I might never have time to start learning another language.

　　有時間的話，我當然想學新語言，但這對我來說幾乎是不可能的事情，我的工作非常忙碌，不僅平日需要加班，連週末也要去公司，要找出幾個小時去上課實在太困難了。此外，我預計明年和女朋友結婚，有了家庭之後，就更不可能有空，這樣一想，我可能一輩子都沒空學新語言了吧。

⑤ **language**
名 語言

⑥ **impossible**
形 不可能的

⑦ **busy**
形 忙碌的

⑧ **during the week**
片 週一至週五

試著更與眾不同

I have been thinking of learning Italian[9] for a long time. I want to do this because of my job. There is a possibility[10] for me to get promoted to the regional[11] manager for our Italian market. It would surely be helpful if I knew how to speak Italian. It's like those foreign businessmen[12] in Taiwan. A lot of them take not only Mandarin Chinese, but also Taiwanese classes in order to do business with us. Maybe I should hire a private[13] tutor to teach me the basic phonic[14] rules of Italian.

　　我想要學義大利語已經很久了，這是為了我的工作，我有可能被升為義大利市場區的經理，如果能懂義大利語，當然會很有幫助。就像來台灣做生意的外國人，很多除了學國語之外，還會學台語，以便和我們做生意。也許我應該請一個私人家教來教我義大利語的基本發音。

⑨ **Italian**
名 義大利語

⑩ **possibility**
名 可能性

⑪ **regional**
形 地區的

⑫ **businessman**
名 商人

⑬ **private**
形 個人的；私人的

⑭ **phonic**
形 語音的

Key Points

答題TIPS看這裡！

每個人想學語言的理由都不同，有些人是為了工作（job），也有人是為了偶像（idol）或迷上該國文化（如：電視劇），在答題時當然要盡量敘述自己之所以想學某個語言的理由。

Words & Phrases 與學語言有關的詞彙

1 textbook
教科書

2 phonic rules
發音規則

3 pronunciation
發音

4 vocabulary
單字

5 abbreviation
縮寫

6 grammar
文法

7 part of speech
詞性

8 sentence pattern
句型

進階實用句 More Expressions

I bought a few French textbooks for self-studying.

為了自學，我買了幾本法文的教科書。

In order to catch up with my classmates, I force myself to memorize ten vocabulary words every day.

為了趕上我同學，我強迫自己每天背十個單字。

I found it difficult to improve my pronunciation and accent. Maybe I should go find a stricter tutor for it.

我覺得要矯正發音和口音很困難，也許我應該找個更嚴厲的家教。

UNIT 15

談論工作的制服

Q Do you think uniforms for all workers should be required?

你覺得規定工作的制服有必要嗎？

 你可以這樣回答

 MP3 075

To be honest, I hate my uniform[1]. I think uniforms are not for everyone. Our uniforms are not custom-made[2]. They come in two sizes, but neither of them fits me well. I am a short person with a chubby[3] build[4]. When I tried the different sizes on, I got upset. The small one is too tight[5], but the large one is too loose[6]. Anyway, I am forced to wear a uniform that makes me look stupid. How am I suppose to feel good about working in the office?

老實說，我討厭我的制服，制服真的不是每個人都能穿。我們的制服不是為每個人量身訂製的，只有兩種尺寸可以選擇，但我穿起來都很難看。我算矮胖型的，當我試穿的時候，真的感到很心煩。小號的太小，大號的又太鬆。總之，我必須穿著那套讓我看起來很蠢的制服，這樣上班怎麼開心得起來呢？

❶ **uniform**
名 制服

❷ **custom-made**
形 訂製的

❸ **chubby**
形 圓胖的

❹ **build**
名 體型

❺ **tight**
形 緊身的

❻ **loose**
形 鬆的；寬的

 換個立場講講看

I actually prefer to work in a company that provides uniforms so that I don't need to worry about buying something suitable[7] to wear. I used to work in a company without uniforms, and the clothing became a competition for some of my co-workers[8]. It was quite[9] bothersome[10] to me. On the other hand, uniforms won't cause this kind of problem since everyone wears the same outfit. In addition, I can save a lot of time and money on ironing[11] and laundry[12] with a uniform. Those will be done for me at work.

我其實比較喜歡在有提供制服的公司上班，這樣我就不用思考要買什麼樣的衣服才適合。我曾經在一家沒有制服的公司上班，服裝對某些同事來說，變成一種競賽，那讓我覺得相當困擾。另一方面，有制服的話，因為每個人穿的都一樣，所以就不會產生類似的問題。此外，我還能省下熨衣服和洗衣服的時間和費用，因為那些公司都會幫我做。

❼ **suitable** 形 合適的	❽ **co-worker** 名 同事	❾ **quite** 副 相當；頗
❿ **bothersome** 形 麻煩的	⓫ **ironing** 名 熨衣服	⓬ **laundry** 名 送洗的衣服

 試著更與眾不同

I prefer to wear my own clothes to work because that makes me feel more confident. I can't imagine wearing something that was picked out[13] for me but not designed[14] for me. I stopped wearing the clothes which my mother picked since I was twelve years old. The style[15] she prefers is totally different from mine. Luckily[16], the companies I used to work for did not require wearing uniforms.

我喜歡穿自己的衣服去上班，因為這能讓我更有自信。讓別人幫我挑衣服，但衣服卻並非為我量身打造，這種事情我完全無法想像。我從十二歲開始就不穿我媽媽挑的衣服了，她對衣服的偏好和我完全不同。幸運的是，我工作過的公司都沒有要求穿制服。

⓭ **pick out** 片 挑選	⓮ **design** 動 設計
⓯ **style** 名 風格	⓰ **luckily** 副 幸運地；幸好

> **延伸note**
> 對衣服的偏好每個人都不同，比如：brand(品牌)、pattern(圖樣)、fashion(流行)…等等。

235

答題TIPS看這裡！

穿制服與否與產業（industry）和公司制度（regulation）有關。對許多老闆而言，穿制服會令客人覺得公司比較有制度，也能提升服務人員的專業形象（professional image）。更重要的是，一眼就能區分員工與客戶，因此在老闆的眼裡，穿制服往往有助於提升企業形象，至於員工喜不喜歡，就另當別論。因此，如果你工作的地方剛好有規定穿制服，大可直接說出你對制服的觀感。

Words & Phrases　描述衣服的相關資訊

1 **free size**
單一尺寸

2 **extra large/small**
特大號/特小號

3 **material**
質料

4 **design**
款式；設計

Words & Phrases　穿上衣物的各種說法

1 **dress up**
盛裝打扮

2 **button up**
扣鈕子

3 **put on**
穿上；戴上

4 **try on**
試穿

進階實用句 More Expressions

The uniform is free size, which means one size fits all.

制服沒有分尺寸，大家都穿同一種尺寸。

I don't like the material of my uniform. It makes my body itchy.

我不喜歡制服的質料，因為會讓我的身體發癢。

I don't mind wearing uniforms as long as they don't make us pay for themsw.

我不介意穿制服，只要別叫我付錢買就好。

Part 6

人際關係

Building Relationship

 動　動詞
 名　名詞
 副　副詞

 形　形容詞
 介　介系詞

 連　連接詞
 片　片語

UNIT 01

對網路交友的看法

Q **Do you believe in online friendship?**
你相信網路交友的關係嗎？

你可以這樣回答

MP3
076

I actually met my boyfriend online through one of those dating websites[1]. I know there are many people who are not who they say they are online, but meeting friends online or face to face[2] is actually very similar[3]. You have to be careful of[4] strangers. I only trust certain prestigious[5] websites because they seem to be more secure. However, it is still important to be careful. I spent almost a year observing[6] my boyfriend.

　　我和我男朋友就是在交友網站上認識的。我知道有很多人在網路上都會吹噓，但線上交友跟實際面對面其實很相似。無論如何，你都必須小心陌生人。我只相信有公信力的網站，因為看起來比較安全。當然，小心一點還是最重要的，我當時花了幾乎一年的時間觀察我男友的為人。

❶ **website** 名 網站	❷ **face to face** 片 面對面	❸ **similar** 形 相似的
❹ **be careful of** 片 小心	❺ **prestigious** 形 有名望的	❻ **observe** 動 觀察

換個立場講講看

I know people seem to have negative[7] feelings towards online friendships[8], but I think as long as you are careful and know what to look out for, it should be quite okay. There could be risks[9] since you can only know others through their words. But that doesn't mean you can't trust anyone online. The principle[10] is not to meet with your online friends alone and avoid meeting them in private[11] or isolated[12] areas. I do have an online friend. I met him through playing an online game. I think he is quite nice actually.

我知道大家對網路交友的印象都滿負面的，但我覺得只要你夠小心，知道要注意什麼，就沒問題。只透過文字去認識一個人當然會有風險，但那並不代表你不能相信所有網路上的人。有一個大原則是，別單獨和網友見面，而且要避免約在私人或人少的地方。我就有一個網友，我們是玩線上遊戲認識的，他人就滿好的。

❼ negative	**❽ friendship**	**❾ risk**
形 反面的；消極的	名 友誼	名 危險；風險
❿ principle	**⓫ private**	**⓬ isolated**
名 原則；原理	形 私下的	形 隔離的

試著更與眾不同

I don't believe in online friendships at all. There are so many scams[13] and liars[14] out there. He can say he is the Prince of Nigeria who is in trouble[15] and needs to borrow[16] some money from me! They might be nice to start with and say things you want to hear to gain your trust. However, once you let your guard[17] down, you become the catch of the day. If he lived overseas, there would be no way to verify[18] the story he told me. Therefore, I'd rather stay away from online friendships.

我完全不相信線上交友這回事，那上面有太多騙局和騙子了。他甚至可以說自己是奈及利亞的王子，有困難需要跟我借錢。這些人剛開始的態度都很好，會講你想聽的話，藉此獲得你的信任，可是，一旦你放下心防，可就變成他釣到的大魚了。如果對方住在海外，那我根本無法證實他的話，所以我不碰這種東西。

⓭ scam	**⓮ liar**	**⓯ in trouble**
名 陰謀；騙局	名 騙子	片 有困難
⓰ borrow	**⓱ guard**	**⓲ verify**
動 借；借入	名 警戒；防護物	動 證明；證實

答題TIPS看這裡！

線上交友有利有弊，總的來說，安全性（security）是一般人最大的考量。雖然相關社會案件不在少數，但實際上願意嘗試的人還是很多，尤其是年輕族群，也可以針對這個現象加以分析，如：It is very popular for young people to meet others through online games, but you have no idea who you are talking to.（年輕人流行藉由線上遊戲認識其他人，但你其實無法得知那些人的身分。）

Words & Phrases 詐騙與網路交友安全

1 **online scam**
網路騙局

2 **cyber crime**
網路犯罪

3 **personal profile**
個人資料

4 **report to the police**
報警

Words & Phrases 在網路上註冊帳號

1 **registration**
註冊

2 **user ID**
使用者名稱

3 **password**
密碼

4 **verification**
證明；核實

進階實用句 More Expressions

You need to watch out for online scams.

小心網路騙局。

Some of the online personal profiles look too good to be true.

有些線上交友的對象看起來實在太優秀，感覺不像是真實資訊。

I am quite open to online friendships as long as money is not involved.

只要不涉及金錢，我可以接受網路交友。

交友的廣泛度

Q **Do you prefer few or many friends?**
你喜歡朋友少一點，還是交友廣泛呢？

你可以這樣回答

MP3
077

I like to have as many friends as possible. I am a party animal; I love to be surrounded[1] by a lot of friends. It is much more fun than being alone. Therefore, I always invite[2] a lot of friends to my birthday party. I especially like going to the KTV with them, singing and screaming[3] together. If my friends could not come, I would feel very lonely[4]. That's also the reason I love making new friends, so that I can always find someone who is free to party.

我喜歡朋友越多越好。我熱愛派對，喜歡被許多朋友包圍的感覺，那樣比一個人要有趣多了。因此，我生日的時候總是會邀請很多朋友來參加派對，我尤其喜歡和他們去KTV，一起唱歌、尖叫。如果朋友無法前來，我就會感到寂寞，這也是我之所以喜歡交朋友的原因，這樣的話，就能確保有一起玩樂的人。

❶ **surround**
　動 圍繞

❷ **invite**
　動 邀請；招待

❸ **scream**
　動 尖叫

❹ **lonely**
　形 寂寞的；孤寂的

延伸note
熱愛派對的人會invite(邀請)許多賓客，注意此時發出的邀請函在英文稱作invitation。

換個立場講講看

Having many friends might be better for some people. However, I think finding someone I can actually talk to or share my feelings[5] with is much more important. I don't want to have friends who just pretend[6] they care about me, but actually say bad things about me behind my back[7]. To me, they aren't real "friends". Compared to the quantity[8] of friends one has, the quality[9] of friendships is more important. Instead of having a lot of fair-weather friends[10], I'd rather have one who is one of the best.

也許有些人喜歡擁有很多朋友，但我覺得找到真正能談心與分享心情的朋友比較重要。我不想要有那種假裝很在乎我，卻在背地裡講我壞話的朋友，這種人根本稱不上朋友。和數量相比，友誼的質量更為重要，和擁有一堆酒肉朋友相比，我只想要一個知心的朋友。

❺ share one's feelings
片 分享心事

❻ pretend
動 假裝

❼ behind one's back
片 在⋯背後

❽ quantity
名 數量

❾ quality
名 品質

❿ fair-weather friend
片 酒肉朋友

 ## 試著更與眾不同

To me, having more friends is ideal[11]. Not all my friends enjoy doing the same things. Some of them enjoy doing quiet things, such as going to the movies, whereas[12] others prefer doing more active[13] things, such as swimming and playing basketball. My interests are quite extensive[14], so I have friends with different interests. It's good for me since I can always find someone who shares the same enthusiasm[15]. I could spend hours discussing[16] a movie with my friends, for example.

就我而言，擁有很多朋友當然是最好不過。不是每個朋友都喜歡做同樣的事，有些朋友喜歡做些類似看電影的靜態活動，也有些人偏好游泳和打籃球這類的運動。我的興趣相當廣泛，所以我有許多興趣各異的朋友。我覺得這是好事，因為我總是能找到和我興趣相投的人，我甚至能花好幾個小時和朋友討論電影呢！

⑪ ideal
形 理想的；完美的

⑫ whereas
連 反之；卻；而

⑬ active
形 活躍的；活潑的

⑭ extensive
形 廣大的；廣泛的

⑮ enthusiasm
名 熱情；熱忱

⑯ discuss
動 討論；商討

Key Points 答題TIPS看這裡！

喜歡呼朋引伴（outgoing）的人一般朋友都比較多，但每個人對朋友的定義不同。有的人覺得知心才算朋友，有的人則覺得能一起做某件事的就是朋友，甚至有的人可能不喜歡與人交往（unsociable）呢！

Words & Phrases 與朋友的互動

1 exchange ideas
討論

2 argue
吵架

3 have a chat
談心

4 be there for each other
彼此鼓勵

Words & Phrases 不受歡迎的類型

1 two-faced
雙面人的

2 hypocrite
偽君子

3 stingy
小氣的；斤斤計較的

4 calculating
愛算計的

🎤 進階實用句 More Expressions

Most of my friends are very outgoing.

我大部分的朋友們都很外向。

The new student seems a bit shy; I hope I can make friends with her.

新來的同學好像有點害羞，我希望能跟她交朋友。

My friends like to be around me because I am always friendly and bubbly.

我的朋友很愛和我待在一起，因為我不僅個性友善，還很活潑。

UNIT 03 和家人的關係

Q Are you close to your family members?
你和家人的關係親密嗎？

你可以這樣回答

MP3 078

Yes, I am very close to my family members[1]. I grew up[2] in a small family; I only have a younger sister other than my parents[3]. My sister and I used to fight a lot when we were little. However, as we grew older, I realized having a sister is really great. She knows me very well, and we share our feelings towards everything. She has left home for graduate school[4]. And when she comes back, we always share a room and can't stop chatting.

是的，我和家人的關係很親密。我在一個小家庭長大，除了我爸媽之外，就只有一個妹妹。我們小時候經常吵架，不過，隨著年紀漸長，我發現有姊妹是件很棒的事，她很了解我，我們會分享對事物的感想。為了唸研究所，她離開家裡。每次她回來，我們都要擠同一個房間，而且總是聊到停不下來。

❶ **member**
名 成員

❷ **grow up**
片 成長；長大

❸ **parent**
名 父親；母親

❹ **graduate school**
片 研究所

延伸note
兄弟姊妹共享同一間房，經常會利用上下舖來節省空間，這種上下舖的床稱為bunk bed。

換個立場講講看

Not really. I am an only child[5] and I think my mother interferes[6] in my life too much. She wants to know everything I am doing and is very opinionated[7]. I sometimes hide the truth from her in order not to be nagged[8]. Luckily, I live in the

school dormitory[9] now. I am closer to my father. He is always supportive of what I do. I believe that he will always encourage[10] me to pursue my dreams.

不太親，我是獨生子，我覺得我媽媽太愛干涉我的生活了。她想知道所有的事情，意見又很多，我有時候甚至會為了不被嘮叨而隱瞞事情。幸運的是，我現在住在學校的宿舍。我和我爸爸的關係比較親，他總是很支持我，我相信他會鼓勵我去追求夢想。

⑤ only child 片 獨生子；獨生女	**⑥ interfere** 動 介入；干涉	**⑦ opinionated** 形 堅持己見的
⑧ nag 動 不斷嘮叨	**⑨ dormitory** 名 宿舍	**⑩ encourage** 動 鼓勵

試著更與眾不同

Well, I am very close to my parents, but not so close to my siblings. I am the youngest in the family. I have two older brothers, but they are a lot older than me. They were college students when I was still a toddler[11]. I don't know if it's because of the sex difference or the generation gap[12]. We don't have much in common. However, I am very close to my parents. They treat me like a princess[13]. My aunt told me that I was totally spoiled[14] when I was in junior high. Fortunately, I've changed a lot.

我和父母的關係非常親，但和兄弟姊妹就不怎麼親了。我是家裡排行最小的。我有兩個哥哥，但他們的年紀和我差很多，我還在學走的時候，他們就已經是大學生了。我不知道是因為性別還是代溝，我們的共通點並不多。不過，我和父母的關係很親密，他們像對待公主般地寵我，我阿姨說國中時期的我根本就是個被寵壞的小孩，幸運的是，我改變了很多。

⑪ toddler 名 學步的小孩	**⑫ generation gap** 片 代溝
⑬ princess 名 公主	**⑭ spoiled** 形 被寵壞的

> **延伸note**
> 講人有「公主病」，也可以用spoiled girl來說；另外還有princess complex（公主情節）的說法。

答題TIPS看這裡！

問題的重點在於和家庭成員的關係，通常會專注在父母以及兄弟姊妹上，兩者可以分開討論。親戚（relative）的部分一般不用特別說，但如果你和某位親戚特別親密，倒是可以多加闡述，解釋之所以這麼親密的原因，例如：I am very close to my aunt because she took care of me when I was little.（我跟阿姨的關係很好，因為我小時候都是她在照顧我。）

Words & Phrases　介紹家庭成員們

1. **sibling**
   兄弟姊妹
2. **cousin**
   表/堂兄弟姊妹
3. **stepfather**
   繼父
4. **stepmother**
   繼母

Words & Phrases　形容家庭關係

1. **loving and caring**
   很關愛的
2. **harmonious**
   和樂的；和諧的
3. **cold**
   冷漠的
4. **dysfunctional**
   不正常的；失衡的

 進階實用句 More Expressions

My family members are very loving and caring towards each other.

我的家人會互相關懷。

I don't know why my brother is cold to me.

我不知道我哥哥對我為何這麼冷淡。

I would say my household is pretty dysfunctional; my father never shows up when we need him.

要我說的話，我家並非正常的家庭，我爸爸從來沒在我們需要他的時候出現過。

UNIT 04

因遲到而讓別人等待

Q How do you feel if others have to wait for you?
讓別人等你的時候，你會有什麼感覺？

你可以這樣回答

MP3 079

I feel terribly sorry when I am running late[1] and make others wait[2] for me. Honestly, I am chronically[3] late. Even though I set an alarm[4] in advance, I still have to rush at the last minute. I don't want to be late, but I just can't help it. Maybe I should adjust my clock twenty minutes earlier. That way, I will think I am running late and actually leave home early and get to where I want to go on time.

因為遲到而讓別人等待時，我會感到非常地抱歉。老實說，我是會習慣性遲到的人，就算我事先設定鬧鐘，還是會在最後一分鐘衝向目的地。我不想要遲到，但就是會變成那樣，也許我應該把時鐘的時間調快二十分鐘，這樣的話，我就會以為自己遲到，但實際上比平常早出門，也就能準時抵達約會地點了。

① **run late**
片 遲到

② **wait**
動 等待

③ **chronically**
副 長期地

④ **alarm**
名 鬧鐘

> **延伸note**
> chronically late是指無論如何，都會拖延到最後一刻的人，因而有習慣性遲到的問題。

換個立場講講看

If I had an appointment[5], I would check the route beforehand[6] and head to the place early. And if the traffic got jammed up[7], which is very likely to cause a delay, I would call the person straight away to let him know that I was running late. No matter if it's with my clients or friends, I always try to be on time. To me, being punctual[8] is just the basic manners. I really don't like being late. By the same token, I do not appreciate it when other people are late, either.

如果我有約，我會事先查好路線，並提早出門。如果遇到很可能會讓我遲到的塞車情況，我會立刻打電話，告訴約會對象我會遲到。不管對方是客戶還是朋友，我都會盡量準時。對我來說，準時是基本禮儀，我很不喜歡遲到，同樣的，也不喜歡別人遲到。

⑤ **appointment**
名 （會面的）約定

⑥ **beforehand**
副 預先；事先

⑦ **jam up**
片 （口）阻塞

⑧ **punctual**
形 準時的

試著更與眾不同

I like to take my time. All my friends know I usually arrive a little bit late. Of course, I won't make them wait too long. It's usual for me to be ten minutes or so late. Most of my friends are quite patient[9]. They don't mind when I am late. They sometimes take their time as well. Meeting with friends is not like visiting[10] a client. I don't want to be too nervous[11] in my private life. Being strict[12] with time is just not my style. I don't mind waiting for people, so I think they should have the same attitude.

我喜歡慢慢來，我的朋友們也知道我通常會遲到。當然，我不會讓他們等太久，通常都晚個十分鐘左右而已。我的朋友大部分都很有耐心，不會介意我遲到，有時候，他們也會慢慢來。和朋友有約又不像是去拜訪客戶，我不想在私人時間裡也那麼緊繃，對時間斤斤計較不符合我的個性，我不介意等人，所以他們也應該也要能等我吧。

⑨ **patient**
形 有耐心的

⑩ **visit**
動 拜訪；探望

⑪ **nervous**
形 緊張不安的

⑫ **strict**
形 嚴格的；嚴厲的

Key Points 答題TIPS看這裡！

因為每個人的性格不同，對準時的定義和接受程度也大不相同，為了守時因素而翻臉的朋友也不在少數。想一下你是否會介意朋友遲到，無論答案為何，都建議加上具體的例子，讓回應更加活潑。

Words & Phrases　常見的遲到原因

1. **traffic jam**
   塞車
2. **car accident**
   車禍
3. **unexpected delay**
   突然有事
4. **work overtime**
   加班

Words & Phrases　對他人遲到的感受

1. **worried**
   擔心的
2. **anxious**
   焦慮的
3. **upset**
   不高興的
4. **annoyed**
   心煩的

進階實用句 More Expressions

I got caught up in traffic and was late for the meeting.

我遇上塞車，結果來不及趕上會議開始的時間。

I don't know what to do when my friend gets upset with me for being late.

如果我朋友因為我遲到而火冒三丈，我會不知道怎麼處理。

I get really worried if my friend is running late. I would wonder if there is an accident.

如果我的朋友遲到，我會很擔心，不知道是不是發生了什麼意外。

面對老闆時的態度

What would you do when you disagree with your employer?

當你不贊同老闆的觀點時，你會怎麼做？

 你可以這樣回答

MP3
080

I actually won't say a thing if I disagree with my employer. The company belongs to[1] him. He surely[2] can make decisions that he wants. If he made a stupid[3] decision, he should live with the consequences himself. I will do whatever he asks me to do even when it doesn't seem workable[4]. My boss is a very stubborn[5] person. Unless he feels the same way as you, he does not listen to you at all. Therefore, I won't bother[6] trying to persuade him, either.

當我不同意老闆的觀點時，我其實什麼也不會說。公司是他的，他當然有決定權。如果他真的做了很愚蠢的決定，那也應該自己承擔後果，我會照他的吩咐執行，就算看起來不可行，我也還是會照著做。我的老闆很固執，除非你的意見跟他想的相同，不然他根本不會聽，所以，我才不會耗費精力在說服他這件事情上。

❶ **belong to** 片 屬於	❷ **surely** 副 確實；無疑	❸ **stupid** 形 愚蠢的；笨的
❹ **workable** 形 切實可行的	❺ **stubborn** 形 倔強的	❻ **bother** 動 煩惱；擔心

 換個立場講講看

I will raise[7] the points and analyses[8] for my boss and show him there is a better way to do things. If he does not want to take my word for it, I'll be fine with that, too. As an employee, I can't really force[9] my boss to do anything. I hope things can work out[10] well for the company, so I give my perspectives[11] at the meetings. However, the final decision is still up to my boss. I will do what I can to make things go smoothly[12].

　　我會提出意見和分析給我的老闆，讓他知道有更好的處理方式。如果他不相信我，那也沒關係。身為員工，我其實無法左右老闆的決定。我希望公司的一切都很順利，所以會在會議上提出我的觀點，但最終決定權還是在老闆的身上，我會盡量努力，讓事情順利進行。

7 raise
動 提出；發出

8 analysis
名 分析；解析

9 force
動 強迫；迫使

10 work out
片 能夠解決

11 perspective
名 看法；觀點

12 smoothly
副 平穩地；順利地

試著更與眾不同

If I were hired to run the business for my boss as the general[13] manager, I would try to convince[14] him to release some of the power to me. In that case, I could really start to make adjustments[15] and improvements[16]. Of course, I would write reports and discuss the business with him. However, he should also trust me since that is what I was hired for. I would definitely say something if I disagreed with him.

　　如果我今天是老闆請來當總經理的，那我會試著說服他下放部分權力給我。這樣的話，我就能做一些改變及調整。當然，我也會用書面的方式向老闆報告進度。但既然我是被請來當經理的，他就應該要對我有一定的信任度，當我不同意他的做法時，我一定會向他反應。

13 general
形 首席的；總的

14 convince
動 使信服

15 adjustment
名 調整；調節

16 improvement
名 改進；改善

> **延伸note**
> adjust to為常見用法，意指「改變…以適應」，如：adjust myself to the life here。

Key Points

答題TIPS看這裡！

要跟老闆或上司說實話並不是每個人都做得到的事，最簡單的方法可能是順老闆的意，但老闆的想法有時候不一定周全，遇到這種情況，每個人會有不同的做法。選擇不直接與老闆溝通的人，背地裡有可能會批評老闆，口試的時候，最好不要讓面試官對你產生「不獨立思考」或「兩面人」的負面印象。

Words & Phrases 觀點與表達意見

1 point of view
觀點；立場

2 in one's shoes
站在某人的角度

3 bear with
忍受；忍耐

4 in one's opinion
就某人而言

Words & Phrases 意見不同時的做法

1 convince
說服

2 survey
調查

3 observation
觀察

4 execution
執行

進階實用句 More Expressions

My boss makes the decision, and I will handle the execution.

老闆做了決定之後，我就會執行他的決定。

Without a detailed analysis, we are not able to make an accurate anticipation.

如果沒有詳細的分析資料，我們就無法做出準確的預測。

I tried very hard to convince my manager that it was not a good idea, but he just wouldn't listen.

我試圖說服經理那並非好辦法，可他就是不聽。

UNIT 06

現代人的晚婚趨勢

Q Do you think people get married late nowadays? Why?

你認為現代人都晚婚嗎？為什麼？

你可以這樣回答

MP3 081

For sure! Just take a look at my friends; most of them are still single[1]. There are only a handful[2] of them who have a partner. They will probably plan to get married in the next couple of years. However, for those who are still single, I have no idea whether they can meet their Mr. or Ms. Right. Some of them keep complaining[3] that it is so hard to find someone suitable[4] at their workplace. However, there are also some who really enjoy the life of being single.

　　當然！看看我的朋友圈，大部分都還單身，只有幾個人有固定的交往對象，那些應該再過幾年就會結婚。但針對那些沒有對象的，我不知道他們究竟是否能遇到心目中的理想情人。有些老是在抱怨在職場上很難找到對象，但有些是真的非常享受單身的生活。

❶ **single**
形 單身的

❷ **handful**
名 少數；少量

❸ **complain**
動 抱怨

❹ **suitable**
形 適當的；合適的

延伸note
講人single(單身的)，在英文裡面還有bachelor(單身漢)與bachelorette(未婚女子)的說法。

換個立場講講看

Absolutely! Especially for those people who spent most of their time building up a career. The financial pressure[5] plays an important role[6] in our lives. Most people worry about certain realistic[7] issues, such as the ability to afford a nice house and a quality life. Therefore, most people around my age would choose to focus on[8] their careers while they are young. By the time they can support[9] a family, there might not be suitable candidates[10] for them.

那是肯定的！特別是那些把時間都花在建立事業的人。財務壓力對現代生活的影響很大，大多數人都擔心現實面的問題，像是自己是否有能力買房子或維持一定的生活水準。因此，和我差不多年紀的人大多會在年輕時專心衝刺事業，等到他們終於有能力成家立業時，卻可能根本找不到適合的對象了。

❺ **pressure** 名 壓力	❻ **role** 名 角色	❼ **realistic** 形 現實的
❽ **focus on** 片 專注在	❾ **support** 動 扶養；贍養	❿ **candidate** 名 候選人；候補者

試著更與眾不同

It seems to be common in modern[11] society. However, this doesn't happen in my family. Most of my family members got married at an early[12] age. My parents married[13] each other when they were twenty. And both of my sisters got married not long after they graduated from university. They both married their high school sweetheart. For those who could not find someone suitable, they might have been studying too hard when they should have been dating[14].

這個現象在現代社會似乎很普遍，但我家完全不是這樣。我家的人都很早婚，我爸媽二十歲就結婚，我的兩個姐姐也是大學畢業沒多久就嫁了，兩個都嫁給高中時期就交往的男朋友。那些找不到對象的人搞不好是因為太專心讀書，該約會的時候都沒有行動，所以後來才找不到對象。

⓫ **modern** 形 現代的；近代的	⓬ **early** 形 早期的	**延伸note** 表示女性晚婚，則用marry at a later age。敘述年齡也很類似，例：at my late 30s(將近四十歲)。
⓭ **marry** 動 與…結婚	⓮ **date** 動（口）約會	

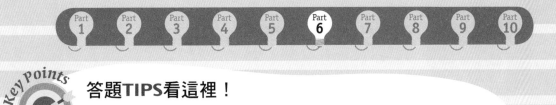

Key Points

答題TIPS看這裡！

晚婚似乎是社會的普遍現象，對女性來說更是一種壓力。坊間也有很多服務因而誕生，如婚友社（match making agency）及線上交友網站之類的；換桌約會（speed dating）或是六人晚餐（dinner for six）也是很風行的聯誼活動。

Words & Phrases　不同的交友方式與平台

1 matchmaker
媒人

2 dating site
交友網站

3 a blind date
盲目約會（透過他人介紹）

4 set sb. up
湊合別人（事先不知情的約會）

Words & Phrases　找對象時的各種態度

1 take control of
主控；主導

2 initiative
主動

3 passive
被動的

4 too cool for school
自視甚高的

進階實用句 More Expressions

I don't want to get married at an early age.

我不想太早結婚。

It's time for me to take control of my own fate. I take more initiative.

該是主控自己命運的時候了，我必須更主動一點。

My mother thinks I am too picky. I never like those men she tried to set me up with.

我媽說我太挑剔，她介紹的那些男生，我沒有一個看上眼的。

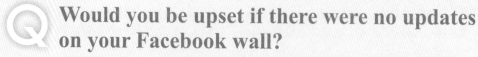

UNIT 07 網路社群的動態

Q **Would you be upset if there were no updates on your Facebook wall?**

如果你臉書上的動態消息沒有任何更新，你會失落嗎？

 你可以這樣回答 MP3 082

No, I wouldn't be. I am not a big Facebook user. I have a Facebook account[1], but I don't often update[2] the details[3] of my daily life[4]. I have some of my relatives as friends on Facebook, and I don't want them to see what I am doing in my spare time. They might call my mother and ask about it. I really don't want to hear my mother ask, "Who was that guy you were with last weekend?"

　　不，我不會感到特別失落，我不常用臉書。我有臉書帳號，但我不常在上面更新我的生活動態。我有加一些親戚為臉書好友，我不想讓他們知道我空閒時的行程，他們可能會打電話問我媽媽，我實在不想聽到我媽問我：「上禮拜跟你出去的那個男生是誰？」

❶ **account**
名 帳號；帳戶

❷ **update**
動 更新

❸ **detail**
名 細節；詳情

❹ **daily life**
片 日常生活

延伸note
ask會隨著搭配的介系詞而產生不同的意思。例：ask about(詢問)、ask for(要求)。

 換個立場講講看

Well, upset[5] is a strong word. Personally, I feel a little bit down[6] when there are no updates on my Facebook wall. I am kind of addicted to[7] Facebook. One thing that I must do before going to bed is go on Facebook. It has become a routine[8] for me. I go on it mostly to check what others have been doing and update

my status[9], too. I usually hear back from my friends pretty quickly. And if I didn't receive their feedback before I fell asleep, I would be kind of[10] disappointed.

　　講失落是太嚴重了一點。就我個人而言，如果我臉書的動態消息上面完全沒有更新，我會感到有點失落。我有輕微上臉書成癮的症狀，每天睡前一定要做的事就是上臉書，都已經變成我的例行工作了。我在上面通常會確認其他人做了些什麼事，以及更新我的狀態。一般而言，我朋友很快就會留言給我，如果在睡前都沒有回應的話，我會覺得有點失望。

⑤ upset
形 心煩的；苦惱的

⑥ down
形 情緒低落的

⑦ be addicted to
片 耽溺於…

⑧ routine
名 日常工作

⑨ status
名 狀態；情形

⑩ kind of
片 有一點

試著更與眾不同

I don't think it would happen to me. I am the Facebook queen[11]. I spend quite a lot of time on Facebook checking every update and leaving my comments[12] for my friends. My best friend does the same thing, too. She replies[13] to Facebook messages even in the middle[14] of the night. So even if I didn't receive any replies from others, I would still have one from her. There was one time that we chatted for the whole night because we enjoyed it so much!

　　我覺得那不太可能發生在我身上。我是臉書女王，我花很多時間在臉書上，看別人的動態更新和留言給朋友，我最好的朋友也是這樣，她就算半夜也會回覆臉書的訊息。所以就算其他人都沒有回應我的動態，我的好友也一定會有回應，我們還曾經因為聊得太開心而整個晚上都沒睡覺呢！

⑪ queen
名 女王

⑫ comment
名 意見；評論

⑬ reply
動 回覆

⑭ middle
名 中部；中途

延伸note
在臉書上po文的英文寫法為post，例如：post a video/picture…等等。

答題TIPS看這裡！

　　臉書是很受歡迎的社群網站，實際上沉迷臉書的人也不在少數。如果因為沒有人回應動態更新，就會感到很失落，這樣的人大概無時無刻都在留意個人的臉書動態，要形容這種沉迷於臉書的人，英文裡會用Facebook junkie這個詞彙。情緒被臉書牽動其實一點也不誇張，相信這樣的人我們身邊都有，可以拿來舉例。

Words & Phrases　與社群網路有關的詞彙

1 **text**
傳簡訊

2 **share an article**
轉貼文章

3 **press like**
按讚

4 **add location**
打卡

Words & Phrases　描述情緒的高低起伏

1 **feel down**
情緒低落

2 **feel blue**
感到憂鬱

3 **cheer up**
高興

4 **feel hyper**
心情很嗨

 ## 進階實用句 More Expressions

I would feel annoyed if no one replied to my post.

如果沒有人回應我貼的文章，我會感到很煩躁。

I turn off the Facebook message notification sound at work.

我工作時會關掉臉書留言的通知鈴聲。

In order to keep in touch with my friends, I log into Facebook every day.

為了與朋友保持聯繫，我每天都會登入臉書。

UNIT 08

培養溝通能力

Q How can you develop good communication skills in English?

你能如何培養英語的溝通能力呢？

 你可以這樣回答

 MP3 083

I listen to the radio[1] quite a lot to practice[2] my listening. If I want to answer[3] a question, I must understand what others are talking about first. Sometimes I will write down the questions I hear on the radio and try to answer them briefly[4]. At first, I could only give some key words. However, as I got used to this exercise, I could elaborate[5] on the questions further and make them into complete sentences. This is how I develop[6] my communication skills.

　我滿常藉由聽廣播來訓練聽力的。如果我想要回答問題，首先必須做的就是了解對方在聊什麼。我有時候會寫下在廣播中聽到的問題，並試著簡答。起初，我只能給出一些關鍵字，不過，在我習慣這種練習之後，就能進一步以完整句闡述，我就是這樣培養溝通能力的。

❶ **radio**
名 廣播電台

❷ **practice**
動 練習；學習

❸ **answer**
動 回答

❹ **briefly**
副 簡潔地；簡短地

❺ **elaborate**
動 詳細闡述

❻ **develop**
動 發展

 換個立場講講看

I like to watch TV and try to understand the storyline[7]. If I don't understand what the characters say, I will observe their facial expressions[8] and body language. It works quite well. After three months of practice, I found myself understanding more of the lines. If I watched a DVD, I would pause from time to time and imitate[9] the intonation[10]. My listening and speaking skills improved a lot after I tried this.

　　我喜歡看電視，並試著理解劇情。當我聽不懂裡面的角色在說什麼時，我會觀察演員的臉部表情和肢體語言，這對我來說很有用，練習了三個月之後，我發現我能聽懂的台詞越來越多。如果是看DVD，我會不時暫停，並模仿他們說話的語調，我的聽寫能力因此進步了許多。

延伸note
line在此處指「台詞」；寫滿台詞的劇本或舞台劇台本則要說script。

⑦ storyline
片 情節

⑧ expression
名 表達；表示

⑨ imitate
動 模仿

⑩ intonation
名 語調；聲調

試著更與眾不同

I like to read novels and try to memorize[11] the sentences I like. I started to keep a diary[12] in English when I was in high school. At the beginning, I could only write a few sentences. After several months, I then moved on to short paragraphs[13]. Now, I can even finish a composition[14] on certain topics. To me, memorizing new vocabulary as much as possible is very helpful; I highlight[15] the words I don't know while reading. Thanks to this, I can communicate with my foreign clients fluently[16] through emails.

　　我喜歡閱讀小說並記下我喜歡的句子。我從高中開始寫英文日記。一開始，我只能寫幾個句子，幾個月之後，我就能寫一小段文字，現在我甚至能針對特定主題寫文章。對我來說，擴充單字量很實用，閱讀時，我通常會標註看不懂的單字。也幸好我有這樣訓練自己，所以我能用電子郵件和外國的客戶溝通。

⑪ memorize
動 記住；背熟

⑫ keep a diary
片 寫日記

⑬ paragraph
名 段落

⑭ composition
名 作文；作品

⑮ highlight
動 使顯著

⑯ fluently
副 流暢地

Key Points 答題TIPS看這裡！

所謂的溝通能力並不只侷限於單一領域，聽、說、讀、寫都算是溝通能力的一環，只是每個人重視的區塊不同，建議依個人經驗來舉例。輕鬆如聽流行歌曲（listen to the pop songs）的方式，也是許多人會採用的方法。

Words & Phrases 培養溝通能力的方式

1 learn new words
學新的字

2 recite along
跟著朗誦

3 take a course
上課

4 make notes
記下重點

5 practice
多練習

6 imitate
模仿

7 attend the seminars
聽演講

8 make a speech
演說；演講

 進階實用句 More Expressions

When I write abstracts, I always keep them simple.

當我在寫大綱時，一定會讓大綱的內容簡單扼要。

I like to watch "Friends" and imitate the way Joey speaks.

我喜歡看《六人行》，學喬伊的說話方式。

I listen to ICRT an hour a day. I hope that I can improve my listening in the near future.

我每天聽一個小時的ICRT，希望我的聽力很快就會進步。

UNIT 09

和誰相處最自在？

 你可以這樣回答

 MP3 084

I prefer to be with my friends. Some of my relatives are very competitive[1]. They like to compare everything, starting from jobs to boyfriends or girlfriends. Sometimes they even talk behind our back. This is what really annoys[2] me. Being with my friends, on the other hand, makes me feel a lot more comfortable[3]. Some of my friends are as close as my family members. They always help me out[4] when I am in trouble. That's what real friends are for.

我比較喜歡跟朋友在一起，我的某些親戚很愛比較，什麼東西都能拿來比，從工作比到我們交往的對象，有時候甚至會在背後說我們的壞話，這是真正惹惱我的地方。和朋友相處就舒服多了，我和某些朋友的關係親密得像真正的家人，我有困難的時候，他們都會來幫我，這才是真正的朋友。

❶ **competitive** 形 好競爭的	❷ **annoy** 動 惹惱；使生氣
❸ **comfortable** 形 舒適的	❹ **help sb. out** 片 幫助某人擺脫困難

延伸note
遇到在背後說人壞話的情況，我們都會寧願對方say it to my face(當著我的面說清楚)。

 換個立場講講看

I prefer to be with my relatives such as my cousins from my father's side. We are the same age, so we grew up together. I am especially close to my younger cousin. We played together when we were little and we even went to the same

primary[5] school. I remember there was one time that I spent the whole summer vacation[6] with him. Even though they relocated[7] to a different area[8] several years ago, we still see each other at family gatherings.

　　我喜歡跟我爸爸那邊的親戚一起，例如我的堂兄弟。我們的年紀相近，所以是一起長大的。我跟我小堂哥的關係特別好，我們小時候一起玩，還上同一間小學，我以前還曾經一整個暑假都和他待在一起呢！雖然他們後來搬到不同區，家族聚會的時候，我們還是會見面。

延伸note
講到年齡差距，如果是剛好相差一歲，可以說A and B are (exactly) one year apart.。

❺ **primary**
形 初等的

❻ **vacation**
名 假期

❼ **relocate**
動 重新安置

❽ **area**
名 地區；區域

試著更與眾不同

I'd rather spend time with my friends than relatives. For some reason, I feel uncomfortable when I am with my relatives. We don't meet each other often, only once or twice a year on Tomb[9] Sweeping[10] Day and Chinese New Year. Therefore, we don't have much to talk about. I feel so awkward[11] when we all go to my grandparents' place. I usually bring a novel or my iPad to avoid[12] talking to them.

　　與其和親戚見面，我寧願和朋友相處。不知為何，和我親戚在一起會讓我感到很拘束。我們不常見面，就清明節和農曆春節時見面，一年大概一兩次而已，所以沒什麼話題好聊。每次去我爺爺奶奶家時，我都覺得很尷尬，我通常會帶小說或iPad去，以避免和他們聊天。

❾ **tomb**
名 墓碑；墳地

❿ **sweep**
動 清掃；打掃

⓫ **awkward**
形 尷尬的

⓬ **avoid**
動 避免

延伸note
清明節掃墓時，常做的事有weed(拔除雜草)、broom(掃地)、以及pay respect to(祭拜亡者)⋯等。

答題TIPS看這裡！

就現代人而言，因為大部分都是小家庭（small family），也很少有機會和其他親戚碰面，所以大多數人和親戚的關係比較冷淡，可能只有逢年過節時會有接觸，覺得陌生也無可厚非。但要是有從小一起長大的親戚，那就另當別論，回答時可以特別提出來。目前大部分的家庭結構為核心家庭（core-family）意指只有父母及子女的組成的家庭，和傳統的大家庭完全不同。

Words & Phrases　與人相處的感覺

1 **awkward**
尷尬的

2 **uncomfortable**
不舒服的

3 **pleasant**
愉快的

4 **relaxed**
放鬆的

Words & Phrases　人際互動的模式

1 **be supportive**
支持的

2 **engage in conversation**
主動談話

3 **give compliments**
讚美別人

4 **joke around**
開玩笑

 ## 進階實用句 More Expressions

My cousin always speaks in such a formal and polite way.

我表哥講話總是很正式、有禮。

I can joke around with my friends, but I can't do that with my relatives.

我可以和朋友亂開玩笑，但我沒辦法跟親戚這樣做。

I struggle to engage in conversation with my relatives because I don't know much about them.

我很難跟親戚一直聊下去，因為我對他們的了解不多。

UNIT 10

最佳的求助對象

Q If you had a problem, would you go to your friends or family? Why?

當你有問題時，你會向朋友還是家人求助？為什麼？

MP3 085

你可以這樣回答

I would go to my family for help for sure[1]! My parents and other family members are very supportive[2]; I couldn't find anyone who loves me as much as they do. My father is always very protective[3] of my brother and me. He wants us to remember that we can count on[4] him no matter what happens. I feel secure when I am with him. Even though I am an adult[5] now, my parents still treat me as their little girl. I love them so much, and they are definitely my first preference[6].

我一定會向家人求助，我爸媽和其他家人都很支持我，我找不到像他們那樣愛我的人了。我爸從小就很保護我和我哥，他總是希望我們記得，無論發生什麼事，我們永遠都可以依靠他。和爸爸在一起的時候，我就很有安全感。儘管我現在已經是成人了，我爸媽依然把我看做他們的小公主。我很愛我的家人，他們肯定會是我第一個求助的對象。

❶ for sure 片 肯定；無疑	❷ supportive 形 支援的	❸ protective 形 保護的
❹ count on 片 依靠	❺ adult 名 成年人	❻ preference 名 偏愛的事物或人

換個立場講講看

If I had a problem, I would usually keep my family out of it as much as possible[7]. My parents worry about me a lot. If I asked for their help, they would immediately[8] think that I were seriously in trouble. I know they care about me, but sometimes they are just overreacting[9]. Therefore, I would like my family to stay out of my business as much as possible unless it involves[10] money.

如果我遇上什麼問題，我通常不會讓家人知道。我爸媽很不放心我，如果我向他們求助，我爸媽會馬上認為有很嚴重的事情發生。我知道這是關心我的表現，但他們有時候真的是太反應過度了。所以，除非牽扯到錢的問題，否則我盡量不讓他們插手我的事情。

延伸note
business有「分內事」之意，常見的用法為none of one's business(與某人無關)。

❼ possible
形 可能的

❽ immediately
副 立刻

❾ overreact
動 反應過度

❿ involve
動 牽涉

 試著更與眾不同

I think it depends on what the problem is. If it is something technical[11], such as how to fix my computer or modify[12] my scooter[13], I would go to my friends for help because my family doesn't know much about machinery[14]. There's no way they could help me in this. My parents are public servants[15] and work in the national tax[16] office. Unless I needed to know how to get my tax return, I usually wouldn't ask for their help.

我會看情況。如果是技術方面的問題，比如修電腦和改裝摩托車，我就會向朋友求助，因為我的家人對機械沒什麼研究，根本就幫不上忙。我的父母都是公務員，他們在國稅局上班，除非我想知道該如何申請退稅，否則我通常不會找他們幫什麼忙。

⓫ technical
形 技術性的

⓬ modify
動 更改；修改

⓭ scooter
名 機車

⓮ machinery
名 機器；機械

⓯ public servant
片 公務員

⓰ tax
名 稅；稅金

Key Points

答題TIPS看這裡！

若是比較古板或性格保守的（conservative）家人，有些人就比較不願意讓他們插手自己的事情，甚至可能會比較依賴朋友。不過，本題並非二選一的題目，看事情選擇求助對象也許是最實際的做法。

Words & Phrases　需要人協助的情況

1 money problem
金錢問題

2 relationship advice
感情上的建議

3 business matter
工作上的問題

4 legal trouble
法律問題

Words & Phrases　幫助他人的表達

1 offer help
提供幫助

2 assistance
幫忙；協助

3 do sb. a favor
幫某人的忙

4 lend sb. a hand
幫某人一把

🎙 進階實用句 More Expressions

Would you mind telling me where the nearest bank is?

可以麻煩你告訴我最近的銀行在哪裡嗎？

I seek help from my co-workers, even for personal problems.

需要幫忙的時候，我會請教同事，就算是私人問題也一樣。

My father is very kind. He would offer help once someone asks him for help.

我的爸爸很仁慈，有人請他幫忙時，他都會伸出援手。

267

Q What is the most effective method of communication in your view?

就你而言,最有效的溝通方式為何?

你可以這樣回答

MP3
086

Talking on the phone is very convenient for me. However, to make the communication more effective[1], I write a summary[2] of the conversation[3] right away. I find this useful because it is likely for us to mishear[4] or misinterpret[5] what people say on the phone. If we can follow up with a memo[6] and confirm what has been discussed, there won't be any misunderstanding.

　　講電話對我而言非常方便,不過,為了讓溝通更有效率,我會在結束對話之後,立即寫一份摘要,列出剛剛對話的重點。我發現這樣做很有幫助,因為講電話的時候很容易聽錯或想錯,因而誤解對方的意思。如果能在講完電話後寫下重點,和對方確認,就不會造成誤會。

❶ effective 形 有效的	❷ summary 名 總結;摘要	❸ conversation 名 對話
❹ mishear 動 誤聽;聽錯	❺ misinterpret 動 誤解	❻ memo 名 備忘錄

換個立場講講看

Personally, communicating with others through emails is the most effective way, especially when it is about business. Sometimes the issue involves more than one person. With an email, I can forward[7] it to whoever is involved or needs to be informed[8] about the progress[9]. If I use the phone, I would need to make quite a lot of calls. That is truly a waste[10] of time. Of course, some of my colleagues don't read the emails right away and forget about my message afterwards. In that case, he or she should take the responsibility since I've done my job.

　　我覺得用電子郵件是最有效率的溝通方式，尤其牽涉到公事時更是如此。有時候，與事情有關的人可能不只一個，寄電子郵件的話，我就能轉發信件給所有與工作有關、以及須要知曉進度的人。如果用電話，我就必須為了一件事打好幾通電話，這實在太浪費時間了。當然，我有些同事不會馬上看信，之後也忘了看，但這種疏失的責任在他們，我已經做到我的本份了。

延伸note
forward在電子郵件中是指「以轉寄的方式寄給大家」；如果是要副本給某人，則要說cc。

❼ forward
動 發送；遞送

❽ inform
動 通知；告知

❾ progress
名 進展

❿ waste
名 浪費；損耗

試著更與眾不同

It might sound traditional[11], but I'd prefer discussing something with others face to face. I can observe people's facial expressions and body language. Words can express the information, but they can't show people's true feelings. When I meet someone in person, I can see if he or she is in doubt[12] about what I say. This is not something I can pick up through emailing or calling. Besides, talking face to face builds a solid[13] relationship bonding[14].

　　聽起來或許很傳統，但我比較喜歡和人面對面地討論事情，因為可以藉此觀察對方的臉部表情與肢體語言。語言和文字雖能傳達資訊，但卻無法表示人們內心的想法。當我和某人碰面時，能藉由表情看出對方是否明白我說的話，這種細節不可能透過電子郵件或電話知道。此外，面對面談話能建立真實的人際關係。

⓫ traditional
形 傳統的

⓬ doubt
名 疑問；不確實

⓭ solid
形 堅固的

❹ bonding
名 （人際）結成特別關係

延伸note
body language（肢體語言）中，有一種分類為gesture（姿勢；手勢），經常為說話的輔助。

答題TIPS看這裡！

有效的溝通方式見仁見智。可能與性格有關，較內向或不擅於交際的人會傾向於間接的溝通方式（例如：電子郵件）；不過，有效率的溝通方式也可能因為事情的性質而有不同的選擇。現在有許多通訊軟體可供大眾選擇（例如：Line），只要有智慧型手機，就能隨時聯絡，因為這種即時性，讓智慧型手機取代了許多傳統的溝通方式（如：書信）。

Words & Phrases　常見的溝通媒介

1 fax
傳真

2 telephone
電話

3 communication app
通訊軟體

4 email
電子郵件

Words & Phrases　關於會議、公事的溝通

1 log book
交接日誌

2 meeting minutes
會議記錄

3 phone conference
三方通話（電話會議）

4 teleconference
視訊會議

進階實用句 More Expressions

I need to prepare the agenda for the teleconference.

我必須替視訊會議準備議程表。

I always follow up with a phone call after I send out the email to make sure everyone received it.

我發過電子郵件之後會再打電話，以確認大家都有收到信。

The meeting minutes need to be signed and approved by the manager before being sent out to everyone.

會議紀錄要給經理確認以後，才能寄出去給大家。

UNIT 12

看重的朋友特質

Q What qualities do you look for when making friends?

交朋友的時候，你看重什麼特質？

你可以這樣回答

MP3 087

The most important thing I look for[1] when making friends is reliability[2] and trustworthiness[3]. In my opinion, a true friendship is having someone I can trust fully[4] and being sure that he or she will always have my back[5]. I had a terrible experience with a friend when I was in high school. I thought she was my best friend, but later I found her lying to me. That is why I have become a firm[6] believer in reliability. And I do appreciate the friends who have been by my side.

交朋友時，我最重視的就是信任感，我覺得真正的友誼朋友應該是找到完全可以信任朋友，而且你知道他們會支持你。我在高中時和朋友曾有過很不愉快的經驗，我視她為我最好的朋友，但後來卻發現她騙我，這也是我之所以這麼重視信任感的原因，也很珍惜一直陪在我身邊的朋友們。

❶ **look for** 片 尋找	❷ **reliability** 名 可信賴性	❸ **trustworthiness** 名 可靠
❹ **fully** 副 完全地；徹底地	❺ **have one's back** 片 支持某人	❻ **firm** 形 堅定的；堅決的

換個立場講講看

What I look for when making friends[7] are people who share common[8] interests with me. I enjoy outdoor[9] activities[10] like camping and mountain hiking. And if my friends also enjoy the same things, we have so much fun

271

together[11]. I don't think I can make friends with those who do not share the same interests with me. I would be struggling to come up with[12] some things to talk about.

　　我想找的朋友是和我有共同興趣的人。我喜歡從事戶外活動，像是露營與登山之類的。如果我朋友喜歡的活動和我一樣，那我們在一起的時候就會很有趣。我不覺得自己能和興趣不同的人交朋友，因為我會不知道要跟他們聊什麼。

❼ make friends
片 交朋友

❽ common
形 共同的；共有的

❾ outdoor
形 戶外的

❿ activity
名 活動

⓫ together
副 一起；共同

⓬ come up with
片 想出

 試著更與眾不同

The qualities I look for in friends are a good sense of humor[13] and an open mind. I think of my friends a lot, especially when I had a bad day or need someone to comfort[14] me. I think that is what friends are for. They listen to[15] my problems without judging[16] me and show me a different way of looking at things. It makes me believe what I was upset about is really not that bad compared to what some people have to put up with.

　　我重視的朋友特質是要有好的幽默感，以及開放的心態。我如果有一天過得不如意或需要人安慰的時候，就會特別想念我的朋友。我覺得能在我低潮時給予安慰的，才是真正的朋友，他們會聆聽我的問題，而不會批評我，而且會引導我用輕鬆的心態來看待事情，讓我相信自己遇到的事情其實沒有那麼糟，因為那和某些人要忍受的事相比，只是小事一椿。

⓭ humor
名 幽默感

⓮ comfort
動 安慰；慰問

⓯ listen to
片 聽

⓰ judge
動 判斷；認為

延伸note
a sense of後面加不同名詞，就能衍生出不同意思。例：a sense of satisfaction (滿足感)。

Key Points

答題TIPS看這裡！

每個人挑朋友的出發點不同，不見得每個人都喜歡良師益友，有些人重視能一起狂歡的朋友（hang out together）；也有不少人是因為有過去的經歷，才了解自己想要怎樣的朋友，回答時不妨多多舉例。

Words & Phrases　難以忍受的缺點

1　**bad hygiene**
　　衛生習慣不好

2　**bad manners**
　　沒有禮貌

3　**aggressive**
　　很兇的

4　**evil**
　　邪惡的

Words & Phrases　朋友間的爭執與溝通

1　**fight with sb.**
　　與某人吵架

2　**punch-up**
　　打架

3　**misunderstanding**
　　誤會

4　**lie to sb.**
　　對某人說謊

🎤 進階實用句 More Expressions

My best friend donates to charities twice a year.

我的好朋友一年會捐兩次錢給慈善機構。

What amazes me most is how I always see eye to eye with my best friend.

最讓我驚訝的是，我和我的好友總像有心電感應似的。

My best friend helped me a lot and didn't expect anything in return.

我的好朋友幫了我很多忙，而且不求回報。

273

手寫信的魅力

Q **Why do people feel better when receiving a hand-written letter?**

收到手寫信時，人們的感覺為什麼會比較好呢？

你可以這樣回答

MP3
088

Comparing with¹ texting or emailing, I am happier when receiving a hand-written letter from my friend. It's much more convenient than texting, so I can really feel the warmness² through his or her words. Because it takes quite a lot of time to do it, I treasure³ those letters more. I even have a box for the hand-written letters from my friends. Unfortunately, it has become a rare⁴ thing nowadays. Most people just don't do it anymore.

　　和簡訊與電子郵件相比，從朋友那裡收到手寫信會更讓我開心。打簡訊其實更方便，所以我能從手寫信的文字中感受到溫度。親筆寫會花很多時間，所以我更珍惜這些親筆信，我甚至有專門放朋友手寫信的盒子呢！可惜的是，現在已經看不太到手寫信，大部分的人都不願意寫了。

❶ **compare with**
片 和⋯相比

❷ **warmness**
名 溫暖；熱情

❸ **treasure**
動 珍藏

❹ **rare**
形 稀有的；罕見的

延伸note
compare with/to都可以用來「比較兩物之間的差異性」；但比喻的用法只能用compare to。

換個立場講講看

Social media⁵ seems to replace⁶ all the old-fashioned⁷ ways of communication. Technology has surely brought significant⁸ changes to our lifestyle. Nobody would deny that our lives have become more and more convenient. However, it has also taken away a lot of things that we were used to. Hand-written letters are a typical[9] example. Whenever I see the cards my friends have given me, I can't stop smiling[10]. You just can't replace the human touch with technology.

　　網路媒介似乎已經替代了以往的溝通方式，科技對我們生活型態的影響很大，大家都會認同生活因為有了科技而越來越便利。不過，科技也讓我們過去所習慣的事物漸漸消失，典型的例子就是手寫信。每次看到朋友給我的卡片，我都忍不住微笑，科技還是沒有辦法取代這種人與人之間的細膩情感。

⑤ media
名 大眾傳媒

⑥ replace
動 取代

⑦ old-fashioned
形 過時的

⑧ significant
形 重要的；重大的

⑨ typical
形 典型的

⑩ smile
動 微笑

試著更與眾不同

We live in such a convenient society that efficiency[11] has become the most important thing to most people. Because of it, writing a letter just doesn't seem worth the hassle[12] anymore. I personally prefer texting and emailing because it suits my fast-paced[13] lifestyle. Although some people think a hand-written letter shows real warmness, I don't agree with this. Emails and messages from friends also show thoughtfulness to me. I don't see a magnificent[14] difference between an email and a written letter.

　　現代生活非常便利，對大多數的現代人來說，效率才是最重要的事。也因此，不太有人會想花那麼多精神去寫一封手寫信。我個人比較喜歡傳簡訊及電子郵件，因為這比較適合快速的生活步調。雖然有些人覺得手寫信比較有人情味，但我不這麼覺得。朋友寄的電子郵件和簡訊同樣能表達他們對我的關懷，我不覺得兩者有那麼大的差別。

⑪ efficiency
名 效率

⑫ hassle
名 麻煩；困難

⑬ fast-paced
形 步調快的

⑭ magnificent
形 壯觀的

延伸note
efficient指「效率高的」；effective則指「有效的」。前者著重於過程，後者則重視結果。

Key Points 答題TIPS看這裡！

和冷冰冰的手機訊息或電子郵件相比，手寫信的價值在傳遞出來的濃厚人情味。在這個科技日新月異的時代，人們反而會懷念這種簡樸的溫度。但喜好科技及講求效率的人可能會覺得手寫信已失去價值，通訊軟體才是王道。如果你講不出原因，不妨直接講你個人喜不喜歡，以及什麼時候會寫手寫信；除此之外，還可以分析通訊軟體的優點。

Words & Phrases 形容手寫信

1. **valuable**
值得珍惜的

2. **retrospective (retro)**
復古的

3. **human touch**
人情味

4. **personalized**
個人化的

Words & Phrases 各種紙張媒介

1. **postcard**
名信片

2. **letter**
信件

3. **birthday card**
生日卡片

4. **memo**
便條紙

 進階實用句 More Expressions

Snail mail is a retro thing. I prefer sending emails.

傳統信件太過時了，我比較喜歡寄電子郵件。

Although it is not time-effective, I still prefer snail mail to email.

雖然沒有時效性，但與電子郵件相比，我還是比較喜歡傳統信件。

I always look forward to the surprises that come with the mail; my friends always put something little in there for me.

我總是很期待信裡面的驚喜，我的朋友都會放點小東西進信封。

對派對的想法

Q **Do you like hosting parties or going out for parties?**

你喜歡舉辦或參加派對嗎?

你可以這樣回答

MP3
089

I like to be invited to go to a party, but I don't enjoy hosting[1] one. Hosting a party costs quite a lot of money. You have to provide enough drinks and some finger food[2]. The most tiring thing is spending time on shopping, not to mention the decorations[3] and clean-up after the party. If I attend a party as a guest[4], all I have to do is to dress up and be there on time. However, in order to show my appreciation, I bring a present for the host.

　　我喜歡參加派對,但卻不喜歡舉辦派對。舉辦派對得花不少錢,你必須提供足夠的飲料和點心,最累人的是得花時間去採買,更不用說布置以及派對後的清理了。如果我只是以賓客身分出席派對的話,我唯一得做的就是打扮得美美的,並準時抵達會場。不過,為了表達我對主辦人的謝意,我會準備禮物前去。

① **host**
動 主辦;舉辦

② **finger food**
片 點心

③ **decoration**
名 裝飾

④ **guest**
名 客人;賓客

> 延伸note
> dress up指正式的打扮,女生也許會穿evening dress(晚禮服),男生就是tuxedo(燕尾服)。

換個立場講講看

I like to host parties because I can decide the theme[5] of the party. My favorite is a 70s party. I can dress up like Bob Marley with a big wig[6], colorful[7] clothes and some big bling[8]. I definitely invite lots of friends. It is always a good night!

However, if you asked me to organize[9] a company function, it would be a different story. I organized one several years ago, and it was really tiring. Every colleague had his or her preference. It was impossible to satisfy[10] everyone.

我喜歡舉辦派對，因為我可以自行決定派對的主題。我最喜歡的主題是七〇年代的派對。我可以穿的像巴布‧馬利一樣，帶上大假髮、穿五顏六色的衣服和誇張的飾品。我絕對會邀請很多朋友，每次我辦派對都很好玩！但如果要我舉辦公司的派對，那就完全不同了，我幾年前曾舉辦過一次，那實在太累人了，每個同事的喜好都不同，根本不可能讓所有的人滿意。

⑤ **theme**
名 主題

⑥ **wig**
名 假髮

⑦ **colorful**
形 鮮豔的

⑧ **bling**
名 珠光寶氣

⑨ **organize**
動 組織；安排

⑩ **satisfy**
動 使滿足

 **試著更與眾不同**

I like to be invited to go to a party; it makes me feel very special. Besides, I enjoy a good social occasion[11]. I like to host parties with funny[12] themes, such as a cartoon[13] characters party. All my friends invited must dress in a cartoon character's costume[14]. I always dress up as Snoopy. The fun I have is good for relieving work pressure. We take lots of photos and post them on Facebook.

我喜歡被邀請參加派對，這會讓我覺得被對方重視。而且，我很喜歡開心的社交場合。主題搞笑的派對很合我的胃口，比如卡通人物的主題派對。被邀請的朋友都必須穿上卡通人物的服裝，我都是扮史奴比。我覺得這種派對真的很好笑，能讓我從工作的壓力中解放。在派對上，我們會拍一堆照片，再上傳到臉書。

⑪ **occasion**
名 場合

⑫ **funny**
形 滑稽可笑的

⑬ **cartoon**
名 卡通

⑭ **costume**
名 服裝

延伸note
藉由派對狂歡，並get in a good laugh with friends(與朋友聊天、開懷大笑)也可以舒壓。

Key Points

答題TIPS看這裡！

派對可以辦得輕鬆或複雜，看個人的選擇。比較仔細或完美主義的人可能會因為辦派對這件事而緊張。但對於不愛熱鬧的人來說，除了不喜歡辦派對之外，可能也不好參與，因為人群會讓他們感到不自在。

Words & Phrases　常見的派對主題

1 pyjama party
睡衣派對

2 70s party
七〇年代派對

3 masquerade ball
假面舞會

4 Christmas party
聖誕舞會

Words & Phrases　派對的服裝要求

1 costume
化裝舞會的服裝

2 dress code
衣著標準

3 wig
假髮

4 accessory
配件

進階實用句 More Expressions

I made a beautiful mask for the annual masquerade ball.

我為了今年的假面舞會做了一個很美的面具。

I am going to a work function; I am not sure about the dress code.

我要去參加公司舉辦的餐會，我不確定應該穿什麼衣服比較適當。

I have never been invited to a pyjama party. I think I should host one.

我從來沒有被邀請去參加睡衣派對過，我覺得我應該舉辦一個。

UNIT 15

改變你的某個人

你可以這樣回答

MP3 090

My mother has been a very influential[1] person to me. I always look up to[2] her because she is a person who supports others and never expects anything in return[3]. My father passed away[4] when I was ten, and my mother has supported the family on her own ever since. Although my sister and I didn't see her a lot when we were younger, we knew she was busy working and made sure we could have a better life. And that's the reason why I am very close to my family.

　　我媽媽對我的影響很大，我一直都很尊敬她，因為她是那種願意支持他人，卻不求回報的人。我爸爸在我十歲的時候就過世了，從那時候起，我媽媽就獨立扶養我們，雖然我妹妹和我小時候很少見到她，但我們知道她忙於工作是為了要給我們一個更好的生活環境，這也是我之所以和家人如此親密的原因。

❶ influential
形 有影響的

❷ look up to
片 尊敬

❸ return
名 報答

❹ pass away
片 過世

延伸note
提到人過世，雖然有kick the bucket(翹辮子)的用法，但此說法較為不慎重，因此要小心使用。

換個立場講講看

One of my high school teachers has influenced me a lot. I was never good at studying, and most my teachers seemed to give up[5] on me. A lot of them didn't even try to push me because they thought it wouldn't make any difference.

Therefore, I kind of gave up trying myself and mixed⁶ in with the wrong people. In my final year of high school, my music teacher showed her belief⁷ in me and kept encouraging me to pursue further⁸ study. If it were not for her, I couldn't have become a college student.

　　我的一位高中老師對我的影響很大。我書讀得不好，大部分的老師都直接放棄我，很多根本就不想理我，因為他們認為我不會有什麼改變。因此，我當時算是已經自我放棄了，和一些不好的人混。直到高三那年，我的音樂老師相信我能做到，一直鼓勵我繼續唸書，如果沒有她，我不可能成為大學生。

延伸note
講到學年時，美國一般都是用數字表示：7年級到9年級(國中)以及10年級到12年級(高中)。

⑤ **give up**
片 放棄

⑥ **mix**
動 使混和

⑦ **belief**
名 相信；信任

⑧ **further**
形 進一步的

試著更與眾不同

My boyfriend has influenced me a lot. We were introduced to each other by a mutual⁹ friend. Well, we were very different. He is a vegetarian¹⁰, but I am not. It does cause some problems when we date. Every time we go to a restaurant, I need to make sure that they offer food for vegetarians. He never forces me to be a vegetarian, but I think he makes a valuable¹¹ point about the environment¹². Because of him, I am eating less meat now.

　　我男友對我的影響很大。我們是由一個共同的朋友介紹交往的，但我們其實非常不一樣。他是素食者，但我不是，當我們出去約會時，這點不同的確造成不少麻煩。每次去餐廳，我都得確定餐廳有供應素食。他從來不強迫我吃素，但我也認同吃素對環境有益，也因為他，我現在比較少吃肉。

⑨ **mutual**
形 共同的

⑩ **vegetarian**
名 素食者

⑪ **valuable**
形 有價值的

⑫ **environment**
名 環境

延伸note
吃素原因有：for the environment(環境)、for one's health(健康)和for religious reason(宗教)。

答題TIPS看這裡！

有影響力的人不一定是偉人或大企業家，日常生活中給你啟發的人，也可能來自於你周遭的市井小民。可能是因為他們對你的信任或是期望，或是講了正面鼓勵你的話，這些都可能影響你做的決定，甚至成為你人生的轉捩點，如：My friend encouraged me to take up the course to be a pastry chef.（我朋友鼓勵我去上烘焙相關的課程。）

Words & Phrases 帶給人的各種影響

1 positive thinking
正面思考

2 negative thinking
負面思考

3 long-lasting
長久的

4 inspiring
有啟發性的

Words & Phrases 表達影響的相關詞彙

1 impact on
影響…

2 be affected by
被…影響

3 be inspired by sb.
受某人啟發

4 under the influence of
在…的影響之下

進階實用句 More Expressions

One of my teachers once said something very valuable.

我的老師曾經說過一些很有價值的話。

My father never realized that he made such an impact on me.

我的父親從來不知道他對我的影響有這麼大。

I always try to stay positive because I know there are people who struggle more than me.

我總是盡量保持正面、積極的態度，因為我知道有很多人比我更辛苦。

Part 7

科技發展
Technology

 動 動詞   **形** 形容詞   **連** 連接詞

 名 名詞   **介** 介系詞   **片** 片語

 副 副詞

UNIT 01
紙本或電子地圖

Q **What do you prefer, paper or electronic maps?**
你比較喜歡用紙本地圖還是電子地圖？

你可以這樣回答

MP3
091

I know almost every car owner owns a GPS now, but I still prefer paper maps. With a paper map, I can see where I am and where I want to go at a glance[1], and I can work out the general direction[2] of my destination[3]. I can choose whatever route I want. On the contrary, I feel insecure[4] while using GPS because I don't get the general idea of the direction. I might end up in a graveyard[5] when my GPS picks up[6] the wrong directions.

　　我知道現在幾乎每一個開車的人都有GPS，但我還是比較喜歡用紙本地圖，因為我一眼就可以看出我目前所在的位置和要去的地點，還能看出大概的方向，自由選擇行車路線；相較之下，GPS看不出整體的路線，所以我會覺得很沒安全感，方向一指錯，我就可能被GPS帶到墓園去。

❶ **glance** 名 一瞥；掃視	❷ **direction** 名 方向	❸ **destination** 名 目的地
❹ **insecure** 形 侷促不安的	❺ **graveyard** 名 墓地	❻ **pick up** 片 挑選

換個立場講講看

I can't live without GPS now, especially when I go to a place I have never been. It is really handy to use because it reads out the directions to me while I am driving[7]. If I use a paper map, I must pull my car over[8] to look at a map.

Otherwise[9], it would be very dangerous and unsafe. On the other hand, GPS gives me directions while I am driving. Besides, bringing a paper map could be bothersome[10] when I am out, so I prefer GPS.

　　我沒有GPS就不行，尤其是當我要前往從沒去過的地方時，更需要它。GPS真的很方便，因為它會在我開車時指示方向，如果要查看紙本地圖，我還必須先把車停靠在路邊，否則就很危險。GPS就不一樣了，它在我開車時會告訴我行車方向。除了這一點之外，出門在外，還要帶紙本地圖有時候很麻煩，所以我還是比較喜歡GPS。

延伸note
與地圖(map)相關的詞彙還有atlas(地圖集；圖解集)；若是掛圖，要說wall map。

⑦ drive
動 開車

⑧ pull over
片 靠路邊停車

⑨ otherwise
副 否則；不然

⑩ bothersome
形 麻煩的

 試著更與眾不同

I prefer GPS because it updates automatically[11]. I have a paper map from 2008, and a lot of new roads are not listed[12] on it. There is no way you can update a paper map unless you buy a new one. GPS doesn't have this problem. Since it is based on[13] satellite[14] navigation[15], it is more reliable. However, you need to be careful when you set your destination. There was one time that I ended up on the opposite[16] side of town from the place I wanted to go.

　　我比較喜歡使用GPS，因為它會自動更新。我有一本二〇〇八年的紙本地圖，可是有很多新路線都沒有列出來。除非買一本新的，否則你根本不可能更新紙本地圖。GPS就不會有這個問題，它是由衛星導航，所以比較可靠。不過，設定目的地時要注意一點，我有一次就被帶到市區的另外一頭。

⑪ automatically
副 自動地

⑫ list
動 列舉

⑬ be based on
片 根據

⑭ satellite
名 人造衛星

⑮ navigation
名 航空；航行

⑯ opposite
形 相反的

Key Points

答題TIPS看這裡！

比較傳統的紙本地圖與電子地圖，最大的不同點就是電子地圖可以隨時更新，紙本地圖則不行，隨著道路設施的增建，紙本地圖的內容只會變得越來越老舊，到最後也許只能提供一個大概的方向。想要更新的話，就只能買一本全新的地圖了。除此之外，GPS所鬧出的笑話也不在少數，對於不怎麼信任GPS的人來說，舉實例也是個很好的方法。

Words & Phrases 道路封閉與其他狀況

1. **road work**
   修路

2. **breath test**
   酒測

3. **detour**
   繞路；繞道

4. **random check point**
   臨檢

Words & Phrases 道路或公路上的設施

1. **speed camera**
   測速照相

2. **toll booth**
   公路收費站

3. **street signs**
   街道標示牌

4. **traffic lights**
   紅綠燈

進階實用句 More Expressions

There is some road work ahead. We have to take a detour.

前面在修路，我們必須繞道而行。

I wish GPS could also tell me where the speed cameras are.

我希望GPS也能告訴我設有測速照相機的地點在哪裡。

All the toll booths have been taken down and replaced by the ETC system.

所有的收費站都被撤掉，被ETC系統取代了。

UNIT 02

打簡訊 vs. 電話

Q **Do you prefer to text people or call them?**
你比較喜歡打簡訊，還是直接用電話溝通？

MP3 092

你可以這樣回答

I normally text my friends instead of calling because I am not sure whether[1] they are free to talk or not. I don't want to interrupt[2] them when they are busy. Texting, on the other hand, is more flexible[3]. As long as they see my text, they will text or call me back when they are available[4]. Most of my friends work in an office. Using their mobiles[5] for personal matters is not acceptable[6]. Therefore, texting is a better way to communicate with them.

　　我通常不會直接打電話給朋友，我會傳簡訊，因為我不確定他們當下方不方便講電話，我不喜歡在朋友正忙碌的時候打擾他們。傳簡訊就沒有這個問題，只要他們看到簡訊，自然會在方便的時候回我。我大部分的朋友都在辦公室上班，不能用手機處理私人事情，所以還是傳簡訊比較好。

❶ **whether**	❷ **interrupt**	❸ **flexible**
連 是否	動 打斷；中斷	形 靈活的
❹ **available**	❺ **mobile**	❻ **acceptable**
形 有空的	名 手機	形 可接受的

換個立場講講看

It depends. If it were an urgent[7] matter, I would call them straight away. Sometimes when I can't get hold of my friends, I leave a voice[8] message and text them to explain[9] what is going on. Texting is convenient for sure, but calling is more efficient when I need them to respond[10] immediately. However, if it were not so urgent, I might choose texting or call them after work.

要看情況，如果是急事，我會馬上打電話。當我聯絡不到他們時，我會留語音信箱，再傳簡訊解釋發生了什麼事。傳簡訊是很方便沒錯，但當我需要朋友立即回覆我的時候，直接打電話顯然更有效率。不過，若不是急事，我會選擇傳簡訊，或下班之後再打電話給他們。

延伸note
講述事情的優先順序，可用priority這個單字；依事情的輕重緩急，則會用到urgency(緊急)。

⑦ **urgent**
形 緊急的；急迫的

⑧ **voice**
名 聲音

⑨ **explain**
動 解釋

⑩ **respond**
動 做出反應

 試著更與眾不同

I would call straight away because I am very slow[11] at typing. It is very hard for me to text my friends. I once even spent an hour and a half to notify[12] my friends about the dates and restaurant for our gathering. This is nothing compared to having serious discussions with them. I could be stuck[13] to the screen[14] of my cell phone for hours. Texting should be a tool for modern people. However, it obviously[15] doesn't suit me, so I would rather make phone calls[16] when I need to talk to my friends.

我會立即打電話，因為我打字非常慢，傳簡訊給朋友對我來說實在太麻煩了。我曾經為了通知朋友聚會的日期和地點，在那裡打了一個半小時的簡訊。這和討論嚴肅的事情相比，根本就還只是小意思，如果要做深入的討論，我可能會花好幾個鐘頭黏在手機螢幕前面。傳簡訊對現代人來說是一種方便的工具，但它顯然不適合我。當我需要和朋友講話的時候，我還是比較喜歡打電話。

⑪ **slow**
形 慢的；緩慢的

⑫ **notify**
動 通知；告知

⑬ **stick**
動 黏住；釘住

⑭ **screen**
名 螢幕

⑮ **obviously**
副 明顯地

⑯ **make phone calls**
片 打電話

Key Points 答題TIPS看這裡！

一般而言，公司會禁止員工在上班時間接私人電話或處理私事。即便現在通訊軟體（communication apps）非常發達，這項原則也沒有改變。但如果是突發的緊急狀況（emergency），就另當別論了。

Words & Phrases 簡訊相關單字

1 text
打簡訊

2 typo
打錯字

3 voice message
語音留言

4 leave a message
留言

Words & Phrases 打電話與人溝通

1 put sb. on hold
請某人稍等

2 hang up
掛掉電話

3 a wrong number
打錯電話

4 get through
接通電話

🎙 進階實用句 More Expressions

The person's line was busy. I kept being put on hold.

對方忙線中，一直叫我稍等。

It was an emergency, but I couldn't get through to my friend.

我有急事要找我的朋友，但電話就是打不通。

After several calls, I finally got through. But the person answering the phone told me that I had the wrong number.

在打了好幾通電話之後，終於順利接通，但對方卻和我說我打錯了。

UNIT 03
發明的進展

Q Can you compare the inventions of the past and those nowadays?

你能比較一下過去與現在的發明嗎？

 你可以這樣回答

 MP3 093

Certainly. Most of the inventions[1] of the past aimed to solve basic problems. For example, the light bulb[2] was invented so that people could utilize[3] the time after sunset. Of course, it came with the discovery[4] of electricity[5]. But it was surely invented because people needed something like it. On the contrary, most inventions now focus on certain improvements. For example, people expect newer computers[6] because we hope they will be "better".

當然可以，過去的發明主要是為了解決基本需求。比方說，為了讓人們能善用日落之後的時間，才有了燈泡。當然，燈泡和發現電的事實密不可分，但很顯然是因為人們有需要，才出現這項物品。相反的，現代發明的重點在於「改善」，例如，人們之所以想要擁有更新的電腦，是因為期望它變得「更好」。

❶ **invention** 名 發明	❷ **light bulb** 片 燈泡	❸ **utilize** 動 利用
❹ **discovery** 名 被發現的事物	❺ **electricity** 名 電；電力	❻ **computer** 名 電腦

 換個立場講講看

I can't imagine how difficult life would be without the gas stove[7] or the electric hotplate[8]. Gas stoves and hotplates these days even come with temperature[9] control[10] and so many fancy[11] functions that I am not able to name them all. I am

290

sure the person who invented the wood fire stove was very proud of[12] himself, but he probably didn't realize one day the wood stove would not be practical at all.

我無法想像沒有瓦斯爐和電磁爐的生活。現在的瓦斯爐和電磁爐甚至還可以控溫，具備我講都講不完的其他功能。我確定發明爐灶的人一定很為自己感到驕傲，但他應該沒想到爐灶有一天會變得這麼不實用。

❼ **gas stove** 片 瓦斯爐	❽ **hotplate** 名 加熱板	❾ **temperature** 名 溫度
❿ **control** 名 調節；支配	⓫ **fancy** 形 別緻的	⓬ **be proud of** 片 為…感到驕傲

試著更與眾不同

It is hard to picture what our lives would be like without the MRT. When I graduated from senior high, buses and trains were the most common public transportation[13]. Things like the MRT were like a sci-fi[14] to me. I never thought one day we could take the MRT to work. However, it actually happened[15] ten years later. The MRT is such a great invention; it is more reliable[16] than buses and trains. Now I don't need to worry about getting stuck in the traffic or missing the trains.

很難想像沒有捷運的生活會是什麼樣子。我剛從高中畢業的時候，公車和火車是最常見的大眾交通工具，捷運那種東西對我來說簡直就像科幻小說一樣，從來沒想過有一天會搭捷運去上班。不過，僅僅花了十年，這件事就成真了。捷運實在是很棒的發明，和公車與火車相比，捷運可靠多了，現在我完全不用擔心會被困在車陣中，或是錯過火車班次。

⓭ **transportation** 名 運輸工具	⓮ **sci-fi** 名 科幻小說	**延伸note** 對外國人直接說MRT(捷運)，對方可不一定了解，建議改用subway或metro。
⓯ **happen** 動 發生	⓰ **reliable** 形 可靠的	

答題TIPS看這裡！

日新月異的科技在生活中帶給我們很大的影響，尤其是電子產品（electronics）和家電用品（domestic white goods）。可以選擇一項自己熟悉的產品（例如：手機、電腦和電視），闡述過去到現在，這些產品有什麼大改變，或者是為現代生活帶來何種便利性。除此之外，也可以談改變不大的產品（例如：機車），這類發明除了外觀之外，功能性和設計原理並沒有什麼改變。

Words & Phrases 改變很大的發明

1 TV / smart TV
電視 / 智慧型電視

2 cell phone / smartphone
手機 / 智慧型手機

3 CD player / MP3 player
收音機 / MP3播放器

4 bullhorn / loudspeaker
大聲公 / 擴音器

Words & Phrases 發明與創新的目標

1 functionality
功能性

2 principles of design
設計原理

3 appearance
外觀

4 dimension
尺寸

進階實用句 More Expressions

The size of the latest cell phone is only as big as my palm.

最新款手機的尺寸不過就我的手掌般大。

I never thought that the company would release the latest model so fast.

我從來沒想過那間公司這麼快就推出新款式。

Although my scooter looks a little bit outdated, it still works quite well.

雖然我的機車看起來有點過時，但性能還是相當不錯的。

UNIT 04　網路對你的影響

Q Does social networking play an important role in your daily life?

社交網路對你日常生活的影響大嗎？

 你可以這樣回答

Yes, social networking[1] has become a very important part of my life. I use it to communicate with my relatives and co-workers. I am a sales representative[2], and I am out visiting clients most of the day. If there is something they need to notify me of, they send me messages through social networking. By doing so, they can reduce[3] the phone bill[4] if they have unlimited[5] Internet data plans. I also check my messages constantly[6] in order not to miss certain information.

　　是的，社交網路在我生活中佔有很重要的角色。我和親戚及同事都是用社交網路來聯絡的。我是一名業務，大部分的時間都在外面拜訪客戶，如果他們需要與我聯繫，就能直接用網路傳訊息給我，只要他們有網路吃到飽，這麼做就能省電話費，我也會一直確認訊息，以免漏看什麼資訊。

❶ **networking** 名 網絡	❷ **representative** 名 代表	❸ **reduce** 動 減少；縮小
❹ **bill** 名 帳單	❺ **unlimited** 形 無限制的	❻ **constantly** 副 不斷地

 換個立場講講看

Not really, I have a smartphone, but I am a technology moron[7]. I am not familiar with the social networking apps. I downloaded[8] Line and Facebook as well, but the system interfaces[9] look complicated. I spent quite a lot of time

293

learning how to call my friends via[10] the apps. I have been using them to call other people. The reception[11] is actually better than I expected. It is just like a normal[12] phone. I'd better learn more about apps.

不算有很大的影響。我有智慧型手機，但我是科技白癡，不熟悉那些社交網路APP該怎麼應用。我有下載LINE和Facebook，但系統介面看起來好複雜，我花了滿久的時間才搞清楚怎麼用APP打電話給朋友。我有用這些社交軟體打電話給別人，收訊其實比想像中好，就像一般電話一樣，我最好還是來學一下APP的其他功能。

⑦ moron
名（口）傻瓜

⑧ download
動 下載

⑨ interface
名 介面

⑩ via
介 藉由；憑藉

⑪ reception
名 收訊

⑫ normal
形 正常的

試著更與眾不同

Definitely! I downloaded various[13] social networking apps because not all of my friends use the same app. I am used to talking to my friends through these social networking apps. As long as I can connect[14] to the Internet, I can share my feelings with everyone around the world. In addition to chatting, sharing articles[15] I love has become more convenient. Honestly, I have been updating my blog[16] since last year.

這是一定的啊！我下載了各種不同的社交網路APP，因為不是每個朋友都用相同的軟體。我已經習慣用這些社交APP和朋友聯繫了，只要我連上網路，就能與世界各地的人分享我的心情。除了聊天之外，分享文章也變得更方便，老實說，我從去年開始就一直有在持續更新我的部落格。

⑬ various
形 各式各樣的

⑭ connect
動 連接；連結

⑮ article
名 文章

⑯ blog
名 部落格

延伸note
blog為web log(網路日誌)的縮寫，現在還有video log(影音部落格)，稱為vlog。

Key Points

答題TIPS看這裡！

現在幾乎每個人都將手機升級為智慧型手機，因為可以用社交網路來聯絡，節省手機的通話費，而且用社交網路還可以上傳照片，分享的功能更強大，因此成為與家人、朋友聯繫的主要媒介。

Words & Phrases　社交網路的設定與互動

1 friend invite/request
好友邀請

2 accept
接受

3 reject
拒絕

4 privacy setting
隱私設定

5 registration
註冊；申請新帳號

6 user name
使用者帳號

7 password
密碼

8 log in
登入

進階實用句 More Expressions

I received a friend invite from someone I don't like. I am going to reject it.

我收到一個不怎麼喜歡的人傳來的好交邀請，我打算拒絕接受。

I need to come up with a new user name and password to register for this new app.

為了申請這個APP，我必須想新的使用者名稱和帳號。

I am going to change my privacy setting on Facebook so that only my friends can view my profile.

我要更改臉書的隱私設定，這樣就只有朋友才看得到我的個人檔案。

UNIT 05 科技發展的缺點

Q **What's the disadvantages or negative influences of technological development?**
科技發展有什麼缺點或不良影響？

你可以這樣回答

MP3 095

I think technology has actually brought us more advantages[1] than disadvantages[2]. For example, I can talk to my brother who lives in the UK through FaceTime, so it does not cost me a cent[3] to make an international call. We can chat freely as long as I can connect to the Internet. As well, I don't need to worry about the time difference[4] when I leave him a message through an app. I can only feel the convenience technology brings us.

我覺得科技帶來的好處遠超過壞處。舉例來說，我可以跟住在英國的哥哥用FaceTime通話，完全不用花錢打國際電話，只要連上網路，我們就可以很自由地聊天。除此之外，當我在APP軟體上留言給他時，不用擔心時差的問題。我只感受到科技所帶來的便利性。

❶ **advantage**
名 優點

❷ **disadvantage**
名 缺點

❸ **cent**
名 分（美加的貨幣單位）

❹ **time difference**
片 時差

延伸note
即便題目問的是缺點，如果你真的認為科技發展的好處比較多，大可表達正面的觀點。

換個立場講講看

I think technological development[5] has got everyone addicted to his or her smart phone. Wherever I go, I see people staring at their cell phones, sending and receiving messages on Line or Facebook. Some experts[6] say that there are people

who actually feel more comfortable chatting through the apps than doing so in person. They are not used to talking to people face to face anymore. This might create[7] a serious social problem in the future[8].

我覺得科技的發展讓大家都沉迷於自己的智慧型手機。無論我到哪裡，都能看到人死盯著手機，不停在收發LINE和臉書訊息的景象。部分專家說有些人甚至更偏好用APP軟體來溝通，而不習慣面對面的溝通方式，這種現象以後可能會造成嚴重的社會問題。

延伸note
我們一般所說的「低頭族」除了smartphone addict，還有phubber這個最新說法。

⑤ development
名 發展；發達

⑥ expert
名 專家

⑦ create
動 創造

⑧ future
名 未來

 試著更與眾不同

I worry about security[9] issues[10] because almost everything can be done online nowadays. What concerns me the most are credit card transactions[11]. I have no idea who else has access[12] to the information or whether someone is trying to hack into the system to steal[13] the information. Technological development in general is a positive thing. It has improved our lives a lot. However, it has also brought a lot of unknown[14] risks.

我擔心網路安全的問題，因為現在幾乎所有的事都能在網路上處理。我最擔心的是信用卡交易，我不知道有誰能看到我的資訊，也無法確保是否有駭客正在嘗試入侵系統、竊取資訊。整體而言，科技發展的利多於弊，因為它的確改善了我們的生活品質，但同時也帶來許多潛在風險。

⑨ security
名 安全

⑩ issue
名 問題；爭議

⑪ transaction
名 交易；買賣

⑫ access
名 進入

⑬ steal
動 偷；竊取

⑭ unknown
形 未知的

答題TIPS看這裡！

科技帶來的正負面影響見仁見智，有些人對於過去習慣的做法被淘汰抱持著感傷。但是也有很多人享受科技帶來的便利性。科技帶來的缺點和不良影響很可能與控管有關，例如：資訊安全、機械設計上的缺陷、或是人為操控的疏失…等等，答題時可以從這些層面去聯想。

Words & Phrases　網路的便利性

1 informative
有教育性的

2 search engine
搜尋引擎

3 instant update
即時的更新

4 platform for friendship
交友平台

Words & Phrases　科技發展的問題

1 unable to spell
無法拼字

2 loss of traditional value
失去傳統價值

3 Internet security issues
網路安全問題

4 system malfunction
系統錯誤

進階實用句 More Expressions

I am so used to the funny spelling online.

我很習慣網路上奇怪的拼字法。

I am worried that computers might take over all our jobs one day.

我擔心有一天電腦會接手我們的工作。

Although life has become a lot more convenient, some people still miss how life used to be.

雖然生活很方便，但還是有人懷念以前的日子。

使用電腦的習慣

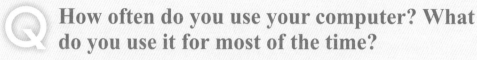

Q **How often do you use your computer? What do you use it for most of the time?**
你多常使用電腦？大部分拿它做什麼呢？

 你可以這樣回答

MP3
096

I use the computer every day because I am an engineer[1]. It's my duty[2] to check and test the computers at work[3]. I help my co-workers with problems related to their computers. I also need to maintain[4] the company database[5] from time to time. It is actually a very demanding[6] job. It's like racing against time because your customers won't be willing to wait for too long. They always expect you to serve them as soon as possible.

　　因為我是工程師，所以我每天都會用到電腦。在上班時間檢查與測試電腦就是我的工作，我幫忙同事處理與電腦有關的問題，也必須負責維修公司的電子資料庫。這份工作其實很忙，總是在跟時間賽跑，因為客戶都不願意等你太久，他們會期望你盡快服務他們。

❶ **engineer**
名 工程師

❷ **duty**
名 義務；本分

❸ **at work**
片 上班

❹ **maintain**
動 維修；保養

❺ **database**
名 資料庫

❻ **demanding**
形 高要求的

 換個立場講講看

Well, I spend several hours on my computer every day. I not only use it to check my emails, but also check out the updates on Facebook. I am currently doing my masters[7], so I have to do a lot of research[8] for my studies. There are various documents[9] stored in my computer. I also need my computer to do the assignments[10]. Of course, my computer is not only for academic[11] use. When I get tired of my studies, I will watch a movie that I downloaded online[12].

我每天會用好幾個小時的電腦。我不僅用它查看電子郵件，還會上網看臉書的動態。我目前在攻讀碩士，必須查很多資料，我的電腦裡也因此存有各式各樣的檔案，我也需要用電腦做作業。當然，除了課業用途之外，當我對研究感到厭倦時，我也會開啟電腦，選部我下載的電影來觀賞。

❼ **master**
名 碩士

❽ **research**
名 研究；調查

❾ **document**
名 文件

❿ **assignment**
名 作業；功課

⓫ **academic**
形 學術的

⓬ **online**
副 連線地

試著更與眾不同

I work as a waitress[13] in a restaurant[14], so I don't have access to computers during[15] working hours. I don't own a computer at home, either. Instead, I use my smartphone to go online to check my emails and chat with my friends. I also like to do online shopping because I don't often get weekends off. Even if I had a day off, I'd rather stay at home. Therefore, online shopping is the best choice[16] for me.

我是一名餐廳服務生，所以上班時間當然不可能用電腦。我家裡沒有電腦，我都用智慧型手機上網查看電子郵件、和朋友聊天。我也喜歡在線上購物，因為我週末通常都要上班，就算我休假，我也寧願待在家裡，所以，線上購物對我來說是最好的選擇。

⓭ **waitress**
名 女服務生

⓮ **restaurant**
名 餐廳

⓯ **during**
介 在…期間

⓰ **choice**
名 選擇

延伸note
新興字彙showrooming表示「先在實體商店看，再透過網路，以更低廉的價格入手商品」。

 答題TIPS看這裡！

現代人幾乎每天都會使用電腦，答題時可分為兩個切入點：上班（work）或是休閒（for leisure time）。除了專業性的用途之外，用電腦來放鬆的人可能還更多呢！例如：觀看影集、和朋友聊天、玩電腦遊戲…等等。

Words & Phrases 與電腦有關的詞彙

1 turn on
開機

2 screen saver
螢幕保護程式

3 Wi-Fi
無線網路

4 router
網路分享器

Words & Phrases 利用電腦做的事情

1 download music
下載音樂

2 play online games
玩線上遊戲

3 online dating
線上交友約會

4 pay the bills
付帳單；轉帳

進階實用句 More Expressions

I like to download music in my spare time.

平常沒事的時候，我喜歡下載音樂。

All I use the computer for is to play online games.

我的電腦單純只是用來玩線上遊戲的。

I am trying this online dating site to see if I can meet somebody.

我正在使用這個線上交友網站，看是不是可以遇到適合的對象。

UNIT 07
相片的適量性

Q **Do you think people take too many pictures nowadays?**

你認為現代人照太多相片了嗎？

你可以這樣回答

MP3 097

Yes, I think people are taking way too many pictures these days. I don't mind[1] the selfies[2] and photos with friends because they are part of the memory[3], especially when we go on vacation. To some extent[4], they are like souvenirs[5]. What I can't put up with are the pictures of food. I really don't see a point of it. I mean, you are not trying to put a menu[6] together. Why bother taking so many pictures of the dishes?

是的，我覺得現代人真的拍太多照片了。我不介意那些自拍照以及和朋友的合照，因為那當中包含著回憶，尤其是出去遊玩的照片更是如此，某種程度上，那些照片就像是出去玩的紀念品一樣。我真正受不了的，是拍餐點的照片，我真的不懂那有什麼意義，又不是在設計菜單，為什麼要拍這麼多食物的照片呢？

❶ **mind**
動 介意

❷ **selfie**
名 自拍照

❸ **memory**
名 回憶；記憶

❹ **extent**
名 程度；範圍

❺ **souvenir**
名 紀念品

❻ **menu**
名 菜單

換個立場講講看

Well, I really enjoy taking photos[7] and I have never thought I was taking too many pictures. Every time I look back to the photos, it always brings back the memory of that moment[8]. It is something that can't be replaced. I post[9] updates and new photos almost every day, so my friends can share the joy[10] with me. I always get a lot of feedback from my friends. I think they appreciate the photos, too.

嗯，我很喜歡照相，從來不覺得自己拍太多照片。每次看到那些照片，我就會回憶起當時的情景，這是無法取代的。我幾乎每天都會更新動態，並上傳照片和朋友分享，我總會從朋友那裡得到許多回應，我覺得他們一定也很喜歡我拍的照片。

延伸note
喜愛拍攝食物的人往往也是藉由delicacy(佳餚)記錄生活，回答時大可靈活替換關鍵字。

⑦ take photos
片 拍照

⑧ moment
名 時刻

⑨ post
動 在網路上發文

⑩ joy
名 歡樂；高興

試著更與眾不同

I think the popularity[11] of smartphones really influences people's habits[12] of taking pictures. In the old days, people wouldn't carry a camera around unless there were a special occasion like a birthday. However, ever since smartphones have gotten more and more popular, taking photos have become convenient. It's like everyone has a portable[13] camera. You can even upload[14] the photos immediately for your friends to see. Our lives have surely changed a lot during these last several years.

我覺得智慧型手機的普及確實影響了人們的拍照習慣。在以前，除非是有類似生日的特殊場合，否則大家不會帶著相機趴趴走。但是，自從智慧型手機開始普及化之後，照相變得方便許多，就像人手一台攜帶型相機似的，你甚至可以立即上傳照片，與朋友分享。過去幾年來，人們的生活確實有很大的改變。

⑪ popularity
名 普及；流行

⑫ habit
名 習慣

⑬ portable
形 便於攜帶的

⑭ upload
動 上傳

延伸note
在網路上常見的幾項更新動作有post(發文)、share(分享)、update(更新)…等等。

答題TIPS看這裡！

提到拍照，除了隨手可及的智慧型手機以外，現在也有很多人使用專業的數位單眼相機（digital SLR）。無論是藉由手機或專業相機，都有越來越多人在社群網站上分享照片，包括生活照（happy snaps）、專業個人寫真（glamorous photos）、婚紗照（wedding photos）、懷孕寫真（pregnancy photos），尤其是自拍照（selfie），近年來更是風行。

Words & Phrases　拍照的相關器材

1. **selfie stick**
   自拍神器
2. **memory card**
   記憶卡
3. **flash**
   閃光燈
4. **tripod**
   相機的腳架

Words & Phrases　相片與後製處理

1. **photo album**
   攝影集；相簿
2. **group photo**
   團體照
3. **selfie**
   自拍
4. **airbrush**
   修圖；修片

進階實用句 More Expressions

I love taking selfies and posting them on Facebook.

我喜歡自拍，再分享到臉書上。

My puppy is so photogenic. I love posting its photos online.

我的小狗真是太上相了，我超愛上傳牠的照片。

Many foreigners haven't seen a selfie stick; I think it is the greatest invention ever!

很多外國人沒有見過自拍神器，我覺得那是有史以來最棒的發明！

寄信的媒介

UNIT 08

Q **What is the best way of sending mail, using a mobile phone or emailing via a computer?**
寄信的最佳媒介為何？手機，還是用電腦寫電子郵件？

你可以這樣回答

MP3
098

I prefer sending emails via my computer because I can actually sit down and type properly[1]. Mobile phones are convenient for receiving and reading emails. However, the layout[2] of the keypad[3] can cause me problems when I want to reply with a lengthy email. If it's a brief[4] email from my friends, I may reply to him or her through my cell phone. But if it's about business, I would definitely use my computer instead.

　　我比較喜歡用電腦寄電子郵件，因為我可以坐下來好好打字。就收發郵件而言，手機當然很方便，不過，如果想要寫一封內容很長的電子郵件，手機上的按鍵就可能造成困難。如果從朋友那裡收到內容很短的郵件，我會用手機回覆；但若是與公事相關的信件，我就一定會用電腦回覆。

❶ **properly**
　副 適當地

❷ **layout**
　名 安排；設計

❸ **keypad**
　名 電腦小型鍵盤

❹ **brief**
　形 簡短的

延伸note
即便手機發達，還是有人習慣以電腦回覆email，原因各異，如：can type quickly(打字快)。

換個立場講講看

I actually prefer to use my mobile phone to email people because I can do it anytime and anywhere I want. In that case, I don't have to wait until[5] I get home. Most of the emails I receive are work-related[6] and require[7] an immediate

305

reply. I am a businessman[8] and spend a lot of time going on business trips to visit my clients. However, things need to be dealt with[9] even when I am not in the office[10]. To me, using a mobile phone is the best way.

　　我比較喜歡使用手機寄送電子郵件，因為隨時隨地都能回覆，不用等到回家。我大部分收到的郵件都與公事有關，需要即時回覆。我是一名商人，經常需要出公差、拜訪客戶，但是，就算我不在辦公室，也還是得處理公事，因此，用手機對我來說是最方便的方式。

⑤ until 連 直到…時	⑥ relate 動 有關；涉及	⑦ require 動 需要
⑧ businessman 名 商人	⑨ deal with 片 處理	⑩ office 名 辦公室

 試著更與眾不同

I am an interior[11] designer[12]. I carry my tablet[13] with me everywhere I go because I need to show my clients my latest designs. I also use it to send and receive emails because the screen is much bigger than a mobile phone's. When I send an email to a client, I usually have to attach[14] photos. I wouldn't be able to do that with my cell phone since all my photos are saved in the memory[15]. Anyway, my cell phone isn't a tool[16] I use to send my emails.

　　我是一名室內設計師，我會隨身攜帶我的平板電腦，因為不管到哪裡都可以使用。我必須給客戶看我的最新設計，所以我會用平板電腦來收發電子郵件，而且平板的螢幕比手機大得多。寄郵件給客戶時，我通常都需要附上照片，因為我的照片都存在硬碟裡，所以我不會用手機處理。總而言之，手機不會是我寄電子郵件時採用的工具。

⑪ interior 形 內部的	⑫ designer 名 設計師	⑬ tablet 名 平板電腦
⑭ attach 動 附加	⑮ memory 名 記憶體	⑯ tool 名 工具

答題TIPS看這裡！

　因為螢幕尺寸的關係，所以並不是每個人都偏好用手機寫信；另一方面，電腦體積又太大，不方便攜帶，因此，筆記型電腦（laptop）和平板電腦（tablet）變成許多人的最佳選擇。

Words & Phrases　電腦與手機的類型

1 desktop computer
桌上型電腦

2 laptop
筆記型電腦

3 tablet
平板電腦

4 smartphone
智慧型手機

Words & Phrases　功能與周邊產品

1 touch screen
觸碰式螢幕

2 blue-tooth
藍芽

3 portable power supply
行動電源

4 transfer cable
傳輸線

進階實用句 More Expressions

My smartphone is linked to my desktop computer.

我的手機與我的桌上型電腦有連結。

I found using a touch screen tablet is an easier way to send emails.

我覺得用觸碰式螢幕的平板來寄電子郵件比較適合。

I always carry a portable power supply with me in case I run out of battery power.

我會隨身攜帶行動電源，以防電池沒電。

網路資訊的可靠性

Q **Do you think Internet sources provide reliable information?**

你覺得網路上的資訊可靠嗎？

你可以這樣回答

MP3
099

Well, looking for information[1] on the Internet is surely efficient and convenient. I utilized it while I was in graduate school. However, I needed to be really careful because it was difficult to find the origin[2] of the information. I normally used it as a rough[3] guideline[4] to get a general idea. If I needed to use the data in my paper, I would cross-reference[5] it with books or other trustworthy sources. The Internet is a virtual[6] world; you have no idea where the information comes from.

　　從網路上找資料確實很有效率，也很方便。我唸研究所的時候，也經常用網路搜尋資料。但是，因為很難確認網路資訊的來源，所以真的要很小心。我通常只會做參考，如果是我必須用在研究裡面的資料，我就會和書籍或其他來源可靠的資料交叉比對。網路畢竟是虛擬世界，資訊從何而來，我們根本就無從得知。

❶ **information** 名 資料；資訊	❷ **origin** 名 起源；由來	❸ **rough** 形 粗略的；初步的
❹ **guideline** 名 指導方針	❺ **cross-reference** 動 互相參照	❻ **virtual** 形 虛擬的

換個立場講講看

If I had to do research on the Internet, I would only use the information from government[7] websites or that recommended by a government authority[8]. A lot

of the information on the Internet is based on personal[9] experiences. Some may have been exaggerated[10] and lost its true value. When I look at something on the Net, I am not able to[11] determine if it is truly correct[12]. Therefore, I only use the information from a reliable source.

　　如果我需要從網路找資訊，我只會採用政府網站或政府部門所推薦的網站。網路上的資訊很多都只是個人經驗，有些甚至言過其實，因而失去真實性，當我在看網路上的文章時，根本無法斷定哪些才是正確的資訊，因此，我只參考能信賴的資料來源。

❼ **government**
名 政府

❽ **authority**
名 官方；當局

❾ **personal**
形 個人的

❿ **exaggerate**
動 誇張；誇大

⓫ **be able to**
片 能夠

⓬ **correct**
形 正確的

 ## 試著更與眾不同

I like to do my research online because I can always find the things I want to know on different blogs. When I Google the recommended restaurants or certain popular items[13], there can be thousands[14] of results[15] for it. As I narrow the search down[16] to "feedback", I can see others' articles and how they feel about the products. Some may even write articles with photos and reviews.

　　我喜歡在網路上搜尋，因為可以在不同的部落格中找到我想要的資訊。當我利用搜尋引擎找「推薦餐廳」或「某些時下流行的產品」時，可能會出現好幾千條的搜尋結果。當我進一步增加「心得」的條件時，就能看到其他人對該項產品的評價，有些部落客甚至還會在文中附上照片呢！

⓭ **item**
名 項目；品目

⓮ **thousand**
名 一千；一千個

⓯ **result**
名 結果

⓰ **narrow down**
片 減少；縮小

延伸note
由網路寫手所寫的「看似心得，實則廣告」的文章，英文稱為advertorial（社論式廣告）。

答題TIPS看這裡！

大家都曉得網路上的資訊不見得可靠，有的還是請專業寫手做的商業廣告（commercial advertisement）。但還是有許多人會將之視為參考資訊，因為內容及呈現方式很吸引人。但現在大多數人在瀏覽網站文章時，都會自行斟酌。另一方面，如果是學術性的研究，一般不太會完全參考網路上的資訊，還是會選擇具權威性的書籍作為參考資料。

Words & Phrases 網路資訊的真實性

1 **trustworthy**
可以信任的

2 **truthful**
真實的

3 **myth**
謠言；迷思

4 **Internet rumor**
網路謠言

Words & Phrases 介紹產品的網路文章

1 **advertisement**
廣告

2 **review**
使用心得

3 **unboxing**
開箱文

4 **feedback**
評價

進階實用句 More Expressions

There are many commercial advertisements hidden in blogs.

部落格中往往包含許多的商業廣告文。

I would double-check the authenticity of the information I find on the Internet.

我會再三確認網路資訊的真實性。

A lot of recommendations from the Internet are disappointments once you go and try the products out.

有很多網路的推薦產品，在你真的用過之後，就會覺得很後悔。

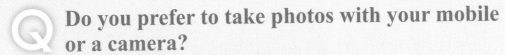

UNIT 10 手機 vs. 傳統相機

Q **Do you prefer to take photos with your mobile or a camera?**

你喜歡用手機拍照，還是用相機呢？

 你可以這樣回答

MP3
100

I actually prefer to take photos with my smartphone because I can upload my photos straight away. I moved out after I graduated from high school and went to university. It's far away[1] from my parents, so I try to take photos and upload them on Facebook. For my personal use, my smartphone is totally[2] enough[3]. There are also some classmates[4] who bring their DSLR cameras when we go out together. Honestly, I don't see the need for doing that.

　　我其實喜歡用智慧型手機拍照，因為照完就可以直接上傳。為了唸大學，我高中畢業後就搬出家裡，離我父母親很遠，所以我會盡量多拍照、上傳照片到臉書上。如果只是一般個人用途，我覺得手機就綽綽有餘了。我有些同學會在我們出去玩的時候攜帶單眼相機，老實說，我看不出有特別帶一台相機的必要。

❶ **far away**
片（離…）很遠

❷ **totally**
副 完全；整個地

❸ **enough**
形 足夠的

❹ **classmate**
名 同班同學

> 延伸note
> the need for表示「有…的必要」，相關變化有 needless(不必要的)，用法為：It's needless to…。

 換個立場講講看

I prefer taking photos with my DSLR camera. The pixels[5] and colors are of such high quality that normal cameras or mobile phones just can't compete[6]. I bought a digital[7] camera because I want to save the photos on a good memory system. It is more convenient for viewing them. When there are photos that I love very much, I just print them out[8] and display[9] them around the house. To me, decorating my house with actual photos seems better than viewing them by clicking[10] a mouse.

我喜歡用數位單眼相機拍照,高品質的像素和顏色是普通相機和手機無法比擬的。因為想要把照片存在良好的記憶體裡,所以我買了一台數位相機,瀏覽照片的時候很方便。如果有我特別喜愛的相片,我會把它印出來放在家裡,對我來說,用相片裝飾家裡比用按滑鼠瀏覽的感覺好。

❺ **pixel** 名 (電腦)像素	❻ **compete** 動 媲美	❼ **digital** 形 數位的
❽ **print out** 片 印出來	❾ **display** 動 陳列;展出	❿ **click** 動 發出卡嗒聲

試著更與眾不同

I prefer taking photos with my mobile phone because I love taking selfies and posting them online. If I used a traditional[11], non-digital camera, the only way to view the photos would be to develop them. It would be very troublesome[12] for me. Some friends suggested I buy a digital camera. But then I would have to find a transfer[13] cable[14] to upload my pictures onto the computer to share them online.

我很愛自拍上傳,所以我比較喜歡用手機拍照。如果是用傳統相機的話,看相片的唯一方式就是把它們沖洗出來,這對我來說很麻煩。有些朋友建議我去買一台數位相機,但這樣的話,我就必須準備一條傳輸線,把相片傳到電腦裡,才能上網分享。

⓫ **traditional** 形 傳統的	⓬ **troublesome** 形 麻煩的;棘手的	**延伸note** 除了傳輸線外,常見的手機周邊線材還有plug adapter(轉接頭)、extension cord(延長線)。
⓭ **transfer** 名 搬;轉換	⓮ **cable** 名 電纜	

Key Points

答題TIPS看這裡！

手機的拍照功能之所以這麼受歡迎，是因為它的便利性，拍完可以直接上傳。回答時可比較單眼相機（SLR camera）與數位單眼相機（DSLR camera），同時具備傳統相機與手機的優點，因而越來越受歡迎。

Words & Phrases 數位相機的特性

1 **resolution**
解析度

2 **megapixel**
畫素

3 **autofocus**
自動對焦

4 **chromatic aberration**
色差

Words & Phrases 與傳統相機有關的詞彙

1 **negatives**
一般傳統底片（負片）

2 **exposure**
曝光

3 **Polaroid**
拍立得

4 **develop photos**
沖洗相片

進階實用句 More Expressions

Some people are obsessed with taking selfies.

有些人超迷自拍照的。

I enrolled in a class to learn how to take photos with a digital SLR.

我報名了一個教你如何用數位單眼相機拍照的課程。

The traditional camera, which uses negatives, is very rare nowadays.

傳統底片式的相機現在很少見了。

UNIT 11

在網路上的消費

Q Do you think online shopping has increased people's spending?

你覺得網路購物增加了人們的花費嗎？

你可以這樣回答

MP3 101

Definitely! Online shopping is what I usually do at home. I find it amazing. However, with its convenience, I lose control[1] every now and then. Online shopping is just one click away from purchase. I don't feel like I'm actually spending money. Therefore, I often feel shocked[2] when I receive my credit card bills. I have even thought about having a calculator[3] with me while I browse[4] clothing on the Internet.

　　絕對有！我在家時經常會利用網路購物，我覺得那很方便，不過，也因為線上購物的便利性，所以我有時候會失控。只要按一個鍵，東西就買好了，沒有花錢的真實感，所以每當收到信用卡的帳單時，我都會很驚訝。我還想過要在瀏覽網路商品時，在旁邊放一台計算機呢！

❶ **lose control**
片 失控

❷ **shocked**
形 震驚的

❸ **calculator**
名 計算機

❹ **browse**
動 瀏覽

延伸note
收到的帳單，在英文裡要用bill；另一個常被混用的單字payment，是指要支付的款項。

換個立場講講看

No, I don't think so. I have never been a big fan of online shopping because you can't really touch or feel the products[5] before you buy them. The photos sometimes are deceptive[6], especially things like clothes and shoes. I tried online shopping several times, but I was never satisfied with[7] the quality of what I bought. The photos on the website always look so attractive[8], but whenever I got my product, I wondered if they had sent me the wrong item. It was nothing like what I saw online.

　　不，我不覺得。我沒喜歡過線上購物，因為購物之前無法親自確認商品的好壞。照片都很容易欺騙人，尤其是衣服和鞋子的圖。我曾經試過幾次線上購物，但從來沒滿意過商品。網站上的照片看起來都很吸引人，但當我拿到實際商品時，我都會懷疑商家是不是寄錯東西了，和我看到的照片根本完全不一樣。

> **延伸note**
> 誇張不實的報導為 exaggerated ad.；a tall tale指誇張的故事，並沒有負面的涵義。

⑤ product
名 產品

⑥ deceptive
形 虛偽的；欺詐的

⑦ be satisfied with
片 對…感到滿意

⑧ attractive
形 有吸引力的

 試著更與眾不同

Yes, I do think so. Online shops usually provide[9] a variety of[10] options. Once you start browsing, you might find something that you didn't think you need but want when you see it! For example, I was going to buy a sheet[11] set for my bed, but ended up buying a lot more than it. I also bought a new quilt[12] and some pillows[13]. It seemed a really good bargain[14] that I shouldn't miss at the time. However, I haven't taken them out from my closet yet!

　　是的，我同意。線上商店通常會提供很多選擇。當你開始逛之後，你可能還會想買原本不覺得自己有缺的東西！例如，我之前想要替自己的床購買一個床套組，但我最後買了一堆東西，還另外加買了棉被及枕頭。當時覺得這樣買超划算，但其實我根本就還沒從衣櫃中拿出來用呢！

⑨ provide
動 提供

⑩ a variety of
片 各種各樣的

⑪ sheet
名 床單；床套

⑫ quilt
名 被褥

⑬ pillow
名 枕頭

⑭ bargain
名 買賣；交易

答題TIPS看這裡！

線上購物的方便性讓人又愛又恨。一不注意，很容易就刷下大筆的金額（pay by card），直到收到帳單時，才驚覺自己花了這麼多錢；或是付帳時才發現信用卡已經刷爆了（max out）；相比之下，用現金付款（pay by cash）比較有花錢的感覺，比較能讓人有所警覺，看到錢包瘦身了，購物時就會更加注意自己的預算（budget）。

Words & Phrases 網路購物的單據

1 shipping advice
出貨通知

2 invoice
帳單

3 packing list
包裝單（貨物明細）

4 payment receipt
收據

Words & Phrases 包裝商品與寄送

1 shipping cost
運費

2 packaging
包裝

3 parcel
小包貨物

4 courier
快遞

進階實用句 More Expressions

You have to watch the shipping cost.

要注意運費的問題。

I am always excited if I know the courier is delivering a parcel today.

如果知道快遞今天要來送包裹，我就會很期待。

It is very troublesome to organize an exchange when I don't like the item I bought online.

當我不喜歡從網路上購買的商品時，要換貨很麻煩。

UNIT 12

萬能的翻譯軟體？

你可以這樣回答

MP3
102

No, I don't think so. There is no way that translation applications[1] would take the lead[2]. Languages are used by human beings[3] and they transform[4] over time. You can't have one dictionary[5] that covers every language use. Instead, you'll have to be familiar with a certain culture to know a language well. When you are doing an assignment, it is natural to look up the vocabulary[6] in the dictionary. However, you can't have a conversation with someone purely by relying on a translation app. It just won't work.

　　不，我不這麼認為，翻譯軟體不可能成為主流。語言是人用以表達的工具，會隨著時間而有所改變，所以，你不可能找到一本囊括所有語言用法的字典。相反地，要真正了解一個語言，你反而須要通曉該語言的文化。做作業的時候，查字典是很自然的事情，但你不可能單純用翻譯軟體和人對話，這根本行不通。

❶ application 名 應用程式	**❷ take the lead** 片 主導	**❸ human being** 片 人類
❹ transform 動 使變換	**❺ dictionary** 名 字典	**❻ vocabulary** 名 詞彙

換個立場講講看

I think using a translation app might work as long as the person I am talking to does not care about my slow response[7]. I know this is not the best solution, but not everyone is good at learning languages. Even if I were a genius[8], it would still take me some time to learn and master another language. That's why I have a pretty positive[9] attitude towards translation apps. As long as I can get the general idea, it is enough. I don't need the translation to be 100% accurate[10].

只要對方不介意我回應的速度慢一點，我覺得用翻譯軟體溝通是滿可行的方法。我知道這不是最理想的解決辦法，但不是人人都擅長學語言。而且就算我是天才，要精通另外一個語言，也需要花時間學習，所以我對翻譯軟體的印象很正面。只要我能理解大概的意思就夠了，不需要百分之百準確的翻譯。

延伸note
翻譯出來的文章，除了accurate(準確的)之外，也會重視是否smooth(流暢的)。

❼ **response**
名 回答；答覆

❽ **genius**
名 天才

❾ **positive**
形 積極的

❿ **accurate**
形 準確的；精確的

 ## 試著更與眾不同

I don't think translation apps can translate everything correctly. They make assumptions[11] about what you want to say. However, what they show could be totally wrong. And you might not notice the sentences were translated incorrectly[12]. For example, I once saw a bike[13] rental[14] billboard[15] that said, "Previous[16] hour free". It makes no sense in English. The correct way to say it is, "The first hour is free."

我覺得翻譯軟體無法準確地翻譯出每句話。它會推測你要講的意思，但最後的翻譯可能完全錯誤，而且你搞不好還看不出錯誤在哪裡。例如，我之前看到一個腳踏車出租店的招牌，上面寫著「Previous hour free」，英文完全錯誤，正確的說法應該是「The first hour is free.（前一小時免費。）」

⓫ **assumption**
名 假定；假想

⓬ **incorrectly**
副 不正確地

⓭ **bike**
名 腳踏車

⓮ **rental**
名 租賃；出租

⓯ **billboard**
名 廣告牌

⓰ **previous**
形 先的；前的

答題TIPS看這裡！

大家一定都有使用翻譯辭典或翻譯軟體的經驗，結果翻譯出來的文章或句子牛頭不對馬嘴，因而鬧笑話。或是看到很不通順的英文翻譯，便知道是用翻譯軟體的傑作。其實這些經驗都可以拿出來舉例。

Words & Phrases　具權威性的翻譯品質

1 evaluation
審核

2 certification
認證

3 authentication
鑑定

4 recognition
合格；認可

Words & Phrases　與翻譯相關的詞彙

1 oral interpretation
口譯

2 misinterpret
翻譯錯誤

3 interpreter
翻譯人員

4 lost in translation
溝通有誤

 進階實用句 More Expressions

If you used a translation app, it might make no sense.

如果你使用翻譯軟體，可能會詞不達意。

He misinterpreted what I said and thought I was judging him.

他誤會我的意思，以為我在批評他。

The waitress told me this is Mexican beef, but it is actually grilled chicken. Something was lost in translation.

女服務生和我說這是墨西哥炒牛肉，但送來的是烤雞，溝通上到底出了什麼問題。

UNIT 13

換手機的頻率

MP3
103

Q Do you like changing your mobile phones often?

你喜歡經常換手機嗎？

 你可以這樣回答

I don't change my mobile phone unless it has some unfixable[1] problem. I found most phones can last[2] quite long without major[3] problems. I don't see the need to change a mobile when it can work well. Some people change their cell phones for the sake[4] of fashion, but I don't do that in general[5]. However, if somebody gives his or her old phone to me, I don't turn down[6] the offer. For example, I got an iPhone 5 from my cousin because she wanted the latest iPhone.

　　除非我手機出現什麼無法維修的問題，否則我不會換手機。我發現大部分的手機用很久也不會有什麼大問題，手機還可以用的話，我不覺得有必要換新的。有些人會為了趕流行而換手機，但我基本上不會那麼做。不過，當別人要送我他的舊手機時，我可不會拒絕，像我之前就因為表妹想要換最新的iPhone，因而撿了她的舊iPhone 5用呢！

❶ unfixable 形 無法維修的	❷ last 動 保持良好狀態	❸ major 形 主要的；重要的
❹ sake 名 目的；理由	❺ in general 片 通常	❻ turn down 片 拒絕

 換個立場講講看

I change my mobiles quite often. I enjoy having the latest model[7] with the best functions. In addition[8], I think having the latest model is a status[9] symbol[10]. Not

everyone can afford changing phones so often, so this makes me proud. Besides, I use quite a lot of app software. In order to make sure they work well, I need to update the software. However, some updates can't be applied to the old cell phones. If this happened to me, I would be very upset.

　　我經常換手機，我喜歡擁有那些功能更進階的最新款式。此外，我覺得擁有最新型的手機也是地位的象徵，不是每個人都能負擔，這讓我覺得很驕傲。而且，我使用很多APP應用程式，為了確保這些程式順利運作，我必須更新軟體。不過，有些軟體更新不適用於舊手機，如果發生這樣的情況，我會感到很不高興。

延伸note
人人在意的特色不同：bluetooth enabled(支援藍芽)、polyphonic ringtone (和弦鈴聲)…等。

⑦ **model**
名 型號；樣式

⑧ **in addition**
片 除此之外

⑨ **status**
名 情形；狀態

⑩ **symbol**
名 象徵

 試著更與眾不同

Well, whenever a new model is released, I am always eager[11] to have one. However, the newest one usually means the most expensive one. It might cost me an arm and a leg, so I consider[12] it carefully. I bought an apartment[13] last year and have to pay my mortgage[14]. The burden[15] of paying it is not easy for me. I don't have much spare money for luxuries[16]. If changing my cell phone becomes necessary, I will have to save up hard for it.

　　當有新款手機上市時，我都很想要，但新手機通常會是昂貴手機的同義詞，價格可能昂貴到不行，所以我會很仔細地考量。我去年才買了公寓，還有貸款要還，負擔就已經夠重了，根本就沒什麼閒錢買奢侈品。如果真的需要換手機，我必須很認真存錢才行。

⑪ **eager**
形 渴望的；急切的

⑫ **consider**
動 考慮；細想

⑬ **apartment**
名 公寓

⑭ **mortgage**
名 抵押借款

⑮ **burden**
名 負擔

⑯ **luxury**
名 奢侈品

答題TIPS看這裡！

換手機往往是很多人都想要的事，在描述新手機的好處時，常見的有：體積較小、照相機像素較高、操作更加便利…等等，可盡量著重在進步的特色上；但是，即便新手機人人想要，但讓人猶豫的因素也不少，最常見的考量是昂貴的價格，或是用慣了一定的品牌或是款式，並不是每個人都很習慣智慧型手機的操作，所以也就不是人人都會更換手機。

Words & Phrases　新款手機的常見賣點

1. **lightweight**
   重量輕的

2. **waterproof**
   防水的

3. **kid-proof**
   防摔的

4. **large screen**
   大螢幕

Words & Phrases　手機的常見款式

1. **bar phone**
   直立式手機

2. **flip phone**
   掀蓋式手機

3. **slider phone**
   滑蓋式手機

4. **swivel phone**
   旋轉式手機

進階實用句 More Expressions

I have my eye on a new HTC phone.

我想要買支新的HTC手機。

The battery doesn't last long. I wonder if there's any problem with it.

這個電池沒辦法使用多久，我在想會不會是電池有問題。

I don't want to change my phone because I would lose the photos I took.

我不想換手機，因為這樣會失去我之前照的照片。

UNIT 14 科技影響社交性？

MP3 104

Q **Do you think technology has turned people into introverts?**

你認為科技讓人們變得內向、封閉嗎？

你可以這樣回答

Yes, I think so. Ever since the smart phone was introduced, more and more people use the communication applications to keep in touch with others. Some may even get used to not actually hearing[1] or seeing people, but chatting through the phone or computers[2]. I once watched a soap opera[3] called "Modern Family". The daughter told her parents to text her when she is in her bedroom. I think that is ridiculous[4] for a family to do.

是的，我覺得科技的確有這方面的影響。自從智慧型手機上市之後，越來越多人使用通訊軟體來和人保持聯繫，有些人甚至很習慣於這種用手機和電腦、不與人面對面接觸的聯繫方式。我曾經看過一齣叫《摩登家庭》的影集，裡面的女兒要求她爸媽在她待在臥室裡時，傳簡訊和她說話，我覺得這種方式對同住一個屋簷下的家庭來說實在太詭異了。

❶ **hear**
動 聽見；聽

❷ **computer**
名 電腦

❸ **a soap opera**
片 肥皂劇；連續劇

❹ **ridiculous**
形 可笑的；滑稽的

> **延伸note**
> 有些人認為科技的發展造成現代人只關心自己的事（mind one's own business），可由此切入。

換個立場講講看

Technology definitely makes our life more and more convenient, but it also has taken away a lot of human contact[5] from our lives. For example, I can choose to deal with an ATM instead of a bank teller[6]. I can reserve[7] a theater[8] ticket and have it mailed to my house without speaking to other people. This kind of lifestyle even affects the younger generation's[9] social skills. If a person was an introvert[10] before, he or she only becomes more introverted through advanced technology.

科技讓我們的生活變得更加便利，這是無庸置疑的事實。但它同時也帶走了許多人與人之間的相處機會。比方說：我可以去自動提款機領錢，而不用和銀行員接觸；買電影票時也完全不用與人接觸，預訂電影票之後，讓對方把票寄到我家就可以。這種生活型態甚至影響了年輕一代的社交能力，如果是本來個性就內向的人，只會因此變得更加封閉而已。

⑤ contact
名 交往；聯繫

⑥ a bank teller
片 （銀行）出納員

⑦ reserve
動 預約；預定

⑧ theater
名 電影院；戲院

⑨ generation
名 世代

⑩ introvert
形 內向的人

 試著更與眾不同

I don't think there's a relationship between technology and introversion. Some things are easier to deal with though a standard[11] computer procedure[12]. For example, if I told a customer service person that I would like to return[13] a shirt, he or she would try to convince me to keep it or swap it for[14] something else. On the contrary, I can avoid the sales pitch[15] and the awkward[16] conversation if I returned the goods online. Things like this do not reflect on my personality at all.

我不覺得科技和個性內向有什麼關聯。有些事情用標準電腦程序來處理會比較容易。就像如果我跟客服人員說我想要退一件衣服，他們會想辦法說服我不要退貨，或是以換貨取代；如果我利用線上程序退貨，就可以省掉被推銷的過程，也能避開尷尬的對話，這種事情和我的性格一點關係也沒有。

⑪ standard
形 標準的

⑫ procedure
名 程序；手續

⑬ return
動 退回；歸還

⑭ swap for
片 與…交換

⑮ pitch
名 （口）推銷；叫賣

⑯ awkward
形 尷尬的

Key Points 答題TIPS看這裡！

一般人會覺得抱怨的話很難說出口，所以如果面對面想表達對事情的不滿，可以用 I would like to make a complaint about... 來開頭，明確表達讓自己不滿的事項，同時用 would like 來緩和說話的語氣。

Words & Phrases 個性內向與行為

1. **unsociable**
   不善交際的
2. **self-centered**
   自我中心的
3. **isolation**
   孤立
4. **keep things to oneself**
   不願意分享

Words & Phrases 一些想表達的情緒

1. **complaint**
   抱怨
2. **compliment**
   讚美
3. **opinion**
   意見
4. **advice**
   勸告

進階實用句 More Expressions

I can't imagine life without technology.

我無法想像沒有科技的生活會是什麼模樣。

I like to do online shopping because I don't want to speak to a salesclerk.

我不想和售貨員講話，所以比較喜歡在網路上購物。

If I had a choice, I would avoid talking to people because I am lacking in self-confidence.

如果能選擇，我會避免跟人講話，因為我沒什麼自信。

325

UNIT 15 將手機關機的理由

MP3
105

When do you usually turn your mobile phone off? Why?

你什麼時候會將手機關機？為什麼？

你可以這樣回答

I normally turn off my cell phone before I go to bed because I don't want to be woken up[1] by the notification[2] sounds in the middle of the night. I like to talk to my friends, but some of them stay up really late to chat. If I stayed up late[3], the tiredness[4] I feel would influence my working efficiency. Therefore, a good sleep is definitely more important to me.

我睡前通常會把電話關機，因為我不想半夜被訊息的通知聲吵醒。我喜歡和朋友聊天，但他們有些人可以為了聊天而熬夜到很晚。如果我也跟著熬夜的話，疲倦感會嚴重影響到我的工作效率，所以好好睡一覺對我來說比較重要。

❶ **wake up**
片 醒來

❷ **notification**
名 通知；通告

❸ **stay up late**
片 熬夜

❹ **tiredness**
名 疲倦

延伸note
形容熟睡的狀態，英文用 sound/deep sleep；淺眠則用 light sleep，皆當名詞使用。

換個立場講講看

I never turn my phone off. I want to be available all times in case there is an emergency. I will turn the volume[5] down before going to bed, so the ring tone[6] would not wake up everyone else. If I am in an exam[7], I turn the phone on vibrate[8]. I still keep it on to ensure[9] that others can reach me. Besides that, I check my phone constantly to see if there is a missed call or message. My friend said

that this might make me nervous, but it's not true. I tried to turn off my cell phone before, but I figured out[10] that only made me even more anxious.

　　我從來不關手機。我要確保別人隨時可以找到我，以防有什麼突發事件。睡前我會把手機音量關小，以免鈴聲吵醒其他人。如果我在考試，我會把手機調成震動模式，但我依然會開著手機，這樣其他人才找得到我，而且我還會一直查看手機，確認自己沒有漏接電話或簡訊。我朋友說這樣的做法會讓我心情緊張，但事實並非如此。我曾經試著把手機關機，但發現那讓我更焦慮。

⑤ volume
名 音量

⑥ ring tone
片 鈴聲

⑦ exam
名（口）考試

⑧ vibrate
動 震動

⑨ ensure
動 保證；擔保

⑩ figure out
片 理解；明白

 **試著更與眾不同**

I think the only place I would turn off my cell phone is when I am on an airplane[11]. There is no reception in the air. Besides, there isn't much I can do besides reading novels or magazines[12]. I am happy to turn my cell phone off to enjoy peace and quiet. I can actually sit down and watch a movie while the flight attendant[13] serves[14] me a glass of red wine without interruption. Turning off my phone is not such a bad thing.

　　我想我唯一會把手機關掉的地方應該是坐飛機的時候。因為那時候手機沒有收訊，而且除了看雜誌之類的事情之外，我能做的事很有限。我很樂意關掉手機，享受片刻的寧靜，我可以安穩地坐在位子上，不被打擾地看完一部電影，而且期間空服員還會送紅酒來。把手機關機其實是很不錯的一件事。

⑪ airplane
名 飛機

⑫ magazine
名 雜誌

⑬ flight attendant
片 空服員

⑭ serve
動 為…服務

延伸note
飛機take off(起飛)和land(降落)的時候特別危險，為了乘客安全，所以會要求關機。

答題TIPS看這裡！

手機對現在人來說是不可或缺的必備品，但過度便利的情況也成為生活的壓力來源，有些人會在情況容許時，將手機關機，好讓自己放鬆一下；不習慣或是礙於工作而無法關機的人，也會視情況將手機轉成靜音（silent）或震動（vibrate）。現在還有smart watch這種產品，就算手機關機，依然能用smart watch替代，但要查看未接來電，還是必須用手機才行。

Words & Phrases　需要關機的場合

1. **in a meeting**
   會議上
2. **on the airplane**
   坐飛機
3. **during an exam**
   考試期間
4. **go to the movies**
   看電影

Words & Phrases　常見的手機操作

1. **unlock**
   解鎖
2. **type in**
   輸入
3. **turn up the volume**
   （音量）轉大聲
4. **turn down the volume**
   （音量）轉小聲

進階實用句 More Expressions

I use the pattern lock as my screen lock.

我用圖形鎖來當我的螢幕鎖。

For some reason, I have no phone reception in my hotel room.

不知道為什麼，我的手機在飯店房間收不到訊號。

I miss phone calls from time to time because I turn my phone on silent mode.

因為我把手機調成靜音，所以有時候會漏接電話。

Part
8

自然與環境
About The Nature

 動 動詞 　　 形 形容詞 　　 連 連接詞

 名 名詞 　　 介 介系詞 　　 片 片語

 副 副詞

UNIT 01 最喜歡的季節

Q **What's your favorite season?**
你最喜歡的季節是什麼？

你可以這樣回答

MP3 106

Summer[1] is my favorite season because I love going to the beach to enjoy water sports. Wearing my favorite bikini[2] and getting a nice suntan[3] are usually what I do there; it makes me feel relaxed and stress-free. My boyfriend took me surfing[4] last summer. It was truly exciting, and we plan to do that again this year. In contrast, I don't like winter much. I can't stand wearing thick layers[5] of clothes and a big jacket. I always plan a holiday to a tropical[6] island in winter.

　　夏天是我最喜歡的季節，因為我喜歡去海邊玩水上活動，我通常會在海邊穿我最喜歡的比基尼做日光浴，這樣能令我放鬆舒壓。我男友去年夏天帶我去衝浪，那真的很刺激，我們計劃今年再去一次。相反的，我就不怎麼喜歡冬天，我受不了穿厚重的衣物和大外套。冬天的時候，我總會計劃到熱帶小島避寒。

❶ **summer** 名 夏天	❷ **bikini** 名 比基尼	❸ **suntan** 名 曬黑
❹ **surfing** 名 衝浪	❺ **layer** 名 層；階層	❻ **tropical** 形 熱帶的

換個立場講講看

Well, I'd say winter. I enjoy the scenery[7] of a mountaintop covered[8] in snow. It is just calming[9] and peaceful[10]. I like to go to the mountains when it snows. The dreamlike snow scenes make the mountaintops look like heavenly places. The cold doesn't seem to bother me. It is a shame that we don't get enough snow for skiing or other activities here in Taiwan. I've been to the United States before. Building a snowman and having a snowball fight with my roommates made my life full of joy.

　　我會選冬天。我喜歡山頭白雪皚皚的景象，那令人感到沉靜、平和。我喜歡在下雪的時候上山，夢幻的雪景使山頭看起來就像天堂。我不太怕冷，可惜的是台灣的下雪量不夠，不能做滑雪之類的活動。我之前去過美國，堆雪人、和室友打雪仗讓我的生活充滿了樂趣。

延伸note
在國外，冬天的遊戲還有snow angels，人倒在雪地中，攤開(或揮動)四肢，做出「雪天使」。

7 scenery
名 風景；景色

8 cover
動 遮蓋；覆蓋

9 calming
形 使人平靜的

10 peaceful
形 平靜的；安寧的

試著更與眾不同

My favorite season is spring[11]. Everything looks so lively[12] during that time. It makes me very cheerful[13] to see the new leaves[14] starting to grow back. When the flowers blossom, I can really see the beauty of nature. What I enjoy the most are the cherry blossoms. I always plan a trip to Wu Ling Farmland[15] every spring to see the cherry blossoms and have a picnic under the trees like the Japanese people do. I wish I could visit Japan to do it the real Japanese[16] way.

　　我最喜歡的季節是春天。萬物生意盎然，看葉子開始重新發芽的模樣，心情就會跟著開心起來，花開的時候，真的能感受到大自然之美。我最喜歡的是看櫻花盛開，我每年都會計劃到武陵農場賞櫻，像日本人一樣，在櫻花樹下野餐，希望有一天我可以親自到日本，體驗一次真正的賞花風情。

11 spring
名 春天

12 lively
形 精力充沛的

13 cheerful
形 興高采烈的

14 leaf
名 葉子

15 farmland
名 農田

16 Japanese
形 日本（人）的

答題TIPS看這裡！

Key Points

一年四季都有吸引人的地方，重點在明確地指出喜歡的季節，以及之所以喜愛的原因。講述原因時，可以從當季的活動切入，例如：My favorite season is autumn because I love to watch the leaves fall.（我最喜歡的季節是秋天，因為我喜歡看落葉。）如果有與某季節相關的重要回憶（memory），當然也是延伸話題的好方法。

Words & Phrases　描述四季給人的感覺

1 brisk
生氣勃勃的

2 thriving
繁榮的

3 peaceful
平靜的

4 depressing
憂鬱的

Words & Phrases　植物成長的過程

1 sprout
發芽；生長

2 blossom
開花

3 bear fruit
結果實

4 wither
枯萎；凋謝

進階實用句 More Expressions

It amazed me when I saw all cherry blossoms together.

看到櫻花齊開的景象，讓我感到很驚奇。

I like to watch the leaves falling in autumn. The streets look so beautiful.

我喜歡秋天落葉的景象，街景看起來好美。

I think winter is the most depressing season because it gets windy and cold.

我覺得冬天是最令人感到憂鬱的季節，因為風很大、天氣又很冷。

332

UNIT 02

來去鄉下住一晚

MP3
107

Q What do you think about living in the countryside?

你對住鄉下的看法如何？

你可以這樣回答

I actually don't mind living in the countryside[1] for a short while. Staying for three to six months is acceptable to me. However, I don't think I could do it for too long because I am so accustomed to[2] the hustle and bustle[3] of the city. Of course, living in the countryside would be a nice break from my job and other duties. But I can't stand the inconvenience there. I don't even want to imagine[4] a life without 7-Eleven. I would definitely get annoyed by the lack of convenience.

　　我其實不介意在鄉下小住一陣子，三到六個月我都可以接受。但是，我不覺得自己能待在鄉下太久，因為我很習慣都市的熱鬧感。當然，到鄉下住的確可以讓我從工作和其他責任當中跳脫出來，好好休息一下，但我無法忍受不便利的生活，我甚至不願意去想像沒有7-11的日子，不便的生活絕對會讓我很快就厭倦的。

❶ **countryside**
名 鄉下

❷ **be accustomed to**
片 習慣於…

❸ **hustle and bustle**
片 喧鬧；熱鬧

❹ **imagine**
動 想像

> **延伸note**
> 如果你從小就住在都市，
> 習慣都市的步調與生活，
> 那麼你可以稱自己為city
> boy/girl。

換個立場講講看

I have always dreamt of moving to the countryside and opening up a B&B[5]. I love the country style very much, so I would decorate my house with nice wooden[6] furniture[7], and flowery[8] pattern curtains[9] and tablecloths[10]. Also, I would love to have a vegetable garden, so I could make special and healthy breakfasts for the guests staying at my B&B. Honestly, I've been saving up for this. Hopefully, my dream can come true in the near future.

我總夢想著搬去鄉下開民宿，我很喜歡鄉村風格，所以我會用原木傢俱、小花圖案的窗簾及桌巾來裝潢我的民宿。我還想要有一個菜園，這樣我就可以替來住宿的房客準備特別又健康的早餐。說實話，我已經有在存錢，希望不久後我就能夢想成真。

❺ **B&B**	❻ **wooden**	❼ **furniture**
名 民宿	形 木製的	名 傢俱
❽ **flowery**	❾ **curtain**	❿ **tablecloth**
形 多花的	名 窗簾	名 桌巾

 試著更與眾不同

I couldn't think of anything worse than moving to the countryside. Some people think the sound of birds singing is very pleasant[11] to hear; but I just find it annoying because it keeps me awake. The other thing that annoys me are the insects[12] in the countryside. I always get bitten by the mosquitoes[13] when I visit the countryside. Although I have covered myself with thick layers of insect repellent[14], it still doesn't work. Being itchy[15] sometimes drives me nuts, especially when I don't have my ointment[16].

我無法想像比搬去鄉下更糟的事，有些人認為鳥叫聲很愉悅，但我只覺得很刺耳，因為那聲音搞得我無法好好睡覺。另一件令我討厭的東西就是鄉下的蚊蟲。每次我到鄉下去，就一定會被蚊子咬，就算我已經塗了厚厚幾層的防蚊液，依然沒效，那種癢癢的感覺真的很令我抓狂，尤其當我沒帶藥膏的時候更是如此。

⑪ **pleasant**	⑫ **insect**	⑬ **mosquito**
形 令人愉快的	名 昆蟲	名 蚊子
⑭ **repellent**	⑮ **itchy**	⑯ **ointment**
名 驅蟲劑	形 癢的	名 藥膏

Key Points

答題TIPS看這裡！

鄉下總是令人聯想到自然清新的空氣，蟲鳴鳥叫，遠離塵囂、回歸自然的生活方式，可是並不是每個人都會喜歡這種生活型態。放棄都市的便利性其實對很多人是很大的挑戰，變成什麼都要自己來。

Words & Phrases　鄉下吸引人的優點

1　**fresh air**
空氣清新

2　**slower-paced life**
生活步調慢

3　**friendly people**
友善的人們

4　**items at lower prices**
較低廉的物價

Words & Phrases　鄉村生活的樣貌

1　**fruit orchard**
果園

2　**fertilize**
施肥

3　**harvest**
收穫

4　**self-sustaining**
自給自足的

進階實用句 More Expressions

I like the peacefulness in the countryside.

我喜歡鄉下的恬靜。

I can have my fruit orchard if I live in the countryside.

如果我住在鄉下，就能擁有自己的果園了。

I wish I could move to the countryside one day and live a self-sustainable lifestyle.

我希望有一天我能搬去鄉下，過自給自足的生活。

UNIT 03

談論替代性能源

What kind of alternative energy do you prefer? Why?

你推崇哪種替代性能源？為什麼？

 你可以這樣回答

MP3 108

I prefer solar power because it doesn't have any negative impacts on the environment. However, solar power can't generate[1] enough power without a large quantity of solar panels[2]. This kind of product is not common in Taiwan. Besides, the solar panels are expensive to install[3]. Solar power is difficult to promote unless our government is willing to subsidize[4] the cost of installation. However, once the equipment[5] is set up, it would be sustainable[6]. I think it's worth the cost.

我推崇太陽能，因為它不會對環境帶來負面的影響。不過，如果缺少大量的太陽能板，那麼太陽能所產生的電力也不敷使用。太陽能板之類的產品在台灣不常見，要安裝也很昂貴，除非政府願意提供安裝的補助經費，否則要推動太陽能發電是很困難的。但一旦安裝了設備，就可以永續使用，我覺得這筆花費很值得。

❶ generate 動 產生；發生	❷ panel 名 嵌板	❸ install 動 安裝
❹ subsidize 動 補助；資助	❺ equipment 名 設備；配備	❻ sustainable 形 可持續發展的

 換個立場講講看

I think biofuel[7] is an ideal alternative[8] to replace gasoline[9] because it is renewable[10]. However, the cost of making biofuel might be a lot higher than traditional gasoline; but I guess that is how much energy[11] is going to cost when we completely run out of gasoline. At this stage, the performance of biofuel is still not as good as traditional gas, but I am sure the scientists[12] who are working on it will find a way to improve its quality.

我覺得生化燃料能替代汽油，因為它可以透過重製的過程，不斷循環利用。不過製造生化燃料的費用遠比一般傳統汽油高，我覺得當有一天石油都用完之後，替代性能源的價格就是會這麼高。目前而言，生化燃料的性能還沒有像傳統汽油那麼好，但我相信研究燃料的科學家們一定會找到方法改善它的品質。

⑦ **biofuel**
名 生物燃料

⑧ **alternative**
名 替代品

⑨ **gasoline**
名 （美）石油

⑩ **renewable**
形 可更新的

⑪ **energy**
名 能源

⑫ **scientist**
名 科學家

試著更與眾不同

I think we should utilize the power of wind to supply our energy needs. I think it is very beneficial[13] for both the environment and the tourism[14] industry[15]. The wind power generators[16] are actually pretty. A wind farm can turn into a hot spot[17] for tourism in the future. However, the cost of production and installation of the wind power generators are still the major concerns. Besides, they require maintenance on a regular basis[18].

我覺得我們應該利用風力來供應用電量，這不管是對環境或觀光業都很有益處。風力發電器的外型很美，風力發電廠可能在未來轉變為熱門景點。不過，製造和安裝風力發電器的費用還是主要的考量，而且風力發電器還需要定期保養維修。

⑬ **beneficial**
形 有益的

⑭ **tourism**
名 旅遊

⑮ **industry**
名 產業

⑯ **generator**
名 發電機

⑰ **a hot spot**
片 熱門景點

⑱ **on a regular basis**
片 定期

Key Points 答題TIPS看這裡！

聽到這個問題，不用想得太複雜。替代性能源在我們的生活周遭都會看到，只是我們有時候沒有注意到而已。最為大家熟悉的，大概就是太陽能與風力。可惜的是，替代性能源現階段尚未成主流，除了費用（cost）偏高之外，發電的效能仍不及核能發電（nuclear power）。

Words & Phrases　各種替代性能源

1 **nuclear power**
核能發電

2 **wind power**
風力發電

3 **coal energy**
媒能發電

4 **water power**
水力發電

Words & Phrases　替代性能源的優點

1 **eco-friendly**
環保的

2 **energy conservation**
節約能源

3 **sustainability**
永續性

4 **reduce imports**
減少進口

🎤 進階實用句 More Expressions

Not everyone is willing to pay more for power.

不是每個人都願意多付電費。

I don't think coal energy is a good alternative because it creates air pollution.

我覺得煤能發電不是個好的替代能源，因為它會造成空氣汙染。

The solar system in my house is only enough to power a toaster. We still need to rely on traditional electricity.

我家的太陽能系統只能供電給烤土司機，我們還是必須依賴一般用電。

338

保護環境的做法

Q Describe one thing you do to protect the environment.

請描述一件你為了保護環境而採取的行動。

 你可以這樣回答

MP3
109

In order to protect the environment, I always make sure that I recycle[1] recyclables[2] such as paper and plastics[3]. I know what I do is only a small amount, but if everyone took recycling seriously like I do, the amount of rubbish[4] would be reduced significantly. By recycling plastic, the amount of toxic[5] pollutants[6] being released into the air would be reduced, too. It is not only good for the environment, but also good for our health.

　　為了保護環境，我總是確保自己有把回收做確實，分好紙類及塑膠之類的可回收物品。我知道一個人的力量有限，但如果大家都像我一樣認真做回收，垃圾量就會大大地減少。藉由回收塑膠，空氣中有毒氣體的排放量也會減低，這不只是為了環境，同時也是為了我們的健康。

❶ recycle
動 回收

❷ recyclable
名 可回收物

❸ plastics
名 塑膠

❹ rubbish
名 垃圾

❺ toxic
形 有毒的

❻ pollutant
名 汙染物

 換個立場講講看

One thing I do for our environment is water conservation[7]. A lack[8] of water has been a problem in Taiwan. Even if it rains heavily, it doesn't mean there will be enough water to use freely. It must rain in the right areas; otherwise, there will still be droughts[9]. The idea of conserving water is heavy promoted[10] by the government because the reservoirs[11] have hit record lows recently[12]. I now take short showers and do my laundry weekly instead of daily.

為了對環保盡一份力，我節約用水。缺水一直是台灣的問題，下很多雨並不表示能有充足的用水，雨一定得下在對的區域，否則還是會出現乾旱。政府現在很重視省水的概念，因為最近水庫的水量時不時就過低，我現在洗澡都採用快速的淋浴，衣服也不再天天洗了，一星期洗一次。

---

⑦ conservation
名 保存

⑧ lack
名 缺乏；缺少

⑨ drought
名 乾旱

⑩ promote
動 提倡；促進

⑪ reservoir
名 水庫

⑫ recently
副 最近；近來

試著更與眾不同

I always make sure I take the rubbish home or to a trash can[13]. I think littering[14] is a big problem and goes against environmental protection. Sometimes I see people throwing their plastic bags into the ocean. It is such a terrible thing to do. Things like plastic bags might cause fish to suffocate[15]. If the fish get eaten by birds, it could cause the birds to die. As part of the food chain, human beings are affected[16] as well. I think it's time for us to take this issue seriously.

我總會確保我把垃圾帶回家，或者是將之都進垃圾桶。我覺得隨地亂丟垃圾很不環保。有時候，我會看到人們隨意把塑膠袋丟進海裡，這種舉動真的很糟糕。像塑膠袋這種東西，可能會讓魚窒息，如果這條魚被鳥吃掉，也可能會導致鳥類死亡。身為食物鏈中的一份子，這也會影響到人類，我覺得是該認真看待這件議題的時候了。

---

⑬ a trash can
片 垃圾桶

⑭ litter
動 亂丟（雜物）

⑮ suffocate
動 窒息

⑯ affect
動 影響

延伸note
海灘的汙染問題日益嚴重，現在也會有團體發起 clean up the beach(清理海灘)的活動。

Key Points

答題TIPS看這裡！

保護環境的行為並不需要是多偉大的事項，從日常生活中隨手可做的事來舉例即可，例如：回收、捐舊衣舊鞋、節省水資源、不亂丟垃圾、走路上班、隨手關燈…等皆可，如果有當過環境清潔志工，也可以拿來舉例。

Words & Phrases　身體力行做環保

1 make a donation
捐款

2 sponsor a tree
樹木認養

3 energy saving
省電

4 reduce one's carbon footprint
節能減碳

Words & Phrases　常見的汙染類別

1 air pollution
空氣汙染

2 water pollution
水汙染

3 noise pollution
噪音汙染

4 soil pollution
土壤汙染

 ### 進階實用句 More Expressions

I make a regular donation to the renewable energy foundation.

我會定期捐款給再生能源協會。

In order to reduce my carbon footprint, I try to walk to work.

為了節能減碳，我盡量走路去上班。

I have replaced the traditional light bulbs with energy saving light bulbs.

我把傳統燈泡全部換成省電燈泡。

UNIT 05

對公園/花園的偏好

Q Do you like to visit parks or gardens?
你喜歡參觀公園或花園嗎？

你可以這樣回答

MP3
110

Speaking of visiting parks or gardens[1], I must introduce my favorite park — The Wetland Park. You can find pelicans[2] and other species of birds there. My favorite is the swans[3]. They sometimes will come up to the visitors begging for food. At first sight, you might find them a little bit daunting[4] because they are sizable[5] birds. However, it is quite enjoyable to get close to wildlife. It means we are doing a good job in maintaining their habitats[6].

說到參觀公園或花園，我一定要介紹我最愛的公園 — 溼地公園。在那裡可以看到鵜鶘還有其他鳥類。我最喜歡天鵝，牠們有時候會過來跟你要東西吃，第一眼看到天鵝，你可能會覺得牠們有點嚇人，因為身形很大隻，但能和野生動物親近其實是很棒的一件事，代表我們維護動物棲息地的工作做得很成功。

❶ **garden**	❷ **pelican**	❸ **swan**
名 花園	名 鵜鶘	名 天鵝
❹ **daunting**	❺ **sizable**	❻ **habitat**
形 令人卻步的	形 相當大的	名 （動物的）棲息地

換個立場講講看

Personally, going to parks or gardens is not that appealing to me. It gets quite boring just to walk through the flower patches[7]. I prefer something more interactive[8], such as a man-made[9] lake where I can do rowing[10]. I think Central park in Kaohsiung does a pretty good job. It combines[11] the natural garden and the recreational[12] side of the park. I went there with my friends before, and I will definitely visit there again with my girlfriend.

　　去公園或花園不怎麼吸引我，在花圃間走來走去其實很無聊。我喜歡比較有互動的東西，像是可以划船的人造湖之類的。我覺得高雄的中央公園就設計得很好，結合自然的花園和人工的娛樂。我之前是和朋友一起去的，我一定要再和我女朋友去一趟。

❼ patch
名 小塊土地

❽ interactive
形 相互作用的

❾ man-made
形 人造的；人工的

❿ rowing
名 划船

⓫ combine
動 使結合

⓬ recreational
形 娛樂的

試著更與眾不同

I like going to parks and gardens because the serenity[13] makes me feel relaxed. I don't know if it's because of my age. I prefer nature to movies or things like that. My favorite thing to do in a park is to have a picnic under the trees. I look after[14] my niece[15] for my sister on the weekends. I usually prepare a picnic and take her to a park. She loves to run around and fly a kite[16], and I will read a novel in the shade. We both enjoy our time there.

　　我喜歡去公園及花園，因為平穩寧靜的環境會讓我覺得很放鬆。我不知道是不是年紀的關係，和電影這種娛樂相比，我比較喜歡親近大自然。我最愛到樹下野餐，週末的時候，我會幫忙我姊姊照顧我的姪女，我通常會準備野餐組，帶她去公園。她喜歡跑來跑去放風箏，我則會在樹蔭下閱讀小說，我們兩個都很享受在公園的時間。

⓭ serenity
名 安詳；寧靜

⓮ look after
片 照顧

⓯ niece
名 姪女；外甥女

⓰ fly a kite
片 放風箏

延伸note
in the shade是指「在陰涼處」；反之則為in the sun（在大太陽底下）。

答題TIPS看這裡！

參觀公園或花園不再只是老人家與小孩的專利，年輕人有約會或野餐聚會時，也會選擇去公園或花園。有些公園或花園的設施齊全，可以照顧到每個人不同的需求。但若不喜歡去那種地方，舉例時可以解釋你不喜歡的原因，像是更喜歡室內活動，或者更喜歡人工的遊樂設施，都可以當作理由。

Words & Phrases 各種形容公園的詞彙

1. **crowded**
   擁擠的
2. **spacious**
   寬敞的
3. **hilly**
   有點坡度的
4. **artificial**
   人工的

Words & Phrases 與花有關的英文俚語

1. **fresh as a daisy**
   容光煥發
2. **shrinking violet**
   害羞靦腆的人
3. **nip in the bud**
   防患未然
4. **not all roses**
   事情不盡如人意

進階實用句 More Expressions

I like to go to Yang Min Mountain for the cherry blossoms.

我喜歡去陽明山賞櫻。

What I like the most is the spacious grassy area in the park.

我最喜歡的是公園寬廣的草地。

The park near my house is very recreational; there is a skating rink for the children.

我家附近的公園很有娛樂性，其中有個兒童溜冰場。

UNIT 06

保存古蹟建築

MP3
111

Q Do you think it's important to maintain historical buildings?

你認為保存古蹟重要嗎？

你可以這樣回答

Yes, it is very important to maintain historical buildings. They are not simply buildings, but represent part of our culture[1] and history. However, it is a pity[2] that a lot of the buildings have been knocked down[3] due to safety reasons. It requires a lot of work to maintain the structure and appearance[4]. That is also the reason why historic monuments[5] are valuable. I always admire the technique and wisdom[6] behind the buildings.

是的，保存古蹟很重要，因為那不只是建築，還代表我們一部分的文化與歷史。可惜的是，很多古蹟都因為安全考量而被拆除，要維持建築物的結構和外觀需要花很多精力，這也是古蹟之所以珍貴的原因，我總會讚嘆那些古蹟建築背後所蘊含的技術與智慧。

❶ culture	❷ pity	❸ knock down
名 文化	名 可惜的事	片 拆卸
❹ appearance	❺ monument	❻ wisdom
名 外觀；外表	名 歷史遺跡	名 智慧

換個立場講講看

Well, I don't think it is important to maintain historical buildings. Most of them are not up to the current building code and might cause some safety problems. In my opinion, those old buildings should be refurbished[7] or turned into housing estates[8] to produce more accommodation[9] for people. It is a waste to keep buildings that nobody lives in when we can turn them into residential[10] buildings and accommodate 100 or more people.

　　我不覺得保存古蹟有什麼重要，大多數的舊建築都不符合當今的建築法規，反而可能造成安全問題。在我看來，那些舊建築應該要翻修或改建為住宅，這樣就能解決更多人的住宿問題。明明可以改建為住宅大樓，提供住處給一百人(甚至更多人)時，卻選擇留著一棟沒人住的建築，是件很浪費的事情。

❼ refurbish
動 整修

❽ estate
名 地產

❾ accommodation
名 住處

❿ residential
形 住宅的

 ## 試著更與眾不同

I would agree with the idea of keeping historical buildings only if they are still in good condition. If it takes more effort[11] to renovate[12] one than tear it down[13], then it would be better to demolish[14] it. It's meaningless to keep something that is broken and unsafe[15] since you won't open it to the public for viewing. However, I know there are countries that keep certain[16] historical spots to remind people of some events like a war. That is a different story.

　　如果那些古蹟的情況良好，那我會同意保存。但如果維修起來比拆掉更費時費事，那我覺得直接拆除會更好。留著殘破的危險建築一點意義也沒有，因為也不可能開放給大眾參觀。不過，我知道有些國家保留特定歷史古蹟是為了提醒人們一些事件，比如曾經發生過的戰爭等等，那種情況就另當別論。

⓫ effort
名 努力；盡力

⓬ renovate
動 整修

⓭ tear down
片 拆卸

⓮ demolish
動 毀壞；破壞

⓯ unsafe
形 不安全的

⓰ certain
形 某些

答題TIPS看這裡！

保存古建築其實影響的層面很大，建築本身如果年久失修，要不要保存就更具爭議性。進行維修可能會失去原始建築的意義；不維修又可能造成危險，對市容也無益，這些不同的理由都可以納入討論。

Words & Phrases　考古與歷史的遺跡

1 **archaeology**
考古學

2 **excavate**
發掘（古物）

3 **historical relic**
歷史文物

4 **historical remains**
遺跡

Words & Phrases　與建築有關的詞彙

1 **foundation**
地基

2 **a steel bar**
鋼筋

3 **cement**
水泥

4 **brick**
磚頭

 ## 進階實用句 More Expressions

The house is old and dated; it needs a full refurbishment.

這間房子已經很舊又過時了，需要重新翻修。

A lot of historical buildings do not have a strong foundation to allow them to last a long time.

很多古蹟都沒有很強健的地基來維持穩固性。

I am upset about the government's decision to tear down the old theater on that street.

我很難過政府決定拆除那條街上的古戲院。

UNIT 07 對回收的概念

Q **Do you think people's attitude towards recycling has changed?**

你認為人們對回收的概念有改變嗎？

你可以這樣回答

MP3 112

Most definitely. In the old days, people just threw everything out as rubbish. Recycling was something to help the helpless[1] old ladies. Nowadays[2], people actually recognize[3] the issue of environmental protection as being important. Reducing the amount of rubbish has become everybody's responsibility[4]. In addition, donating[5] old clothes and shoes has also become popular because it is not only recycling, but also a charitable[6] act.

　　當然有，以前大家什麼都當垃圾丟掉，回收好像只是為了幫忙那些無助的老婆婆。現在人們的環保意識抬頭，每個人都有責任減少自己的垃圾量。除此之外，捐贈不用的衣服與鞋子也變得普遍了，因為那不再只是回收利用，更是做善行。

❶ **helpless** 形 無助的	❷ **nowadays** 副 現今；時下	❸ **recognize** 動 承認（事實）
❹ **responsibility** 名 責任	❺ **donate** 動 捐獻	❻ **charitable** 形 慈善的

換個立場講講看

No, I don't think it has changed much. I have been doing recycling and separating[7] my trash into recyclables and non-recyclables before the government made it compulsory[8]. I would gather[9] cardboard[10] boxes and plastic bottles for the lady who does the recycling in our neighbourhood. I started doing it when I was in primary school because my teachers and parents are all advocates of recycling. I think the idea of recycling hasn't changed much. The only difference is there are more people doing it now.

　　不，我覺得沒變那麼多，在政府還沒硬性規定回收之前，我就開始做回收了，我會把垃圾分成可回收和不可回收兩類。因為我的老師和父母都提倡資源回收，從國小開始，我就會幫我們這一區做回收的太太留紙箱和塑膠瓶。大家對回收的概念並沒有什麼改變，頂多就是現在做回收的人比較多而已。

延伸note
其他項目：aluminum cans(鋁罐)、textiles and fabrics(舊衣類)、batteries(廢電池)⋯。

7 separate
動 分隔；分割

8 compulsory
形 強制的；強迫的

9 gather
動 收集

10 cardboard
形 硬紙板製的

試著更與眾不同

Yes, I think so. However, it has nothing to do with people's attitudes towards recycling, but the awareness[11] of various environmental issues. Experts[12] have emphasized[13] that a lot of damage[14] we have caused over the years is not reversible[15]. All we can do now is to not make the situation worse. In order to achieve this goal[16], people have started to do more recycling. By reducing the amount of rubbish, we can reduce the pollution.

　　是的，我覺得有，但那和對回收的態度有沒有改變無關，而是因為大眾注意到許多的環境問題。專家們也一直強調很多已經造成的傷害都是無法修補的。我們現在能做的，就是不要讓情況惡化，為了達成這個目標，所以民眾已經開始更注重回收工作。藉由減少垃圾量，就能降低環境污染。

11 awareness
名 察覺；體認

12 expert
名 專家

13 emphasize
動 強調

14 damage
名 傷害；損害

15 reversible
形 可逆的

16 goal
名 目標

Words & Phrases 資源回收的項目

1 **aluminium cans**
鋁罐

2 **tin cans**
罐頭

3 **paper and cardboard**
廢紙類

4 **glass**
玻璃類

5 **PET bottles**
寶特瓶類

6 **compost**
堆肥

7 **pig fodder**
豬飼料

8 **Styrofoam**
保麗龍

 進階實用句 More Expressions

I always buy things made of recycled materials.

我總是會買用回收原料做的東西。

Nowadays, you can see recycling bins in most places.

現在到處都看得到回收桶。

Aluminium cans have become a popular material used by artists.

鋁罐已經變成藝術家愛用的材料之一。

UNIT 08 喜歡的公園型態

Q Do you prefer parks with open spaces or facilities? Why?

你喜歡公園內有寬廣的空間，還是完善的設施？為什麼？

你可以這樣回答

MP3 113

I prefer parks with open spaces because I don't have any kids, and there is no need for me to use the facilities[1]. What I enjoy doing in a park is to have a picnic on the grass. Living in the city, I sometimes get tired of seeing all the tall buildings. Some studies say that getting close to nature can help people release[2] the pressure[3]. That's what I feel like when I go to a park. By feeling the breeze[4] and sunshine[5], I can get away from the daily trifles[6] and refresh myself.

　　我比較喜歡空間寬敞的公園，因為我沒有小孩，也用不上什麼公園設施。在公園裡，我最喜歡的事情就是坐在草地上野餐。住在城市，我有時候會很厭倦一成不變的大樓風景。有些研究顯示，接近大自然能幫助人們釋放壓力，我去公園的時候，就有這樣的感覺。感受微風和和煦的陽光，我就能從日常瑣事中解脫，恢復精力。

❶ **facility** 名 設備；設施	❷ **release** 動 釋放；解放	❸ **pressure** 名 壓力
❹ **breeze** 名 微風	❺ **sunshine** 名 陽光	❻ **trifle** 名 小事；瑣事

換個立場講講看

Well, I can't really choose between those two options. If you ask me, a mixture[7] of open area and facilities is perfect. A park is a public[8] area for everyone living in the same neighborhood[9]. Therefore, it should fit the residents'[10] needs. For example, I like to go to parks with lots of trees and flowers. I enjoy sitting on the bench[11] watching the squirrels[12] jumping from one tree to the other. However, a park with various exercise facilities is ideal for my sister.

　　我沒有辦法從中選一個，如果你問我，兩者兼顧的公園我覺得是最理想的。公園是同一區的人們共享的公共區域，因此，它應該要能滿足所有居民的需求，比方說，我喜歡去很多花草樹木的公園，我很享受坐在長椅上，看松鼠在樹梢間跳躍的感覺，不過，我姐姐就覺得運動設施多元的公園比較好。

❼ **mixture** 名 混合	❽ **public** 形 公共的	❾ **neighborhood** 名 鄰近地區
❿ **resident** 名 居民	⓫ **bench** 名 長椅	⓬ **squirrel** 名 松鼠

試著更與眾不同

I like parks with lots of facilities, such as a playground[13] for the kids or a basketball court. It is hard to find a place to exercise after work unless I join a gym[14]. I prefer playing basketball, but all the courts are usually taken when I get there. In that case, I could only go to a park to use the fitness[15] equipment. I think it would be great if our mayor[16] could build basketball courts in all the parks.

　　我喜歡有完善設施的公園，像兒童遊戲場和籃球場。除非我去健身房，否則下班後很難找到可以運動的場地。我想打籃球，但當我抵達的時候，籃球場通常都被占滿了，那個時候我就只好去公園使用運動器材。如果市長可以把所有公園與籃球場結合，那肯定很棒。

⓭ **playground** 名 運動場；遊戲場	⓮ **gym** 名 健身房
⓯ **fitness** 名 健身	⓰ **mayor** 名 市長

延伸note
公園的運動設施可能還包括 tennis court(網球場)、baseball field(棒球場)、golf course(高爾夫球場)等。

Key Points 答題TIPS看這裡！

大家想去公園的原因或理由都不同，喜歡寬敞空間的人可能只想到公園裡找一片寧靜；但公園最大宗的用戶往往是上了年紀的人（the elders）跟小孩（kids），所以現代人也越來越重視公園的設施。

Words & Phrases　公園內的常見設施

1 entrance
入口

2 trail
步道

3 pavilion
涼亭

4 fountain
噴水池

Words & Phrases　各種兒童遊戲器材

1 playground slide
溜滑梯

2 swing
鞦韆

3 see-saw
蹺蹺板

4 merry-go-around
旋轉木馬

進階實用句 More Expressions

There are many designated bike lanes through the park.

公園裡有很多腳踏車專用道。

I think a well-designed park should include disabled access.

我覺得一個好公園應該要有無障礙空間。

Surprisingly, there were quite a lot of people at the track and field event.

令人驚訝的是，田徑賽上還滿多人的。

UNIT 09

瀕臨絕種的動物

Q Do you think endangered animals should be kept in zoos? Why?

你認為瀕臨絕種的動物應該放在動物園裡嗎？為什麼？

 你可以這樣回答

Yes, I think endangered[1] animals should be kept in zoos. Generally speaking, endangered animals have trouble multiplying[2]. Even if the babies are born, they might die quickly. Therefore, these animals require some special treatment[3]. I think the best way is to keep them in zoos until their population[4] increases to a certain level[5]. By then, we can release the animals back to the wild; otherwise, they would become extinct[6] very soon.

是的，我覺得瀕臨絕種的動物應該養在動物園裡。一般而言，瀕臨絕種的動物在繁衍後代這方面一定有困難，就算寶寶出生了，也可能很快就死亡。因此，這些動物需要特別的照顧，我覺得最好的方式就是養在動物園裡，直到牠們的數量達到標準後，再放回野外，否則牠們很快就會絕種了。

❶ **endangered**	❷ **multiply**	❸ **treatment**
形 快要絕種的	動 使繁殖	名 對待；待遇
❹ **population**	❺ **level**	❻ **extinct**
名 （動物的）總數	名 標準；水平	形 絕種的

 換個立場講講看

I don't think it is fair to interfere with[7] nature; animals become endangered for various reasons. Take the dinosaurs[8] for example. If the dinosaurs were still alive, our history would be totally different and society might not even be dominated[9] by human beings. To me, the fact that certain species[10] disappear is actually an act of God. There must be a greater reason for it. We just can't see it yet at this stage.

　　我覺得干涉自然世界並不公平，動物們會瀕臨絕種是有各種不同原因的，就像恐龍。如果恐龍沒有絕種，那歷史就會完全不同，人類也不可能主宰這個社會。就我而言，某些物種之所以會消失，都是天意，背後有更大的理由，只是我們目前看不到而已。

延伸note
可以拿來舉例的瀕臨絕種動物有：gavial(長吻鱷)、jaguar(美洲豹)、sea otter(海獺)…等。

7 interfere with
片 干預；妨害

8 dinosaur
名 恐龍

9 dominate
動 支配；統治

10 species
名 種類

試著更與眾不同

Well, I agree with doing something for endangered animals, but keeping them in zoos won't help much. Those animals belong to[11] the wild, so we shouldn't forcefully[12] relocate[13] them to zoos. I think the best solution is to maintain their natural habitats[14] or minimize[15] their natural enemies. However, we should have a careful and detailed evaluation[16] in advance, or the actions might also cause other species to become endangered.

　　我同意要做點什麼來幫助那些瀕臨絕種的動物，但是把牠們養在動物園並沒有多大幫助。那些動物屬於野生大自然的一員，所以我們不應該強制性地把牠們移至動物園。我覺得最好的方式是保護好牠們的棲息地或減少牠們的天敵數量。不過，要做之前，一定要先經過謹慎、詳細的評估，不然這種舉動也可能造成其他物種瀕臨絕種。

11 belong to
片 屬於

12 forcefully
副 強有力地

13 relocate
動 重新安置

14 habitat
名 （動物的）棲息地

15 minimize
動 使縮到最小

16 evaluation
名 評價；估算

答題TIPS看這裡！

瀕臨絕種的動物是否需要人類來保育，是很值得討論的議題（a controversial issue）。因為牽涉的不只有一種物種，為了食物鏈（food chain）的平衡，所以沒有絕對的正確做法。缺了或是多了一種物種，皆會影響生態（ecology），不得不慎。回答時建議選定某一種立場闡述（agree/disagree），再於後面補充說明原因以及此問題的複雜性。

Words & Phrases 家畜與野生動物

1 **domestic**
家飼的

2 **feed**
餵食

3 **reproduce**
繁殖

4 **feral**
野生的

Words & Phrases 瀕臨絕種的台灣物種

1 **Salmo formosanus**
櫻花鉤吻鮭

2 **black-faced spoonbill**
黑面琵鷺

3 **sika deer**
梅花鹿

4 **green sea turtle**
綠蠵龜

進階實用句 More Expressions

Feral animals are natural hunters because they need to get their prey.

野生動物是天生的獵人，因為牠們必須自己捕獲獵物。

Relocating endangered animals is not the only way to help them.

重新安置瀕臨絕種的動物並非唯一幫助牠們的辦法。

Some endangered animals can't be kept domestically.

有些瀕臨絕種的動物不能養在家裡。

UNIT 10 國內的降雨量

Q Do you get a lot of rain in your country?
你國家的降雨量很大嗎？

你可以這樣回答

MP3 115

Yes, we get a lot of rain here in Taiwan, especially in summer. It's the season when we get a lot of typhoons[1]. However, the rainfall[2] does not distribute[3] evenly[4] throughout the year. We either get a lot of rain or nothing at all. I appreciate the rainfall, but it sometimes is too much and causes mudslides[5] in the mountains. There were cases like this in the past. Even some villages disappeared because of the serious natural disasters[6].

是的，台灣夏天的雨量很充足，夏天是我們的颱風季節。但是，一整年降雨量的分布並不平均，有時候下很多雨，有時候卻連一滴雨都沒有。我很感謝有充足的雨量，但有時候下得過多，反而造成山崩。過去幾年，類似的例子屢見不鮮，因為嚴重的天災，甚至有些村落都因而消失了。

❶ **typhoon** 名 颱風	❷ **rainfall** 名 降雨量	❸ **distribute** 動 分布
❹ **evenly** 副 均衡地	❺ **mudslide** 名 山崩	❻ **disaster** 名 災害；災難

換個立場講講看

No, we don't get a lot of rain. The weather is very dry in my country. People suffer from[7] drought almost every year. The mining[8] industry is strong because we are rich in natural resources. However, agriculture[9] seems impossible

due to the climate[10]. Therefore, we rely on importation[11] from other countries for food and water. The government even sets water restrictions for household water usage. I can only water my lawn[12] once a week. I would rather exchange our other natural resources for water.

　　不，我們的雨量稀少，我國的天氣非常乾燥，幾乎年年乾旱，人們過得很辛苦。因為我們有豐富的自然資源，所以礦業很穩固，但因為氣候因素，農業根本不可能在我國發展。因此，我們的食物和水都必須仰賴進口。政府甚至還限制民生用水，所以我一個星期只能替我的草坪澆一次水。我還寧願用我們的其他自然資源交換水呢！

| ⑦ **suffer from** 片 受（某事物）之苦 | ⑧ **mining** 名 採礦；礦業 | ⑨ **agriculture** 名 農業 |
| ⑩ **climate** 名 氣候 | ⑪ **importation** 名 進口 | ⑫ **lawn** 名 草坪 |

試著更與眾不同

It depends on which country you compare with. If you compared the rainfall in my country with somewhere like Africa, we do get a lot of rainfall. However, it seems normal when you compare it with somewhere like Indonesia[13] or the Philippines[14]. The water storage in our reservoirs is much less than the rainfall. However, the rainfall is enough to support the population[15]. And we don't need to worry about the excess[16] rainfall possibly flooding the whole city.

　　看你是跟哪些國家比。如果和非洲比，那我們國內的降雨量真的滿多。但是，如果和印尼或菲律賓那些國家相比，那我們國家的降雨量就只能算中等。我們水庫蓄的水比降雨量少得多，但雨量足夠供國人使用，而且不需要擔心過多的雨量可能淹掉整個城市。

| ⑬ **Indonesia** 名 印尼 | ⑭ **Philippines** 名 菲律賓 |
| ⑮ **population** 名 全部居民 | ⑯ **excess** 形 過量的 |

延伸note
降雨量(rainfall)的多寡和水庫的蓄水量(storage)不是同一回事，可以分開來討論。

Key Points 答題TIPS看這裡！

降雨量如果足夠人民使用，那就是達到最好的平衡。最怕就是雨量充沛可是卻不停帶來洪災（flood）；或因為沒有下在集水區，所以依然不敷使用，後者是台灣常見的情況，因而必須限水（water rationing）。

Words & Phrases 各種雨量失衡的情況

1 **heavy rain** 暴雨
2 **debris flow** 土石流
3 **flood** 淹水；洪水
4 **drought** 乾旱

Words & Phrases 保存水量的相關詞彙

1 **reservoir** 水庫
2 **catchment** 集水（量）
3 **conserve** 保存；節省
4 **water saving** 節約用水

進階實用句 More Expressions

The water level in the reservoir hit a record low.

水庫的水位已經創了歷年來的新低。

It rained so much in the past several hours; half of the city is flooded.

過去一小時內下了好多雨，城市的大半區域都淹水了。

I wish the rain could fall in the catchment area in order to resolve the drought problem.

我希望雨可以下在集水區，以解決乾旱的問題。

UNIT 11 日曬時間的長短

Q How long are you exposed to sunlight daily?
你每天曬到太陽的時間多長？

 你可以這樣回答

MP3
116

I always walk to work from the MRT station[1] to the office. It takes about twenty minutes. This is the only chance to get some sun exposure[2] during the day. By the time I get off work, it is almost dark. Some women are afraid of suntans[3], but I think getting sun exposure is necessary for our health. On the weekends, however, I will put on sunscreen when I go out. Being healthy is important, but getting sunburned[4] is definitely not good.

我總是從車站用走的到辦公室，大約二十分鐘左右，這是我一天中唯一有機會曬到太陽的時間，因為等到我下班，天都已經黑了。有些女性會擔心曬黑，但我覺得曬太陽對健康來說是必要的。不過，週末的時候，我會擦防曬乳，健康很重要沒錯，但曬傷可不太妙。

❶ **station**
名 車站

❷ **exposure**
名 暴露；曝曬

❸ **suntan**
名 曬黑

❹ **sunburn**
動 曬傷皮膚

> **延伸note**
> 以往國人崇尚白皙膚色 (fair)的審美觀，近年來有一些變化，古銅色肌膚 (brunet)也開始被喜愛囉。

 換個立場講講看

I work at Taiwan Power Company as a maintenance engineer. I often need to go out to fix broken cables[5]. On average[6], I spend two to three hours a day under the direct sunlight. In order to avoid being sunburned, I wear a long-sleeved[7]

uniform. However, I get hot and sweaty[8] all the time. Furthermore, I must make sure that I drink plenty of water. One of my colleagues got dehydrated because he was in the sun too long without water. I must say this job is not as easy as it seems.

我是台電的維修工程師，我經常需要外出，修理壞掉的線路，一天平均下來，也要在烈日下曬個兩到三個小時，為了避免被曬傷，我會穿長袖制服，但那也會讓我熱得汗流不止。除此之外，我還必須確保自己有補充水分，我有同事就是因曬太陽太久又沒喝水而出現脫水症狀，我必須說，這份工作沒有想像的輕鬆。

延伸note
因為工作而必須曝曬於烈日下的工作不在少數，如：清潔工(cleaner)…等。

⑤ cable
名 電纜

⑥ average
名 平均

⑦ long-sleeved
形 長袖的

⑧ sweaty
形 滿身是汗的

 試著更與眾不同

Well, I hardly[9] have a chance to be exposed to sunlight. I drive to my university and spend most of the time indoors, either in the classroom or the laboratory[10]. The cafeteria[11] is in the basement[12] of the building, so I don't even need to leave the building for my lunch. I also have a parking space[13] in the underground[14] parking. Come to think of it, that might be the reason why the doctor suggested I do some outdoor activities on weekends.

我幾乎沒有曬到太陽的機會。我開車去大學，大部分的時間都待在室內，不是在教室，就是在實驗室。學校餐廳設在大樓的地下室，所以我甚至不用出去買午餐。我在地下停車場也有一個車位。這麼一想，這也許是醫生之所以建議我週末去做些戶外活動的原因吧。

⑨ hardly
副 幾乎不

⑩ laboratory
名 實驗室

⑪ cafeteria
名 （學校的）餐廳

⑫ basement
名 地下室

⑬ a parking space
片 停車位

⑭ underground
形 地下的

答題TIPS看這裡！

曬太陽的時間長短與每個人的職業或作息有很大的關係，若是屬於室內的行政工作，曬太陽的機會可能只有上下班的時間。如果是外勤人員，曬太陽則變得不可避免。答題時也可以講出自己因曝曬而做的防曬措施，像是擦防曬用品、喝水、撐陽傘（open a parasol）等方法。

Words & Phrases　曝曬過多所造成的問題

1 **dehydration**
脫水

2 **sunstroke**
中暑

3 **age spot**
老人斑；曬斑

4 **skin cancer**
皮膚癌

Words & Phrases　中暑時可採取的處理

1 **rehydration**
補充水分

2 **take a cool shower**
洗冷水浴

3 **fan**
用扇子扇風

4 **cool down**
降溫

進階實用句 More Expressions

I avoid going out from 10 a.m. to 2 p.m., or I might get heatstroke.

早上十點至下午兩點間，我會避免出門，以防中暑。

I found another age spot on my face; I should wear more sunscreen.

我的臉又出現新的曬斑，我應該多擦一點防曬乳。

Dehydration might have serious consequences.

脫水可能會造成嚴重的後果。

UNIT 12 觀光業與環境

Q **Can tourism cause environmental issues?**
觀光業的發展會產生環境問題嗎？

 你可以這樣回答

 MP3 117

Yes, it can. I believe tourism[1] not only brings in[2] money, but also causes damage[3] to our environment. Firstly, having more tourists also means more garbage. The way to deal with the excess amount of garbage is the first challenge. Secondly, not everyone has the same attitude towards environmental protection. Some tourists love to take a piece of nature home as a souvenir. This kind of behavior[4] also does harm to our environment.

會產生問題。我認為觀光業不僅會帶來賺錢的機會，同時也會對環境造成傷害。首先，有更多的觀光客湧進，就代表會製造更多垃圾，該如何處理過量的垃圾會是首要挑戰；第二，並不是每個人都有環保意識，有些觀光客還很喜歡帶回一些自然的產物留作紀念，這類型的行為也會對環境造成傷害。

❶ **tourism**
名 觀光業

❷ **bring in**
片 帶來；引進

❸ **damage**
名 損害；損失

❹ **behavior**
名 行為；舉止

> 延伸note
> do harm to sth./sb.意指「危害某物/某人」；類似的表達還有轉成形容詞的 It is harmful to...。

 換個立場講講看

I am afraid that that is a fair[5] statement[6]. Of course, we don't notice the problems when there are just a small number of tourists. However, as more and more foreigners[7] come for a visit, the problems become obvious. For example, all tourists have to use toilets[8]. Therefore, we must handle the increased amount of sewage[9]. I know tourism brings in benefits to the economy, but there should be a balance[10] between economic growth and environmental protection.

　　這恐怕是事實。當然，觀光客的數量還很少的時候，我們不會注意到有問題，但當有越來越多外國人來國內參觀時，問題就會變得很明顯了。比方說，所有觀光客都需要上廁所，所以我們肯定會面臨到處理大量汙水的問題。我知道旅遊業替經濟帶來益處，但在經濟發展和環境保護之間，應該要有個平衡點。

5 fair 形 公正的	**6 statement** 名 敘述；描述	**7 foreigner** 名 外國人
8 toilet 名 廁所；洗手間	**9 sewage** 名 汙水	**10 balance** 名 平衡；均衡

 試著更與眾不同

In my opinion[11], there should not be any serious environmental issues[12] as long as we make a detailed and complete plan in advance. For example, we can put the recycling bins[13] and normal garbage bins together. This can remind[14] people to do recycling when they throw away garbage. Also, we can put up signs that ask tourists to respect[15] nature. I believe that we can minimize the impact to the environment once we take some measures[16].

　　我覺得只要我們事先做好詳盡且完整的規畫，就不會造成太嚴重的環境問題。比方說，我們可以同時裝設回收桶和一般的垃圾桶，以提醒丟垃圾的人作好資源回收；也可以設立告示牌，要求觀光客們尊重自然環境。只要採取一些措施，就能將對環境的衝擊減到最低。

11 in one's opinion 片 就某人看來	**12 issue** 名 議題	**13 bin** 名 箱子；容器
14 remind 動 提醒	**15 respect** 動 敬重；尊敬	**16 measure** 名 手段；方法

答題TIPS看這裡！

對於一個社區來說，如果突然增加很多外來的人口，他們設施就會不夠用，更何況是大量的觀光客。為了觀光發展而增加的交通接駁車，或是垃圾量及汙水量，都是會造成環境汙染的問題。

Words & Phrases　常見的觀光類型

1 **culture / heritage tour**
文化之旅

2 **ecotourism tour**
生態觀光

3 **educational tour**
修學旅行

4 **industrial tourism**
產業觀光

Words & Phrases　一些可去的觀光景點

1 **recreational farm**
休閒農場

2 **scenic area**
風景區

3 **hot spring area**
溫泉區

4 **offshore island**
離島

進階實用句 More Expressions

Some tourists engrave their names on trees.

有些遊客會在樹上刻他們的名字。

Tourism results in an increasing amount of greenhouse gas emission.

旅遊業造成了更多的溫室氣體排放。

Our government decided to have more shuttle buses during the high peak of tourism.

我們政府決定在觀光的高峰期增加接駁車的數量。

UNIT 13 氣候的轉變

MP3
118

Q Has the weather changed in the past ten years in your country?

過去十年當中，你國家的天氣有產生變化嗎？

你可以這樣回答

I am not quite sure, but I did notice that it gets hotter in summer. I think the high temperature[1] is different from the time I was little. When I was still a kid, 33 degrees[2] meant an unusually[3] hot day. However, 33 degrees seems quite[4] normal nowadays. The temperature even goes up to 40 degrees, which is really unbearable[5] for me. This kind of climate change also makes me stay indoors as much as I can. I can't imagine life without air-conditioning[6].

　　我不太確定，但我有發現夏天變得更熱了。高溫的程度和我小時候的情況完全不同，當我還小的時候，三十三度就已經是不尋常的高溫，但現在，三十三度似乎很尋常，甚至還可能上升到四十度，我根本無法忍受這種熱度。炎熱的氣候變遷使我能待在室內就不出門，實在無法想像沒有空調該怎麼過。

---

❶ **temperature**
名 溫度

❷ **degree**
名 度；度數

❸ **unusually**
副 不尋常地

❹ **quite**
副 頗；相當

❺ **unbearable**
形 不能忍受的

❻ **air-conditioning**
名 空調

換個立場講講看

I don't think the weather has changed much, but the air quality has truly gotten worse compared to the situation[7] ten years ago. Dust[8] storms[9] come across the Taiwan Strait[10] and affect the air quality very much. All the dust makes the sky unclear[11] like a cloudy day. Even if there isn't a dust storm, air pollution is becoming more and more serious. I hope our government can do something before the conditions get worse[12].

　　我不覺得天氣有什麼特別大的改變，但空氣品質確實比十年前要差。沙塵暴經由台灣海峽吹過來，對空氣品質的影響非常大。那些沙塵導致天空一片霧濛濛，像陰天一般。就算沒有沙塵暴，空氣汙染的情況也越來越嚴重，希望我們政府能在情況惡化之前，採取一些行動。

❼ situation
名 情況

❽ dust
名 灰塵；塵土

❾ storm
名 暴風雨

❿ strait
名 海峽

⓫ unclear
形 不清晰的；不清楚的

⓬ get worse
片 變得更糟

試著更與眾不同

I can't really tell because the weather varies[13] every year. In some years, we get colder winters, and in some years, we get lots of rain. These kinds of differences are normal[14], so I can't say it has something to do with a significant weather change. One thing I am sure about is that the river[15] near my place has become cleaner because there were not any fish in it ten years ago. However, it's because our government has put a lot of effort into river dredging[16].

　　天氣每年都會變化，所以我沒有辦法判斷。有幾年，我們的冬季會遇到嚴寒，也有幾年會下很多雨。這類的變化很正常，所以我沒有辦法判定天氣有很重大的變化。我唯一可以確定的是，我家附近的河流變得乾淨許多，因為那條河在十年前根本就沒有魚。不過，這是因為我們政府花了很大的精神去整治它。

⓭ vary
動 變化

⓮ normal
形 正常的

⓯ river
名 河流

⓰ dredging
名 挖泥

> **延伸note**
> A vary with B表示A隨著B變化，通常用來表示隨著環境不同而引起的變化。

答題TIPS看這裡！

要談論天氣變化，除了自己的感覺外，可能還要參考一些數據，才能精確地知道是不是有變化，或是有了什麼樣的變化。不過，在完全沒有概念的情況下，也可以運用實際的生活經驗和觀察，例如：空氣汙染（air pollution）導致呼吸道過敏；水汙染（water pollution）影響生態；土壤汙染（soil pollution）使得農作物的化學物殘量增加…等等。

Words & Phrases　空氣汙染可能帶來的影響

1	**allergy** 過敏	**2**	**short of breath** 呼吸急促
3	**runny nose** 流鼻水	**4**	**itchy eyes** 眼睛癢
5	**skin rash** 皮膚過敏	**6**	**cough** 咳嗽
7	**sore throat** 喉嚨痛	**8**	**mucus** 痰；鼻涕

進階實用句 More Expressions

As soon as the dust storm hits, I get a sore throat and start coughing mucus.

只要沙塵暴一來，我就會喉嚨痛，開始咳出痰來。

The rainfall has dropped a lot over the past five years. We have been in drought conditions since then.

雨量在過去五年內少了很多，我們從那時候就開始出現乾旱的現象。

We started to import rice three years ago. Some farmers decided not to grow rice due to the water shortage.

我們大概三年前開始進口稻米。因為缺水，有些農夫決定不種稻米了。

UNIT 14
補救已受損害的環境

Q How can you compensate for environmental damage?

你能如何補救對環境造成的損害呢？

 你可以這樣回答

Unfortunately, most of the damage is irreversible[1]. In other words, there is no way to reverse it once the damage is done. In order to remedy[2] the situation, the best thing we can do is to not make conditions worse. Thanks to the experts' warnings[3], there are more and more people who recognize the importance of protecting our environment. There have even been activities that encourage[4] people to plant more trees.

可惜的是，大部分的損害都是不可逆的。換句話說，一旦造成損害，就沒有辦法彌補了。為了補救，我們唯一能做的就是別讓情況變得更糟。多虧專家們的提醒，現在有越來越多人開始認清保育環境的重要性，甚至還有鼓勵人們多種樹的活動呢！

❶ **irreversible**
形 不可逆的

❷ **remedy**
動 補救

❸ **warning**
名 警告

❹ **encourage**
動 鼓勵

> 延伸note
> thanks to為「幸虧」之意，但thanks for sth.意指「為…表示感激」，後面的sth.表示原由。

 換個立場講講看

In order to do something about the environment, I volunteered[5] to participate in[6] the Beach Clean-up Day. By picking up the rubbish in the ocean[7], we can save the marine[8] life. I don't know if you watched the Disney movie "Happy Feet". If you did, you would know this kind of selfish[9] behavior will do harm to the ecology eventually[10]. It's never late to do something about it. What an individual can do might be limited, but it can make a big difference once there are thousands of people doing the same thing.

　　為了替環保盡一份力，我自願當「海灘清潔日」的志工。只要撿起海裡的垃圾，我們就能拯救海洋生物。我不知道你有沒有看過迪士尼的動畫《快樂腳》，如果你看過，你就會知道這種自私的行為最終會損害生態。行動永遠不嫌晚，一個人能做的或許有限，但如果有好幾千人都在做同樣的事情，就會有很大的改變了。

❺ volunteer 動 自願（做）	❻ participate in 片 參與	❼ ocean 名 海洋
❽ marine 形 海的；海產的	❾ selfish 形 自私的	❿ eventually 副 最終；終於

 試著更與眾不同

I used to drive to work. However, I changed and now ride[11] my bicycle instead. Because in this way, I believe I can reduce greenhouse[12] gas emissions[13]. I started cycling because of the environmental concerns at first[14], but I figured that it is also healthful. Therefore, I've been thinking about encouraging my colleagues to do the same thing. I can even invite them to go cycling together on weekends. If there were more people doing this, it would surely make a difference to the environment.

　　我以前都開車上班，不過後來我改變了，現在我都改騎腳踏車，因為我相信這樣能減少溫室氣體的排放量。起初，我是為了環境考量才改騎腳踏車，但後來我發現這也有益健康，所以我一直想要鼓勵我的同事響應，我甚至可以約他們週末的時候一起去騎腳踏車。如果有越來越多人這麼做，那肯定對環境更好。

⓫ ride 動 乘坐	⓬ greenhouse 名 溫室
⓭ emission 名 散發	⓮ at first 片 起初

延伸note
溫室效應氣體的種類很多，人為來源主要為車輛（vehicles）和工廠（factory）的排放氣體。

答題TIPS看這裡！

有很多環境損壞雖然無法回復，但人們依然能盡一己之力，盡量補救。其中一個例子是臭氧層破洞（the ozone hole）的問題，因為各國皆配合作為，所以臭氧層破洞的情形有很大的改善。如果能舉出實際例子，當然會更有說服力。

Words & Phrases　大自然被破壞的現象

1 **global warming**
全球暖化

2 **climate change**
氣候變遷

3 **greenhouse effect**
溫室效應

4 **desertification**
沙漠化

5 **ocean acidification**
海水酸化

6 **overexploitation**
過度開採

7 **habitat destruction**
棲息地破壞

8 **ozone depletion**
臭氧層破壞

進階實用句 More Expressions

Global warming is a warning for human beings.

全球暖化的現象是對人類的警告。

We must take environmental damage seriously and do something about it.

我們必須認真看待環境損壞這件事，並做些什麼來改善它。

Some developing countries have serious water contamination because of the enormous factories.

因為大量的工廠，水汙染的情形在部分開發中國家很嚴重。

UNIT 15

冬天、夏天二選一

Do you enjoy summer or winter more? Why?
夏天跟冬天相比,你更喜歡哪一個?為什麼?

 你可以這樣回答

MP3
120

I definitely enjoy summer more than winter. I like to go traveling. Summertime is better for me because it's when I can bring some light[1] baggage[2] with me. However, if I travel in winter, I have to bring sweaters[3], thick pants and my down jacket[4]. All of these will make my luggage really heavy. Besides, traveling in winter doesn't seem appealing to me. I don't want to stay in a hotel for the whole day. It feels boring just sitting there and watching the scenery.

和冬天比起來,我肯定比較喜歡夏天,我喜歡旅行,夏天去旅行比較好,因為我可以帶輕便的行李。但是,如果冬天出去旅行,我就必須帶毛衣、厚褲和羽絨大衣,這些東西會讓我的行李很重。而且,冬天旅行不怎麼吸引我。我不想待在旅館一整天,坐在那邊看風景實在太無聊了。

❶ **light**
形(重量)輕的

❷ **baggage**
名 行李

❸ **sweater**
名 毛衣

❹ **down jacket**
片 羽絨外套

延伸note
機場的行李則分為carry-on baggage(手提隨身行李)和 checked baggage(托運行李)兩種。

 換個立場講講看

I definitely like summer more. There are a lot of activities I can do in summer. I especially enjoy going to the beaches and checking out the girls in the bikinis[5]. This year, I am going to the gym regularly[6] to ensure I look good. When the summer comes, I will wear stylish[7] boardshorts and cool sunglasses[8]. I am sure that there will be girls looking at me, too! I can't wait for the summer to come. Maybe I will find myself a girlfriend this year! Of course, I don't dislike winter. But indoor activities are just not my type of thing.

　　我當然比較喜歡夏天，夏天能從事的活動很多。我尤其喜歡去海邊看比基尼辣妹。我今年會固定上健身房運動，以確保我的體態。夏天到的時候，我會穿上有形的海灘褲、戴上看起來很酷的太陽眼鏡，到時候肯定也會有注意我的女孩！真期待夏天到來，我今年搞不好能替自己找個女朋友呢！當然，我並不討厭冬天，但室內活動就是不符合我的胃口。

延伸note
夏天是玩水的季節，很多人這時都會特別想要 keep in good shape(保持良好的身材)。

5 bikini
名 比基尼

6 regularly
副 有規律地

7 stylish
形 時髦的

8 sunglasses
名 太陽眼鏡

試著更與眾不同

I enjoy winter a lot more than summer because I can wear thick clothes. I am not very confident[9] about my body shape[10]. I always try to cover[11] it as much as I can, even in summer. However, I get hot wearing a long-sleeved shirt in summer. I get sweaty all over[12]. On the contrary, winter suits[13] me better. It might sound awkward, but I feel secure[14] in my coat.

　　我喜歡冬天多過於夏天，因為我可以穿上厚重的衣物，我對我的身材沒有自信，總是希望可以全部包起來。可是在夏天穿長袖衣物真的很熱，我會因此汗流浹背，相較之下，冬天就比較適合我，聽起來或許很怪，但穿著大外套會讓我覺得比較有安全感。

9 confident
形 自信的

10 body shape
片 身材

11 cover
動 遮掩；遮蓋

12 all over
片 到處；各處

13 suit
動 適合

14 secure
形 安心的

答題TIPS看這裡！

如果只是比較夏天與冬天，舉例的時候就需要用極端比較的例子，例如只能在夏天或冬天才能做的事情。舉例來說，喜歡冬天的人可能喜歡看雪景，這就是夏天沒有辦法做的事；而夏天和冬天也各有缺點，夏天時可能酷暑難耐（sultry），冬天則因為太冷，人會變得比較懶散（inactive），也比較不便於從事戶外活動。

Words & Phrases 夏日的海邊行

1. **go to the beach**
   去海邊

2. **wear a bikini**
   穿比基尼

3. **get a nice tan**
   曬成古銅色

4. **enjoy the sea breeze**
   吹海風

Words & Phrases 冬天的推薦活動

1. **go skiing**
   去滑雪

2. **watch the snow flakes**
   看雪花飄

3. **build a snowman**
   堆雪人

4. **go to a hot spring**
   泡溫泉

進階實用句 More Expressions

Skiing is my favorite sport; I always look forward to the winter.

滑雪是我最喜歡的運動，我總是很期待冬天的到來。

I like working on a nice tan during summer.

我夏天的時候喜歡把皮膚曬成古銅色。

I enjoy winter a lot more than summer because I don't like being sweaty.

我喜歡冬天遠勝過夏天，因為我不喜歡汗流浹背的感覺。

374

Part 9

政治與媒體
Politics and Media

 動 動詞 　　 形 形容詞 　　 連 連接詞

 名 名詞 　　 介 介系詞 　　 片 片語

 副 副詞

UNIT 01 關於社交軟體

Q What do you think of social media?
你對社交軟體的看法如何?

MP3 121

你可以這樣回答

Social media[1] has become part of our life. All my friends are regular[2] social media users. We can share our lives and all kinds of information on it even though we live in different cities. I can even know where they are because they update[3] their location[4] all the time. If they met a good-looking[5] guy, they might even post a photo of him. By seeing the picture[6], I feel I am with them right there and then.

社交網路軟體已經是我們生活的一部分了。我的朋友都是社交軟體的高頻率使用者。就算我們各自住在不同的城市,也可以在上面分享生活點滴和各式各樣的資訊。因為他們常常打卡,所以我甚至會知道他們的所在地。如果他們遇到帥哥,也很可能上傳對方的照片,看到照片,就會讓我有種和他們在一起的感覺。

❶ media 名 媒體	❷ regular 形 固定的	❸ update 動 更新
❹ location 名 地點	❺ good-looking 形 好看的;漂亮的	❻ picture 名 圖片;照片

換個立場講講看

I think the biggest concern of using social media is Internet safety. I like to post everything about my day on Facebook, but I am not sure whether the information will be used in an illegal[7] way or not. A lot of fraud[8] has happened through the Internet, so we must be careful about this. In addition, I have no idea who is seeing the messages[9] I post. I got comments from my friend's friends before. I didn't know who they are. Not until then did I realize that even strangers[10] can see my posts.

我覺得社交網路平台最大的問題是網路安全。我很喜歡在臉書上分享生活點滴,但卻無法確保我分享的東西不會被人拿來利用在不法的事情上。網路詐騙的例子很多,所以我們必須很小心謹慎。除此之外,我也不能確定有誰能看到我的文章。我之前曾經看到我朋友的朋友寫回應給我,但我根本不知道他們誰,那時候我才發現連陌生人都看得到我的文章。

延伸note
詐騙集團(fraud gang)除了詐騙電話(a fraud call),還會利用網路進行網路詐騙。

⑦ **illegal**
　形 不合法的

⑧ **fraud**
　名 欺騙(行為);騙局

⑨ **message**
　名 訊息

⑩ **stranger**
　名 陌生人

試著更與眾不同

I really regretted[11] adding some of my relatives as my Facebook friends. It is like they are watching what I have been doing recently[12]. The moment I posted something, I would get a reply from this particular person that I really don't like. I feel bad deleting[13] her from my friend list, but I got so sick of[14] it. At last, I registered[15] for another account that only adds[16] a small number of friends.

我實在很後悔把親戚加入臉書好友,因為他們好像在監看我的一舉一動。只要我一更新動態,馬上就會有個我很不喜歡的人回應,我不好意思將她從我的好友名單裡刪除,但又實在很受不了這種情況。所以,我最後又申請了一個新帳號,這個帳號只加少數的好友。

⑪ **regret**
　動 後悔

⑫ **recently**
　副 最近;近來

⑬ **delete**
　動 刪除

⑭ **get sick of**
　片 厭倦

⑮ **register**
　動 註冊

⑯ **add**
　動 增加;添加

答題TIPS看這裡！

現在這個時代，不單單只有年輕人懂得如何操作智慧型手機，很多長輩也開始用社群網站來跟兒女們連絡，功能比傳統的簡訊齊全多了。不過，五花八門的功能卻也可能讓人眼花撩亂，部分對科技不熟悉的人，也會為了操作不順而苦惱，例如：I want to share my selfie, but I don't know how to do that.（我想分享自拍照，但我不知該如何操作。）

Words & Phrases　認識臉書的各種設計

1　**news feed**
動態時報

2　**profile picture**
大頭照

3　**chat box**
聊天視窗

4　**fan page**
粉絲專頁

Words & Phrases　臉書上常見的動作

1　**update one's status**
更新動態

2　**give sb. a thumbs-up**
按讚

3　**unfriend**
刪除好友

4　**tag**
標記

進階實用句 More Expressions

I always chat with my parents via video calls.

我都是打視訊電話跟我爸媽聊天。

I posted a selfie with my puppy and got 1000 likes.

我上傳的我跟小狗的自拍照，有一千人按讚。

I like to add my location on Facebook, so my boyfriend knows where I am.

我喜歡在臉書上打卡，這樣我男朋友就知道我在哪裡。

UNIT 02

看報紙的偏好

Q **Do you read the newspapers? Which page do you like to read?**

你會看報紙嗎？喜歡閱讀哪一刊？

你可以這樣回答

MP3 122

Yes, I read newspapers[1], but I usually won't go out of my way to buy them. I read newspapers when I find them on a train or in a restaurant. When I read them, I go to the entertainment[2] page immediately. Celebrity[3] gossip[4] is a lot easier to read than politics. The former takes no brainpower to process[5]. It is a perfect way to kill time[6] while I am waiting for the train or traveling somewhere.

　我會看報紙，但我通常不會特別去買，如果在火車上或餐廳裡看到報紙，我才會拿來翻一下。閱讀報紙的時候，我會直接翻到影視娛樂版，名人的八卦比政治新聞容易閱讀多了，看八卦總是比較不須要用大腦。等火車或旅行的時候，用這個來打發時間的效果最好。

❶ newspapers 名 報紙；新聞	**❷ entertainment** 名 娛樂	**❸ celebrity** 名 名人
❹ gossip 名 八卦	**❺ process** 動 處理	**❻ kill time** 片 打發時間

換個立場講講看

Certainly. I buy newspapers quite often[7], especially the day after a big sports event[8]. I like to read about the scores[9] and the comments on the performance of the athletes[10]. Sometimes when I am eager[11] to know the scores, I turn to the Internet so that I won't need to wait until the next day. If there's nothing special in the sports pages, I will read the lifestyle[12] pages. However, I don't read political news because it would only bore me.

　　當然，我常買報紙，尤其是重要比賽的隔天。我會看最終比數，也愛看有關運動員表現的評論。有時候，當我迫不急待想知道比賽的結果時，我會去查網路資訊，這樣就不用等到隔天了。如果體育版沒有特別的新聞，我就會看生活版。不過，我絕對不看政治新聞，那只會讓我覺得很無趣。

7 often
副 經常

8 event
名 事件；（比賽）項目

9 score
名 得分；比數

10 athlete
名 運動員

11 eager
形 渴望的

12 lifestyle
名 生活方式

試著更與眾不同

Not really. I don't buy newspapers often. Instead, I prefer to read the news online. In addition to the fact that it is free, I don't need to worry about recycling the newspapers after I am done with them. My favorite is the political news because I don't have time to watch the evening[13] news on television. The political[14] news in Taiwan sometimes is quite entertaining[15]. You would not believe some of the things those politicians[16] say.

　　不太會，我不怎麼買報紙，我比較喜歡閱讀網路上的新聞。除了因為是免費的之外，也不需要擔心之後的回收問題。我最喜歡看的是政治版，因為我沒時間看電視上的晚間新聞。台灣的政治新聞真的很能夠娛樂讀者，那些政客說的話有時候真的讓人瞠目結舌。

13 evening
名 傍晚；晚間

14 political
形 政治的

16 entertaining
形 有趣的

17 politician
名 政客

> **延伸note**
> 政客常見的負面形容詞包括radical(激進的)、windy(空談的)、tricky(奸詐的)…等。

Key Points

答題TIPS看這裡！

因為網路的便利性，會買實體報紙的人減少，可是餐廳還是會提供實體報紙。若是會定期買報紙的人，應該都有自己偏好的版面。不過，如果是免費發放（for free）的報紙，大家也可能會全部快速瀏覽一遍。

Words & Phrases	認識報紙的細節
1 **headline** 標題	2 **subheading** 副標題
3 **photo credit** 圖片來源	4 **caption** 照片描述

Words & Phrases	報紙各個版面
1 **front page** 頭版	2 **entertainment page** 娛樂版
3 **sports page** 體育版	4 **classified ad.** 分類廣告

 進階實用句 More Expressions

I can't wait until the day after to read the news.

我無法等到隔天再看新聞。

I read the finance pages like a Bible because I have invested in the stock market.

我天天看金融版，因為我有投資股票。

I can view other perspectives towards certain issues by reading the editorial page.

藉由閱讀社論，我可以學到其他人對某些議題的看法。

UNIT
03
電視、廣播與網路

Q **What's the main difference between TV, radio and the Internet?**

電視、廣播與網路最大的差異在哪裡？

你可以這樣回答

MP3
123

I believe the main[1] difference between TV, radio and the Internet is credibility[2] and reliability[3]. To me, the Internet is the least trustworthy[4] source of information. Anyone can write his or her opinions on a specific issue. Even hackers can hack into[5] any websites and change the information. So there's no way we can recognize the truthfulness[6] of the information online. On the contrary, TV and radio are more reliable.

　　我認為電視、廣播以及網路最大的不同在於信任度以及可靠度。在我看來，網路上的資料是最沒什麼可信度的。任何人都能針對某個議題高談闊論，連駭客都能駭進網站竄改資訊，我們根本就無從判斷網路資訊的真實性。相比之下，電視和廣播就可靠多了。

❶ **main**
形 主要的

❷ **credibility**
名 可信性

❸ **reliability**
名 可靠度

❹ **trustworthy**
形 可信的

❺ **hack into**
片 侵入（別人的電腦系統）

❻ **truthfulness**
名 真實

換個立場講講看

The main difference between TV, radio and the Internet is the level[7] of animation[8]. I think TV is the most attractive and entertaining source of information. There is a lot of audio[9] and visual[10] stimulation[11]. Radio, on the other

hand, offers only audio stimulation to the audience. I sometimes fall asleep when I am listening to it. However, radio has its advantages[12]. I can listen to it when I drive, but I can't carry a television with me everywhere.

電視、廣播和網路最大的不同在其生動的程度。我覺得電視最吸引人，也最具娛樂性，電視會有很多影音刺激，相比之下，廣播就只能提供聲音方面的刺激給聽眾，我聽廣播有時候還會睡著。不過，廣播也是有優點的，我開車的時候就可以聽廣播，畢竟我不可能隨身攜帶一台電視。

⑦ level
名 程度；標準

⑧ animation
名 生氣；活潑

⑨ audio
形 聽覺的；聲音的

⑩ visual
形 視覺的

⑪ stimulation
名 刺激

⑫ advantage
名 優點；優勢

試著更與眾不同

Well, I don't think that TV, radio and the Internet are really that different. All of them offer[13] us information. The only difference among these three is the type of medium[14]. Different users will choose the most convenient one for themselves. For example, if I am out, I can only watch shows[15] via the Internet. However, television is my first choice while I am at home. I can alternate[16] one with the other freely based on where I am.

我不覺得電視、廣播和網路有很大的不同，三個都能提供資訊。唯一的不同就是媒介的型態，不同的使用者會選擇最方便、最適合自己的媒介。比方說，如果我人在外面，我就只能透過網路看節目；但如果我在家裡，電視就會是我的最佳選擇。我會根據我所在的地點，自由地選擇最適合當下情境的工具。

⑬ offer
動 給予；提供

⑭ medium
名 媒介

⑮ show
名 表演；演出節目

⑯ alternate
動 使交替

> **延伸note**
> 與show相關的節目有：talk show(脫口秀)、variety show(綜藝節目)、game show(益智問答)…等。

答題TIPS看這裡！

比較電視，廣播及網路，可以從兩方面下手，第一是可信度，例如: 網路的訊息很容易被駭客入侵。第二點是在何種情況下使用的方便性，例如開車的時候聽廣播比較安全，這樣就容易比較。另外，網路與電視、廣播最大的差別在於，網路能讓使用者鎖定特定類型的節目收看。現在，也開始出現純網路的節目與電視劇，這也可能會變成未來的主流。

Words & Phrases 消息來源的可信度

1 credibility
信任度

2 reliability
可靠度

3 verify
求證；驗證

4 source
消息來源

Words & Phrases 各種主持人的說法

1 host
廣播、電視節目主持人

2 (news) anchor
新聞主播

3 DJ (= disc jockey)
音樂節目主持人

4 commentator
實況解說員（尤指運動賽事）

進階實用句 More Expressions

We must be careful of the scams online.

我們必須小心網路上的騙局。

I always wonder how to verify the information published online.

我總是在想線上公開的資訊要怎麼求證其可信度。

Although I watch TV every day, I don't find all the information reliable.

雖然我每天看電視，但並非所有資訊都很可靠。

UNIT 04 限制網路的必要性

Q **Is there a need to have government restrictions on the Internet and TV?**

政府有必要限制網路與電視節目嗎？

 你可以這樣回答

 MP3 124

In my opinion, restrictions[1] on TV and the Internet would not really work these days. There are more and more people used to watching TV programs[2] via YouTube. Even if you block[3] certain sites for some reasons, it might not work because there are quite a lot of people good at cracking[4] security. These are no longer[5] the martial[6] law days. Even my 60-year-old mother has an iPhone to Google with. Having restrictions is not going to work.

就我看來，限制電視節目和網路不會有什麼用。越來越多人習慣在Youtube上觀看電視節目，就算你為了一些原因而封鎖某些網站，也不一定有用，因為懂得破解的人也很多。現在已經不是戒嚴時期，就連我六十歲的母親都有一台iPhone，知道怎麼上網，限制不可能有用。

❶ **restriction**
動 限制；約束

❷ **program**
名 節目；演出

❸ **block**
動 阻擋；限制

❹ **crack**
動 破解（密碼等）

❺ **no longer**
片 不再

❻ **martial**
形 軍事的

 換個立場講講看

Sure. I agree that there should be some restrictions on TV and the Internet; otherwise, they would create[7] some problems for society[8]. I don't want my kids to watch the programs with violence[9] or adult[10] themes[11]. How can I stop them from watching that if it is available to them on TV and the Internet? Furthermore, if the government has no knowledge of what kind of information people are receiving, it might make it very hard to enforce the legislation[12].

當然,我同意電視節目和網路都必須被限制,不然社會將產生問題。我並不希望我的小孩看到涉及暴力及成人主題的節目,但如果那些節目充斥在電視及網路上,我要如何避免呢?除此之外,如果政府不清楚人民接收到什麼樣的資訊,推動政令時可能會變得很困難。

❼ create
動 引起;產生

❽ society
名 社會

❾ violence
名 暴力

❿ adult
形 成人的

⓫ theme
名 主題

⓬ legislation
名 法律;法規

試著更與眾不同

I personally believe there should be some restrictions on TV and the Internet, but they have to be fair and honest. Otherwise, those mediums will lose credibility[13] with people. For example, a news channel[14] in a communist country is used more as a tool for the government to promote communism[15] rather than for reporting the truth. In that case, the information is biased[16], and the Internet is controlled by the government, too. This is not what people want or expect.

我個人認為電視節目和網路的確應該要有一些限制。前提是,必須公平且誠實。否則,人民將會對其誠信失去信賴。舉例來說,共產國家的新聞台就像政府提倡共產主義的工具,不會報導真相。在這種情況下,大眾接收到的資訊都會很偏頗,而且,網路也被政府控制,這並非人民想要的結果。

⓭ credibility
名 可信度;可靠性

⓮ channel
名 頻道

⓯ communism
名 共產主義

⓰ biased
形 存有偏見的

延伸note
講到政體,和民主國家 (democracy)相對的,是一人或少數人專政的極權國家(dictatorship)。

Key Points

答題TIPS看這裡！

想想看網路和電視節目的影響力有多大，指出實際影響的層面，就你的角度及生活經驗來舉例，例如Facebook, Line, Twitter...等等，這些通訊軟體都可以應用在對話之中，這樣就可以輕而易舉地回答。

Words & Phrases　電影分級的說法

1 general (G)
普遍級

2 parental guidance (PG)
輔導級

3 mature audience (MA)
15歲以下兒童不適合收看

4 restricted (R)
限制級

Words & Phrases　過當的網路監控

1 human rights
人權

2 hacker
（電）駭客

3 monitor
監控；監聽

4 block
阻擋；妨礙

 ## 進階實用句 More Expressions

I busted my brother trying to get on to restricted websites.

我發現我弟弟想偷上有管制的網站。

There will always be a hacker who knows the way to crack a code.

總會有駭客知道破解的方法。

The government can only control the media to a certain degree. There is so much more online nowadays!

政府限制媒體最多也只能到某個程度，網路上限制不到的還多著呢！

UNIT 05

喜歡的節目類型

 你可以這樣回答

 MP3 125

My favorite kind of TV programs are comedic[1] talk shows; I like the way the hosts throw in jokes here and there when they are interviewing[2] the celebrities. In order to make the show funny, the hosts sometimes make fun of the guests[3]. However, he might embarrass[4] the guest if the jokes are not planned carefully. I think you need to be very talented to be a comedian[5]. It is hard to say something funny but not offensive[6].

　　我最喜歡的節目是喜劇的脫口秀，我喜歡看主持人採訪名人時開玩笑的輕鬆氣氛。為了讓節目有趣，主持人有時候會開來賓的玩笑，但是，如果沒有拿捏好，這些玩笑就會讓來賓感到很尷尬，我覺得要成為諧星必須很有天分，說的話必須搞笑，但又不能讓人覺得失禮，要恰到好處其實不容易。

❶ **comedic**	❷ **interview**	❸ **guest**
形 喜劇的	動 採訪	名 來賓
❹ **embarrass**	❺ **comedian**	❻ **offensive**
動 使窘	名 丑角式人物	形 冒犯的

 換個立場講講看

I enjoy watching the singing competitions[7]. It is very entertaining listening to the beautiful voices. I like singing myself, too. I can learn some singing skills by watching the competitions because the judges[8] give out a tip or two. Sometimes

they even demonstrate⁹ how to express the songs with more feelings and a better tone of voice. Of course, there might be some competitors¹⁰ I don't like. It's always interesting to discuss the ones I like the most with my friends.

　　我很喜歡看歌唱比賽的節目，聽到美麗的歌聲總是很能放鬆，我自己也喜歡唱歌，我可以藉由看比賽學到一些歌唱技巧，因為評審會指點一二，評審有時候甚至會當場示範更富情感的唱歌方式，以及更加優美的音調。當然，我也會有不喜歡的參賽者，和朋友討論自己最支持的參賽者總是很有樂趣。

延伸note
如果有特定觀賞的歌唱比賽節目，不妨舉實例，如：American Idol(美國偶像)。

❼ **competition**
名 比賽；競賽

❽ **judge**
名 評審

❾ **demonstrate**
動 示範

❿ **competitor**
名 參賽者

試著更與眾不同

I love to watch the Korean¹¹ soap operas¹². For some reason, Korean soap operas are more attractive¹³ than the Taiwanese TV series. Maybe it has something to do with how good-looking and stylish¹⁴ the actors are. I think we should try to support our domestic¹⁵ TV industry¹⁶. If we can improve the quality, we can also attract a larger audience. Recently, I've seen some Korean soap operas adapted from Taiwanese scripts. I feel happy about this.

　　我喜歡看韓劇，奇怪的是，韓劇就是比台劇要吸引人，可能是因為裡面的演員都很帥氣、有形的關係吧。我覺得我們也應該要扶植國內的電視產業。如果我們能提升品質，就能吸引更多的觀眾。最近看到台劇受到青睞，被改編成韓劇，這讓我感到很開心。

⓫ **Korean**
形 韓國（人）的

⓬ **soap opera**
片 連續劇

⓭ **attractive**
形 吸引人的

⓮ **stylish**
形 時髦的；流行的

⓯ **domestic**
形 國內的

⓰ **industry**
名 企業；行業

答題TIPS看這裡！

各式各樣的節目都有人喜愛，只要明確的指出喜歡的節目是哪一種類並加以解釋，就能輕鬆答題。例如：I love watching the news because I found the reporters of the news channels are very pretty.（我喜歡看新聞，因為我覺得新聞台的主播都很漂亮。）如果平常不怎麼看電視，也可以用 I don't watch TV very often.開頭，再詳加敘述。

Words & Phrases 家庭常看的電視節目

1 talk show
脫口秀

2 sitcom
情境喜劇

3 cartoon
卡通節目

4 TV series
影集

Words & Phrases 電視的周邊產品

1 remote control
遙控器

2 wide screen
寬螢幕

3 DVD player
DVD放映機

4 speaker
揚聲器；音響喇叭

進階實用句 More Expressions

I especially like watching travel shows.

我特別喜歡看旅遊節目。

The Discovery Channel is my favorite. I love the documentaries in particular.

《探索頻道》是我的最愛，我尤其喜歡看紀錄片。

Have you ever watched a talent show? There are a lot of people who amaze me.

你有看過達人秀嗎？節目上會出現很多讓我讚嘆不已的人。

UNIT 06 與朋友談政治

Q **Do you talk about politics with your friends?**
你會與朋友談政治嗎？

你可以這樣回答

MP3 126

No, I think politics¹ are too sensitive² to talk about with my friends. Not everyone feels the same about the various political parties. Unless I am absolutely sure about my friends' preference, I do not mention it at all; otherwise, we might end up fighting and arguing about the politics and politicians. Couples have even divorced³ over political issues. My motto⁴ is: never discuss politics if you still want to be friends.

　　不會，我覺得和朋友談政治信念實在太敏感了。不是每個人都支持一樣的政黨。除非我確定朋友的偏好，否則我不會提起政治話題。否則，我們最後可能會為了談論政治與政客而大吵一架，以前甚至還發生過夫妻因政治立場而離婚的呢！我的座右銘是：如果還想要維持友誼，就不要討論政治。

❶ **politics**
名 政治

❷ **sensitive**
形 敏感的

❸ **divorce**
動 離婚

❹ **motto**
名 座右銘

> **延伸note**
> end up後面接動名詞，表示「最後在做什麼」；後面接名詞表示「最後到達什麼狀態」。

換個立場講講看

Absolutely! My grandfather⁵ was in the air force⁶, so I have lived in the air force community with them since I was born⁷. Most of the people here seem to have the same political beliefs, and what my grandfather and his friends like to do is to sit around in the courtyard[8] and criticize the Democratic[9] Progressive[10] Party. However, things have changed now. Our neighbors seem to criticize our president more than anyone else.

當然會，我的爺爺以前是空軍的一員，所以從我出生後，我們家就一直住在空軍眷村。大部分眷村的人都擁有相同的政治傾向，我爺爺和他朋友最喜歡做的事，就是坐在中庭批評民進黨。不過，時空背景已經不同了，我們的鄰居現在最常做的，就是批評總統。

5 grandfather 名 祖父；爺爺		**6** air force 片 空軍		**7** born 形 出生的	
8 courtyard 名 庭院		**9** democratic 形 民主的		**10** progressive 形 進步的；革新的	

試著更與眾不同

I think there is no point arguing[11] about political issues. To some extent, politics is like a religion[12]. Once you believe in it, no one can talk you out of it. It is a very personal matter[13]. I would discuss with my friends about a particular political matter such as a new law or regulation[14]. However, I would try to avoid showing my political party preference. I think everyone has the right[15] to believe in whatever they want. We should respect[16] that.

我覺得為了政治議題而與人爭執是件很沒有意義的事。就某部分來說，政治與宗教信仰其實有相似之處，一旦你相信了，就沒有人能改變你的想法，這是很私人的事。我會和朋友討論像是新法律或法規這類的政治議題，但我會避免顯露個人的政治傾向。我覺得每個人都有權利選擇自己想相信的，我們應該尊重這一點。

11 argue 動 爭執		**12** religion 名 宗教		**13** matter 名 事務	
14 regulation 名 規章；條例		**15** right 名 權利		**16** respect 動 尊重	

Key Points

答題TIPS看這裡！

政治是個很敏感的話題，可它同時也是人們喜歡在茶餘飯後討論的事。大家對政治的堅持與狂熱，從外表有時看不太出來，為了政治立場不同而爭吵者大有人在，這也可能是政論節目之所以風行的原因。

Words & Phrases 政府機關與元首

1 **parliament**
國會

2 **legislative**
立法機關

3 **president**
總統

4 **prime minister**
首相；總理

Words & Phrases 選舉候選人的作為

1 **hustings**
政見發表會

2 **debate**
辯論

3 **solicit votes**
拜票

4 **publicize**
廣告宣傳

進階實用句 More Expressions

The politicians are pressing defamation charges against each other.

政治人物正在互相告毀謗。

I watch political commentary to hear the experts' opinions.

我看政論節目，因為我想聽聽專家的看法。

I normally keep my political preference to myself. I don't like arguing it with my friends.

我會隱藏自己的政治傾向，因為我不喜歡和朋友爭論。

UNIT 07 影響投票的因素

What factor(s) will affect your vote in an election?

影響你選舉會投誰的因素是什麼？

 你可以這樣回答

MP3
127

The candidates[1] policy proposals[2] would be something that affects my vote in an election[3]. Through their proposals, I can see what the politicians are going to do once they are elected. However, if a politician is running for re-election[4], I would carefully evaluate his or her performance during the term of office[5]. This would be a good indicator[6] to see whether the politician is trustworthy enough to be elected the second time.

候選人的政見會影響我的投票意願。根據他們的政見，我就能知曉候選人選上之後打算做些什麼事。不過，如果候選人是要競選連任，那我就會評估他任期內的表現，這是一個很好的指標，能看出候選人能不能被託付。

❶ **candidate**
名 候選人

❷ **proposal**
名 建議；提議

❸ **election**
名 選舉

❹ **re-election**
名 重新當選

❺ **the term of office**
片 任期

❻ **indicator**
名 指示物；指標

 換個立場講講看

The political party would be something I look for in an election. In general[7], I agree with the ideology[8] of the Democratic Progressive Party more than any other parties. I believe they need to have more seats[9] in the Legislature to be able to pass and execute the policy they wish to promote. This goal[10] is not easy, but I believe the situation would change gradually[11]. Therefore, I always vote for the candidates who belong to[12] the Democratic Progressive Party.

政黨會是我投票的參考因素。和其他政黨相比,我通常比較認同民進黨的意識形態。我認為他們必須在立法院當中取得更多的席次,才有辦法通過並施行他們想推動的政策。這個目標並不容易,但我覺得情況將能逐漸改變,因此,我每次都會投給民進黨的候選人。

7 in general
片 通常

8 ideology
名 意識形態

9 seat
名 席次

10 goal
名 目標

11 gradually
副 逐漸地

12 belong to
片 屬於

試著更與眾不同

Scandals[13] like bribery[14] would definitely affect[15] my vote in an election. For example, if one candidate got busted[16] taking a bribe, I would not vote for him or his party at all. I think remaining uncorrupted[17] is a key factor in being a statesman[18]. Having this personal belief would mean that a politician would work hard for all people, not just for his own benefit. However, a politician with a corrupt mind would do the things opposite. It would be such a terrible thing for a country and its people.

收賄之類的醜聞絕對會影響我的投票意願。比方說,如果有候選人被踢爆收賄,我就絕對不會投給他,也不可能投給他隸屬的政黨。我覺得要成為政治家,清廉是一個非常關鍵的特質,表示這名政治家不會只考量自己的利益,而會為了全體人民的福祉而努力。相比之下,會貪污的政客所做的就完全相反,對國家和人民來說是件很可怕的事。

13 scandal
名 醜聞

14 bribery
名 行賄;收賄

15 affect
動 影響

16 bust
動 使爆裂

17 uncorrupted
形 未被收買的

18 statesman
名 政治家

答題TIPS看這裡！

影響選舉的原因有很多，有些人是選人不選黨，有人是選黨不選人，有些人相信政見，有些人在乎人格清廉。其實時事也是影響選舉的很重要原因，如果候選人選前被爆出收賄，或是執政黨被發現與官商勾結（collusion），甚至是候選人有緋聞（love affair / scandal），都可能影響選民的支持度。

Words & Phrases　與投票有關的詞彙

1 poll worker
選務人員

2 voting booth
投票亭

3 ballot paper
選票

4 cast a vote
投票

Words & Phrases　候選人的負面新聞

1 bribery
賄賂

2 violence
暴力事件

3 corruption
貪汙

4 accusation
指控；誣告

進階實用句 More Expressions

I would not vote for members who betrayed their own party.

我不會投給背叛自己政黨的人。

There will be a lot of accusations when the election is approaching.

隨著選舉的接近，法律指控也會越來越多。

Politicians do not appreciate any negative news because it might destroy their reputation in an instant.

政客們都不願意有負面新聞，因為他們的名聲可能毀於一旦。

UNIT 08

抗議和請願

Are protests and petitions effective ways to express different voices?

抗議和請願是表達不同意見的有效手段嗎？

 你可以這樣回答

MP3
128

I think protests[1] and petitions[2] are very effective[3] in terms of expressing people's different voices, especially when the events draw wide attention[4]. If no one knows about the protest or petition, it might not make a difference. Therefore, the media always plays an important role. With a lot of media exposure[5], people can understand what the protesters' appeal[6] is. That is how it works in a democratic country.

　　人民想要發聲的話，抗議和請願是很有效的手段，尤其是當抗議本身引起廣泛的關注時更有效。如果沒有人知道抗議或請願的事，最後就可能會不了了之。因此，在抗議行動裡，媒體總是扮演著很重要的角色，因為有大量的媒體曝光，所以大眾能了解抗議者的訴求是什麼，這就是民主國家的運作方式。

❶ protest 名 抗議	❷ petition 名 請願	❸ effective 形 有效的
❹ attention 名 注意；關注	❺ exposure 名 曝光；曝露	❻ appeal 名 訴求

 換個立場講講看

I don't think protests and petitions are effective in expressing different voices. Quite a lot of protests lose their true value[7] once they got more attention. For example, the 318 Sunflower[8] Student Movement[9] was meant to be a protest against the fact that the Legislative[10] Yuan passed the Cross-Strait Service Agreement in a ridiculous[11] manner. However, people seem to only remember the riot[12] at the end. The reason behind the protest seems to be lost.

想要表達不同的訴求，我不覺得抗議和請願會有效。有相當多的抗議活動都會在關注度提高之後，失去了其訴求的核心價值。就像318太陽花學運原本是為了抗議立法院以不合規定的方式，強行通過兩岸貿易協定，但到最後，人們似乎只記得暴動，抗議真正的意義反而沒人記得。

7 value
名 重要性；價值

8 sunflower
名 向日葵

9 movement
名 運動；活動

10 legislative
形 立法的

11 ridiculous
形 可笑的；荒謬的

12 riot
名 暴動

試著更與眾不同

I don't think protests and petitions make any difference at all. I think their only purpose[13] is to make the protestors feel better about themselves. It makes them feel that they are doing something about the situation they are in. Just think about the protests formed[14] by laid-off employees[15]. They did everything they could to draw more attention, but I have never seen the employers[16] come out to give the workers what they wanted.

我不覺得抗議和請願有什麼效果，我覺得唯一的作用只是自我安慰，讓抗議者覺得替自己做了些什麼，只要看看被解雇員工所發起的抗議行動就能理解。他們會盡己所能地取得關注，但我從來沒有看過有哪個老闆跳出來答應這些員工的訴求。

13 purpose
名 目的

14 form
動 形成；構成

15 employee
名 雇員；員工

16 employer
名 雇主；老闆

> **延伸note**
> sit-in為「靜坐抗議」。如果是一整夜都不離開的靜坐抗議，稱為overnight sit-in。

Key Points

答題TIPS看這裡！

抗議和請願並非相同的概念，一般街頭看到的抗議行為稱作protest，這種活動涉及集會結社相關的法律；但請願（petition）指的是利用請願書等法律途徑，向政府表達意見的流程，舉例或解釋的時候一定要分清楚。

Words & Phrases 抗議與請願

1. **protestor**
   抗議者
2. **political appeal**
   政治訴求
3. **media coverage**
   媒體報導
4. **fight against**
   抗爭

Words & Phrases 抗議造成的結果

1. **outcome**
   結果
2. **arrest**
   逮捕
3. **mutual benefit**
   雙贏；共同的利益
4. **conflict**
   衝突

進階實用句 More Expressions

The police arrested a few protestors after the conflict.

在那場衝突之後，警方逮捕了一些抗議者。

I don't think the government changed its attitude after the protest demonstration.

我覺得在抗議遊行結束後，政府依然沒有改變其態度。

Protests might create more conflicts between the two parties involved.

抗議可能會讓雙方人馬的對立情況變得更嚴重。

UNIT 09 看新聞的重要性

Q **Do you think it's important to follow news?**
你認為注意新聞重要嗎？

你可以這樣回答

MP3 129

I do think it is important to follow the news. I watch the international news every day. Through the news, I realize what is going on around the world. Sometimes it informs us of the changes which affect our daily lives[1], such as fluctuations[2] in petrol prices. Besides that, it's also a good topic to start a conversation[3] with. If you don't follow the news, you might feel bored while others are exchanging[4] their opinions on a specific event.

　　我覺得注意新聞很重要，我每天都看國際新聞。藉由新聞，我能了解世界上正在發生的事情。有時候，新聞會報導一些和我們生活息息相關的事情，例如油價上漲之類的。除此之外，新聞也是能開啟對話的工具，如果你沒在注意新聞，那當其他人都在針對某個事件交換意見時，你就會感到特別無聊。

❶ **daily life**
片 日常生活

❷ **fluctuation**
名 波動；變動

❸ **conversation**
名 對話；會話

❹ **exchange**
動 交換

延伸note
講到汽油，美式的說法為 gas；petrol 則為英式說法，可依照情況自行替換。

換個立場講講看

Honestly, I don't see the importance of following the news. I spend a lot of time working overtime. I don't have the energy[5] to catch up with[6] the latest news after a whole day's hard work. Even though I don't follow the news, I don't think I miss out[7] on anything. That is, not knowing about the latest news makes no difference to my life. I know that the next election is not until next year. This is all the news I need to know at this stage[8].

說句實在話，我實在看不出新聞有什麼重要的。我加班的時間很多，經過一整天的忙碌洗禮，實在也沒那個精神去看新聞。不過，就算沒看新聞，我也不覺得自己錯過了什麼，新聞內容對我來說一點都不重要。我知道明年要選舉，就現階段而言，我覺得自己只要知道這個就夠了。

延伸note
有一種對政治冷感的人，不會關心時事，英文稱這種現象為political alienation(政治冷感)。

❺ **energy**
名 能量；能源

❻ **catch up with**
片 趕上

❼ **miss out**
片 失去…的機會

❽ **stage**
名 階段；時期

試著更與眾不同

I don't have much interest in news. However, I think it is a good way to start a conversation with others. When I run out of[9] things to say, I always remark[10] and comment[11] on the news I have seen lately[12]. It works well every time. I know there are people who don't follow the news, but most people I meet do. Even though they might not follow the details, most people will have a general idea of the big events.

我對新聞沒什麼興趣，但是，我覺得新聞是與別人聊天的好話題。當我沒話講的時候，我就會主動評論我最近看的時事新聞，這招每次都有效。我知道不是每個人都會看新聞，但我遇到的大部分人都會看，就算他們不曉得細節，也會對重大事件有基本的概念。

❾ **run out of**
片 用光；耗盡

❿ **remark**
動 評論；議論

⓫ **comment**
動 解釋；評論

⓬ **lately**
副 最近

延伸note
談論新聞(the news)和談論政治(politics)不同，新聞不一定涉及政治立場，因此能成為聊天話題。

答題TIPS看這裡！

看新聞除了可以與社會和國際接軌之外，對人際關係也很有幫助，是一個很好聊天的話題，因為大部分的人都會看新聞，就算他們沒有看，你也可以扮演告知的角色。有關新聞的話題不見得都很嚴肅，像生活方面的新聞，或是影劇新聞，都是能開啟對話的好主題。

Words & Phrases 描述政治情況的詞彙

1. **play politics**
   玩弄政治手段

2. **flip flopper**
   立場不一致的人

3. **pork barrel**
   政治酬庸

4. **lobbyist**
   說客

Words & Phrases 敘述國際財金情勢

1. **referendum**
   公投

2. **standoff**
   僵局

3. **debt-stricken**
   負債累累的

4. **bailout**
   緊急（財政）援助

進階實用句 More Expressions

I listen to a news channel on the radio every day.

我每天都會聽新聞廣播。

I have to work overtime tonight, so I will miss out the evening news.

我今天晚上要加班，所以沒辦法看晚間新聞了。

CNN has very detailed coverage on most international matters.

CNN對大部分的國際事件都有很詳盡的報導。

402

UNIT 10

眼中的電視廣告

Q **What do you think about advertisements on TV?**

你對電視廣告的看法為何？

你可以這樣回答

MP3 130

I know some people dislike[1] advertisements because they interfere with their TV watching enjoyment. I actually don't mind watching advertisements. Some of them are quite creative. Advertising agencies put in a lot of effort to create the 30-second advertisement, trying to increase[2] sales[3] for their clients. Because the company needs to compress[4] all the ideas within 30 seconds[5], the ads are very creative[6]. There are quite a lot of good advertisements on TV.

我知道有些人不喜歡廣告，會覺得廣告打斷他們看電視節目的趣味，但我其實不介意看廣告，有些廣告很有創意。廣告公司會花很多心血打造這短短的三十秒，希望藉由廣告帶動產品銷量。因為公司必須把所有想法濃縮在這三十秒當中，所以廣告都會很有創意，優秀的電視廣告其實還滿多的呢！

❶ dislike 動 不喜歡	❷ increase 動 增加	❸ sale 名 銷售量
❹ compress 動 濃縮	❺ second 名 秒	❻ creative 形 有創意的

換個立場講講看

I get annoyed whenever an advertisement comes on. All I want is to watch the show, but I get interrupted constantly[7] every fifteen to twenty minutes by advertisements. I know they are the most effective way to promote products.

When the same advertisement keeps repeating[8] itself, I feel like I am being brainwashed[9]. No wonder[10] companies are willing to spend a lot of money on TV advertising.

　　每次看到廣告，我都覺得很煩，我只是想要好好看個節目，但每十五到二十分鐘就會被廣告打斷。我知道這種推銷方式其實是最有效的，當同一個廣告重複播放時，感覺自己像被洗腦一樣，難怪廠商會願意花大錢在電視上打廣告。

延伸note
hard sell除了強迫推銷外，還指「產品很難賣出」的情況。soft sell則指「說服性推銷」。

⑦ **constantly**
副 不斷地；時常地

⑧ **repeat**
動 重複

⑨ **brainwash**
動 對（人）實行洗腦

⑩ **no wonder**
片 難怪

試著更與眾不同

I love watching new advertisements on TV. They always draw my attention[11]. My favorite ads are funny[12] and creative. They leave a good impression though I might not be able to buy their products in my lifetime[13]. My least favorite advertisements are about automobiles[14]. Most of them only focus on the functionality[15] of the car. None of them make a distinctive[16] impression, so they all seem the same to me.

　　我喜歡看電視廣告，每次看到，我都會特別注意。我最喜歡那些有創意又有趣的廣告，那讓我留下很深刻的印象，就算我可能一輩子都不會買那家公司的產品，我也依然會很喜愛。我最不喜歡汽車廣告，大部分的汽車廣告都只強調車子的性能，廣告一點都不特別，所以看起來都一樣。

⑪ **draw one's attention**
片 吸引某人注意

⑫ **funny**
形 有趣的；好笑的

⑬ **lifetime**
名 終身

⑭ **automobile**
名 （美）汽車

⑮ **functionality**
名 功能

⑥ **distinctive**
形 有特色的

Key Points

答題TIPS看這裡！

若在看節目看得入迷時，突然跳出廣告，的確會讓許多人覺得掃興。但現在其實有很多廣告都相當有創意（creativity），高價品牌廣告的質感也特別好（high quality），由此切入，或許就能有不同的回應。

Words & Phrases 吸引人的好廣告

1 creative
有創意的

2 original
有原創性的

3 impressive
令人印象深刻的

4 persuasive
有說服力的

Words & Phrases 製作廣告的詞彙

1 close-up
特寫

2 sound effect
音效

3 edit
剪輯

4 on air
播出中；錄製中

進階實用句 More Expressions

It is difficult to differentiate your product from the rest.

要把自家產品跟其他人的做區隔，其實很困難。

I bought this oven because of a persuasive ad.

因為廣告很有說服力，所以我買了這台烤箱。

Some advertisements are very creative. They are a pleasure to watch.

有些廣告很有創意，看那種廣告是種享受。

UNIT 11 政府的教育補助

Does the government provide enough support to education in your view?

你認為政府給予的教育輔助足夠嗎？

你可以這樣回答

MP3 131

Well, I think the government does not provide enough support for education[1]. In the past few years, the education system has changed so much that I have problems keeping up with[2] the newest system. They get me so confused[3]. Luckily, my kid is still in kindergarten[4]. Otherwise, I would become one of those parents who complains[5] about this. In my opinion, the system wasn't properly[6] thought out before the execution of it.

　　我覺得政府沒有提供足夠的教育輔助。在過去的幾年中，教育體制改了又改，我都跟不上制度更新的速度了，這些不斷改變的制度真的讓我感到困惑。還好我的孩子還在上幼稚園，否則我就會成為那些不停抱怨的家長們之一。就我看來，這個制度在實施之前，並沒有經過完善的評估。

❶ education	❷ keep up with	❸ confused
名 教育	片 跟上（形勢）	形 困惑的
❹ kindergarten	❺ complain	❻ properly
名 幼稚園	動 抱怨	副 恰當地

換個立場講講看

Our government does provide some supports in terms of education, but it could be better. I am a college student who is lucky because I don't need to worry about my tuition[7]. My parents will support me fully[8]. However, some of my friends have to apply for[9] student loans for their studies. It causes a lot of pressure[10] for them because it will increase their living expenses. I think the government could try to do something about that.

　　我覺得政府有提供一些教育上的輔助，可是並不足夠。我是一個大學生，我覺得自己很幸運，有我父母幫我付學費；不像我的一些朋友，需要申請助學貸款，因為這會增加他們的生活費，所以導致更大的壓力，我覺得政府應該正視這個問題並採取行動。

延伸note
apply for後面接的是「想申請的目標物」；apply to則要接你「提出申請的單位」。

7 tuition
名 學費

9 apply for
片 申請

8 fully
副 完全地；徹底地

10 pressure
名 壓力

 試著更與眾不同

I think government is trying its best to support education. However, there can't be an executive order[11] that satisfies everyone. For example, I know some people are upset about recruiting[12] Chinese students to Taiwan. To me, this might be necessary because of the low birth rate[13]. Some schools might have to close down[14] in the future. And there will be less demand[15] for teachers. As I am studying to be a qualified[16] teacher, keeping the number of students is highly relevant to my job.

　　我覺得政府對於教育補助這一塊，已經很盡力了，但是，不可能有一個行政命令能讓所有人滿意。比方說，我知道有些人不滿政府開放陸生來台，但這或許是很必要的措施。因為隨著出生率降低，部分學校將會面臨關閉的命運，對教師的需求也會跟著減少。我現在正在唸教育學程，有一定的學生數量將與我的工作息息相關。

11 order
名 命令

14 close down
片 停業

12 recruit
動 補充

15 demand
名 需求；需要

13 birth rate
片 出生率

16 qualified
形 合格的

答題TIPS看這裡！

政府對教育的補助可以從不同的角度切入，例如：政策上的補助（如開放僑生的制度）、金錢上的補助（如助學貸款）、制度上的補助（如加權平均）…等等。例句如：I wish the government would offer more financial support to the students who live far away from their schools.（我希望政府能提供更多財務上的補助給那些為了求學而遠離家鄉的學生。）

Words & Phrases 財務方面的補助

1 government incentive
政府獎勵

2 special grant
特別獎助

3 allowance
津貼

4 scholarship
獎學金

Words & Phrases 畢業與相關要求

1 credit
學分

2 curriculum
全部課程

3 diploma
畢業證書

4 dissertation
學位論文

進階實用句 More Expressions

I have to study hard to keep my grades up.

我必須很努力念書來提升成績。

Our student dormitory is heavily subsidized by the government.

我們的學生宿舍獲得很多政府的補助。

The government brought in a special grant to waive tuitions for students in need.

政府推行了特別獎助給那些貧困的學生，讓他們得以免學費。

UNIT 12

對食品安全的措施

Q **Should the government have strict food safety regulations?**

政府應該制定嚴格的食品安全規範嗎？

你可以這樣回答

MP3
132

Absolutely. I think the government hasn't been doing its job well when it comes to food safety regulations. Problems are not isolated[1] incidents[2]; there have been a series of food items that were found to contain preservatives[3] or improper chemicals[4]. What scares the public most is the fact that those chemicals were not meant for human consumption[5]. I don't understand why the government has not learned its lesson. These kinds of events shouldn't happen repeatedly if our government supervises[6] things well.

當然，我覺得過去幾年政府根本沒有盡到監督食安的責任，這不是單一的突發事件，已經有一連串的食物添加防腐劑或不適當的化學物品，讓大眾感到恐慌的是，這些物質根本就不能給人類食用。我不了解為什麼政府沒有學到教訓，如果政府的監督做得更好，類似的事件根本就不會重複發生。

❶ **isolated**	❷ **incident**	❸ **preservative**
形 分離的	名 事件	名 防腐劑
❹ **chemical**	❺ **consumption**	❻ **supervise**
名 化學製品	名 消耗；耗盡	動 監督

換個立場講講看

Speaking of food safety, I have lost faith[7] in our government. I think having a tougher law doesn't equal[8] safety. If we don't have the right person to execute the law, it is useless[9]. The main problem is with law enforcement[10]. The government seems corrupt[11]. It has sided with big enterprise[12]. Instead of tougher regulations, tougher public servants will make the real difference.

　　說到食品安全，我對政府真的是完全失去信心。有嚴格的法律不等於安全，如果沒有適當的執法者，那法令也毫無用武之地。最主要的問題出在執法者身上。政府似乎滿貪腐的，只選擇站在財閥那一邊。與其設立更嚴格的政令，還不如有一個嚴格的執法者，這才能改變現況。

7 faith
名 信心

8 equal
動 等於

9 useless
形 無用的；無效的

10 enforcement
名 實施；執行

11 corrupt
形 貪腐的

12 enterprise
名 企業；公司

 試著更與眾不同

It is very disappointing[13] to see things like food safety become such a big issue in Taiwan. Everyone is questioning[14] the food that we are eating. I prepare my lunch box every day now because I am concerned about the additives. Introducing stricter regulations is necessary. The food safety regulations might need to be reviewed[15] and amended[16]. I hope I can say that I have no more concern about the food in Taiwan in the near future.

　　台灣的食安問題變得這麼嚴重，真令人感到失望。大家都質疑我們在吃的食物，不知道裡面放了些什麼原料。我現在每天都自己準備午餐，因為我擔心添加物的問題。加入更嚴格的法令是一定要做的事，食安法令可能需要重新審視，並加以修改。我希望不久後就能向別人說，我對台灣的食物已經沒有疑慮了。

13 disappointing
形 令人失望的

14 question
動 質疑

15 review
動 再檢查

16 amend
動 修改

延伸note
一連串的食安風暴(food safety issues)讓民眾不安，尤以之前的地溝油(guter oil)最嚴重。

Key Points

答題TIPS看這裡！

食安風暴的問題在這幾年真的讓民眾感到相當不安，進而引發對政府的不滿。當然，一般人都會同意要制定更嚴格的法令。但回答時可以更進一步，思考「如果只有制定嚴格的法律，真的夠嗎？」

Words & Phrases　與食安相關的詞彙

1 artificial additive
人工添加物

2 gutter oil
餿水油

3 chemicals
化學原料

4 extract
萃取物；抽出物

Words & Phrases　身體不適的反應

1 upset stomach
胃痛

2 vomit
嘔吐

3 diarrhea
腹瀉

4 dehydration
脫水

進階實用句 More Expressions

I prepare my own meals now.

我現在都自己煮飯。

I think we should increase the penalty for people who breach food safety regulations.

我認為應該要加重那些違反食品安全法者的刑責。

If you read the food labelling carefully, you'll realize that there are a lot of artificial additives in the food.

如果你認真看食品標示，你會發現食物裡有很多人工添加物。

UNIT 13 新聞照片的可信度

Q How much can we trust photographs presented by journalists?

關於新聞的照片，我們能相信幾分呢？

 你可以這樣回答

 MP3 133

In my opinion, the photographs[1] presented on the news channel are trustworthy. The training programs for journalists[2] not only cover writing and interviewing[3] skills, but also ethics[4]. Journalists are acting as the audiences' eyes. They should tell the stories as close to the truth[5] as possible. However, photos can only tell us part of the truth. We still need more description[6] in words to get the whole picture.

在我看來，新聞台所發布的照片應該都很有可信度。要訓練一個新聞工作者，除了加強寫作與問話的技巧外，倫理道德標準也必須訓練。新聞工作者等於是觀眾的眼睛，他們必須盡量呈現真實。不過，照片只能表示一部分的真實，我們還是需要敘述的補助，以了解事件的全貌。

❶ **photograph** 名 照片	❷ **journalist** 名 新聞工作者	❸ **interview** 動 訪問
❹ **ethics** 名 道德標準	❺ **truth** 名 事實；真相	❻ **description** 名 描寫；敘述

 換個立場講講看

I have quite a lot of confidence[7] in the news footage[8] and the photographs presented by journalists. The photographs are taken at the scene[9], so they can present the truth in some sense. However, the remarks[10] that are put together with the photographs might not be so reliable[11]. It might be from the journalist's point

of view[12]. Therefore, it sometimes becomes biased. However, I think journalists report on stories as close to the truth as possible.

我對新聞報導的影片和照片有相當大的信心，照片是在現場拍的，所以能表現出部份的真相，但對於照片所提供的註解，就有令人質疑的成分。文字敘述可能來自新聞工作者本身的觀點，所以有時候會帶有偏見，但我想記者們會盡量以貼近真相的方式報導。

7 confidence
名 信心

8 footage
名 （影片的）連續鏡頭

9 scene
名 場面；事件

10 remark
名 評論

11 reliable
形 可信賴的

12 point of view
片 觀點

試著更與眾不同

I used to trust[13] everything journalists said because of their professional[14] image[15]. However, my thinking totally changed after a serious incident. A senior reporter from NBC got busted for making up stories about what happened in a warzone. That really destroyed[16] all my trust in journalism. NBC has been a prestigious news channel. This scandal truly damaged its reputation[17]. I think NBC did the right thing in suspending[18] the journalist for six months.

我以前百分之百相信新聞記者，因為他們的形象很專業，但在一件嚴重的事件過後，我就不再這麼信任記者了。有一位NBC（美國國家廣播公司）資深的新聞記者被踢爆報導假的戰地新聞，這讓我對新聞界的信心完全瓦解，NBC一直以來都是這麼有聲望的新聞台，這件醜聞重重地打擊了他們的名聲。我覺得NBC將這名記者停職半年是很正確的處理方式。

13 trust
動 相信；信任

14 professional
形 專業的

15 image
名 形象

16 destroy
動 破壞

17 reputation
名 名譽；名聲

18 suspend
動 使中止

答題TIPS看這裡！

對於新聞報導的照片，一般人其實都會覺得有一定的可信度。第一個原因是「眼見為憑」的影響，不太可能是為了報導，就捏造出一個不存在的場面；第二是媒體一般還是被認為具備專業度，新聞也應該有審議的程序。但也有專業記者被拆穿報導假新聞，其中包含他所拍攝的照片內容。所以對觀眾來說，願意相信到什麼程度，就見仁見智了。

Words & Phrases 媒體的偏頗報導

1 alter
修改

2 make up
捏造

3 slander
誹謗；詆毀

4 garble
對…斷章取義

Words & Phrases 媒體報導的相關類型

1 breaking news
最新消息

2 in-depth coverage
深入報導

3 report live
現場報導

4 exclusive interview
獨家訪問

進階實用句 More Expressions

As long as the photograph is genuine, it is trustworthy.

只要照片是真的，那就可以信任。

Anyone who makes up news should be suspended if not fired straight away.

對於編造新聞的人，如果沒有直接辭退，也應該被停職。

News from warzones is valuable because the journalists risk their lives for the news.

戰地新聞很珍貴，因為記者們需要冒生命危險去報導。

報紙照片的角色

Q What is the role of photographs in newspapers?

報紙的照片扮演什麼樣的角色呢？

你可以這樣回答

Newspapers[1] are one of the oldest ways for people to obtain[2] information. However, photographs can explain the situation better than a thousand words. It also makes the reading more interesting because there are pictures to fill in the blanks[3]. Therefore, the description in words will have a concrete[4] image. From the photographs, you can see the facial expressions of some politicians clearly. That will make the stories even livelier.

　　報紙是一種很傳統、老舊的資訊傳播媒介。但是，加上照片，就比單純的文字敘述更有說服力了。照片會讓讀報紙這件事變得更有趣，因為圖像能滿足空白的想像空間，進而讓文字敘述擁有一個鮮明的形象。藉由照片，你可以很清楚地看到政客們的表情，這讓新聞敘述變得更加生動。

❶ **newspapers**
名 報紙

❷ **obtain**
動 得到；獲得

❸ **blank**
名 空白

❹ **concrete**
形 具體的

> 延伸note
> 除了社論版(editorial page)之外，現在的報紙版面多半都會附上照片，不再純由文字主宰。

換個立場講講看

I don't think anyone would deny[5] the important role of photographs in newspapers. It is like supporting evidence[6] for the coverage. Credibility will increase if there are photos presented. Having photos also means more visual[7] stimulation[8] for the readers. As the technology develops, various types of media appear. This has made it tough for newspapers. They also need to make themselves more appealing to the public, and presenting the photos is definitely a way.

　　我覺得沒有人能否認照片在報紙裡所扮演的重要角色。它就像報導的輔助證據，如果有附上照片，新聞的可信度就會跟著提高。附上照片也表示將帶給讀者更多的視覺刺激。隨著科技的發展，各式各樣的媒體如雨後春筍般出現，這讓報紙陷入了困境，變得需要讓它看起來更吸引大眾，為了達成目的，附上照片絕對會是一個方法。

⑤ deny
動 否認

⑥ evidence
名 證據

⑦ visual
形 視覺的

⑧ stimulation
名 刺激

試著更與眾不同

I think photographs are necessary for most pages. Coverage with photographs surely is more attractive to most readers[9]. However, I don't need many pictures while reading. I enjoy reading the columnists'[10] pieces[11] in particular[12]. Columnists' opinions are what I want to read. Photos are unnecessary when I am reading. However, I noticed that there are fewer and fewer people like me. Most people enjoy photos more than the words themselves.

　　對大多數的報紙版面而言，照片是必要的。一則附上照片的報導絕對會吸引更多讀者。但是，我閱讀的時候並不需要太多照片。我特別喜歡看專欄作家的文章，那些作家的觀點是我想看的內容，照片對我來說不怎麼重要。不過，我發現越來越少人會和我一樣，和單純的文字相比，大多數人都比較喜歡有照片的新聞。

⑨ reader
名 讀者

⑩ columnist
名 專欄作家

⑪ piece
名 一則消息；報導

⑫ in particular
片 特別

Key Points

答題TIPS看這裡！

報紙如果沒有照片的加持，只有純文字的報紙一定乏味不少。有些讀者是被聳動的標題還有照片吸引來購買報紙，尤其是頭版（front page）新聞更是如此。現在媒體競爭激烈，電子媒體的興起也對傳統平面報紙帶來不小的衝擊。

Words & Phrases　對照片的觀感與印象

1. **bloody**
   血腥的
2. **touching**
   感人的
3. **inspirational**
   鼓勵人心的
4. **hidden message**
   隱藏的訊息

Words & Phrases　拍照的主題和內容

1. **theme**
   拍攝主題
2. **landscape**
   風景
3. **portrait**
   肖像
4. **reflection**
   倒影

🎤 進階實用句 More Expressions

There are some hidden messages in that photo.

那張照片有些隱藏訊息。

Seeing that touching news and the inspirational photo really made my day.

看了那則感人的新聞以及鼓勵人心的照片，讓我一整天的心情都很好。

The photos of the war look bloody. They remind people of the cruel nature of a war.

這場戰爭的照片看起來很血腥，提醒了人們戰爭的殘酷。

417

UNIT 15　國內 vs. 國際新聞

Q Do you watch local or world news mostly?
你比較常看國內新聞還是國際新聞？

 你可以這樣回答

MP3
135

I watch local[1] news mostly because Taiwanese news channels don't seem to cover a lot of international news. Of course, news on CNN or other professional news channels is authoritative[2], but I don't see it often. First, local news sometimes covers the news that is more interesting[3]. I don't want to know about those sad conflicts[4] between countries all the time[5]. Second, watching news in my mother tongue[6] is much more comfortable.

　　我比較常看國內新聞，因為台灣新聞台似乎不太會報導國際新聞。當然，像CNN那樣的專業新聞台具備權威性，但我不怎麼看。首先，國內新聞的報導有時候更有趣，我可不想老是看些讓人感傷的國際衝突；第二、以自己母語播報的新聞，看起來當然更舒服。

❶ local
形 國內的

❷ authoritative
形 權威性的

❸ interesting
形 有趣的

❹ conflict
名 衝突

❺ all the time
片 總是

❻ mother tongue
片 母語

 換個立場講講看

I like to watch international news because I want to know what is going on around the world; I don't want to be a person with tunnel[7] vision[8]. Through the international news, I can see what really matters[9] or has impact. I sometimes find the local news boring and pointless[10]. Knowing things about my country is important, but I just don't see the point of hearing about a politician's private life[11]. It is not helpful to enhancing[12] my international perspective.

　我喜歡看國際新聞，因為我想要知道全球發生了什麼事。我不想要成為眼界狹窄的人。藉由國際新聞，我能得知真正重要、帶來重大影響的事件。我有時候會覺得國內新聞毫無意義。知道自己國家的事的確很重要，但我不曉得知道政客的私生活有何意義，對培養國際觀一點幫助也沒有。

❼ tunnel 名 隧道	**❽ vision** 名 洞察力；眼光	**❾ matter** 動 有關係；要緊
❿ pointless 形 無意義的	**⓫ private life** 片 私生活	**⓬ enhance** 動 強化

試著更與眾不同

Generally[13], I like to watch local news. But I also watch the international news on CNN when I have time. To be honest, world news sometimes just bores[14] me. I struggle[15] to stay focused[16] while watching it. However, it's a good way to develop an international perspective. When I speak to a foreigner, there's no way that he or she will know what happened in my country in detail[17]. International news is definitely a proper[18] topic for foreigners.

　基本上，我喜歡看國內新聞，但有空的時候，我也會看CNN的報導。老實說，國際新聞有時候只讓我覺得無趣，看的時候我得試圖保持清醒，但那是培養我國際觀的好方法。當我與外國人聊天時，對方不可能清楚知道我國家內部的事情，在那種時候，國際新聞絕對是更適當的聊天主題。

⓭ generally 副 通常；一般地	**⓮ bore** 動 使厭煩	**⓯ struggle** 動 努力；掙扎
⓰ focused 形 專心的	**⓱ in detail** 片 詳細地	**⓲ proper** 形 適當的

419

答題TIPS看這裡！

其實對國內新聞和國際新聞的喜好見仁見智。最大的不同點除了內容（content）外，就是報導的方式。有些國內的新聞報導偏向輕鬆生活的路線，會比較有娛樂性（entertaining）。相較之下，國際新聞的報導就嚴肅許多，不管議題、還是報導時的態度，都會比國內新聞要嚴謹。

Words & Phrases　新聞所涵蓋的區域大小

1 global
全球的

2 international
國際的

3 domestic
國內的

4 local
地方性的

Words & Phrases　選擇看國際新聞台的原因

1 authority
權威；影響力

2 widespread
普遍的

3 neutral
中立的

4 credibility
公信力

進階實用句 More Expressions

I have always wanted to become a news reporter.

我總是想成為新聞主播。

The presidential election in Malaysia made international headlines.

馬來西亞的總統大選登上國際頭條。

The breaking news is about the death of the former prime minister, which was later confirmed to be a rumor.

快報是有關前總理辭世的消息，後來證實那只是謠言。

Part 10

假設與看法
Various Opinions

 動 動詞   形 形容詞   連 連接詞

 名 名詞   介 介系詞   片 片語

 副 副詞

傳統服飾的消失

Q Is it a good thing that people no longer wear their traditional costumes?

人們不再穿傳統服飾是好事嗎？

 你可以這樣回答

There are people who are concerned[1] about this very much, but I have a different opinion. As with changing attitudes towards technology, people's taste[2] towards clothing also change over time. I mean, why bother putting on a cheongsam[3] when I can wear a simple shirt and jeans[4]? Besides, not wearing a traditional costume[5] doesn't mean I don't know my culture. I still have an interest in knowing more about my ancestors[6].

有很多人擔心這件事，但我的想法不同。就像對科技發展的態度隨著時間而有所不同，人們對衣著的品味當然會改變。我的意思是，當我能穿簡單的T恤和牛仔褲時，為什麼我必須費那個精神穿旗袍呢？況且，不穿傳統服飾並不代表我不了解自己的文化，我還是對祖先很有興趣。

❶ concern 動 擔心	❷ taste 名 品味	❸ cheongsam 名 旗袍
❹ jeans 名 牛仔褲	❺ costume 名 服裝	❻ ancestor 名 祖先

 換個立場講講看

In my opinion, it is not good that people no longer[7] wear their traditional costumes. Wearing traditional costumes reflects an appreciation for one's culture. It plays an important role in the inheritance[8] of the culture by the next generation[9]. It also shows that people are still proud of who they were and who they are. I think they would gain[10] a lot more respect from others by preserving[11] their history. Even the government should encourage[12] people to wear traditional costumes.

　　我不覺得人們不再穿他們的傳統服飾是件好事，我覺得穿傳統服飾反映人們重視自身的文化。在傳承文化給下一代這方面扮演很重要的角色，也表示他們對自己的根感到驕傲。這樣反而會比較受人尊重，政府應該鼓勵人們穿他們的傳統服飾。

⑦ **no longer** 片 不再	⑧ **inheritance** 名 繼承物	⑨ **generation** 名 世代
⑩ **gain** 動 獲得	⑪ **preserve** 動 保存；維護	⑫ **encourage** 動 鼓勵

試著更與眾不同

I think some traditional costumes are actually designed[13] to suit the lifestyle of the old days when people were hunting[14] and gathering[15]. It seems somehow out of place if people wear traditional costumes in modern[16] society. For example, it is not appropriate to wear them to certain places or on cercain occasions like the office or weddings[17]. No matter how much you love your culture, you should still wear something that shows proper manners[18].

　　我覺得有些傳統服飾的設計符合古早的生活方式，像打獵或採集那樣的生活型態。如果你穿到現代社會，看起來就很突兀。比方說，穿著那樣的服裝到公司或參加婚禮就很不適當，不管你多熱愛自己的文化，穿衣服還是要符合禮節。

⑬ **design** 動 設計；構思	⑭ **hunt** 動 打獵；追獵	⑮ **gather** 動 採集；收割
⑯ **modern** 形 現代的	⑰ **wedding** 名 結婚典禮	⑱ **manner** 名 禮節

答題TIPS看這裡！

傳統服飾不再受歡迎有它們原因，最常見的理由是不合時宜，比方說：在百貨公司看到穿著旗袍的人，不免會引起他人側目；除此之外，政府的態度也會影響人民對傳統的觀感，若有大力推崇傳統活動，自然增加年輕人對自己傳統的歸屬感。全球化（globalization）帶來更多文化交流的機會，但在這波主流下，如何維持自身的傳統文化，也是一項重要的課題。

Words & Phrases　亞洲的傳統服飾

1 **kimono**
日本和服

2 **Indian Saree**
印度沙麗

3 **cheongsam**
中式旗袍

4 **burka**
伊斯蘭全身罩袍

Words & Phrases　傳統服飾的作用

1 **tradition**
傳統

2 **culture**
文化

3 **handicraft**
手工藝

4 **solemnity**
莊重；莊嚴

進階實用句 More Expressions

Almost every woman wears the traditional Saree in India.

在印度，幾乎每個婦女都穿傳統沙麗。

I don't think wearing traditional costumes means you are old-fashioned.

我覺得穿傳統服飾並不表示落伍。

In Japan, you will see people wearing kimonos on formal occasions.

在日本，你會看到人們在正式場合中穿和服。

UNIT 02 遇上塞車的反應

Q How would you deal with getting stuck in a traffic jam?

遇上塞車，你會如何面對？

你可以這樣回答

MP3 137

I would get really annoyed if I got stuck[1] in a traffic jam. The most depressing[2] part is: there would be nothing I could do. Therefore, I would try to entertain myself, trying to make it less unpleasant[3]. I would turn the radio on and sing along[4] with the music. Somehow, I feel better when I sing out loud. It makes me feel like I'm having my own concert[5]. I would avoid complaining about the traffic because it would only make the whole process[6] seem longer.

我覺得遇上塞車很煩，最讓人沮喪的是：根本一點辦法也沒有。因此，我會試著讓自己開心一點，以讓塞車沒那麼討人厭。我會打開廣播，跟著音樂唱歌。不知為何，當我跟著大聲唱時，會覺得舒服很多，那讓我感覺像是在開自己的演唱會。我會盡量避免抱怨，因為那只會讓我覺得塞車的時間很長而已。

❶ **stick**	❷ **depressing**	❸ **unpleasant**
動 使停止；阻塞	形 令人沮喪的	形 使人不愉快的
❹ **sing along**	❺ **concert**	❻ **process**
片 跟著唱	名 演唱會	名 過程

換個立場講講看

Luckily, I don't normally drive a car; I prefer to ride my scooter[7]. Although I run into traffic jams sometimes, it is much easier to get around via my scooter. If the traffic were very bad, I would turn into a little alley[8] to avoid the heavy traffic. I know a lot of short cuts[9]. On the contrary, cars lack this kind of mobility[10]. If I were driving a car, the only thing I could do is sit there and wait for the traffic to get better.

幸好我不常開車，我比較喜歡騎機車。雖然騎機車有時候也會遇到塞車，但機車比較容易行動。如果車況很塞，我會轉進小巷內，以避開車潮。我知道很多捷徑。相反的，車子就缺乏這種機動性，如果我開車的話，唯一能做的就是坐在車內，等待車潮減少。

⑦ scooter
名 機車

⑧ alley
名 小巷子

⑨ short cut
片 近路；捷徑

⑩ mobility
名 機動性

試著更與眾不同

If I got stuck in traffic while I was driving to work, I would send a LINE message[11] to my manager immediately. It is important to let him know that I would be late so that my manager could handle[12] the situation properly. And once I send the message, I wouldn't panic or be upset[13]. I would turn on the radio and catch up on the news. However, I still hope this doesn't happen. I wouldn't want to mess up[14] a morning meeting because of the traffic.

如果上班遇到塞車，我就會立刻傳LINE訊息給我的經理。讓他知道我會遲到很重要，這樣經理才能掌握情況。而且，通知他以後，我就不會感到那麼焦慮或生氣。我會打開廣播聽新聞，不過，我還是希望別發生這種情況，我可不想因為交通而搞砸一場早晨會議。

⑪ message
名 訊息

⑫ handle
動 處理

⑬ upset
形 心煩的；苦惱的

⑭ mess up
片 搞砸

Key Points 答題TIPS看這裡！

遇上塞車，大部分的人除了無奈還是無奈，同樣是待在車上，有些人會用不同的心境去面對。如果是與人有約，或趕著上班，先通知對方就可以不用那麼著急。當然，也有人會找事情做，如聽個歌之類的來放鬆心情。

Words & Phrases 塞車造成的情緒與行為

1 impatient
不耐煩的

2 worried
憂慮的

3 honk the horn
按喇叭

4 change lanes
變換車道

Words & Phrases 準時與遲到的說法

1 punctual
準時的

2 on time
準時的

3 in time
及時的

4 be late for
遲到

🎤 進階實用句 More Expressions

I don't own a car, so I take the MRT to get around town.

我沒有車，都是靠捷運在市區趴趴走。

I ran into an old friend of mine. We caught up over coffee for almost two hours.

我巧遇老朋友，我們去喝咖啡，聊近況聊了快兩個小時。

I am so sick of being stuck in traffic; I wonder how long it will take for me to get to my office.

塞在車陣中真的好煩，到底還要花多久時間才能到公司啊？

UNIT 03

約會對象遲到時

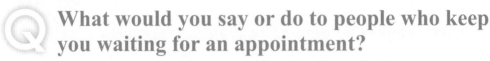

Q What would you say or do to people who keep you waiting for an appointment?

約好見面的對象讓你等了許久,你會有何反應?

 你可以這樣回答

 MP3 138

It depends on who that person is. If it is a person who is famous[1] for being late, I would definitely give him a hard time and warn[2] him not to be late next time. I can't stand[3] people with this chronic problem. However, if it is someone who is usually punctual for our appointments, I wouldn't mind that much because there must be a reason for that. I have a friend like this. And I sometimes even ask her to take her time because I don't want her to be too rushed[4].

　　要看對象是誰。如果對方是出了名的愛遲到,那我一定會讓他很不好過,而且會警告他下次不准再遲到,我無法忍受會習慣性遲到的人。不過,如果對方是那種通常都會準時赴約的人,我就不會太介意,因為一定有原因。我有一個朋友就是這樣,我有時候甚至會叫她慢慢來,因為不希望她太過倉促。

❶ **famous**
形 出名的

❷ **warn**
動 警告

❸ **stand**
動 忍受

❹ **rushed**
形 匆忙的

延伸note
give sb. a hard time表示「讓某人很不好過」,可能涉及言語(如責備)或行為(如不理會對方)。

 **換個立場講講看**

I think being late happens to everyone, so I wouldn't be really mad at this. However, if I waited for the person for more than half[5] an hour without any messages, I would stop waiting and leave right away. Being late is one thing, but not sending[6] any messages to explain[7] the reason[8] is another. I can be considerate[9] only if that person shows his or her politeness[10]. Almost everybody has a cell phone today. I don't think sending a message to me would be that difficult.

　　如果我準時抵達，但跟我約好的那個人遲到超過半小時以上，卻都沒有通知我，那我就直接放棄，不等了。遲到是件很沒禮貌的事，如果連通知對方這件事都沒有做，那就更糟糕。我知道每個人都可能會因為塞車而遲到，但我受不了對方不通知我，一直讓我等下去。

⑤ **half**
名 一半；二分之一

⑥ **send**
動 寄送

⑦ **explain**
動 解釋

⑧ **reason**
名 原因；理由

⑨ **considerate**
形 體諒的

⑩ **politeness**
名 有禮貌

 試著更與眾不同

Whenever my boyfriend is running late for our date, I wait for him anyway. However, I am usually really angry[11] with him once he arrives. I make him apologize to me with a bouquet[12] and a present[13] later. I really don't understand[14] what takes him so long. I mean, boys need to wait for their dates most of the time. However, it's the exact opposite situation with my boyfriend and me. It sometimes drives me crazy.

　　每次我男友遲到，我都會等他，但是當他抵達的時候，我通常會非常火大。我會要他拿著花束和禮物向我道歉。我實在無法理解他為什麼都會弄這麼久，我的意思是，大部分的時候，都是男生在等待和自己約會的女孩吧？但我男友和我的情況卻完全相反，這有時候真的令我感到很抓狂。

⑪ **angry**
形 生氣的

⑫ **bouquet**
名 花束

⑬ **present**
名 禮物

⑭ **understand**
動 理解

延伸note
遲到除了口頭上的 apology(道歉)之外，以行動表現更能打動人心(如：buy sb. a meal 請人吃飯)。

答題TIPS看這裡！

等人的經驗大家難免都會遇到，大家對於遲到的容忍度（tolerance）都不同。不過，無論是脾氣多好（have good temper）的人，應該也不會享受這種經驗吧。所以，可以先表達你對遲到這件事的觀感，再以實際例子補充。對於遲到的人，大部分的人都會先問原因，給別人解釋的機會。如果能在遲到前先通知一下對方，大多能大事化小。

Words & Phrases	遲到後採取的行動

1 apologize
道歉

2 explain
解釋

3 be one's treat
請客

4 make a promise
承諾

Words & Phrases	可能遲到的理由

1 family urgency
家裡有急事

2 get lost
迷路

3 car accident
車禍

4 sleep over
睡過頭

進階實用句 More Expressions

I don't like to go out with Joe. He is famous for being late.

我不喜歡和喬出去，他可是出了名的遲到大王。

My friend did not show up yesterday. I later discovered he was hospitalized.

我朋友昨天沒有到場，我後來才知道他住院了。

I was supposed to meet with my friend twenty minutes ago, but I got so lost.

我二十分鐘前就該與朋友碰面了，但我完全性地迷路。

UNIT 04 他人對你的負評

Q **When someone complains about you, what do you do?**

當有人抱怨你時，你會怎麼反應？

你可以這樣回答

MP3 139

If I heard someone is complaining about me, I would be very surprised[1] and embarrassed[2]. I would wonder how many people he had spoken to about me. I care about others' attitudes towards me quite a lot, so I would worry that others might be influenced by his words. I would not confront the person because I am too shy[3]. However, I would ask others what exactly he complained about. And I would try to be more careful to avoid making the same mistake[4].

如果聽到有人在抱怨我，我會很驚訝，並感到丟臉。我會想知道他和多少人談過我的事。我很介意他人對我的態度，所以會擔心其他人受到他的影響。我不敢直接找對方講開，因為我很害羞，但我會問其他人，搞清楚他究竟為何不滿，並盡量小心，以免再犯相同的錯誤。

❶ **surprised**
形 驚訝的

❷ **embarrassed**
形 尷尬的

❸ **shy**
形 害羞的

❹ **mistake**
名 錯誤；過失

延伸note
對於內向的人(introvert)來說，要當面講開本來就很困難，但無論如何，別忘了提出解決之道。

換個立場講講看

If someone complained about me, I would ask him what I did wrong in person[5]. I wouldn't get too upset before I knew what exactly made him dislike me. If there were a misunderstanding between us, it could be resolved[6] easily once we had a serious talk. If I did something wrong, I would be willing to[7] apologize to him. Who knows? I might make friends with that person afterwards. To me, this is why communication[8] matters in friendship.

如果有人抱怨我的事情，我會當面問他我哪裡做錯了。在沒有弄清楚他為什麼不高興之前，我不會生氣。如果是誤會造成的，那只要認真談過之過，就能馬上解決。如果我哪裡做錯了，我會很樂意向他道歉，誰知道呢？我們事後搞不好還能成為朋友呢！對我而言，這就是為何溝通在友誼裡扮演如此重要角色的原因。

延伸note
有話直說的人（be straightforward)與拐彎抹角(beat around the bush)只是性格的差異。

❺ **in person**
片 當面

❻ **resolve**
動 解決

❼ **be willing to**
片 樂意

❽ **communication**
名 溝通

試著更與眾不同

I don't really care if people complain about me. Sometimes when you want to get things done, it is impossible to please[9] everyone. I can't satisfy all people's expectation[10] when everyone's need[11] is different. Take our mayor[12] for example. There are a lot of people complaining about him because he has been very strict[13] in enforcing the new regulations. I would not say he is popular, but he is definitely a capable[14] person.

當有人抱怨我的時候，我其實不會很在意。想要成就大事，不可能取悅每一個人。當每個人的需求都不同時，我不可能滿足所有人的期待。就舉我們的市長為例。因為他在推行政務時非常嚴苛，所以有很多人都對他不滿，我不會說他很受人歡迎，但他絕對算是個能幹的人。

❾ **please**
動 取悅

❿ **expectation**
名 期待；預期

⓫ **need**
名 需求；需要

⓬ **mayor**
名 市長

⓭ **strict**
形 嚴苛的

⓮ **capable**
形 有能力的

Key Points

答題TIPS看這裡！

大家對於處理抱怨的態度都不同，這其實與每個人的情緒智商（EQ）有關，並沒有什麼對錯之分，有些人喜歡講開、有些人不願意撕破臉、有些人會感到丟臉、有些人則根本不在意，按自己的個性答題即可。

Words & Phrases　人際矛盾與解決之道

1. **misunderstand**
誤會；誤解

2. **resolve the issue**
解決問題

3. **confront**
勇敢地面對

4. **intervention**
調停；斡旋

Words & Phrases　不受歡迎的八卦舉動

1. **slander**
誹謗；詆毀

2. **gossip**
八卦；閒言閒語

3. **rumor**
流言；謠言

4. **talk behind one's back**
在某人背後講閒話

進階實用句 More Expressions

I hate people talking behind my back.

我討厭人家在我背後說閒話。

David got pissed off when he realized his co-workers complained about him.

當大衛得知同事抱怨他的時候，他很生氣。

After hearing lots of complaints, we decided to do something to help John's addiction to alcohol.

在收到許多抱怨之後，我們決定替約翰的酗酒問題做點什麼。

433

UNIT 05

與旅伴發生爭執

Q **What would you do if you had an argument with your friend while you were traveling?**

旅途中，與朋友發生爭執時，你會怎麼做？

你可以這樣回答

I think traveling would be the worst timing[1] to have an argument with my friend. It's possible that my companion[2] is the only person I would be traveling with. If we had a serious fight and decided[3] to go separate[4] ways, I would be on my own[5]. That's the worst situation I can imagine. To avoid this, I would sit down with my friend and try to work out a way that is acceptable[6] to both of us. I really don't want to be stuck in a foreign country by myself.

我覺得旅途中發生爭執是最糟的時間點，因為那個旅伴很可能是我唯一的旅行對象。如果我們談不攏，最後決定各走各的路，那我就會變成自己一個人。為了避免這種情況，我想我會坐下來，好好跟他談出一個我們對方都能接受的方式，因為我真的不想一個人困在陌生的國家。

❶ **timing** 名 時間的安排	❷ **companion** 名 同伴；朋友	❸ **decide** 動 決定
❹ **separate** 形 個別的	❺ **on one's own** 片 獨自	❻ **acceptable** 形 可接受的

換個立場講講看

If I had an argument with my friend while we were traveling, I might put up with him until the end of the trip. All the travel planning was done based on[7] the right number of people. If one of us pulled out[8] half way, the rest of us would have to pay more for the accommodation and maybe some penalty[9] because we were one person short[10]. I wouldn't want others to feel uncomfortable just because of my emotions[11]. After all[12], I can say goodbye to the person I dislike once the trip is over.

如果我與朋友起了爭執，我可能會盡量忍耐，直到旅程結束。旅程的計畫都必須按人數安排，如果我們當中有任何一個人突然不去，剩下的人就必須負擔更多的住宿費，甚至可能因為少一個人而有罰金，我可不希望因為自己的情緒，害其他人不開心。畢竟，只要旅程一結束，我就可以揮別我不喜歡的某人啦。

⑦ be based on	⑧ pull out	⑨ penalty
片 根據	片 退出	名 罰金
⑩ short	⑪ emotion	⑫ after all
形 短缺的；不足的	名 情緒	片 畢竟

試著更與眾不同

If that happened, I might go my own way. It takes me a long time to save up[13] for a trip, so I don't want to ruin the trip simply[14] because of a fight. There's no need to put up with each other if we really can't stay together. If it's alright[15] with my friend, I would definitely suggest we separate. That way, we could still enjoy[16] our trip and see the things that we had planned.

如果真的吵起來，我應該會選擇分開旅行吧。我花了很久時間存錢，才有辦法出來旅遊，所以我不想讓一個小小的爭吵毀了這一切。如果我們真的無法忍受對方，那就沒必要勉強。只要我朋友能接受，我就會建議各走各的。這樣的話，我們都可以享受旅程，去看之前計劃好要看的東西。

⑬ save up	⑭ simply
片 存錢	副 僅僅；只不過
⑮ alright	⑯ enjoy
形 沒問題的	動 享受

延伸note
對於個性比較獨立（independent）的人來說，分開旅行並非情緒化，而是能解決問題的手段。

Key Points

答題TIPS看這裡！

旅行中的爭吵其實很難處理，可能要看是大事還是小事。如果是為了行程該怎麼走，那很可能就會拆夥，各走各的。但如果是小事，因為只須忍耐一下，就會過去，所以大多數人應該會選擇忍耐。若是團體旅遊，因為拆夥最先面臨的問題就是花費，所以若牽涉到成行的人數，就必須考量其他人必須分攤的成本。

Words & Phrases　吵架詞彙與用語

1 be sick of
厭倦

2 Knock it off.
少來。

3 Leave me alone.
走開。

4 Get over yourself.
少自以為是。

Words & Phrases　令人害怕的旅伴類型

1 emotional
情緒化的

2 picky
挑剔的

3 whine
嘟囔

4 stubborn
頑固的；固執的

進階實用句 More Expressions

It rained for three days. The weather totally ruined the trip.

一連下了三天雨，把我們的旅程都毀了。

We'd better make sure that we are on the same page before we go traveling.

在出發之前，最好確認我們彼此的認知是一樣的。

We'd better be more considerate of each other; otherwise, we might get into a fight sooner or later.

我們最好能更體諒對方，不然遲早可能吵架。

UNIT 06 安排七天的假期

Q If you had a week's holiday, how would you like to spend it? Why?

如果你有一星期的假期，你會如何度過？為什麼？

MP3 141

你可以這樣回答

If I had a week's holiday, I would book[1] myself an overseas[2] trip to somewhere exotic[3]. However, one week is not long enough to visit a country where it is hard to get around, so it must have good public transportation[4]. I think Tokyo would be ideal because it only takes three hours on the plane[5]. Furthermore, I could take the express[6] around the city. It would save me time on transportation. I could enjoy my trip more.

　　如果我有一個星期的假，我會出國，找一個有異國風情的地方度假。不過，一個星期其實滿短的，所以無法去難以行動的地方，交通設施便利的地點比較適合。我覺得東京很理想，坐飛機只要三個小時，除此之外，搭新幹線就能到城市的各處觀光，省下很多交通時間，讓我能更享受這趟旅程。

❶ book 動 預約	**❷ overseas** 形 海外的	**❸ exotic** 形 異國情調的
❹ transportation 名 交通工具	**❺ plane** 名 飛機	**❻ express** 名 快車

換個立場講講看

I am really busy at work, so it is not often that I get a holiday[7] like that. If I really got seven days off, I would spend the first three days sleeping and enjoying a leisurely[8] life at home. If I felt like it, I might rent a car and drive to the east coast[9]

437

to check out the beautiful scenery[10]. I would find a nice resort[11] to enjoy the facilities. I know this would cost me an arm and a leg, but I do need to reward[12] myself sometimes.

　　我的工作很忙，所以不太有機會取得這種長假。如果我真的能休七天假，前三天我會待在家裡睡覺，享受這種悠閒的感覺。如果我想的話，可能會租一輛車，開車到東海岸欣賞美景。我會找一家很不錯的度假飯店，享受飯店的設施。當然，這可能會非常昂貴，但我有時候的確需要好好犒賞自己一下。

❼ holiday	❽ leisurely	❾ coast
名 假期	形 悠閒的	名 海岸
❿ scenery	⓫ resort	⓬ reward
名 風景	名 度假勝地	動 獎勵

 試著更與眾不同

If my boyfriend could take the same days off as me, we would definitely go somewhere together since it is hard to get a long holiday like that. However, this wouldn't happen most of the time, so another way to enjoy my holiday would be with my mother. I would plan a cruise[13] vacation[14] for my mother. Going on a cruise would be ideal for her because everything she needed would be provided. She is suffering[15] from arthritis[16], so a trip requiring lots of walking wouldn't be suitable.

　　如果我男友也能請假的話，那我們肯定會一起去旅行，因為這樣的長假實在太少見了。不過，這基本上不會發生，另外一個享受假期的方式，就是找我母親一起。我會替母親規劃郵輪之旅，對她而言，郵輪會比較理想，因為船上什麼都有提供。她受關節炎所苦，因此，需要走很多路的行程並不適合她。

⓭ cruise	⓮ vacation
名 郵輪	名 假期
⓯ suffer	⓰ arthritis
動 受苦；患病	名 關節炎

延伸note
郵輪觀光通常會停靠於各國的港口，讓旅客上岸觀光，稱為shore excursion。

 Key Points

答題TIPS看這裡！

除了春節，一般人很難有長達七天的假期。被問到這個問題，一般人會回答自己想去哪裡玩，不過，只想悠閒地待在家裡的人也不在少數。建議選擇一個點（go on vacation / stay at home），做延伸發揮，會比較有內容。

Words & Phrases　休假時的各種行動

1 travel abroad
出國旅遊

2 sleep in
補眠

3 go to the movies
看電影

4 take a walk
散步

Words & Phrases　描述旅遊的相關花費

1 an admission ticket
門票

2 a concession ticket
有折扣的票（如：學生票）

3 accommodation
住宿

4 travel insurance
旅遊保險

🎤 進階實用句 More Expressions

I would utilize my holidays and go out.

我會盡量利用我的假期出去玩。

Every time we go traveling, we end up spending a lot on souvenirs.

每次我們去旅行，都因為紀念品而花了很多錢。

I might go to a theme park because I can get a student discount.

我可能會去主題遊樂園玩，因為我可以買學生票。

UNIT 07 工作熱情與現實

Q **Would you accept a low-paying job if you really liked it?**

你會接受一份你很喜歡，但薪水很低的工作嗎？

MP3 142

你可以這樣回答

I would accept a low-paying job if I really liked it. I just graduated from college this June[1]. It is hard to get a decent job without enough work experience. Therefore, I wouldn't mind spending a couple of years in a low-paying job. Through the years, I would try my best to gain experience and improve my skills[2]. Once I became more professional[3] and was able to prove[4] myself, I would then expect a salary raise.

　　如果我真的很喜歡那份工作，我會願意接受低薪。我今年六月剛從大學畢業，沒有工作經驗，很難找到一份好工作，因此，我不介意花幾年做一份低薪的工作。在這幾年，我會盡我所能地吸取經驗、提升自己的能力。當我變得專業，也能證明自己的能力時，我就會期待公司幫我加薪。

❶ **June**
名 六月

❷ **skill**
名 能力；熟巧

❸ **professional**
形 專業的

❹ **prove**
動 證明

> **延伸note**
> 社會新鮮人(freshman)對於低薪的接受度比較高，以此表達自己積極的心態也是一種方式。

換個立場講講看

This would be a tough[5] decision for me. If the pay were enough to cover my living expenses, I would accept a low-paying job as long as it was something that interested me. However, I definitely wouldn't do it for long because I also expect a better life. As a techie[6], I am always eager to have the newest consumer[7] electronics[8]. Because of this, I would need higher pay. Of course, I could accept lower pay at start[9], but I would definitely expect a raise[10] as I improved my job performance.

這對我來說很難抉擇，如果薪水足夠我生活，那只要這份工作吸引我，我願意接受低薪。但是，我無法長久接受這種情況，因為我也會想要過比較好的生活。身為電子迷，我會很想要擁有最新的3C產品，也因為如此，我需要較高的薪水。當然，一開始我願意接受低薪，但隨著工作表現提升，我會期待加薪。

| ❺ **tough**
形 棘手的 | ❻ **techie**
名 電子迷 | ❼ **consumer**
名 消費者 |
| ❽ **electronics**
名 電子學 | ❾ **start**
名 起初 | ❿ **raise**
名 加薪 |

試著更與眾不同

Honestly, I would not accept a low-paying job even if I liked the job. If I could barely[11] survive[12] with the pay, I wouldn't be happy with what I was doing because of that. Reality[13] would hit strongly when I got my credit card[14] bills. Having dreams is important, but facing reality also matters. I want to be able to afford a nice house and car. Therefore, I would not consider taking a low-paying job in any case.

說實話，不管我再怎麼喜歡一份工作，如果薪水很低，我也不會接受。如果薪水只夠我果腹，那我也不可能喜歡上我在做的工作。收到信用卡帳單的當下，現實就會狠狠地重擊我了。擁有夢想當然很重要，但面對現實也具備同樣的重要性。我想要買好房好車，因此，無論如何，我都不會考慮一份低薪工作。

| ⓫ **barely**
副 幾乎不 | ⓬ **survive**
動 倖存 |
| ⓭ **reality**
名 現實 | ⓮ **credit card**
片 信用卡 |

延伸note
具備類似立場的你，在回答時可盡量聚焦在 be practical上，點出自己的務實性格。

答題TIPS看這裡！

接受一份喜歡、卻低薪的工作實在不是個容易的決定。如果低薪，但還能勉強過活，有些人可能還會接受；但薪水若低到無法生活，或者無法達到自己期望的標準，有些人就會因為現實面（reality）的考量，而拒絕接受。答題時，建議盡量給予原因。單純的Yes, I can.或No, I can't.絕對不是面試官想聽的答案。

Words & Phrases　生活中的支出

1 utility bill
水電費

2 power bill
電費

3 water bill
水費

4 credit card bill
信用卡費

5 phone bill
電話費

6 bank charges
銀行手續費

7 check
餐廳的帳單

8 loan
貸款

進階實用句 More Expressions

I hate the end of the month because I have so many bills to pay.

我很討厭月底，因為有很多帳單要付。

I need at least thirty thousand to cover my monthly expenses.

我一個月至少要三萬塊來負擔我的開支。

One of third of my pay goes to the rent. Therefore, I don't have much left.

我薪水的三分之一要用來繳房租，所以剩下的薪水並不多。

UNIT 08

看書 vs. 看電視

Q What do you prefer, reading books or watching TV?

你比較喜歡看書還是看電視？

 你可以這樣回答

MP3 143

I prefer to read books because they are something I can take with me when I am out. It's a great way to kill time when I wait for the bus or train. I like TV shows as well[1]. However, it's not that convenient compared to reading books. I know a lot of people watch TV shows[2] on their cell phones, but I am not used to it. I tried it several[3] times before, and it only made my eyes dry[4]. Books are much more comfortable to read.

我比較喜歡看書，因為書籍是我外出時能隨身攜帶的東西。在等公車或火車時，看書是個很棒的消遣。我也喜歡看電視節目，但這就沒書籍那麼方便。我知道有很多人會用手機看電視節目，可是我不習慣。我之前試過幾次，每次都覺得眼睛因而變得乾澀，看書的感覺舒服多了。

❶ **as well** 片 也；同樣地	❷ **TV show** 片 電視節目
❸ **several** 形 數個的	❹ **dry** 形 乾澀的

> 延伸note
> 懂得善用(utilize)零碎時間的人，就算只是交通時間，也能陸續看完一本小說的。

 換個立場講講看

I prefer to watch TV because it offers both visual and audio[5] stimulation. This is something reading can't compete with. I read the Harry Potter books, but I enjoyed the movies as well. When I read the book, it was all about the words. I could feel that the story is excellent[6]. But when I watched the movie on TV, I got more excitement[7] from the scenes. I held my breath[8] when danger approached[9] the characters. I think that's what fascinates[10] me the most when I watch TV.

　　我比較喜歡看電視，因為電視能同時滿足視覺與聽覺的享受，這是閱讀無法辦到的事。我之前有看《哈利波特》的小說，但我依然很喜歡電影版本。看小說的時候，都只是文字敘述，我可以感受到故事情節很精彩，但當我在電視上看電影版時，從畫面所感受到的刺激感更強烈，看到危險逼近時，我會隨著角色屏息，我覺得這就是電視的魅力。

⑤ **audio**
形 聽覺的

⑥ **excellent**
形 出色的

⑦ **excitement**
名 興奮

⑧ **hold one's breath**
片 屏息

⑨ **approach**
動 接近

⑩ **fascinate**
動 迷住

試著更與眾不同

Comparing books with TV, I would say watching TV is more appealing. My favorite TV program is the political talk show. They invite experts to share their views on recent[11] political issues. Sometimes they have representatives from different parties[12] and some journalists. Because each of them has a unique[13] standpoint[14], the debate[15] might get pretty sharp[16]. I think it's helpful to me because I can broaden my horizons through their words.

　　書和電視兩相比較之下，我會說電視比較吸引我。我最喜歡看政論節目，他們會邀請一些專家上節目，針對最近的政治議題分享看法。有時候他們會邀請不同黨派的代表和記者，因為每一個都有其獨特的立場，所以辯論可能會變得很激烈。我覺得這對我很有幫助，因為我能藉由他們的論點拓寬自己的視野。

⑪ **recent**
形 最近的

⑫ **party**
名 黨派

⑬ **unique**
形 獨特的

⑭ **standpoint**
名 立場；看法

⑮ **debate**
名 辯論

⑯ **sharp**
形 激烈的

Key Points

答題TIPS看這裡！

因為題目是將兩樣特定的東西提出來比較，因此可以先指出比較喜歡哪一樣，接著再針對喜歡的項目做補充說明，比較常見的切入點為：解釋原因（explanation）、舉實例（example）、比較優劣（advantage vs. disadvatage）…等等。

Words & Phrases 不同的書報種類

1 **periodical**
期刊

2 **magazine**
雜誌

3 **tabloid**
八卦雜誌

4 **children's books**
童書

5 **digest**
文摘

6 **photo album**
攝影寫真書

7 **reference books**
參考書

8 **proceedings**
論文集

進階實用句 More Expressions

I like to fill in my day with lots of reading.

我每天都想要大量閱讀。

There is a really good documentary program on TV. I watch it every night.

最近在演一個很精彩的紀錄片，我每天晚上都會收看。

I like to read the biographies of influential people and find out the secrets to their success.

我喜歡讀名人傳記，並找出他們成功的原因。

445

UNIT 09

最想見一面的人

Q **Describe someone you would like to meet if you had the opportunity.**

如果有機會的話，你會想與哪個人見上一面？

 你可以這樣回答

MP3 144

If I had the opportunity[1], I would love to meet Tom Cruise. I would like to know what his secret is to be so active at his age. He has been in the film[2] business for over thirty years. Although he looks older compared to what he did in his past movies, he is still full of energy[3] and stamina[4]. Have you seen the latest "Mission Impossible"? I was surprised to hear that he didn't use a body double[5] in that movie. I can't believe he is still fit[6] enough to perform in an action movie like that.

　　如果有機會的話，我想見湯姆·克魯斯。我想問他，以他的年紀來看，如何能保持活力。他在電影界的時間超過三十年。和他以前的作品相比，雖然看得出他也有歲月的痕跡，但他依然很有精力。你看過最新的《不可能的任務》嗎？當我聽說他在裡面沒有用替身演員時，真的感到很驚訝，真不敢相信他還有足夠的體力來演出動作片。

❶ **opportunity** 名 機會	❷ **film** 名 電影	❸ **energy** 名 活力；幹勁
❹ **stamina** 名 精力；耐力	❺ **body double** 片 替身演員	❻ **fit** 形 健康的；強健的

 換個立場講講看

I would like to meet our mayor of Taipei, Ko Wen-Je. He has a unique[7] character which is unlike[8] any other politicians who was elected in the past. He dares[9] to take up the responsibility to challenge the big enterprises. Things like that make him so special and controversial[10]. I sometimes think he comes close to the truth. Things might get very ugly because the investigation[11] might cause some politicians to be incarcerated[12].

　　如果有機會，我會想見台北市長柯文哲。他是一個很特別的人，一點都不像以前選出來的政客。他敢擔起責任挑戰財閥，類似這樣的事件顯示出他的特別之處，也讓他飽受爭議。我有時候覺得他快找出事情的真相了。真相也許很醜陋，因為調查結果可能會導致部分政府官員被判刑。

❼ **unique**	❽ **unlike**	❾ **dare**
形 獨特的	形 不同的；不相似的	動 敢；膽敢
❿ **controversial**	⓫ **investigation**	⓬ **incarcerate**
形 有爭議的	名 調查	動 監禁

試著更與眾不同

I wish I could have the opportunity to meet Mark Zuckerberg, one of the co-founders[13] of Facebook. He started as a computer programmer[14], but look what he has achieved[15]. Facebook has become one of the most popular social networking[16] websites in the world. I would really like to find out more about him and what drove him to keep moving forward. As a Facebook user, I find that the website's functions are still improving. No wonder Facebook is so popular.

　　我希望我有機會可以見到馬克・祖克柏，臉書的其中一個創辦人。他出身自軟體工程師，可是卻有今天的成就。臉書是世界上最流行的社交軟體之一，我很想多了解他私下的模樣，以及是什麼推動他堅持下去。身為臉書的使用者，我發現網路上的功能一直在進步，也難怪臉書會這麼受歡迎。

⓭ **co-founder**	⓮ **programmer**
名 共同創辦人	名 程式設計師
⓯ **achieve**	⓰ **networking**
動 達到；贏得	名 網路關係網

延伸note
提出崇拜的對象時，如果不確定名字，可以用描述法，如：a Japanese comedian（日本諧星）。

答題TIPS看這裡！

大部分人想要見的人很可能是各界不同的名人，可能是國家元首（president / prime minister）、政商名流（celebrity）、影視紅星（movie star）、或是一個行為令你崇拜的人。除了現實生活中的人物，也可以發揮創意，無須侷限在這個時代，古人或是書本中捏造的人物也能成為答題的例子。

Words & Phrases 想見的人們類型

1. **movie star**
   電影明星
2. **celebrity**
   名人；名流
3. **the deceased**
   死者
4. **fictional character**
   虛構角色

Words & Phrases 想與人見面的原因

1. **talk to sb.**
   和某人交談
2. **share one's feelings**
   吐露心事
3. **ask for a signature**
   要簽名
4. **exchange opinions**
   意見交流

進階實用句 More Expressions

You will realize that he is very thoughtful.

你之後就會發現他很體貼。

I believe most successful businessmen are calculative and greedy to some extent.

我相信大部分的成功商人在某種程度上，都是城府深且有野心的。

After the interview, I realized that the scientist's success is not based on how clever he is; it is based on how hard he tries.

在訪談過後，我發現這名科學家成功的原因不在他有多聰明，而在於他有多努力。

UNIT 10

國貨還是進口貨

Q Do you prefer local or imported products?
你喜歡本國產品還是進口商品呢？

 你可以這樣回答

MP3
145

When it comes to food, I prefer the imported products. After a series of[1] food safety issues, I have lost faith[2] in locally made products. I know imported products aren't necessarily better. However, most foreign governments take food safety regulations a lot more seriously[3]. I hope our government can do more about food safety so that I don't need to spend more on imported farm produce[4].

　　提到食品，我會買進口產品。經過一連串的食安風暴後，我對本國產品的信心消失殆盡。當然，我知道進口產品的品質不一定就比較好，但大部分的國外政府對食品安全法的態度較為嚴謹。我希望政府能針對食品安全多做改善，這樣我就不用花那麼多錢在國外的農產品上了。

❶ a series of
片 一系列的

❷ faith
名 信心；信念

❸ seriously
副 嚴謹地

❹ produce
名 產品；農產品

延伸note
現在有越來越多人強調有機食品(organic food)的重要性；就連蔬菜，也有人只買有機蔬菜了。

 換個立場講講看

I prefer local products because I can indirectly[5] support the local economy like this. Buying local products keeps our factories[6] open, so workers have jobs to support their families. If I only bought imported products, fewer people would benefit[7] from it. Soon, we would not be able to buy things that were made in

Taiwan because of the number of factories that would have to shut down[8]. If a country relies[9] only on importation, it will do harm to[10] both its economy and its politics.

　　我比較喜歡買本國產品，因為這樣我能間接地促進國內經濟。購買本國產品代表工廠能存活，工人也就能保有這份工作、養活家人。如果我只買進口產品，能因此獲益的人會少很多，很快地，許多工廠會因而倒閉，到時候我們就買不到台灣製的產品了。如果國家只依靠進口，對經濟和政治的傷害都會很大。

⑤ **indirectly** 副 間接地	⑥ **factory** 名 工廠	⑦ **benefit** 動 得益；受惠
⑧ **shut down** 片 （使）關閉	⑨ **rely** 動 依賴；依靠	⑩ **do harm to** 片 傷害；損害

 試著更與眾不同

I prefer to buy local products because the quality is better. Some countries' labor[11] is rather cheap[12], so they can keep costs lower. However, the texture of their clothing is usually rough[13]. I can't stand the quality at all. In contrast, even though local products cost more, they have fine[14] quality. I'd rather buy an expensive[15] but durable[16] item. However, for those who care only about the price, the cheapest might be the most ideal.

　　我比較喜歡當地的商品，因為品質比較好，有些國家的勞工低廉，所以能壓低其產品的價格，但是，衣服的質料卻很粗糙，我完全不能接受那種品質。相比之下，本國製的商品雖然比較貴，但品質卻很好，對我來說，價格貴沒關係，只要產品耐用就好。不過，對那些只在意價格的消費者而言，便宜就是好。

⑪ **labor** 名 勞工；勞方	⑫ **cheap** 形 便宜的	⑬ **rough** 形 粗糙的；粗製的
⑭ **fine** 形 美好的；優秀的	⑮ **expensive** 形 昂貴的	⑯ **durable** 形 耐用的

Key Points

答題TIPS看這裡！

大家會選擇進口商品的原因不外乎兩點。一口品質良好（fine quality）；二則為低廉的價格（cheap），這會涉及到國外的薪資標準。針對本題，選定一個特定的產品（如：食品、衣物、電子產品…等），會比較好分析。

Words & Phrases 商品在市場上的競爭力

1. **competitive**
   有競爭力

2. **premium quality**
   品質優良

3. **unique design**
   設計特殊

4. **affordable**
   負擔的起；價格便宜

Words & Phrases 與進出口貿易有關的詞彙

1. **import**
   進口

2. **export**
   出口

3. **tariff**
   關稅

4. **exchange rate**
   匯率

進階實用句 More Expressions

That 39-dollar shop is full of things that are made in China.

那家39元商店都是大陸製的產品。

I'd rather pay extra to buy items made locally instead of imported items.

我情願多花一點錢來買國內製的產品，也不願意買進口商品。

I think local industry should change its policy and focus on improving quality.

我覺得國內產業應該改變方針，強調改善品質。

UNIT 11
產品品牌的重要性

MP3
146

Q Why is the brand of products important?
產品的品牌為什麼重要？

你可以這樣回答

Building up a trustworthy brand[1] is not an easy task[2]. The meaning behind a big brand is quality and reliability. Companies with big brand names invest[3] a lot of money in quality control[4]. Most of the big brands offer good after-sales service. To make sure the service is accessible[5], they have lots of shops or boutiques[6] in the city. I sometimes purchase products with a famous brand name because of their high-quality.

　　要建立有良好口碑的品牌並非易事，大品牌能讓人對其商品的品質產生信任感。那些耳熟能詳的大品牌會投資許多錢在品管控制上，大部分也都會提供完善的售後服務。為了確保服務的完整性，所以會在市區內設置許多店家。我有時候也會為了品質而去買名牌。

① **brand**
　名 品牌；牌子

② **task**
　名 任務

③ **invest**
　動 投資

④ **control**
　名 控制；支配

⑤ **accessible**
　形 可接近的

⑥ **boutique**
　名 精品店

換個立場講講看

Brand is something that people are willing to pay big money for. Famous brands are also status[7] symbols, especially when people carry them around[8] with them. For example, there are a lot of cell phones on the market. However, the iPhone stands in a unique position[9] not matter what. Having the newest iPhone seems prestigious[10]. People are proud of being an Apple user. I think the marketing[11] campaigns[12] are worth every cent they cost.

　　品牌是大眾願意花大錢的原因，無論到哪裡，只要帶著這些名牌產品，就能象徵你的地位特殊。例如：市場上有很多手機，但iPhone無論如何就是坐擁一個特殊的地位。擁有最新的蘋果手機表示尊貴，人們都以當蘋果的使用者為榮。我覺得蘋果公司花大錢的行銷手段真是值回票價了。

❼ status
名 地位

❽ carry around
片 隨身攜帶

❾ position
名 地位；身分

❿ prestigious
形 有名望的

⓫ marketing
名 行銷

⓬ campaign
名 運動；活動

試著更與眾不同

I think the brand name means a lot to a company[13]. Companies can set higher prices and make bigger profits[14]. Personally, I don't have a brand preference. Therefore, if I can find a cheap alternative[15] with the same functions, I will turn to a generic[16] brand. Products with famous brands are usually fancy[17]. If money were no concern[18], I would love to buy products with famous brand names, too. Unfortunately, this is not the case for most consumers.

　　我覺得品牌對公司來說很重要，因為他們可以藉此提高價格，賺取更多利潤。我對品牌並沒有什麼特別偏好，所以，當我找得到功能相同、價格又便宜的替代品時，我就會去買那些無廠牌的商品。名牌看起來通常都比較精緻，不考慮價格的話，我也想買名牌。可惜的是，大部分的消費者無法不考慮價格。

⓭ company
名 公司

⓮ profit
名 利潤；收益

⓯ alternative
名 替代品

⓰ generic
形 沒有商標名的

⓱ fancy
形 別緻的

⓲ concern
名 關心的事

答題TIPS看這裡！

品牌（brand）是大家購物時會參考的一個重要指標，也是直接影響產品價格的因素。不過所謂的品牌，並不等於名牌（a famous brand）。以3C產品為例，Apple、ASUS、Acer、Samsung…都是出名的品牌，但它們並不一定等於奢侈品（luxury），答題時要注意這一點，不要把兩者混為一談。

Words & Phrases　購買名牌的原因

1 designer
設計師

2 show off
炫耀

3 texture
質地

4 fashion
流行

Words & Phrases　常見的付款方式

1 pay on delivery
貨到付款

2 pay in instalment
分期付款

3 by ATM transfer
ATM轉帳

4 by credit card
刷信用卡

進階實用句 More Expressions

If I wait until the annual sale, I will pay a lot less.

如果我等到週年慶才買，價格就會便宜很多。

It takes a lot of planning and investment to build up a brand.

要建立一個品牌需要很多計畫和投資。

I am willing to pay extra for brand-name items because they are less likely to break.

我情願花多一點錢去買有品牌的產品，因為比較不容易壞掉。

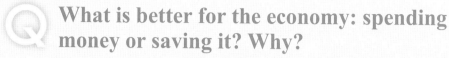

UNIT 12 花錢/存錢之於經濟

Q **What is better for the economy: spending money or saving it? Why?**

你認為花錢與存錢哪個對經濟比較有幫助？為什麼？

 你可以這樣回答

 MP3 147

In my opinion, spending money is definitely more helpful for the economy because it makes money flow[1] through society[2]. For example, let's say I go and get my hair done at a hair salon[3]. Then, the hairdresser[4] goes to a restaurant to buy her meal. After that, the restaurant owner can afford to pay his car loan. The bank can then utilize the capital[5] for investments and earn more money. This is how spending money stimulates[6] the economy.

在我看來，花錢一定對經濟有比較大的幫助，因為那能讓現金在社會流通。比方說：我到美容院做了頭髮，付錢給設計師；設計師接著去餐廳吃飯；用餐過後，餐廳老闆就有錢繳汽車貸款；而銀行就能夠善用這筆資金去做投資，賺更多錢。這就是花錢能刺激經濟的原因。

❶ **flow**	❷ **society**	❸ **salon**
名 流；流動	名 社會	名 沙龍
❹ **hairdresser**	❺ **capital**	❻ **stimulate**
名 美髮師	名 資本；本錢	動 刺激

 換個立場講講看

Well, this is quite complicated since there is no absolute[7] answer to it. In general, spending money is beneficial[8] to the economy. The cash flow matters for the economy. However, the deposit[9] rate also plays a key role in the

455

long-term economic growth[10]. Therefore, I don't think I could choose one over the other when it comes to the economy. The government should decide the proper monetary[11] and financial[12] policy to suit different situations.

這個問題很複雜，沒有絕對正確的答案。一般而言，花錢對社會當然有幫助，現金的流動對經濟的影響很大。不過，就長期的經濟成長而言，儲蓄率的角色也非常關鍵。因此，談到經濟時，我實在無法從中選擇一種做法。政府應該要針對不同的情形，決定適用於當下的貨幣與財政政策。

⑦ absolute
形 絕對的

⑧ beneficial
形 有益的

⑨ deposit
名 存款

⑩ growth
名 成長

⑪ monetary
形 貨幣的

⑫ financial
形 財政的

 **試著更與眾不同**

I think people should care more about their savings[13] instead of spending. It is harder for people to get jobs or get a pay raise when the economy grows slowly. When an economic recession[14] strikes[15], the impact[16] on employment[17] is usually enormous. People might get sacked[18] without advance warning. This creates another social problem for people. Therefore, we should maintain enough savings since you never know what might happen.

在我看來，民眾應該注意存錢，而非花錢。當經濟成長緩慢的時候，人們很難找到工作，也比較難取得加薪的福利。當經濟大蕭條席捲而來，對就業率的衝擊尤其嚴重。人們可能會在不被通知的情況下被裁員，造成更大的社會問題，因此，我們應該要有足夠的積蓄，因為你永遠都無法預測下一刻會發生什麼事。

⑬ saving
名 節約；節儉

⑭ recession
名 衰退

⑮ strike
動 打；擊

⑯ impact
名 衝擊

⑰ employment
名 雇用；受雇

⑱ sack
動 （口）開除；解僱

Key Points

答題TIPS看這裡！

花錢其實對經濟有一定層面的幫助，因為有人願意花錢，其他們人才會有錢賺。可是當經濟不好的時候，大家都沒錢賺，花錢的意願當然就會跟著降低，情願保守一點把錢存下來，該怎麼做，其實很兩難。

Words & Phrases　經濟的景氣與蕭條

1 **bloom**
繁榮；成長

2 **prosperous**
繁榮的

3 **depression**
不景氣

4 **sluggish**
蕭條的

Words & Phrases　與貨幣相關的情況

1 **monetary**
貨幣的

2 **inflation**
通貨膨脹

3 **devaluate**
使（貨幣）貶值

4 **appreciate**
漲價；升值

🎙 進階實用句 More Expressions

A dollar saved is a dollar earned.

沒花掉的錢，就是省下來的錢。

If people don't purchase, it will also slow down the economic growth.

如果大家都不消費，同樣也會導致經濟成長變慢。

The Consumer Confidence Index is an indication of how the economy is performing.

消費者信心指數是觀察經濟表現的指標。

UNIT 13　最想逃避的事

Q Given a chance, what daily task would you like to avoid?

有機會的話，你想避開的日常事務為何？

 你可以這樣回答

MP3
148

If I got the chance, I would definitely avoid¹ the task of vacuuming the floor. In order to do the vacuuming, I have to remove some of the furniture in advance so I can clean most of the corners² in the house. I also need to plug³ the vacuum⁴ into a socket⁵ while using it. It is difficult to move around. I must constantly relocate the vacuum to a different spot. And when I finally finish cleaning, I have to put the furniture back. So, it is tiring⁶.

　　如果可以的話，我絕對會避開吸地板。為了吸塵，我必須事先移開部分傢俱，這樣我才能清理各個角落。此外，使用的時候，吸塵器必須插在插座上，移動很不方便，我必須一直移動吸塵器。當我好不容易打掃完了，還必須把之前移開的傢俱放回去，真是累死人了。

❶ **avoid**	❷ **corner**	❸ **plug**
動 避免	名 角落	動 給…接通電源
❹ **vacuum**	❺ **socket**	❻ **tiring**
名 吸塵器	名 插座	形 累人的

 換個立場講講看

If I had a choice, I would like to avoid driving. Driving takes a lot of concentration⁷. I have to constantly⁸ worry about the pedestrians⁹ and the scooters passing by¹⁰. This is especially tiring when I work overtime the day

458

before. Besides, there are a lot of crazy drivers out there. Some of them are so violent that they even carry weapons[11] with them. You never know what kind of drivers you might run into[12]. Therefore, it would be wonderful if I could avoid driving.

　　如果可以選擇，我想避免開車。開車的時候必須很專心，我得不停地注意路上的行人以及從旁邊經過的機車。若我前一天加班工作的話，這種狀況尤其累人。除此之外，路上還有很多瘋狂的駕駛，有些還很暴力，甚至隨身攜帶武器。你根本無法預料自己會遇上什麼樣的人。如果能不開車的話，就太好了。

❼ concentration
名 專心；專注

❽ constantly
副 不斷地

❾ pedestrian
名 行人

❿ pass by
片 經過；過去

⓫ weapon
名 武器

⓬ run into
片 偶然碰到

 試著更與眾不同

I wish I could avoid doing the washing up. I enjoy preparing a nice meal for my family. However, when I finish the meal, all I want to do is chill out[13] and relax. I like to turn on[14] the television and watch the programs I like. However, my husband[15] always asks me to wash the dishes before he takes out the garbage. I really don't like getting my hands wet[16] and greasy[17]. Recently, I've been thinking about switching[18] tasks with my husband. Maybe he would enjoy washing the dishes more than taking out the garbage.

　　我希望能不用洗碗。我喜歡替家人準備餐點，但是，當我吃完飯後，就只想要放鬆休息。我會打開電視，觀看喜歡的節目，但我先生總會要求我在他出去倒垃圾前洗好碗。我真的不喜歡搞得雙手又濕又油膩。我最近想要和我老公交換工作，搞不好他更喜歡洗碗呢！

⓭ chill out
片 冷靜

⓮ turn on
片 打開

⓯ husband
名 丈夫

⓰ wet
形 濕的

⓱ greasy
形 油膩的

⓲ switch
動 變更；轉換

答題TIPS看這裡！

日常事務的涵蓋範圍很廣，可以是家事（household chores）或是每天必須做的行為（daily routine），如：刷牙洗臉。比較穩健的答題方式為「點出不想做的事情為何，再解釋其原因」，例如：I would like to avoid making breakfast because I am so bad at cooking. I prefer someone else to make it for me.（我不想做早餐，因為我的廚藝很差，希望有人願意煮給我吃。）

Words & Phrases 想避開日常事務的原因

1 time-consuming
浪費時間

2 not good at
不擅長

3 have no interest
沒有興趣

4 troublesome
麻煩

Words & Phrases 勇於承擔的態度

1 face the music
勇於承擔後果

2 take the blame
承擔責任

3 take over
接管；繼任

4 composed
鎮靜的；沉著的

進階實用句 More Expressions

I wish I could avoid going to the bank.

我希望能避免去銀行。

I try to avoid going to the traditional market because it's hard to find a parking space.

我盡量避免去傳統市場，因為停車位很難找。

I don't want to run into one of my neighbors. She always asks questions that I don't want to talk about.

我不想遇到我的一位鄰居，她總是問些我不想談的問題。

不同法律的必要性

Q Why is there a need to have different laws?
不同的法律為何有存在的必要？

你可以這樣回答

MP3
149

If you examine Western countries' laws carefully, you will see an interesting situation. In a country with lots of regions[1], the laws may vary[2] according to the different regions. A constitution[3] sets up the general rules for a country, such as its governmental[4] system. However, when it comes to the specific rules for us to follow, legislative[5] authorities then make all kinds of regulations. All of those should be really clear in order to maintain faith in the social order[6].

如果仔細觀察西方國家的法律，就會發現一個很有趣的情況。包含許多行政區域的國家，會出現州法（各州會訂定不同的法律）。憲法規範國家主要的概念，包含確立政府系統。不過，當涉及讓人民遵從的法律時，立法機構就會制定各種不同的法律。這些法律內容會非常清楚，以便維持社會秩序。

❶ **region**
名 行政區域

❷ **vary**
動 變更；修改

❸ **constitution**
名 憲法

❹ **governmental**
形 政府的

❺ **legislative**
形 立法的

❻ **social order**
片 社會秩序

換個立場講講看

I believe laws were invented[7] to protect[8] citizens[9] and restrict their behavior. All the different laws aim to achieve the same goal. We need various laws to deal with different cases. That's why we have criminal[10] law, civil[11] law and family law. It is impossible to cover all of these in one set of regulations. Instead, separating them into different laws is more efficient[12] for keeping order.

我認為法律是為了保護人民與約束人們的行為，因而被制定出來。不同的法律都是為了達成這同一個目標。我們需要各式各樣的法律來處理不同的案件，這也是為什麼會將法律分成刑法、民法、家事法…等條文。我們不可能把所有的法律規定都放在同一個法規當中，相反地，為了讓其發揮最高的效率，將之分成好幾種不同的法律類型才是最佳做法。

7 invent 動 發明；創造	**8 protect** 動 保護	**9 citizen** 名 公民
10 criminal 形 刑事上的	**11 civil** 形 民事的	**12 efficient** 形 有效率的

試著更與眾不同

Setting up rules for people to follow is a way to stabilize[13] our society. If there were no laws, our lives would be in chaos[14] since people wouldn't be punished[15] after doing something bad. In that case, people might only consider their own interests. There won't be things called illegal[16], so people might do whatever they want. This might lead to anarchy[17], which is very scary to imagine[18]. Therefore, I think all of those different laws are what everyone needs in modern society.

制定法規並讓人民遵守能夠穩定社會情況。如果完全沒有法律，人們不會因為做壞事而被懲戒，那我們的生活將會一團混亂。在那種情況下，大家可能只考慮自身的利益。沒有任何事情會被視為不合法，所以人們將會變得過於隨心所欲，很有可能會導致無政府狀態，光是想像都覺得恐怖。因此，我覺得各式各樣的法律其實是必要的。

13 stabilize 動 使穩定	**14 chaos** 名 混亂	**15 punish** 動 懲罰
16 illegal 形 不合法的	**17 anarchy** 名 無政府（狀態）	**18 imagine** 動 想像

Key Points 答題TIPS看這裡！

為何需要不同的法律是一個觀念上的問題。把法律看成能約束社會行為的工具是個很好的切入點，不管事民生問題、還是刑事責任，幾乎所有事情都需要法律來約束，或作為行為準則，否則社會就會大亂。

Words & Phrases 不同的法律

1 state law
州際法律

2 federal law
聯邦法律

3 international law
國際法

4 civil law
民法

5 criminal law
刑法

6 business law
商業法

7 law of tax
稅法

8 traffic law
交通法規

🎤 進階實用句 More Expressions

Laws are used to protect people's rights.

法律是用來保護人民的權利的。

If you want to sue someone for compensation, you do so under civil law.

如果你想要求賠償的話，那就要告對方民事刑責。

You must obey the traffic laws when you are driving; otherwise, you will get a fine.

開車時必須遵守交通規則，不然會收到罰單。

精緻作品 vs. 藝術

Q **What is the difference between a well-made object and a work of art?**

做工精緻的物品和藝術作品有何不同？

 你可以這樣回答

 MP3 150

I believe the main difference is that well-made objects[1] can be mass[2] produced, while artists[3] don't do the same thing with their works for commercial reasons. When you go shopping, you can see well-made objects in the shops in bulk[4]. This isn't the case with art. Works of art might only be displayed[5] in art galleries[6]. Every work of art has its unique value.

　　我認為最大的不同在於，做工精緻的物品是可以被大量生產的，但藝術家不會為了商業化的理由而對自己的作品如此。逛街的時候，你一定能看到店家裡陳列著大量的精緻商品，而非藝術品。如果是藝術品，可能就只會放在畫廊裡陳列，每一件藝術作品都會有其獨特的價值。

① **object**
名 物體

② **mass**
形 大量的

③ **artist**
名 藝術家

④ **in bulk**
片 大量

⑤ **display**
動 展示

⑥ **gallery**
名 畫廊

 換個立場講講看

I think a well-made object is also a type of artwork because it must be designed[7] and created[8] by someone. It might not be from someone who is famous, but it's still a creation for the designer. There are a lot of people who dream of being artists[9]. However, that is never easy. I believe most give up[10] on the dream and make practical things for a living. To some extent, you can still see the creativity in the products, so I don't see there's a huge difference between the two.

其實我覺得做工精緻的物品也算一種藝術作品,因為那同樣是由某個人設計並創作出來的。當然,創作者可能不怎麼出名,但那還是他的創作。很多人都懷抱著成為藝術家的夢想,但是,這絕非易事,我相信大部分的人到最後都會為了生活而放棄理想。就某種程度而言,你還是能看出那些精緻作品背後的創意,所以我不覺得這兩者有很大的不同。

延伸note
藝術品的價值通常都很高,甚至還會出現 forgery(贗品)。

7 design
動 設計

8 create
動 創造

9 artist
名 藝術家

10 give up
片 放棄

試著更與眾不同

I really don't think a well-made object is different from a work of art. Based on my observations[11], well-made objects are usually appreciated[12] by most people since they fit in with common aesthetics[13]. On the other hand, there are some people who admire[14] actual works of art, whether they be from artists from the past or contemporaries[15] who became famous later. Van Gogh is a typical[16] example of an artist who became famous after he died.

我不覺得做工精緻的物品和藝術品有哪裡不同。根據我的觀察,做工精緻的物品通常會被大眾欣賞,因為它符合主流的審美觀。另一方面來說,有些人欣賞真正的藝術品,無論作品的創作者已故,或是之後才出名。梵谷就是個很典型的例子,他就是在過世之後才變得出名。

11 observation
名 觀察

12 appreciate
動 欣賞

13 aesthetics
名 審美觀

14 admire
動 欣賞

15 contemporary
名 同時代的人

16 typical
形 典型的

答題TIPS看這裡！

作工精細的商品隨處可見，這和藝術品（work of art）當然有差別，不過，喜歡不喜歡是另外一回事。針對自己怎樣都無法理解的藝術作品，也不用勉強自己去讚嘆。越坦承的答題態度，反而越可能讓自己的答案從眾多面試者當中跳出來。不過，無論你的觀點為何，解釋原因、維持清楚的邏輯依然是首要重點。

Words & Phrases 對藝術品的評價

1 one of a kind
獨一無二的

2 valuable
價值連城的

3 priceless
無價的

4 a form of expression
一種表現手法

Words & Phrases 走在藝廊與畫展中

1 art gallery
藝廊

2 art exhibition
畫展

3 artistic
藝術感的；抽象的

4 contemporary
當代的

 進階實用句 More Expressions

This work of art is too abstract to me. I don't get it at all.

這個藝術品太具藝術感了，我完全看不懂。

The painting was done by a famous artist. It is one of a kind.

這幅畫出自一位出名的畫家，是他獨一無二的創作。

Everyone's interpretation will be different. That's why I love art so much.

就算是面對同一件作品，每個人的詮釋也都不同，這是我為何這麼喜歡藝術的原因。

Part 1 性格與特質

① be accustomed to 習慣於⋯⋯

A couple of years after I moved to the UK, I got accustomed to the lifestyle here.

搬到英國住了幾年後，我開始習慣這裡的生活方式了。

② beat around the bush 拐彎抹角

Please be straightforward with me. I don't like people beating around the bush.

請直接跟我說，我不喜歡人家拐彎抹角。

③ change one's mind 某人改變主意

It is very hard to persuade him to change his mind.

要說服他改變心意是很困難的一件事。

④ face up to 勇敢面對；面對事實

I know no one wants to see this happen, but we need to face up to the consequences.

我知道沒有人想看到這種情況，但我們必須面對結果。

⑤ joke around 開玩笑

Tony is such a funny person; he never stops joking around.

東尼的個性很搞笑，總是不停地開玩笑。

Part 2 食物與旅遊

① at the table 在吃飯

No one wants to answer the phone because we are all at the table.

沒有人想去接電話，因為我們都在吃飯。

2 be fond of 喜好;愛好

I am fond of classic ballet. I watched "Swan Lake" several times.

我很喜愛古典芭蕾,看過好多次的《天鵝湖》。

3 dish out 分到個人的盤子裡

My mother dished out the steak to make sure everyone had one piece of it.

我媽媽將牛排分到每個人的盤子裡,以確保大家都有一片。

4 have a good time 玩得開心

We went to Bali for our honeymoon and had a good time.

我們到峇里島度蜜月,玩得很開心。

5 lack of 缺少;不足

I am planning a trip across Europe, but I have lack of money at the moment.

我計劃要橫跨歐洲,但現在缺少經費。

$\mathscr{Part}\ 3$ 音樂與電影

1 be addicted to 沉溺於某種嗜好

I am so addicted to movies, so I love movie marathons.

我很沉溺於看電影,所以很愛電影馬拉松的活動。

2 bring back 再掀風潮;使憶起

The 70s dress the actress wore brought back the fashion again.

那名女演員所穿的七〇年代洋裝再次掀起了流行風潮。

3 come into notice 引起注意

The preview of the new movie came into my notice.

新電影的預告片引起了我的注意。

④ in high/low spirits 心情好／差

I am in high spirits because I might be getting a promotion.

我現在心情很好，因為我可能會被升職。

⑤ name after 以……命名

I was named after my grandmother.

我的名字是以我奶奶的名字命名的。

Part 4 運動與健康

① at times 偶爾

On weekends, I would invite my friends over and play Ma-Jiang together at times.

我有時候會在週末邀請朋友來，一起打麻將。

② catch a cold 感冒；傷風

The weather is windy and rainy. I might catch a cold by the time I get home.

天氣又濕又冷，我可能回家就感冒了。

③ compete with 與……競爭

I am representing my school to compete with the other swimmers in the competition.

我代表學校跟其他游泳選手比賽。

④ in good/bad health 健康狀況佳／差

My grandfather is 85 years old, and he is still in good health.

我爺爺已經八十五歲了，身體還很健康。

⑤ in charge of 照料；管控；負責

I am in charge of three branches in northern Taiwan.

我負責北台灣的三間分行。

Part 5 職業與學習

① be Greek to 一竅不通

I have no idea what this project is about. It is all Greek to me.

我不了解這項企劃的內容，完全一竅不通。

② burn the midnight oil 熬夜

I still have got so much work to do; I have to burn the midnight oil tonight.

我還有很多工作要做，看來今晚得熬夜了。

③ clock in 打卡上班

I might not be able to clock in on time because of the traffic jam.

因為塞車的關係，我應該沒辦法準時打卡了。

④ earn one's living 謀生

Simon is a qualified pastry chef. He opened a small pastry shop to earn his living.

賽門是有執照的點心烘焙師，開了一家小間糕點坊謀生。

⑤ learn one's lesson 藉經驗獲取教訓

I got a ticket for speeding; I really learned my lesson this time.

我被開了超速的罰單，我這次真的學到教訓了。

Part 6 人際關係

① ask after 問候；探問

I haven't seen your family for a long time; please ask after your parents for me.

我很久沒有看到妳爸媽了，麻煩幫我問候他們。

② be fed up with 感到厭煩

Everybody keeps asking me what Eddy did to our manager. I am so fed up with it.

大家一直問我艾迪對經理做了什麼，問得我都厭煩了。

③ clear the air 化解誤會

The manager thought it was me who missed the deadline. I need to clear the air.

經理以為是我錯過了截止日，我必須澄清誤會。

④ come across 意外發現

I came across this really good article when I was looking for some information for my research.

我在找研究資料的時候意外發現這篇文章。

⑤ do sb. a favor 幫某人一個忙

I am flat out at the moment. Can you please do me a favor?

我忙翻了，請問你可以幫我個忙嗎？

Part 7 科技發展

① acquaint with 熟悉；了解

I worked on a similar project before, so I am acquainted with this software.

我以前做過類似的專案，所以我滿熟悉這個軟體的。

② be distinct from 與……區別

The iPhone system is totally distinct from the Android system.

iPhone系統與安卓系統完全不同。

③ for the time being 暫時

I have finally caught up with the schedule for the time being. I can take a break now.

我終於暫時趕上進度，可以休息一下了。

④ get ahead 進步；領先

You need to work extra hard to get ahead, especially when you are competing with so many people.

你必須更努力才能領先，尤其是在跟這麼多人競爭的情況下。

⑤ on the basis of 基於……

On the basis of mutual understanding, we decided to ban the usage of cell phones during work hours.

基於共識，我們決定「上班時間內禁止使用手機」。

Part 8 自然與環境

① at the expense of 以……為代價

This residential estate was built at the expense of natural habitats of an endangered bird.

這片住宅區是犧牲了瀕臨絕種的鳥類棲息地，才得以建成。

② be abundant in 豐富；充裕

Western Australia is abundant in natural resources.

澳洲西部充滿了天然資源。

③ bear the brunt of 首當其衝

Apparently, Hualien city will bear the brunt of the force of the typhoon.

看來花蓮市會首當其衝受到颱風的影響。

4 dry up 乾涸；枯竭

We are in a serious drought at the moment; all the reservoirs are drying up.

我們目前乾旱得很嚴重，所有的水庫都快乾涸了。

5 put emphasis on 強調；重視

I think the government should put emphasis on water conservation before it is too late.

我覺得政府平時就應該強調珍惜水資源，不然等到缺水時就太晚了。

Part 9 政治與媒體

1 appeal to 吸引；訴諸

The candidate's policy proposal appeals to younger voters.

這名候選人的政見很吸引年輕的選民。

2 at first hand 直接地；第一手地

This is exclusive news. I got it at first hand before everyone else.

這是獨家新聞，我搶先一步拿到第一手消息。

3 at issue 爭議中；討論中

Whether to demolish the old building is still at issue. It is inconclusive at this stage.

大家還在討論是否要拆除舊建築物，目前尚未達到共識。

4 come into effect 生效

The new traffic regulations are coming into effect on the 1st of July.

新的交通法規會在七月一日正式生效。

⑤ interfere with 干涉；干預

Mr. Thompson said that he won't interfere with the case this time.

對這次的案子，湯普森先生說他不會出手干預。

Part 10 假設與看法

① according to 根據；按照

According to the latest research, it is not good for your health if you eat too much red meat.

最新的研究顯示，吃太多的紅肉對健康有負面的影響。

② be opposed to 反對

Most people would like to go overseas on the graduation trip, but I am opposed to the idea.

大部分的人畢業旅行都想要出國，但我反對。

③ cannot choose but 只好

Since the decision has been made, I guess I cannot choose but to follow the rules.

既然結果已經出來了，那我就只好遵守規則了。

④ meet halfway 妥協

There is no point in keep arguing. We need to come up with a solution to meet each other halfway.

再吵下去也沒用，我們必須想出一個方法來妥協。

⑤ pros and cons 正反兩方

Everything has its pros and cons. You need to think carefully before you decide.

每件事都有正反兩面，做決定之前，你必須考慮清楚。

1 sb. decided to... 某人決定要……。

This is not the first time Laura busted her boyfriend cheating; therefore, she decided to break up with him.

這不是蘿拉第一次發現她男友在外面有小三,她決定要分手。

2 make sure (that)... 確定……

I just want to make sure this is the way to the museum.

我想要確定這條路會通到博物館。

3 sb. look forward to... 某人期待……。

David really looks forward to all the perks that are associated with his new position.

大衛很期待新工作的相關福利。

4 sb. would rather... 某人寧願……。

This train is packed. I would rather wait for the next one.

這班火車很擠,我情願等下一班。

5 would like to start with... 想先從……開始。

There are quite a lot of tasks in the project; I would like to start with the planning.

這個專案有很多項目要做,我想先從計畫開始。

6 be stuck between...and... 不知該選……還是……。

I am stuck between my mother and my girlfriend; they don't get along with each other well.

我媽媽跟我女朋友處得不好,真的是讓我左右為難。

7 play an important role in... 在……方面扮演重要的角色。

The team leader plays an important role in the negotiation of this project.

在談判方面，這個專案的組長扮演很重要的角色。

8 Would you mind...? 你介意……嗎？

Would you mind passing the ketchup to me?

你介意幫我把番茄醬遞過來嗎？

9 be wondering if...(or not) 在思考是否……／想知道是否……。

I am wondering if you can give me a hand to repair the shelves.

不知道你是否願意幫我一起修理書櫃。

10 sb. have/has no idea... 某人不知道……。

I have no idea where the new building is. I need to check the address.

我不知道新大樓在哪裡，我得確認地址。

11 There's no doubt that... ……是毫無疑問的。

The manager is very supportive. There's no doubt that he would have your back.

經理很支持我們，他絕對會幫你。

12 try one's best to... 盡最大的努力去……。

I am trying my best to put this puzzle together without other people's help.

我盡最大的努力，想獨自把拼圖拼好。

13 In one's opinion,... 就某人看來，……。

In my opinion, we would definitely make a profit.

就我看來，我們一定會賺錢。

14 **express one's gratitude to...** 感謝……。

Professor Lee helped me so much through my university life; I would like to express my gratitude to **him.**

李教授在大學時期幫了我很多，我想向他道謝。

15 **sb. have/has confidence in...** 某人對……有信心。

Tina has always been very careful at work, so I have confidence in **her.**

蒂娜在工作上一直很小心，所以我對她有信心。

16 **Will there be time for...?** 會有……的時間嗎？

Will there be time for **a quick meal after the meeting?**

開完會之後，有時間先去吃個飯嗎？

17 **...have a lot in common** ……有很多共同點。

I met Will at the party for the first time. We have a lot in common.

我在派對上認識威爾，我們有很多共同點。

18 **(It is) no wonder (that)...** 難怪……。

There is one piece missing; no wonder **I couldn't make it work.**

原來是少了一片，難怪我怎麼樣都拼不起來。

19 **It takes time to...** ……很花時間。

It takes time to **get to know a person; therefore, you should not rush into marriage.**

要認識一個人是很花時間的，所以不要趕著結婚。

20 **sth. depend on...** 要看……而定。

The schedule depends on **our flight.**

行程要看班機的時間而定。

國家圖書館出版品預行編目資料

面試零痛點，這樣口說最高分 / 張翔 著. --初版. --
新北市：知識工場出版 采舍國際有限公司發行，
2018.06 面； 公分. --（Master 06）
ISBN 978-986-271-815-5 (平裝)

1.英語　2.會話

805.188　　　　　　　　　　　　107002834

面試"零"痛點，
這樣口說最高分

Let's Stand Out
In Oral Exams.

知識工場 · Master 06

面試零痛點，這樣口說最高分

出 版 者／全球華文聯合出版平台・知識工場
作　　者／張翔　　　　　　　印 行 者／知識工場
出版總監／王寶玲　　　　　　英文編輯／何牧蓉
總 編 輯／歐綾纖　　　　　　美術設計／蔡瑪麗

郵撥帳號／50017206 采舍國際有限公司（郵撥購買，請另付一成郵資）
台灣出版中心／新北市中和區中山路2段366巷10號10樓
電　　話／（02）2248-7896
傳　　真／（02）2248-7758
ISBN-13／978-986-271-815-5
出版日期／2018年6月初版

全球華文市場總代理／采舍國際
地　　址／新北市中和區中山路2段366巷10號3樓
電　　話／（02）8245-8786
傳　　真／（02）8245-8718

港澳地區總經銷／和平圖書
地　　址／香港柴灣嘉業街12號百樂門大廈17樓
電　　話／（852）2804-6687
傳　　真／（852）2804-6409

全系列書系特約展示
新絲路網路書店
地　　址／新北市中和區中山路2段366巷10號10樓
電　　話／（02）8245-9896
傳　　真／（02）8245-8819
網　　址／www.silkbook.com

本書採減碳印製流程並使用優質中性紙（Acid & Alkali Free）通過綠色印刷認證，最符環保要求。

本書為名師張翔等及出版社編輯小組精心編著覆核，如仍有疏漏，請各位先進不吝指正。來函請寄
mujung@mail.book4u.com.tw，若經查證無誤，我們將有精美小禮物贈送！